Ab

Caitlin Crews discov[...] age of twelve and has [...] affair with romance no[...] [...]sts on keeping near her at all [...] [...]urrently lives in the Pacific Northwest, with her animator/comic book artist husband and their menagerie of ridiculous animals.

USA Today best-selling author **Anna DePalo** is a Harvard graduate and former intellectual property lawyer. Her books have won the RT Reviewers' Choice Award, the Golden Leaf, the Book Buyer's Best and the NECRWA Readers' Choice, and have been published in over twenty countries. She lives with her husband, son and daughter in New York. Readers are invited to follow her at www.annadepalo.com, www.facebook.com/ AnnaDePaloBooks, and www.twitter.com/Anna_DePalo

Cat Schield lives in Minnesota with her daughter, their opiniated Burmese cats and a silly Doberman puppy. Winner of the Romance Writers of America 2010 Golden Heart® for series contemporary romance, when she's not writing sexy, romantic stories for Mills & Boon Desire, she can be found sailing with friends on the St. Croix River or in more exotic locales like the Caribbean and Europe. You can find out more about her books at www.catschield.net

The Princes
COLLECTION

Seducing
Her Prince

CAITLIN CREWS

ANNA DEPALO

CAT SCHIELD

MILLS & BOON

First Published in Great Britain 2020
By Mills & Boon, an imprint of HarperCollins*Publishers*
1 London Bridge Street, London, SE1 9GF

SEDUCING HER PRINCE © 2020 Harlequin Books S.A.

A Royal Without Rules © 2013 Caitlin Crews
One Night with Prince Charming © 2011 Anna DePalo
A Royal Baby Surprise © 2015 Catherine Schield

ISBN: 978-0-263-28156-9

MIX
Paper from
responsible sources
FSC™ C007454

Printed and bound in Spain
by CPI, Barcelona

A ROYAL WITHOUT RULES

CAITLIN CREWS

To Megan Haslam who was so enthusiastic about this book even before I wrote it, and to Charlotte Ledger, who claimed Pato might have ruined her for all men. Thanks for being such fantastic editors!

CHAPTER ONE

HIS ROYAL HIGHNESS Prince Patricio, the most debauched creature in the kingdom of Kitzinia—if not the entire world—and the bane of Adriana Righetti's existence, lay sprawled across his sumptuous, princely bed in his vast apartments in the Kitzinia Royal Palace, sound asleep despite the fact it was three minutes past noon.

And he was not, Adriana saw as she strode into the room, alone.

According to legend and the European tabloids, Pato, without the pressure of his older brother's responsibilities as heir apparent, and lacking the slightest shred of conscience or propriety, had not slept alone since puberty. Adriana had expected to find him wrapped around the trollop du jour—no doubt the same redhead he'd made such a spectacle of himself with at his brother's engagement celebration the night before.

Jackass.

But as she stared at the great bed before her, the frustration that had propelled her all the way through the palace shifted. She hadn't expected to find the redhead *and* a brunette, both women naked and draped over what was known as Kitzinia's royal treasure: Prince Pato's lean and golden torso, all smooth muscle and sculpted male beauty, cut off by a sheet riding scandalously low on his narrow hips.

Although *"scandalous"* in this context was, clearly, relative.

"No need to be so shy." Somehow, Adriana didn't react to the mocking gleam in Prince Pato's gaze when she looked up to find him watching her, his eyes sleepy and a crook to his wicked mouth. "There's always room for one more."

"I'm tempted." Her crisp tone was anything but. "But I'm afraid I must decline."

"This isn't a spectator sport."

Pato shifted the brunette off his chest with a consummate skill that spoke of long practice, and propped himself up on one elbow, not noticing or not caring that the sheet slipped lower as he moved. Adriana held her breath, but the sheet *just* preserved what little remained of his modesty. The redhead rolled away from him as Pato shoved his thick, too-long tawny hair back from his forehead, amusement gleaming in eyes Adriana knew perfectly well were hazel, yet looked like polished gold.

And then he smiled with challenge and command. "Climb in or get out."

Adriana eyed him in all his unapologetic, glorious flesh. Prince Pato, international manwhore and noted black sheep of the Kitzinia royal family, was the biggest waste of space alive. He stood for nothing save his own hedonism and selfishness, and she wanted to be anywhere in all the world but here.

Anywhere.

She'd spent the last three years as Crown Prince Lenz's personal assistant, a job she adored despite the fact it had often involved handling Pato's inevitable messes. This paternity suit, that jilted lover's vindictive appearance on television, this crashed sports car worth untold millions, that reckless and/or thoughtless act making embarrassing headlines… He was the thorn in his responsible older brother's side, and therefore dug deep and hard in hers.

And thanks to his inability to behave for one single day—even at his only brother's engagement party!—Pato was now *her* problem to handle in the two months leading up to Kitzinia's first royal wedding in a generation.

Adriana couldn't believe this was happening. She'd been demoted from working at the right hand of the future king to taking out the royal family's trash. After her years of loyalty, her hard work. Just when she'd started to kid herself that she really could begin to wash away the historic stain on the once proud Righetti name.

"Pato needs a keeper," Prince Lenz had said earlier this morning, having called Adriana into his private study upon her arrival at the palace. Adriana had ached for him and the burdens he had to shoulder. She would do anything he asked, anything at all; she only wished he'd asked for something else. Pato was the one part of palace life she couldn't abide. "There are only two months until the wedding and I can't have the papers filled with his usual exploits. Not when there's so much at stake."

What was at stake, Adriana knew full well, was Lenz's storybook marriage to the lovely Princess Lissette, which the world viewed as a fairy tale come to life—or would, if Pato could be contained for five minutes. Kitzinia was a tiny little country nestled high in the Alps, rich in world-renowned ski resorts and stunning mountain lakes bristling with castles and villas and all kinds of holiday-making splendor. Tourist economies like theirs thrived on fairy tales, not dissipated princes hell-bent on self-destruction in the glare of as many cameras as possible.

Two months in this hell, she thought now, still holding Pato's amused gaze. *Two months knee-deep in interchangeable women, sexual innuendo and his callous disregard for anything but his own pleasure.*

But Lenz wanted her to do this. Lenz, who had believed in her, overlooking her infamous surname when he'd hired her. Lenz, who she would have walked through fire for, had he wanted it. Lenz, who deserved better than his brother. Somehow, she would do this.

"I would sooner climb across a sea of broken glass on my hands and knees than into that circus carousel you call your bed," Adriana said, then smiled politely. "I mean that with all due respect, of course, Your Royal Highness."

Pato tilted back his head and laughed.

And Adriana was forced to admit—however grudgingly—that his laugh was impossibly compelling, like everything else about him. It wasn't fair. It never had been. If interiors matched exteriors, Lenz would be the Kitzinian prince who looked like this, with all that thick sun-and-chocolate hair that fell about Pato's lean face and hinted at his wildness, that sinful mouth, and the kind of bone structure that made artists and young girls weep. Lenz, not Pato, should have been the one who'd inherited their late mother's celebrated beauty. Those cheekbones, the gorgeous eyes and easy grace, the smile that caused riots, and the delighted laughter that lit whole rooms.

It simply wasn't fair.

Pato extricated himself from the pile of naked women on his bed and swung his long legs over the side, wrapping the sheet around his waist as he stood. As much to taunt her with the other women's nakedness as to conceal his own, Adriana thought, her eyes narrowing as he raised his arms high above his head and stretched. Long and lazy, like an arrogant cat. He grinned at her when she glared at him, and as he moved toward her she stiffened instinctively—and his grin only deepened.

"What is my brother's favorite lapdog doing in my bedroom this early in the day?" he asked, that low, husky voice of his no more than mildly curious. Still, his gaze raked over her and she felt a kind of clutching in her chest, a hitch in her breath. "Looking as pinch-faced and censorious as ever, I see."

"First of all," Adriana said, glancing pointedly at the delicate watch on her wrist and telling herself she wasn't *pinched* and didn't care that he thought so, "it's past noon. It's not early in the day by any definition."

"That depends entirely on what you did last night," he replied, unrepentant and amused, with a disconcerting lick of heat beneath. "I don't mean what *you* did, of course. I mean what *I* did, which I imagine was far more energetic than however it is you prepare yourself for another day of pointless subservience."

Adriana looked at him, then at the bed and its naked contents. Then back at him. She raised a disdainful eyebrow, and he laughed again, as if she delighted him. The last thing she wanted to do was delight him. If she had her way, she'd have nothing to do with him at all.

But this was not about her, she reminded herself. Fiercely.

"Second," she said, staring back at him repressively, which had no discernible effect, "it's past time for your companions to leave, no matter how energetic they may have been—and please, don't feel you need to share the details. I'm sure we'll read all about it in the papers, as usual." She aimed a chilly smile at him. "Will you do the honors or should I call the royal guard to remove them from the palace?"

"Are you offering to take their place?" Pato asked lazily.

He shifted, and despite herself, Adriana's gaze dropped to the expanse of his golden-brown chest, sun-kissed and finely honed, long and lean and—

For God's sake, she snapped at herself. *You've seen all this before, like everyone else with an internet connection.*

She'd even seen the pictures that were deemed too risqué for publication, which the palace had gnashed its collective teeth over and which, according to Lenz, had only made his shameless brother laugh. Which meant she'd seen every part of him. But she had never been this close, in person, to Prince Pato in his preferred state of undress.

It was…different. Much different.

When she forced her gaze upward, his expression was far too knowing.

"I like things my way in my bed," he said, his decadent mouth crooking into something too hot to be any kind of smile. "But don't worry. I'll make it worth your while if you follow my rules."

That crackled in the air, like a shower of sparks.

"I have no interest in your sexual résumé, thank you," Adriana snapped. She hadn't expected he'd be so *potent* up close. She'd assumed he'd repulse her—and he did, of course. Intellectually. "And in any case it's unnecessary, as it's been splashed on the cover of every tabloid magazine for years."

He shocked her completely by reaching over and tugging gently on the chic jacket she wore over her favorite pencil skirt. Once, twice, three times—and Adriana simply stood there, stunned. And let him.

By the time she recovered her wits, he'd dropped his hand, and she glanced down to see that he'd unbuttoned her jacket, so that the sides fell away and the silk of her thin pink camisole was the only thing standing between his heated gaze and her skin.

Adriana swallowed. Pato smiled.

"Rule number one," he said, his husky voice a low rumble that made her wildly beating heart pump even faster. Even harder. "You're overdressed. I prefer to see skin."

For a moment, there was nothing but blank noise in her head, and a dangerous heat thick and bright everywhere else.

But then she made herself breathe, forcing one breath and then the next, and cold, sweet reason returned with the flow of oxygen. This was Pato's game, wasn't it? This was what he did. And she wasn't here to play along.

"That won't work," she told him coolly, ignoring the urge to cover herself. That was undoubtedly what he thought she'd do, what he wanted her to do before she ran away, screaming, like all the previous staff members Lenz had assigned him over the years. She wasn't going to be one of them.

His golden eyes danced. "Won't it? Are you sure?"

"I'm not your brother's lapdog any longer." Adriana squared her shoulders and held his gaze, tilting her chin up. "Thanks to your appalling behavior last night, which managed to deeply offend your soon-to-be sister-in-law and her entire family—to say nothing of the entire diplomatic corps—I'm yours until your brother's wedding."

If anything, Pato's eyes were even more like gold then, liquid and scalding. As wicked as he was, and her whole body seemed to tighten from the inside out.

"Really." He looked at her as if he could eat her in one bite, and would. Possibly right then and there. "All mine?"

Adriana thought her heart might catapult from her chest, and she ignored the curl of heat low in her belly, as golden and liquid as his intent gaze. *This is what he does,* she reminded herself sternly. *He's* trying *to unnerve you.*

"Please calm yourself," she said with a dry amusement she wished she felt. "I'm your new assistant, secretary, aide. Babysitter. Keeper. I don't care what you call me. The job remains the same."

"I'm not in the market for a lapdog," Pato said in his lazy way, though Adriana thought something far more alert moved over his face for a scant second before it disappeared into the usual carelessness. "And if by some coincidence I was, I certainly wouldn't choose a little beige hen who's made a career out of scowling at me in prudish horror and ruffling her feathers in unspeakable outrage every time I breathe."

"Not when you breathe. Only when you act. Or open your mouth. Or—" Adriana inclined her head toward his naked torso, which took up far too much of her view, and shouldn't have affected her at all "—when you fling off your clothes at the slightest provocation, the way other people shake hands."

"Off you go." He made a dismissive, shooing sort of gesture with one hand, though his lips twitched. "Run back to my drearily good and noble brother and tell him I eat hens like you for breakfast."

"Then it's a pity you slept through breakfast, as usual," Adriana retorted. "I'm not going anywhere, Your Royal Highness. Call me whatever you like. You can't insult me."

"I insulted the easily offended Lissette and all of her family without even trying, or so you claim." His dark brows arched, invoking all manner of sins. Inviting her to commit them. "Imagine how offensive I could be if I put my mind to it and chose a target."

"I don't have to imagine that," Adriana assured him. "I'm the one who sorted out your last five scandals. This year."

"Various doctors I've never met have made extensive claims in any number of sleazy publications that I'm an adrenaline junkie," Pato continued, studying her, as if he knew perfectly well that the thing that curled low and tight inside her was brighter now, hotter. More dangerous. "I think that means I like a challenge. Shall we test that theory?"

"I'm not challenging you, Your Royal Highness." Adriana kept her expression perfectly smooth, and it was much harder than it should have been. "You can't insult me because, quite honestly, it doesn't matter what you think of me."

His lips quirked. "But I am a prince of the realm. Surely your role as subject and member of staff is to satisfy my every whim? I can think of several possibilities already."

How was he getting to her like this? It wasn't as if this was the first time they'd spoken, though it was certainly the longest and most unclothed interaction she'd had with the man. It was also the only extended conversation she'd ever had with him on her own. She'd never been the focus of all his attention before, she realized. She'd only been *near* it. That was the crucial difference, and it hummed in her like an electric current no matter how little she wanted it to. She shook her head at him.

"The only thing that matters is making sure you cease to be a liability to your brother for the next two months. My role is to make sure that happens." Adriana smiled again, reminding herself that she had dealt with far worse things than an oversexed black sheep prince. That she'd cut her teeth on far more unpleasant situations and had learned a long time ago to keep her cool. Why should this be any different? "And I should warn you, Your Royal Highness. I'm very good at my job."

"And still," he murmured, his head tilting slightly to one side, "all I hear is challenge piled upon challenge. I confess, it's like a siren song to me."

"Resist it," she suggested tartly.

He gave her a full smile then, and she had the strangest sense that he was profoundly dangerous, despite his seeming carelessness. That he was toying with her, stringing her along, for some twisted reason of his own. That he was something far more than disreputable, something far less easily dismissed. It was disconcerting—and, she told herself, highly unlikely.

"It isn't only your brother who wants me here, before you ask," Adriana said quickly, feeling suddenly as if she was out of her depth and desperate for a foothold. Any foothold. "Your father does, too. He made his wishes very clear to Lenz."

Adriana couldn't pinpoint what changed, precisely, as Pato didn't appear to move. But she felt the shift in him. She could sense it in the same way she knew, somehow, that he was far more predatory than he should have been, standing there naked with a sheet wrapped around his hips and his hair in disarray.

"Hauling out your biggest weapon already?" he asked quietly, and a chill sneaked down the length of her spine. "Does that mean I've found my way beneath your skin? Tactically speaking, you probably shouldn't have let me know that."

"I'm letting you know the situation," she replied, but she felt a prickle of apprehension. As if she'd underestimated him.

But that was impossible. This was Pato.

"Far be it from me to disobey my king," he said, a note she didn't recognize and couldn't interpret in his voice. It confused her—and worse, intrigued her, and that prickle filled out and became something more like a shiver as his eyes narrowed. "If he wishes to saddle me with the tedious morality police in the form of a Righetti, of all things, so be it. I adore irony."

Adriana laughed at that. Not because it was funny, but because she hadn't expected him to land that particular blow, and she should have. She was such a fool, she thought then, fighting back a wave of a very familiar, very old despair. She should have followed her brothers, her cousins, and left Kitzinia to live in happy anonymity abroad. Why did she imagine that she alone could shift the dark mark that hovered over her family, that branded them all, that no one in the kingdom ever forgot for an instant? Why did she still persist in believing there was anything she could do to change that?

But all she showed Pato was the calm smile she'd learned, over the years, was the best response. The only response.

"And here I would have said that you'd never have reason to learn the name of a little beige hen, no matter how long I've worked in the palace."

"I think you'll find that everybody knows your name,

Adriana," he said, watching her closely. "Blood will tell, they say. And yours…" He shrugged.

She didn't know why that felt like a punch. It was no more than the truth, and unlike most, he hadn't even been particularly rude while delivering it.

"Yes, Almado Righetti made a horrible choice a hundred years ago," she said evenly. She didn't blush or avert her eyes. She didn't cringe or cry. She'd outgrown all that before she'd left grammar school. It was that or collapse. Daily. "If you expect me to run away in tears simply because you've mentioned my family's history, I'm afraid you need to prepare yourself for disappointment."

Once again, that flash of something more, like a shadow across his gorgeous face, making those lush eyes seem clever. Aware. And once again, it was gone almost the moment Adriana saw it.

"I don't want or need a lapdog," he said, the steel in his tone not matching the easy way he stood, the tilt of his head, that hot gold gleam in his eyes.

"I don't work for you, Your Royal Highness," Adriana replied simply, and let her profound pleasure in that fact color her voice. "You are simply another task I must complete to Prince Lenz's satisfaction. And I will."

That strange undercurrent tugged at her again. She wished she could puzzle it out, but he only gazed at her, all his shockingly intense magnetism bright in the air between them. She had the stray thought that if he used his power for good, he could do anything. Anything at all.

But that was silly. Pato was a monument to wastefulness, nothing more. A royal pain in the ass. *Her* ass, now, and for the next two months.

"I don't recall any other martyrs in the Righetti family line," he drawled after a moment. "Your people run more to murderous traitors and conniving royal mistresses, yes?" A quirk of his dark brow. "I'm happy to discuss the latter, in case you wondered. I do so hate an empty bed."

"Evidently," Adriana agreed acidly, nodding toward the overflowing one behind him.

"Rule number two," he said, sinful and dark. "I'm a royal prince. It's always appropriate to kneel in my presence. You could start right now." He nodded at his feet, though his gaze burned. "Right here."

And for a helpless moment, she imagined doing exactly that, as if he'd conjured the image inside her head. Of her simply dropping to her knees before him, then pulling that sheet away and doing what he was clearly suggesting she do.... Adriana felt herself heat, then tremble deep inside, and he smiled. He knew.

God help her, but *he knew.*

When she heard one of his bedmates call his name from behind him, Adriana jumped on it as if it was a lifeline—and told herself she didn't care that he knew exactly how much he'd got to her. Or that the curve in his wicked mouth mocked her.

"It looks like you're needed," Adriana said, pure adrenaline keeping her voice as calm and unbothered as it should have been. She knew she couldn't show him any fear, or any hint that she might waver. He was like some kind of wild animal who would pounce at the slightest hint of either—she knew that with a deep certainty she had no interest at all in testing.

"I often am," he said, a world of sensual promise in his voice, and that calm light of too much experience in his gaze. "Shall I demonstrate why?"

She eyed the pouty redhead, who was finally sitting up in the bed, apparently as unconcerned with her nudity as Pato was.

Adriana hated him. She hated this. She didn't know or

want to know why he'd succeeded in getting to her—she wanted to do her job and then return to happily loathing him from afar.

"I suggest you get rid of them, put some clothes on and meet me in your private parlor," she said in a clipped voice. "We need to discuss how this is going to go."

"Oh, we will," Pato agreed huskily, a dark gleam in his gaze and a certain cast to his mouth that made something deep inside her quiver. "We can start with how little I like being told what to do."

"You can talk all you want," Adriana replied, that same kick of adrenaline making her bold. Or maybe it was something else—something more to do with that odd hunger that made her feel edgy and needy, and pulsed in her as he looked at her that way. "I'll listen. I might even nod supportively. But then, one way or another, you'll behave."

Pato rid himself of his companions with as little fuss as possible, showered, and then called his brother.

"All these years I thought it was true love," he said sardonically when Lenz answered. "The descendant of the kingdom's most famous traitor and the besotted future king in a doomed romance. Isn't that what they whisper in the corners of the palace? The gossip blogs?"

There was a brief silence, which he knew was Lenz clearing whatever room he was in. Pato was happy to wait. He didn't know why he felt so raw inside, as if he was angry. When he was never angry. When he had often been accused of being incapable of achieving the state of anger, so offensively blasé was he.

And yet. He thought of Adriana Righetti and her dark brown eyes, the way she'd spoken to him. He pressed one hand against the center of his chest. Hard.

"What are you talking about?" Lenz asked, after a muttered conversation and the sound of a door closing.

"Your latest discard," Pato said. He stood there for a moment in his dressing room, scowling at his own wardrobe. What the hell was the matter with him? He felt…tight. Restless. As if this wasn't all part of the plan. He hadn't expected her to be…*her.* "Thank you for the warning that this was happening today."

"Do you require warnings now?" Lenz sounded amused. "Has the Playboy Prince lost his magic touch?"

"I'm merely considering how best to proceed," Pato said, that raw thing in him seeming to tie itself into a knot, because he knew how he'd *like* to proceed. It was hot and raw inside him. Emphatic. "Yet all I find myself thinking about are those Righetti royal mistresses. She looks just like them. Tell me, brother, what other gifts has she inherited? Please tell me they're kinky."

"Stop!" Lenz bit out the sharp command, something Pato very rarely heard directed at him. "Have some respect. Adriana isn't like that. She never…"

But he didn't finish. And Pato blinked, everything in him going still. Too still. As if this mattered.

"Does that mean what I think that means?" he asked. It couldn't. He shouldn't care—but there was that raw thing in him, and he had to know. "Is it possible? Was Adriana Righetti, in fact, no more than your personal assistant?"

Lenz muttered a curse. "Is that so difficult to believe?"

"It defies all reason," Pato retorted. But he smiled, a deep satisfaction moving through him, and he thought of the way Adriana had looked at him, determination and awareness in her dark eyes. He felt it kick in him. Hard. "You kept her for three whole years. What exactly were you doing?"

"Working," Lenz said drily. "She happens to be a great deal more than a pretty face." He cleared his throat. "Speaking of which, the papers are having a grand time attempting to uncover the identity of your mystery woman."

"Which one?" Pato asked, still smiling.

Lenz sighed. "And still the public adores you. I can't think why."

"We all have our roles to play." He heard the restlessness in his voice then, the darkness. It was harder and harder to keep it at bay.

His older brother let out another sigh, this one tinged with bitterness, and Pato felt his own rise to the surface. Not that it was ever far away. Especially not now.

"I thought it would feel different at this point," Lenz said quietly. "I thought I would feel triumphant. Victorious. *Something.* Instead, I am nothing but an imposter."

Pato pulled on a pair of trousers and a shirt and roamed out of his dressing room, then around the great bedchamber, hardly seeing any of it. There was too much history, too much water under the bridge, and only some of it theirs. Chess pieces put in place and manipulated across the years. Choices and vows made and then kept. They were in the final stages of a very long game, with far too much at stake. Far too much to lose.

"Don't lose faith now," he said, his voice gruff. "It's almost done."

Lenz's laugh was harsh. "What does faith have to do with it? It's all lies and misdirection. Callous manipulation."

"If you don't have faith in this course of ours, Lenz," Pato said fiercely, the rawness in his brother's voice scraping inside him, "then all of this has been in vain. All of it, for all these years. And then what will we do?"

There was a muffled noise that suggested one of Lenz's aides had poked a head in.

"I must go," his brother said after another low conversation. "And this is about sacrifice, Pato, though never mine.

Don't think it doesn't keep me awake, wondering at my own vanity. If I was a good man, a good brother…"

He didn't finish. What would be the point? Pato rubbed a hand over his eyes.

"It's done," he said. "The choice is made. We are who are and there's no going back."

There was a long pause, and Pato knew exactly which demons danced there between them, taunting his brother, dark and vicious. They were his, too.

"Be as kind to Adriana as you can," Lenz said abruptly. "I like her."

"We are all of us pawns, brother," Pato reminded him softly.

"Be nice to her anyway."

"Is that a command?" The raw thing in him was growing, hot and hungry. And Lenz had never touched her.

"If it has to be." Lenz snorted. "Will it work?"

Pato laughed, though it was a darker sound than it should have been. He thought of all the moving parts of this game, all they'd done and all there was left to do before it was over. And then he thought of Adriana Righetti's sharp smile on her courtesan's mouth, then the dazed expression on her face when he'd told her to kneel. And the heat in him seemed to simmer, then become intent.

"It's never worked before," he told his brother. "But hope springs eternal, does it not?"

His certainly did.

He found Adriana waiting for him as promised in the relatively small reception room off the grandiose main foyer of his lavish palace apartment. It was filled with fussy antiques, commanding works of art and the gilt-edged glamor that was meant to proclaim his exalted status to all who entered. Pato much preferred the flat he kept in London, where he wasn't required to impart a history lesson every time a guest glanced at a chair.

She was every bit as beautiful as her famously promiscuous ancestors, Pato thought, standing in the doorway and studying her. More so. She stood at the windows that looked out over the cold, blue waters of the alpine lake surrounding the palace, impatient hands on her hips and her stiff back to the door, and there was nothing in the least bit beige about her. Or even henlike, come to that. She'd refastened her jacket, and he appreciated the line of it almost as much as he'd enjoyed ruining that line when he'd unbuttoned it earlier. It skimmed over the elegant shape of her body before flaring slightly at her hips, over the narrow sheath of the skirt she wore and the high heels that made her legs look long and lean and as if they'd fit nicely wrapped around his back.

And she had in her genetic arsenal the most celebrated temptresses in the history of the kingdom. How could he possibly resist?

Anticipation moved in him, hard and bright. He needed her with him to play out this part of the game—but he hadn't expected he'd enjoy himself. And now, he thought, he would. Oh, how he would.

There were so many ways to be nice, after all, and Pato knew every last one of them.

CHAPTER TWO

TEN DAYS LATER, Adriana stood in the middle of a glittering embassy ballroom, a serene smile pasted to her face, while inside, she itched to kill Pato. Preferably with her very own hands.

It was a feeling she was growing accustomed to the more time she spent in his presence—and the more he pulled his little stunts. Like tonight's disappearing act in the middle of a reception where he was supposed to be calmly discharging his royal duties.

Please, she scoffed inside her head, her gaze moving around the room for the fifth time, holding out hope that she'd somehow missed him before, that he'd somehow blended into a crowd for the first time in his life. *As if he has the slightest idea what the word* duty *means!*

"The prince stepped out to take an important phone call," she lied to the ambassador beside her, when she accepted, finally, what she already knew. Pato had vanished, which could only bode ill. She kept her smile in place. "Why don't I see if I can help expedite things?"

"If you would be so kind," the ambassador murmured in reply, but without the sly, knowing look that usually accompanied any discussion of Pato or his suspicious absences in polite company. Nor did he look around to see if any women were also missing. Adriana viewed that as a point in her favor.

She had kept the paparazzi's favorite prince scandal-free for ten whole days. That was something of a record, if she did say so herself. Her intention was to continue her winning streak—but that meant finding him. And fast.

Because Adriana couldn't kid herself. She hadn't *contained* Pato over the past ten days. He'd laughed at her when she'd told him she planned to try. She'd simply babysat him, making sure he was never out of her sight unless he was asleep. That had involved frustrating days with Pato forever in her personal space, always teasing her and testing her, then doing as he pleased, with Adriana as his annoyed escort. It had meant long nights unable to sleep as she waited for the inevitable phone call from the guards she'd placed at his door to keep Pato in and the parade of trollops out. All she really had going for her was her fierce determination to bend him to her will—his brother's will, she reminded herself sternly—whether he wanted to or not.

Naturally, he didn't want to do anything of the kind.

Though he was always laughing, always shallow and reckless and the life of the party, if not the party itself, Adriana had come to realize that Pato had a fearsome will of his own. Iron and steel, wholly unbendable, beneath that impossibly pretty face and all his trademark languor.

Tonight he'd simply slipped away from the embassy receiving line, showing Adriana that he'd been indulging her this whole time. Allowing her to *think* she was making some kind of progress when, in fact, he'd been in control from the start.

She could practically *see* his mocking smile, and it burned through her, making her flush hot with the force of her temper. She excused herself from the ambassador and his aides, then walked calmly across the ballroom floor as if she was headed nowhere more interesting than the powder room, nodding by rote to those she passed and not even paying attention to the usual swell of her loathed surname like a wake of whispers behind her as she went. She was too focused on Pato, damn him.

He would *not* be the reason she failed Lenz. *He would not.*

But Pato wasn't corrupting innocents in the library, or involved in something sordid in any of the receiving rooms. She checked all of them—including every last closet because, the man was capable of anything—then stood there fuming. Had he *left?* Was he even now gallivanting about the city, causing trouble in one of the slick nightclubs he favored, filled as they were with the bored and the rich? How would she explain that to Lenz when it was all over the tabloids in the morning? But that was when she heard a soft thump from above her. Adriana tilted her head back and studied at the ceiling. The only thing above her was the ambassador's residence....

Of course. That bastard.

Adriana climbed the stairs as fast as she could without running, and then smiled at the armed guard who stood sentry at the entrance to the residence. She waved her mobile at him.

"I'm Prince Pato's assistant," she said matter-of-factly. "And I have His Majesty the King on the line...?"

She let her voice trail away, and had to fight back the rush of fury that swirled in her when the guard nodded her in, confirming her suspicions. She'd wanted to be mistaken, she really had.

And now she wanted to kill him. She *would* kill him.

Once on the other side of the ornate entryway, Adriana could hear music—and above it, a peal of feminine laughter. Her teeth clenched together, making her jaw ache. She marched down the hallway, stopped outside the cracked door where the noise came from, and then had to take a moment to prepare herself.

You already found him in bed with two women, a brisk voice inside her pointed out. *You handled it.*

She tucked her clutch beneath her arm, and wished she was wearing something more like a suit of armor, and not a sparkly blue gown that tied behind her neck, flowed to her feet and left her arms bare. For some reason, it made her feel intensely vulnerable, a sensation that mixed with her galloping temper and left her feeling faintly ill.

He was sleeping *when you saw that,* another voice countered. *He is probably not sleeping now.*

God, she hated him. She hated that this was her life. Adriana steeled herself and pushed through the door.

The music was loud, electronic and hypnotic, filling the dimly lit room. Adriana saw the woman first. She was completely naked save for a tiny black thong, plus long dark hair spilling down to the small of her back, and she was dancing.

If that was the word for it. It was carnal. Seductive. She moved to the music as if it was part of her, sensual and dark, writhing and spinning in the space between the two low couches that took up most of the floor space of the cozy room.

Performing, Adriana realized after a stunned moment. She was performing.

Pato lounged on the far couch, his long legs thrust out in front of him and crossed at the ankle, his elegant suit jacket open over his magnificent chest, and his lean arms stretched out along the back of the seat. He was fully clothed, which both surprised and oddly disappointed Adriana, but he looked no less the perfect picture of sexual indolence even though his skin wasn't showing.

Her throat went dry. The woman bent over backward, her hips circling in open, lustful invitation, her arms in the air before her. The music was like a dark throb, moving inside Adriana like a demand, a caress.

She swallowed hard, and that was when she realized Pato was looking straight at her.

Her heart stopped. Then kicked, exploding into her ribs, making her stomach drop. But Adriana didn't—couldn't—move.

The moment stretched out between them, electric and fierce. There was only that arrogant golden stare of his, as if the woman before him didn't exist. As if the music was for Adriana alone—for him. She had the panicked thought that he'd *wanted* her to find him like this, that this was some kind of trap. That he knew, somehow, the riot inside of her, the confusion. The heat.

Adriana didn't know how long she stood there, frozen on the outside and that catastrophic fire within. But eventually—seconds later? years?—Pato lifted one hand, pointed a remote toward the entertainment center on the far wall and silenced the music. All without looking away from Adriana for an instant.

The sudden silence made her flinch. Pato's mouth curved in one corner, wicked and knowing.

"It's time to go, Your Royal Highness," Adriana said stiffly into the quiet. She was aware, on some level, that the other woman was speaking, scowling at her. But Adriana couldn't seem to hear a word she said. Couldn't seem to see anything but Pato.

"You could come sit down, Adriana." His dark brows rose in challenge as he patted the sofa cushion beside him, and she was certain he knew the very moment her nipples pulled taut in a reaction she didn't understand. He smiled. "Watch. Enjoy. Who knows what might happen?"

"Not a single thing you're imagining right now, I assure you," Adriana said, struggling to control her voice.

She forced her shoulders back, stood straighter. She would not let this man best her. She couldn't let herself feel these

things, whatever they were. She had too much to prove—
and too much too lose. Adriana jerked her gaze away from
him, ignoring his low chuckle, and frowned at the woman,
who still stood there wearing nothing but a black thong and
an attitude.

"Aren't you the ambassador's daughter?" she asked
sharply. "Should we call downstairs and ask your father what
he thinks about your innovative approach to foreign policy?"

The woman made an extremely rude and anatomically
challenging suggestion.

"No, thank you," Adriana replied coolly, unable, on some
level, to process the fact that she was having this conversation while gazing at this woman's bared breasts. Not the first
set of naked breasts she'd seen in Pato's company. She could
only pray it was the last. "But I'm sure that if you walked
into the ballroom dressed like this you'd have a few takers.
No doubt that would delight your father even further."

Pato laughed then, rising from the couch with that sinuous
masculine grace he didn't deserve, and straightened his suit
jacket with a practiced tug. He did not look at all ashamed,
or even caught out. He looked the way he always did: deeply
amused. Lazy and disreputable. Unfairly sexy. His darker-
than-blond hair was long enough to hint at a curl, and he
wore it so carelessly, as if fingers had just or were about to
run through it. That wicked mouth of his made him look like
a satyr, not a prince. And those golden eyes gleamed as he
held her gaze, connecting with a punch to all that confused
heat inside her. Making it bloom into an open flame.

"There is no need for threats, Adriana," he said, sardonic
and low, and she felt it everywhere. "Nothing would please
me more than to do your bidding."

The ambassador's daughter moved then, plastering herself to his long, lean body, rubbing her naked breasts against
his chest as she flung her arms around his neck, hooked one

leg over his hip and pressed her mouth to his. He didn't kiss her the way Adriana had once seen him kiss one of his paramours in an almost-hidden alcove in the palace—carnal and demanding and an obvious, smoking-hot prelude to what came next. This was not *that,* thank goodness. But he didn't exactly fight her off, either.

"Then by all means, let's have you do my bidding, Your Royal Highness," Adriana said icily, everything inside her seeming to fold in on itself, like a fist. "Whenever you can tear yourself away, of course."

Pato set the other woman aside with a practiced ease that reminded Adriana of the same dexterity he'd showed in his bed that other morning. It made that fist curl tighter. Harder. He murmured something Adriana couldn't hear, that made the ambassador's thonged daughter smile at him as if he'd licked her. And then he smoothed down his tie, buttoned his jacket and sauntered toward the doorway as if there wasn't a nearly naked woman panting behind him and a formal reception he was supposed to be attending below.

Adriana stepped back to let him move into the hallway, and took more pleasure than she should have in snapping the door shut behind him. Perhaps with slightly more force than necessary.

"Temper, temper," Pato murmured, eyeing her with laughter in that golden gaze. "And here I thought you'd be so proud of me."

"I doubt you thought anything of the kind." She'd never wanted to hit another human being so much in all her life. "I doubt you *think.* And why on earth would I be proud of this embarrassing display?"

He propped one shoulder against the closed door and waved a languid hand down the length of him, inviting her to take a long look. She declined. Mostly.

"Am I not clothed?" he asked, taunting her. Again. "'Keep

your clothes on, Your Royal Highness,' you said in that prissy way of yours in the car on the way over tonight. I am delighted, as ever, to obey."

"You wouldn't know how to *obey* if it was your job," she snapped at him. "Not that I imagine you know what one of those is, either."

"You make a good point," he said, and that was when it occurred to Adriana that they hadn't moved at all—that they were standing entirely too close in that doorway. His face shifted from pretty to predatory, and her head spun. "I'm better at giving the orders, it's true. Rule number three, Adriana. The faster you obey me, the harder and the longer you'll come. Consider it my personal guarantee."

She couldn't believe he'd said that. Her entire body seemed to ignite, then liquefy.

"Enough," she muttered, but she didn't fool him with her horrified tone, if that flash of amused satisfaction in his gaze meant anything. Desperation made her lash out. "You shouldn't share these sad rules of yours, Your Royal Highness. It only makes you that much more pathetic—the dissipated, aging bachelor, growing more pitiable by the moment, on a fast track to complete irrelevance."

"Yes," he agreed. He leaned closer, surrounding her, mesmerizing her. "That's exactly why you're breathing so fast, why your cheeks are so flushed. You pity me."

Adriana ducked around him and started down the hall, telling herself none of that had happened. None of it. No dancing girl, no strange awareness. No *rules* that made her belly feel tight and needy. And certainly not the look she'd just seen in his eyes, stamped hard on his face. But her heart clattered in her chest, it was as hard to breathe as he'd suggested, and she knew she was lying.

Worse, he was right beside her.

"You're welcome," Pato said after a moment, sounding

smug and irritatingly male. It made her pulse race, but she refused to look at him. She couldn't seem to stop herself from imagining what kind of orders he'd give…and she hated herself for wondering.

"I beg your pardon?" she asked icily, furious with herself.

"Someone needs to provide fodder for your fantasies, Adriana. I live to serve."

She stopped walking, her hand on the door that led out of the residence. When she looked at him, she ignored the impact of that hot golden gaze of his and smiled instead. Poisonously.

"My fantasies involve killing you," she told him. "I spend hours imagining burying you in the palace gardens beneath the thorniest rose bushes, so I'd never have to deal with you again." She paused, then added with exaggerated politeness, "Your Royal Highness."

Pato grinned widely, and leaned down close. Too close. Adriana was aware, suddenly and wildly, of all the skin she was showing, all of it *right there,* within his reach. All that bare flesh, so close to that satyr's mouth of his. That wicked mouth with a slight smear of crimson on it, a sordid little memento that did nothing to detract from his devastating appeal. Or from her insane response to him.

"I knew you fantasized about me," he murmured, his voice insinuating, delicious. Seductive. "I can see it on your face when you think it's not showing."

He ran his fingertip down the sparkling blue strap that rose from the bodice of her gown and fastened at the nape of her neck. That was all. That was enough. He touched nothing but the fabric, up and down and back again, lazy and slow and so very nearly innocuous.

And Adriana burned. And shivered. And hated herself.

"Someday," he whispered, his eyes ablaze, "I'll tell you what you do in my fantasies. They're often…complicated."

Adriana focused on that smear of lipstick on his perfect lips. She didn't understand any of this. She should be horrified, disgusted. She should find him categorically repulsive. Why didn't she? What was *wrong* with her?

But she was terrified that she already knew.

"That's certainly something to look forward to," she said, the deliberate insincerity in her voice like a slap, just as she'd intended, but he only grinned again. "In the meantime, you have lipstick all over your mouth." She kept her expression smooth as she stepped back, away from him. She snapped open her clutch, reached inside with a hand that was *not* shaking, and produced a tissue. "I know you like to trumpet your conquests to all and sundry but not, I beg you, tonight. Not the ambassador's daughter."

"They wouldn't think it was the ambassador's daughter who put her mouth all over me, Adriana." He held her with that golden stare for another ageless moment, so sure of himself. So sure of *her.* He took the tissue from her hand then, his fingers brushing over hers—leaving nothing behind but heat and confusion, neither of which she could afford. "Small minds prefer the simplest explanations. They'd assume it was you."

"You must have done *something*," Adriana's father said peevishly, and not for the first time. "I told you to ingratiate yourself, to be obliging, didn't I? I told you to be careful!"

"You did," Adriana agreed. She didn't look over at her mother, who was preparing breakfast at the stove. She didn't have to look; she could feel her mother's sympathy like a cool breeze through the room. She tried to rub away the tension in her temples, the churning confusion inside her. "But I didn't do anything, I promise. Lenz thinks this is a great opportunity for me."

There was a tense silence then, and Adriana blinked as she realized her mistake. Her stomach twisted.

"*Lenz?*" Her father's brows clapped together. "You're quite familiar with the crown prince and future king of Kitzinia, are you not? I don't need to tell you where that leads, Adriana. I don't need to remind you whose blood runs through your veins. The shame of it."

He didn't. He really didn't, as she was the one who lived it in ways he couldn't imagine, being male. But he always did, anyway. She could see that same old lecture building in him, making his whole body stiffen.

"Papa," she said gently, reaching over to cover his hands with hers. "I worked with him for three years. A certain amount of familiarity is to be expected."

"And yet he insults you like this, throwing you to his dog of a brother like refuse, straight back into the tabloids." Her father frowned at her, and a small chill tickled the back of her neck. "Perhaps his expectation was for rather more familiarity than you offered, have you thought of that?"

It wasn't the first time her father had managed to articulate her deepest fears. But this time it seemed to sting more. Adriana pulled her hands away.

"Eat, Emilio," her mother said then, slipping into her usual seat and raising her brows when Adriana's father only scowled at the cooked breakfast she set before him. "You hate it when your eggs get cold."

"It was never like that," Adriana said, pushed to defend herself—though she wasn't sure she was addressing her father as much as herself. "Lenz is a good man."

"He is a man," her father replied shortly, something she didn't like in his gaze. "A very powerful man. And you are a very beautiful woman with only a terrible history and a disgraced family name to protect you."

"Emilio, please," her mother interjected.

Her father looked at her for an uncomfortable moment, then dropped his gaze to his meal, his silence almost worse. Adriana excused herself, unable to imagine eating even a bite when her stomach was in knots.

She made her way through the ancient villa to her childhood bedroom. It would be easier to leave Kitzinia altogether, she knew. She'd sat up nights as a child, listening to her mother beg her father to emigrate, to live in a place where their surname need never cause any kind of reaction at all. But Emilio Righetti was too proud to abandon the country his ancestor had betrayed, and Adriana understood it, no matter how hard it was to bear sometimes, no matter how she wished she didn't. Because when it came right down to it, she was the same.

She shut the door to her bedroom behind her and sank down on the edge of her bed. She was so tired, though she didn't dare let herself sleep. She had to return to the palace. Had to face Pato again.

Adriana let her eyes drift shut, wishing herself far away from the villa she'd grown up in, surrounded by the remains of the once vast Righetti wealth. If she looked out her window, she could see the causeway the kingdom had built in the 1950s, linking the red-roofed, picturesque city that spread along the lakeside to the royal palace that sat proudly on its own island in the middle of the blue water, its towers and spires thrust high against the backdrop of the snowcapped Alps. The villa boasted one of the finest addresses in the old city, a clear indication that the Righettis had once been highly favored by many Kitzinian rulers.

Now the villa was a national landmark. A reminder. The birthplace and home of the man who had murdered his king, betrayed his country, nearly toppling the kingdom with his treachery. Because of him, all the rest of the Righetti family history was seen through a negative lens. There had been

other royal mistresses from other noble Kitzinian families—
but only the Righettis enjoyed the label of witches. Whores.

There was no escape from who she was, Adriana knew.
Not as long as she stayed here. And she didn't understand
what was happening to her now—what was happening *in*
her. What had ignited in her last night at that embassy party
under Pato's arrogant golden stare. What had stalked her
dreams all through the long night, erotic and wild, and still
thrummed beneath her skin when she woke...

That was a lie, she thought now, cupping a hand over the
nape of her neck as if she could ease the tension she felt.
Adriana knew exactly what was happening. She didn't *want*
to understand it, because she didn't want to admit it. Yet the
way her father had looked at her today, as if she was somehow visibly tainted by the family history, made it impossible
to keep lying to herself.

She'd heard it all her life. It had been flung at her in school
and was whispered behind her back even now. It wasn't
enough that she was assumed to be traitorous by blood, like
all her male relatives. She was the only female Righetti of
her generation, and more, was the very image of her famous
forebears—there were portraits in the Royal Gallery to prove
it. They were well-known and well-documented whores, all
the way down to Adriana's great-aunt, who had famously
beguiled one of the king's cousins into walking away from
his dukedom, disowned and disgraced.

And Adriana was just like them.

She knew exactly how tainted she really was, how very
much she lived down to her family's legacy. Because it wasn't
Lenz who had dreamed of something more familiar. It was
her.

Lenz was good and kind, and he'd believed in her. He'd
given her a chance. Adriana was the first Righetti to set foot
in the palace since her traitorous ancestor had been executed

there a hundred years ago, and Lenz had made that happen. He'd changed everything. He'd given her hope. And in return, Adriana had adored him, happy simply to be near him.

And yet she'd dreamed of Pato in ways she'd never dreamed of his brother. Wild and sensual. Explicit. Maybe it shouldn't surprise her that she couldn't get Pato out of her head, she thought now in a wave of misery. Maybe it was programmed into her very flesh, her bones, to want him. To want anything, anyone royal, moving from one prince to the next. To be exactly what she'd always been: a Righetti.

That was what they said in the tabloids, which had pounced on her switch from Lenz's office to Pato's with malicious glee, after three years of going a bit easier on her. *She's failed to snare Prince Lenz with her Righetti wiles—will the shameless Pato be easier to trap?*

Maybe this had all been inevitable from the start.

Her mobile phone chirped at her from the bedside table, snapping her eyes open. She reached for it and tensed when she saw the name that flashed on the screen. It felt like confirmation that she was cursed. But she picked it up, because Pato was her job. Her responsibility. It didn't matter what she felt.

It only mattered what she did, and she controlled that. Not him. Not the ghosts of her slutty ancestors. Not her own treacherous blood.

Stop being so melodramatic, she ordered herself, pulling in a deep breath. *Nothing is inevitable.*

"It's eight-fifteen in the morning," she said by way of a greeting, and she didn't bother to sweeten her tone. "Surely too early for your usual debauchery."

"Pack your bags," Pato said, sounding uncharacteristically alert despite the hour. "We're flying to London this afternoon. There's some charity thing I had no intention of attending, and now, apparently, must. My brother commands it."

Adriana blinked, and sorted through the possibilities in her head.

"Presumably you mean the Children's Foundation, of which you and your brother are major benefactors," she said crisply. "And their annual ball."

"Presumably," he agreed, that alertness blending into his more typical laziness, and prickling over her skin no matter how badly she didn't want to be affected. "I don't really care, I only follow orders. And Adriana?"

"Yes?" But she knew. She could hear it in his voice. She could imagine that smile in the corner of his mouth, that gleam in his eyes. She didn't have to see any of it—she felt it. Her eyes drifted shut again, and she hated herself anew.

"It's never too early for debauchery," he said in that low, stirring way that was only his. "I'd be delighted to prove that to you. You can make it back to the palace in what? Twenty minutes?"

"You need to stop," she retorted, not realizing she meant to speak, and then it sat there between them. Pato didn't reply, but she could *feel* him. That disconcerting power of his, that predatory beauty. She dropped her forehead into one hand, kept her eyes shut. "I'm not your toy. I don't expect you to make my job easy for me, but this is unacceptable." He still didn't speak, but she could feel the thrum of him inside her, the electricity. "Not every woman you meet wants to sleep with you."

He laughed, and she felt it slide through her like light, illuminating too many truths she'd prefer to hide away forever. Exposing her. Making that curl of heat glow again, low and hot, proving what a liar she was.

"Rule number four," he began.

"Would you like to know what you can do with your rules?" she demanded, desperate.

"Adriana," he chided her, though she could hear the thread

of laughter in his voice. Somehow, that made it worse. "I'm fairly certain I could legally have you beheaded for speaking to me in such an appalling fashion, given the medieval laws of our great kingdom. I am your prince and your employer, not one of your common little boyfriends. A modicum of respect, please."

She was too raw. Too unbalanced. It crossed her mind then that she might not survive him. Certainly not intact. That he might be the thing that finally broke her.

"I apologize, Your Royal Highness," she said, her voice much too close to a whisper. "I don't know what came over me."

"Rule number four," he said again, softly. And meanwhile her heart thudded so hard in her chest that she could feel the echo of it in her ears, her teeth. Her sex. "If you can't muster up the courage to say it to my face, I'm not going to take it seriously."

Because he knew, of course. That she was using this phone conversation to hide, because she doubted her own strength when he was standing in front of her. He'd watched it, hadn't he? Exploited it. He knew exactly how weak she was.

And now she did, too.

"London," she said, changing the subject, because she had to end this conversation right now. She had to find her balance again, or at least figure out how to fake it. "A charity ball. I'll pack appropriately, of course."

"Say it to my face, Adriana," he urged her, and she told herself she didn't recognize what she heard in his voice then. But her skin broke out in goose bumps, even her breasts felt heavy, and she knew better. She knew. "See what happens."

"I should be back in the palace within the hour, Your Royal Highness," she said politely, and hung up.

And then sat there on the edge of her bed, her head in her

hands, and wondered what the hell would become of her if she couldn't find a way to control this. To control *herself*.

Because she was terribly afraid that if she couldn't, Pato would.

CHAPTER THREE

THE CHARITY BALL in London was, of course, as tedious as every other charity ball Pato had ever attended. He smiled. He posed for obligatory photographs with Lenz and the chilly Lissette, as well as with any number of other people whose names he forgot almost before he heard them. He then contemplated impaling himself on the dramatic ice sculpture near the lavish buffet to see if that might enliven the evening in some small way.

"Restrain yourself," Adriana replied, in that stuffy voice that he found amused him far more than it should, when he announced his intentions. Pato angled a look at her.

She stood beside him as she had all evening, never more than three steps away, as if she'd put him on an invisible leash and was holding it tight. Her lovely face was smoothed to polite placidity, she knew exactly how to blend into the background whenever someone came to speak to him, and she held her mobile phone tight in one hand as if she planned to use it to subdue him if he made a break for it. She'd been nothing but irritatingly serene and unflappably professional since she'd returned to the palace with her packed bag this morning. And all this time, across the span of Europe and the whole of London, she'd managed to avoid looking at him directly.

Pato found her fascinating.

"Restraint?" he asked, noting the way her shoulders tensed

beneath the cap sleeves of the elegant black sheath she wore when he spoke. Every time he spoke. It made him want to press his mouth to her collarbone, to lick his way up the curve of her neck to the subdued sparkle of small diamonds at her ears. "I'm unfamiliar with the concept."

She smiled slightly, but kept her attention trained on the dance floor in front of them. "Truer words have never been spoken, Your Royal Highness."

He laughed. He liked it when she slapped at him, when her voice was something more than cool, smooth, bland. He liked when he could sense her temper, her frustration. He found that the more he told her how bored he was, the less bored he actually felt.

Pato knew he was on dangerous ground. He didn't care. He hadn't enjoyed himself so much in years.

A curvy brunette in a slinky dress slithered up to him then, her heavily kohled eyes sweeping over Adriana dismissively before she leaned in close and ran her hands over Pato's chest.

"Your Royal Highness," she purred, her lips painted a sultry red that matched the fingernails she ran along the length of his tie. "We meet again. I knew we would."

Pato smiled indulgently. He had no idea who she was. "And you were right."

Beside him, he felt Adriana bristle, and he enjoyed that immensely, so he picked up the brunette's hand and kissed it, making her lean even more heavily against him.

"Dance with me," she commanded him in a sultry voice.

Pato didn't feel like dancing and he wasn't particularly fond of commands, but he could feel Adriana's disapproval like a cold wind at his back, and so he smiled wider.

"I'm afraid I'm here with my own version of an electronic ankle bracelet," he said blithely, turning slightly. He indicated Adriana with a nod of his head, and was pleased to notice she flushed. At the attention? Or was that the sweet kick of her temper? And why did he want so badly to know? "It's like a walking house arrest."

The brunette blinked, looking from him to Adriana and then back.

"What did you do?" she asked, wide-eyed, no doubt plotting her call to the tabloids as she spoke.

"Haven't you heard?" Pato asked, his eyes on Adriana and the way her hand tensed around her mobile as she glared out at the crowd. "I've been very, very naughty. Again."

The brunette made some reply, but Pato watched Adriana, who dragged her gaze to his then as if it hurt her to do it. Even better, her meltingly brown eyes shot fire at him.

"There you are," he said quietly, with a satisfaction he didn't bother to hide. He smiled when her eyes narrowed. He tried to make his voice sound like a supplicant's, but what came out was more like lazy challenge. "Am I allowed to dance, Adriana? Is that permitted?"

"Stay where I can see you," she ordered him, all smooth command, as if she really did have him under her control. His smile deepened when she turned a cool gaze on the brunette. "Please don't force me to invoke Kitzinian law, ma'am. No leaving the ballroom. No public displays. Keep it clean and polite. Do you understand?"

The woman nodded, looking slightly dazed, and Pato laughed.

"My very own prison warden," he said, as if he approved. "I am duly chastened."

He pulled the brunette into his arms as he took to the floor, but he couldn't seem to take his eyes off Adriana, who stood where he'd left her, looking calm and unruffled. Serene. She even gazed at him across the swell of bodies, a kind of victory in her dark eyes. He felt it like a direct challenge.

When the interminable dance was finished, he murmured the appropriate things to the brunette, forgot her and then prowled back over to the assistant he'd never wanted in the first place. This time, she looked at him as he approached. More than that, she met his eyes boldly. He didn't know why that should affect him far more than the way the lush brunette had leaned against him throughout the dance, trying to entice him with her curves.

"You don't know who that woman is, do you?" Adriana asked when he reached her side, her tone mild. Polite. Pato knew better than to believe it.

"I haven't the faintest idea."

"But you slept with her." Something like panic flared in her dark gaze, intriguing him even as she blinked it away. The tips of her ears were red, he noticed, up there near her swept-back blond hair, and her eyes were too bright. "Didn't you?"

"Probably." He arched a brow at her. "Are you asking that in an official capacity, Adriana? Or are you jealous?"

"I'm merely curious," she said with a sniff, sounding as if she was discussing something as dry and uninteresting as his daily schedule. "I imagine, at this point, you can't walk across a single room in Europe without tripping over legions of former conquests."

"Well," he said. "I rarely trip."

"It must be difficult, at this point, to find someone you *haven't* already been intimate with." She smiled at him, that killer smile he'd seen before, sweet and deadly, which was supposed to be a weapon and instead delighted him. "Then again, it's not as if you can remember, anyway, can you?"

Pato stood there for a moment, that same jagged restlessness beating at him, making him want things he'd given up a long time ago. Making him hard and wild, and shoving him much too close to a line he couldn't allow himself to cross.

And still she smiled at him like that, as if she could handle this kind of battle, when he knew she was completely unaware of how much danger she was in.

"Ah," he said in the low voice he could see made her shiver, and then he smiled as if she was prey and he was already on her. In her. "I see." And he was closer than he should have been. He was much too close and he didn't care at all, because her eyes widened and were that intoxicating shade of the finest Swiss chocolate. "You're under the impression that you can shame me."

They stared at each other, while laughter and conversation and the music kicked around them. Her lovely face flushed red. He saw the flash of that same panic he'd seen before, as if she wasn't at all as controlled as she pretended, but she didn't look away. Brave, he thought. Or foolish.

Pato lost himself in her dark gaze then, electric and alive and focused on him as if nothing else existed. As if he was already buried deep inside her, and she was waiting for him to move.

That image didn't help matters at all. He blew out a breath.

"Come," he said shortly, annoyed with himself. He turned on his heel and started across the great ballroom, knowing she had no choice but to follow, to keep him on that absurd leash of hers. And she did.

"Where are you going?" she asked as she fell into step with him. He didn't think that hint of breathlessness in her voice was from walking, and it carved out something like a smile inside him.

"It's like we're chained together, Adriana." He couldn't seem to find his footing, and that was a catastrophe waiting to happen. And still, he didn't care about that the way he knew he should. "Think of the possibilities."

"No, thank you," she replied, predictably, and he indulged himself and wrapped his hand around her upper arm, feigning solicitousness as he moved her through the door that led out toward the gardens. She jumped when he touched her, electric shock and that darker kick beneath it. He knew because he felt it, too. Her skin was softer than satin, warm and smooth beneath his palm, she smelled faintly of jasmine, and he shouldn't have done it. Because now he knew.

Her eyes flew to his, and it punched through him hard, making him want to push her back against the nearest wall, lift her against him, lose himself completely in the burn of it. In her.

"Are you sure?" he asked, as they moved from the bright light of the ballroom into the soft, cool dark outside. He led her across the wide patio, skirting the small clumps of people who stood clustered around the bar tables that dotted it here and there. "Five minutes ago my sexual escapades were foremost on your mind. Don't tell me you've lost interest so quickly."

He looked down at her, and made no effort to contain the heat in him. The fire. He felt a tremor run through her, and God help him, he wanted her more than he'd wanted anything in years.

"I didn't realize you were so sensitive about your scandalous past, Your Royal Highness," she said, in a rendition of her usual cool he might have believed, had he not been looking into the wild heat in her gaze. "I'll take care not to mention it again."

"Somehow," he murmured, his grip on her arm tightening just enough to make her suck in a breath, just enough to torture himself, "I very much doubt that."

At some point, he was going to have to figure out why this woman got to him like this. But not tonight. Not now.

She pulled her arm from his grip as he steered her between two tables, as if concerned they couldn't make it through the narrow channel side by side. But she rubbed at the place he'd touched her as if he'd left behind a mark, and Pato smiled.

In the deepest, farthest shadows of the patio, he found an empty table, the candle in the center, which should have been glowing, unlit. But he didn't need candlelight to see her as she deliberately put the table between them, keeping as far out of his reach as she could. His eyes adjusted to the dark and he studied the flush on her cheeks, the hectic sparkle in her gaze.

And then he waited, leaning his elbows on the table and watching her. Her pretty eyes widened. She shifted from one foot to the other. He made her nervous, and he couldn't pretend he didn't like it.

"I wasn't trying to shame you," she said after long moments passed, just the two of them in a far, dark corner, all the nerves he could see on her face rich in her voice. And there was something else, he thought as he studied her. Something he couldn't quite identify.

"Of course you were."

"I didn't mean—"

"You did."

She looked stricken for a moment, then dropped her gaze to the tabletop, and he watched as she crossed her arms as if she thought she needed to hold herself together. Or protect herself.

"What are you ashamed of, Adriana?" he asked softly.

She flinched as if he'd slapped her, telling him a great deal more than he imagined she meant to do, but her expression was clear when she lifted her head. That mask again. She let out a breath and then she opened her mouth—

"Don't lie to me," he heard himself say, and worse, he could feel how important it was to him that she heed him. How absurdly, dangerously important. "Don't clean it up. Just tell me."

"I'm a Righetti, Your Royal Highness," she said after a moment, her dark eyes glittering in the shadows. "Shame runs like blood in our veins. It's who we are."

Pato didn't know how long they stood like that, held in that taut, near-painful moment. He didn't know how long he gazed at her, at the proud tilt of her chin and the faintest tremor in her lips, with that darkness in her eyes. He didn't know how she'd punched into him so completely that her hand might as well have ripped through his chest. That was what it felt like, and he didn't want that. He didn't want *this*. He couldn't.

"Adriana," he said finally, but his voice was no more than a rasp. And then he saw figures approaching from the corner of his eye, and he stopped, almost grateful for the intrusion into a moment that shouldn't have happened in the first place.

She dropped her gaze again, and hunched her shoulders slightly as she stood there, as if warding off whoever had come to stand at the table a small distance behind her. Pato didn't spare them a glance. He didn't look away from Adriana for even a moment, and the fact that was more dangerous than anything that had come before didn't escape him.

He wanted to touch her. He wanted to pull her against him, hold her, soothe her somehow, and he felt hollow inside because of it. Hollow and twisted, and stuck where he'd put himself, on the other side of an incidental table and an impossible divide, useless and corrupt and dismissable.

A fine bed he'd made, indeed.

And then she stiffened again, as if she'd been struck, and Pato frowned as he recognized the voices coming from behind her.

"Was that wise, do you think?" The cold, precise tones of Princess Lissette, her faint accent making the words seem even icier. She sounded as blonde and Nordic as she looked, Pato thought uncharitably. And as frigid.

"I'm not sure what wisdom has to do with it."

There was no mistaking his brother's voice, and the ruthlessly careful way he spoke while in public. The dutiful Crown Prince Lenz and his arranged-since-the-cradle bride stood at the next table, a candle bright between them, the warm glow doing nothing to ease their stiff, wary postures.

There were worse beds to lie in than his, Pato knew, eyeing his brother. *Poor bastard.*

"One must strive to be compassionate, of course," Lissette continued in the same measured way. "But even I know of her family's notoriety. Do you worry that it reflects badly on your judgment, your discernment, that you selected her to be your assistant when she is widely regarded as something of a pariah?"

Pato went still. Adriana seemed turned to stone, a statue, her eyes lowered as she bent slightly forward over her crossed arms.

"Look at me," he ordered her in an undertone, but she ignored him.

Behind her, an uncomfortable silence swelled. Pato saw his brother begin to frown, then remember himself and fight it back. His ice princess fiancée only gazed back at him calmly. Pato wanted to order them to stop talking, to point out that Adriana was *right here*—but he didn't trust that the princess would stop. Or that she wasn't already aware that Adriana stood at the next table. And he didn't want Adriana to be any more of a target. A dim alarm sounded in him then, questioning that unusual protective urge, but he shoved it aside.

"This will all go much smoother, I think," Lenz said finally, an edge to his voice, "if you do not speak of things you don't understand, Princess."

"I believe I understand perfectly," she replied with cool hauteur. "You took a traitor's daughter as your mistress and flaunted her in the face of Kitzinian society, for years. What is there to misunderstand?"

"Adriana Righetti was never my mistress," Lenz snapped, his tone scathing. Even derisive. "Credit me with slightly more intelligence than that, Lissette."

There were other voices then, calling out for the happy royal couple from some distance across the patio, and Pato watched in a quiet fury as his brother pasted on his usual public smile, offered his arm to his fiancée—who smiled back in the same way as she took it—before they glided away. He had the wholly uncharacteristic urge to smack their heads together.

Then he glanced back at Adriana, who still hadn't moved a muscle.

"Look at me," he said again, with an odd urgency he didn't understand.

She lifted her head then and the pain on her face stunned him into silence. He could see it in her dark eyes, slicked not with embarrassment but with a kind of grief.

For a moment he was lost. This wasn't the tough, impervious Adriana he'd grown accustomed to over the past days— unflappable, he'd assumed, thanks to growing up a beautiful Righetti girl in the sharp teeth of Kitzinian society. But then, suddenly, he understood.

And didn't care at all for how it made him feel.

"My God," he said flatly. "You're in love with him."

Adriana woke up in a rush and had no idea where she was.

She was on her stomach on an unfamiliar bed in a sunlit room she'd never seen before. She blinked, frowned, and realized as she did both that her head ached and that she'd neglected to remove her eye makeup the night before. What—

There was a slight movement behind her, a small shift against the mattress.

She was not alone in the bed.

Adriana froze. Then, very slowly, her heart pounding, she turned to look, somehow knowing what she would see even as she prayed she was mistaken.

Please not him. Please not him. Please—

Prince Pato lay sprawled out on his back, the sheets kicked off, naked save for a pair of tight navy blue briefs that clung to his narrow hips. The light from the skylights bathed him in shades of gold, and she couldn't quite take in that perfect, hard-packed flesh of his, so close beside her she could almost feel the heat he generated, and could see the rough shadow of his beard on his jaw. She couldn't make sense of all his fine masculine beauty, much less the picture of sheer abandon he made, sun-kissed and golden and stretched out so carelessly against the crisp white sheets.

She was in bed with Pato.

Her mouth was too dry; her eyes felt scraped and hollow. She felt fragile and broken, and had no idea how to pull herself together enough to handle this. Adriana was afraid she might be sick.

In a panic, she whipped her head around, yanked back the sheet and looked down at herself, not sure whether to be horrified or relieved to discover that while she wasn't naked, she wore only the matching cranberry hip-slung panties and bra she'd had on beneath her gown at the charity ball.

The ball. Adriana fought to keep breathing as images from the night before began to flood her head. Those strange, intense moments with Pato. His hand on her arm. The way he'd looked at her, as if he could see straight into her. Then Lenz's voice, so disgusted, so appalled.

She couldn't think about Lenz. She couldn't.

Had she really done this? Had she decided to become what she'd always been so proud she wasn't? With the one person in all the world best suited to debauch her—or anyone, come to that—completely? He did it by rote, no doubt. He could do it in his sleep. No wonder she couldn't recall it.

Adriana turned to look at him again, as if she might see her own actions tattooed on his smooth skin, and she jolted in shock.

Pato was awake. And watching her.

"Oh, my God," she whispered. She pulled the sheets up

to her neck, fought the urge to burst into tears, and stared at him in horror.

Pato's golden eyes were sleepy, his hair a thick, careless mess, and still he fairly oozed the same sensual menace he had the night before, when he'd been dressed so elegantly. He studied her for a long moment, and the great, wide bed felt like a tiny little cot, suddenly. Like a trap. Adriana's pulse beat at her, and she forgot about her headache.

"I hope you appreciate the sacrifice I made to your modesty," Pato said in that drawling way of his, as if he was too lazy to bother enunciating properly. He waved at the form-fitting briefs he wore. At that flat abdomen of his, the crisp dark hair that disappeared beneath the fabric. She jerked her eyes away, and his mouth curved. "I think you know very well I prefer to sleep naked."

Adriana felt dizzy, and part of her welcomed it. Encouraged it. It would be such a relief to simply faint dead away. To escape whatever morning-after this was. She lifted a hand to her head, only belatedly realizing that her hair had tumbled down from its chignon, and was hanging around her face in a wild mess that rivaled Pato's.

Somehow, that made it worse. It made her feel like the wanton slut she must have become last night. Was it possible to share a bed with Prince Pato and *not* be a wanton slut? Her chest felt tight.

He watched her as she pushed the mass of blond waves behind her shoulders, his golden gaze like a flame as it touched her. More images from the previous night flashed through her head then, as if the heat of his gaze triggered her memory, and she frowned at him.

"You got me drunk," she accused him.

Blaming him felt good. Clean. Far better to concentrate on that and not the images flickering in her head. Some dark-paneled pub, or possibly the kind of rich man's club a prince might frequent, thick with reds and woods and the shots of strong spirits Pato slid in front of her, one after the next, his golden gaze never leaving her face. His elegant hands brushing hers. That wicked mouth of his much too close.

"You got you drunk," he corrected, shifting over to his side and propping his head up on one hand as he continued to regard her with that lazy intent that made her belly fold in on itself. "Who was I to stand in your way?"

A dark street, laughter. *Her* laughter, and the wicked current of his voice beneath it. Her arm around Pato's waist and his lean, hard arm around her shoulders. Then being held high against his chest as he moved through some kind of lobby...

This was awful, Adriana thought then, her chest aching with the sobs, the screams, she refused to let out. This was beyond awful.

"My God." She said it again, despite the decided lack of any divine intervention this morning. She squeezed her eyes shut, bracing herself for the blow. Preparing herself, because she had to know. "Did you—? Did we—?"

There was nothing but silence. Adriana dared to open her eyes again, to find that Pato was staring at her in outrage.

She shuddered. "Does that mean we did?" she asked in a tiny voice.

"First of all," he said, in that low voice of his that curled around her like a caress, and she couldn't seem to shake it off, "I am not in the habit of taking advantage of drunk women who pretend to detest me when they are sober, no matter how much they beg."

His gaze was hard on hers, and Adriana felt caught in the heat, the command, that surely a wastrel like Pato shouldn't have at his disposal. Eventually, his mouth moved into a small, sexy grin that shouldn't have tugged at her like that, all fire and need in the core of her, then a shiver everywhere else. She couldn't seem to think, to move. To breathe. She could only stare back at him, her heart going wild, as if he was holding her captive in the palm of his hand.

"And second," he said silkily, "if we had, you wouldn't have to ask. You'd know."

"Oh," Adriana said faintly, not sure she was breathing. "Well. If you're sure…?"

Pato shook his head. "I'm sure."

She believed him. He was only *looking* at her now, all that gleaming attention of his focused on her. He wasn't even touching her, and she felt branded. Scalded. Changed. She had a perfect memory of his hand on her arm, the heat of it, the punch of it, the way everything inside her had wound deliciously tight. She believed him, and yet there was something inside her that almost wished—

Stop, she snapped at herself, off balance and scared and much too close to falling apart.

Adriana realized belatedly that far too much time had passed and she'd done nothing but stare at him, while he watched her and no doubt read every last thought that crossed her mind. He was lethal; she understood that now, in a way she hadn't before. He was lethal and she was in bed with him and somehow by the grace of God she hadn't succumbed to his darker nature or, worse, *hers…*

Adriana frowned. "Did you say I *begged?*"

Pato smiled.

"For what?" she asked in an appalled whisper. "Exactly?"

He smiled wider.

"This can't be happening." She was barely audible, even to her own ears, but she felt each word like a stone slamming through her. "Did I—" But even as she asked, she shut herself off. "No. I don't want to know."

"You begged very prettily," he told her then, that wild gleam in his eyes, which made her feel much too hot, too constricted, as if she might burst wide-open. "If it helps."

It helped confirm that she hated herself, Adriana thought, that old black wave of self-loathing rising in her and then drenching her, drowning her, in all the ways she'd let herself down. *Blood really will tell,* she thought bitterly. *You've been fooling yourself all these years, but in the end, you're no better than any of them. Righetti whores.*

She managed to take a breath, then another one.

And then, through her confusion, one thing became perfectly clear: it was time to accept who she was, once and for all. And that meant it was time to change her life.

"Thank you, Your Royal Highness," she said stiffly, not looking at him. "I'm sorry that I let myself get so out of control and that you had to deal with me. How incredibly unprofessional."

She scrambled to crawl out of the bed, away from him. This had to end. What was she was doing here, disgracing herself with a prince, when she could be living without the weight of all of this in some happy foreign land like her brothers? She'd been so desperate to prove herself—and now she'd proved only that she was exactly who everyone thought she was.

Enough, she thought grimly.

And there was what Lenz had said, the way he'd said it, but she didn't want to think about that. She didn't want to let it hurt her the way she suspected it would when she did.

It seemed to take an hour to reach the edge of the bed, and as she went to swing her feet to the ground, Pato simply reached out and hauled her back by the arm until she was on her side and facing him. No sheet this time to hide behind. Just far too much of her nearly naked body far too near his. Panic screamed through her, making her skin burst into flames.

"You can't just...*manhandle* people!" she exclaimed heatedly.

Pato shrugged, and the total lack of concern in the gesture reminded her forcefully that, black sheep or not, he was a royal prince. Pampered and indulged. Used to getting whatever he wanted. He wasn't required to concern himself with other people's feelings, particularly hers.

That should have disgusted her. It alarmed her that it didn't.

"I think we're a bit past worrying about professionalism," he said, his voice mild, though his eyes were intent on hers, and his mouth looked dangerous in a new way with his jaw unshaved and his thick hair so unruly.

And all of him *so close.*

"I need to leave," she replied evenly. "The palace, the royal family—I should have done it a long time ago." She started to pull away from him, but he only shifted position and smoothed his hand down to the indentation of her waist. He rested it there, almost idly, and she froze as if he was pressing her to the bed with brute force.

It would have been easier if he had been, she recognized on some level. It would have been unambiguous. But instead he was only touching her, *barely* touching her, and she couldn't seem to form the words to demand he let her go. She only trembled. Inside and out.

And he knew. His eyes gleamed, and he knew.

"At least let me get back under the sheet," she said desperately.

"Why?" He shrugged again, so lazy. So at ease. "You're showing less skin than you would if you were wearing a bikini."

"You've never seen me in a bikini," she managed to say. "It would be inappropriate."

His fingers traced the faintest pattern along the curve of her body, and she could no more help the shiver of goose bumps that rose on her skin than she could turn back time and avoid this scenario in the first place. He looked at the telltale prickle of flesh, his hand tightened at her waist and she let out a tiny, involuntary sound that made his golden gaze darken and focus on her, hot and hungry.

But when he spoke again, his voice was light.

"I hate to be indelicate, Adriana, but I've already seen all of this. You're about eight hours too late for modesty."

"It's time for me to leave," she said, desperate and determined in equal measure. "You never wanted an assistant in the first place, and I think it's high time I rethink my career prospects."

Pato only raised a dark brow.

"I have no business being at the palace," she said urgently. "The princess was right. If I'd had any idea that working for your brother would harm *his* reputation, I never would have taken the job in the first place. I would never want people to think less of him because of me. I would never want to compromise his reputation, or—"

"You can't possibly be this naive."

Something Adriana had never seen before moved over Pato's face. His hand tightened briefly, and then he released her and sat up in a smooth roll.

He shoved his hair back and pinned her with a glare when she scrambled away from him and to her knees on the far side of the bed, pulling the sheet back over her as she went. She had never seen him look like that. Brooding, dark. No hint of his famous laughter, his notorious smile.

"I'm being rational, not naive," she countered, unable to tear her eyes away from him when he looked like this, as if he was someone else. Someone ruthless and hard. Not like easy, careless Pato at all. "Your brother was the first person to believe in me, but it was wrong of me to take advantage of that."

Pato shook his head, rubbing at his jaw with one hand as if he was keeping words back manually.

"I abused his kindness," she continued, her unease growing. "His—"

"For God's sake, Adriana," Pato spat out. "He wasn't being *kind*. He was grooming you to be his mistress."

CHAPTER FOUR

FOR A LONG, breathless moment, Adriana could only stare at him, another piece of her world crumbling into dust in this bed, shattering in that relentless golden gaze.

"That's absurd." She felt turned inside out. "He would never do something like that."

"You know all about his previous assistants, I'm sure," Pato said, in that same blunt way, a hard gleam in his gaze and no hint of a curve on that mouth of his. "Did you never question why he cycled so many of them through that position? And why they all had such different sets of credentials? One an art historian, another a socialite? Lenz prefers his mistresses be accessible."

Adriana felt as if she'd slipped sideways into some alternate reality, where nothing made sense any longer. Lenz had wanted her, all this time, as she'd so often daydreamed he might—but not as his mistress. She'd never wanted *that*. And now she sat too close to naked in the morning sun with Pato, of all people, who looked like some harsher version of himself, and she was terrified that he might be right. Hadn't her father said the same thing only yesterday?

"He's a good man," she whispered, shaken.

"Yes," Pato said impatiently. "And yet he's still flesh and blood like all the rest of us."

She shook her head, and looked down at the bed. She'd

done this. She understood that, if nothing else. This was the Righetti curse. *This was her fault.* Her head felt heavy again, and it pounded, but she knew it wasn't a leftover from last night. It was the generations of Righettis running wild in her blood, and her silly notion she could be any different.

"Do people really think that I'm his mistress?" she asked, sounding like a stranger to her own ears. She was afraid to look at Pato then, but she made herself do it anyway. His eyes seemed darker than usual, and they glittered.

"Of course." There was an edge to his low voice then, a darker sheen to that intent way he looked at her. "You are a Righetti, he is a Kitzinian prince, and one thing we know about history, Adriana, is that it repeats itself until it kills us all."

Suddenly, the fact that she was practically naked with this man seemed obscene, disgusting. As if her flesh itself were evil, as if it had made her do this—her body ignoring her brain and acting of its own accord. She slid out of the bed and looked around wildly, her eyes falling on the nearest chair. She walked over and grabbed the oversize wrap that she'd worn against the cool London weather, dropped the sheet that made everything seem too sexual, and covered herself.

It didn't make her feel any better.

Adriana couldn't understand how she'd been so blind, so stupid. How she hadn't known that *of course* people would think the worst of her, no matter if the tabloids had eased off—out of respect for Lenz, she understood now in a miserable rush of insight. No one had cared that she was good at her job, that she'd never so much as touched the future king. Why had she imagined any of that would matter? *Because you wanted to pretend. Because you wanted to believe you could be someone else.*

But she was a Righetti. There was never any mistaking

that. She should have known it would poison everyone and everything she came into contact with. Even Lenz.

She turned then, and Pato still watched her, sitting there on his bed, a vision of indolent male beauty. Every inch of him royal, gorgeous and as utterly, deliberately corrupt as it was assumed she was. He'd chosen it. He was the Playboy Prince, scandalous and dissolute. But he was still a prince.

Adriana blinked. "So are you," she said slowly, as an idea took root inside her, and began to grow. "A Kitzinian prince, I mean."

Pato's mouth crooked. "To my father's everlasting dismay, yes."

It was so simple, Adriana thought then, staring at him as if she'd never seen him before. It could fix everything.

"Then we should make them all think that I'm *your* mistress," she said in a rush. She clutched the wrap tighter around her, drifting closer to the bed as she spoke. "The tabloids are halfway there already."

"I beg your pardon?"

"No one would be at all surprised to discover that *you* were sleeping with a Righetti," she continued excitedly, ignoring the odd, arrested look on his face. "Your brother is much too responsible to make that kind of mistake. But you live for mistakes. You're famous for them!"

"I'm not following you," he said, and she noticed then that his voice had gone low and hot, and not with the kind of heat she'd heard before.

"It wouldn't even take that much effort." She was warming to the topic as her mind raced ahead, picturing it. "One paparazzi picture and the whole world would be happy to believe that history was indeed repeating itself, but with a far more likely candidate than your brother."

Pato only looked at her for a long moment, and Adriana found herself remembering, suddenly, that he was second in line to the throne. One tragedy and he would be king. All of a sudden he looked as commanding, as regal, as a man in such a position should. Powerful beyond measure. Dangerous.

It was as if she hadn't seen him before. As if he'd been hiding, right there in plain sight, beneath the dissipated exterior. But how was that possible?

"It wouldn't be real, of course," she said quickly, confusion making her feel edgy. Or maybe that was him. "All we'd need was a few pictures and some good PR spin."

He laughed then, but it was a low, almost aggressive sound, and it made her whole body stiffen in reaction.

"You can't possibly be suggesting that we pretend you're sleeping with me to preserve my brother's reputation," he said softly, and Adriana didn't miss the fact that the tone he used was deadly. It made her stomach twist. "You are not actually standing here in my bedroom, wearing almost nothing, and proposing such a thing."

She searched his face, but he was a stranger, dark and hard.

"That's exactly what I'm proposing."

His jaw worked. His golden eyes flashed. "No."

She scowled at him. "Why not?"

"Do you really require a reason?" he demanded, and then he got to his feet, making everything that much more tense. "You'd be much better served making certain we both forget this absurd conversation ever happened."

That was when Adriana realized, in a kind of shock, that he was angry. Pato, who famously never got angry. Who was supposed to be carefree and easy in all things. Who had laughed off every sticky situation he'd ever been in.

But not this one. Not today. He was *angry*. And she had no idea why.

She watched him warily as he roamed around the foot of the bed, so close to naked, and now that temper she hadn't known he had spilling out around him like a black cloud.

But she couldn't stop. Not when she'd figured out a way to fix things. And what did he care, anyway? It wasn't as if *his* reputation was at stake.

"I don't understand," she said after a moment, trying to sound reasonable. Rational. "You've gone out of your way to link yourself to every woman with a bad reputation you've ever come across. Why not me? My bad reputation goes back centuries!"

"I actually did those things," he replied, that dark temper rich in his voice, in the narrow gaze he aimed at her. "I didn't pretend for the cameras. I don't apologize for who I am, but I also don't fake it."

Adriana blinked. "So your issue isn't the idea itself, then. It's that you need your debaucheries to be honest and truthful. Real."

The way he looked at her then made a low, dark pulse begin to drum in her, panic and heat and something else she'd never experienced before and couldn't name. It took everything she had not to bolt for the door and forget she'd ever started this.

"My reputation is my life's work," Pato said, and there was a certain harshness in his voice then, dark and grim and tired, that made something clutch hard in Adriana's chest. "It's not a cross I'm forced to bear. It's deliberate."

"Fine," she blurted out. She'd never felt so desperate. She only knew this had to happen, she had to have the opportunity to fix one thing her family name had ruined, just one thing—

"Fine?" he echoed, his golden eyes narrowing, focusing in on her in a way that should have made her fall over in a dead faint. Incinerate on the spot. Run.

Something.

But she met his gaze squarely instead.

"We don't have to fake it," Adriana said, very distinctly, so there could be no mistake. "I'll sleep with you."

All the air in the room evaporated into a shimmer of heat. Into the intensity of Pato's gaze, the electricity that arced between them, the tension bright and taut and very nearly painful.

He laughed, low and dark and wicked, and Adriana felt it like a touch, as if his strong, elegant hands were directly on her skin. It made her feel weak. It made her want to drop the wrap and press herself against him, to see if that might ease the heavy ache inside her, the pulse of it, the need.

But who was she kidding? She knew it would. And so did he.

"You have no idea what you're asking, Adriana," he scoffed. His mouth curved mockingly, knowingly, and that ache in her only grew sharper, more insistent. She suddenly wasn't at all sure what she was desperate for. But she couldn't look away. "You wouldn't know where to start."

Adriana couldn't stop the shivering, way down deep inside her.

Her bones felt like jelly and she didn't know what scared her more—that she might really follow through and throw herself at him, and God only knew what would become of her then, or that the terrible ache inside her might take her to the ground on its own, and then he'd know exactly how much he tormented her.

Though she suspected he already did.

Pato was coming toward her, that sun-kissed skin on careless display, the faint brush of dark hair across his hard pectoral muscles seeming to emphasize his fascinating, unapologetic maleness. And he watched her so intently as he moved, his golden eyes gleaming as if all the wickedness in the world was in him, dark and rich and his to use against her if he chose. All his.

She shouldn't find that at all intriguing. She shouldn't

wonder, now that she'd glimpsed a different side of this man, what else he hid behind his disreputable mask.

This is about Lenz, she reminded herself sharply. She refused to think about Pato's claim that her beloved crown prince had wanted her as his mistress all those years she'd believed they'd been working together in harmony. She couldn't let that matter. This was about saving the one thing she could save, the one thing her family name had blackened that she could actually wash clean.

She couldn't save herself, perhaps. But she could save Lenz's reputation.

"Your brother—" she began.

"Rule number five," Pato said smoothly, but with that alarming kick of dark fire beneath. "When attempting to negotiate your way into my bed, don't bring up my brother. Ever."

Adriana felt her pulse beating too hard inside her neck, her wrists. And lower, where it mixed with that ache in her, gave it bite. She forced herself to stand still as Pato roamed toward her. Forced herself to act as if he didn't, in fact, intimidate her—even when he stopped so close to her that she had to tilt her head back to look at him.

He crossed his arms over his chest, his eyes unreadable.

"Are we negotiating?" she asked, her voice so much smaller than it should have been. Telling him too much she shouldn't let him know.

"I don't take trembling virgins to my bed, Adriana," Pato said, with all that gold in his gaze and that curve to his lips, but still, that new hardness beneath. It almost made her miss what he'd said. Then it penetrated, and her body seemed to detonate into a long, red flush of humiliation—but he wasn't finished. "Particularly not trembling, terrified virgins who imagine themselves in love with my brother and view my bed as a sacrificial altar."

"I—" She'd never stammered in her life. She had to order herself to snap her mouth closed, to calm herself. Or at least to breathe. "I'm not terrified." His gaze never wavered, and yet she was sure it was consuming her where she stood. "And, of course, I'm certainly not a *virgin*."

His dark brows rose. "Convince me."

"How?" she demanded, bright red and humiliated. And trembling, just as he'd accused. He missed nothing. "Not that it would matter if I was or that it's any of your business, let me point out."

"But it is." He was merciless, his hard gaze hot. "You want in my bed? Then I want to know every last detail of your vast sexual experience. Convince me, Adriana. Consider it a job interview—your résumé. After all, you've read all about me in the tabloids. You said so yourself."

She told herself he couldn't possibly be asking that. *This couldn't possibly be happening.* But then, what part of this day so far was at all possible? She didn't drink to excess and wake up in men's beds. She didn't have extended conversations with royal Kitzinian princes in her underwear. And had she really told this man she would sleep with him?

So she took a deep breath and she told him what she thought he wanted to hear.

"I couldn't possibly count them all," she said primly, lifting her chin. "I stopped keeping track when I passed into triple digits."

He only shook his head at her.

"For all I know you and I have already slept together, in fact," she continued wildly. "Didn't you once tell an interviewer that you blacked out the better part of the last decade? Well, you're not alone. Who knows where I've been? You were probably there, too, making a spectacle of yourself."

"And somehow," Pato said mildly, "I remain unconvinced."

"Everybody knows I'm a whore," Adriana forced herself to

say, not wanting to admit how limited her sexual experience really was. She wasn't a virgin, true—but that was more or less a technicality, and deeply embarrassing to boot. "They've been calling me that since I was a child, before I even knew what the word meant. Why shouldn't I embrace it? You do."

"That doesn't answer the question, does it?" His gaze bored into her, not relenting at all. Not even the smallest bit. "You have not had sexual partners numbering in the triple digits, Adriana. I'd be very much surprised if you've had three in the whole of your life."

And then he simply stood there, staring down at her, somehow knowing these things that he shouldn't. It made her feel almost itchy, as if her skin had stopped fitting her properly. As if she was seconds away from exploding, humiliated and laid unacceptably bare.

"One." She bit out the admission, hating him, hating herself. And yet still as determined to go through with this as she was filled with that terrible, gnawing ache that she worried might consume her alive. *Do it for Lenz,* she ordered herself. "There was only one and it—"

He waited, his eyes intent and demanding on hers, and she couldn't do it. She couldn't tell this sleek, sensual, unapologetically carnal creature about that fumble in the dark, the shock of searing pain and then the unpleasant fullness that followed. That vulnerable, exposed feeling. She'd been seventeen. It had taken all of three unremarkable minutes in a bedroom at a party she shouldn't have gone to in the first place, and then he'd bragged to the whole school that the Righetti girl was as much of a whore as suspected.

"And?" Pato prompted her.

"It was mercifully brief."

"I feel seduced already," he said drily. "What a tempting picture you paint. How can I possibly resist the sacrificial near-virgin who wishes to prostrate herself in my bed for my brother's benefit? I've never been so aroused."

Each dry, sardonic word, delivered in that deliberately stinging way of his, made Adriana's fists tighten where she held the wrap around her. She felt that flush of heat that told her she was getting redder, broadcasting the fact he was getting to her. She felt that twist in her gut and still, that ache below. This was a disaster.

But you have to do it. You'll never be able to live with yourself if you don't. This might be the only opportunity you ever have to do something good with all this notoriety...

"Then teach me," she exclaimed, cutting him off before he could continue ripping her to shreds one sardonic word at a time.

For a moment, Pato only looked at her.

And then he closed the distance between them, reaching out to spear his hands into the wild tangle of her hair, making her go up slightly on her toes and brace her hands against the hot, hard planes of his chest or fall completely against him. Her wrap floated to the floor between them, and she forgot it as he held her face still, keeping her captive, a mere breath away from his beautiful mouth.

She heard a sharp, high sound, some kind of gasp, and realized only belatedly that she'd made it. The echo of it made her tremble, or perhaps that was the wildfire in his eyes.

"Teach me everything," she whispered, spurred on by some dark thing inside her she hardly recognized. But she saw the way his eyes flared, and the ache inside her bloomed in immediate response.

His mouth was so close to hers, his face dark and dangerous, that lethal fire in his gaze. And yet he only held her there, taut and breathless, while sensation after sensation shook through her. Towering flames in her throat, her breasts, her belly. That shocking brightness between her legs.

Her lips parted slightly, and she recognized it as the invitation it was. His gaze dropped to her mouth, hungry and hard, and she felt her nipples pull tight. Nothing existed but that pulse of heat that drummed in her, louder and wilder—

And then he dragged his gaze back to hers and let her go.

She caught herself before she staggered backward, but she was shaky, unbalanced, and for some reason felt as if she might burst into tears. She couldn't seem to form the words she needed, and his eyes darkened because, of course, he knew that, too. He'd done this to her deliberately.

"You can't handle me, Adriana," Pato growled. "Look at you. I've barely touched you and you're coming apart."

That dark thing inside of her roared through her, making her bold. Making her stark, raving mad. But she couldn't hold it in check. She couldn't stop.

She didn't *want* to stop, and she didn't want to think about why.

"It looks like you're the one who's coming apart, Your Royal Highness," she hissed. Taunting him. Poking at him, and she knew it. She wanted it—she wanted *him*—and the obvious truth of that was like another explosion, bathing her in a white-hot heat. Adriana had no choice then but to keep talking despite the way he looked at her. "Maybe your reputation is all lies and misdirection. Maybe the truth is *you* can't handle *me*."

When he laughed then, it was darker than what was inside her, darker and far wilder, and it connected to that ache in her, hard. So hard she stopped breathing.

And then he moved.

His arms came around her and his hands slid over her bottom with an easy command, as if he'd touched her a thousand times before and just as carnally, slipping directly into her panties and pausing to test her curves, her flesh, against the heat of his palms. She made a wild sort of sound, but as she did he hauled her to him and lifted her against him, pulling her legs around his waist even as her back hit the wall behind her.

The room seemed to spin around, but that was only Pato, pressing her to the wall of his chest and the wall at her back, molding his hips to hers, the hardest part of him flush against her. Skin. Heat. Fires within fires, and she was afraid she was already burned to a crisp. Everything hurt—but was eased by the heat of him, only to hurt again. And again.

She expected an explosion. A detonation. Something to match that searing blaze in his gaze, the drum of anticipation beneath her skin, that hunger between her legs that he was only making worse. Her eyes were glazed and wide, and she could feel him everywhere. That perfect, lean body pressed against her, into her, so powerful and male, holding her steady so far from the ground.

His hands moved over her skin, leaving trails of fire in his wake. He traced the curve of her breasts, teased the hard tips with his thumbs until she moaned. He moved his hips, rocking against her, making her breath come in desperate pants even as her core ignited into a glorious, molten ache that she never wanted to end, that she wasn't sure she'd survive.

Adriana couldn't think. She could only hold on to his broad, hard shoulders and surrender to the dark exultation that roared in her, that made her try to get closer to him, that made her think she might die if she couldn't taste him. That made her want things she'd only read about before. That made her want everything.

He leaned in close, so close that when his wicked mouth curved again, she felt it against her own lips, and it made her shake against him, the small moan escaping her before she could stop it.

"Let me see if I can handle this," he mocked her.

"I don't think you can," she heard herself say. "Or you already would have."

As if she was as wanton as he was, and as unashamed. As if she knew what she was demanding.

That smile of his deepened, torturing her. Delighting her.

And then, slowly and deliberately, with one hand on her bottom to move her against him in a sinuous rhythm that made her feel weak, the other at her jaw to hold her where he wanted her, Pato took his own sweet time and licked his way into her mouth.

Ruining her, Adriana thought while the world disappeared, forever.

He never should have tasted her.

That it was a terrible mistake was a certainty, but Adriana clung to him like honey, melting and hot, tasting like sugar and fire with her lithe body wrapped all around him. Pato couldn't stop himself. For a heady moment—his mouth angled over hers, tasting her again and again and again—he even forgot why he should.

This was supposed to be a lesson to her. A way to decidedly call her bluff, nothing more.

And yet he wanted to take her where they stood, pressed up against the wall, thrusting into the heat of her he could feel scalding him through the thin layers that barely separated them. She was so soft. So responsive.

Perfect.

But she didn't want *him,* no matter what her body shouted at him. No matter what he felt in his arms, what he tasted.

She met him even as he grew bolder, hotter, more demanding. She kissed him as if she'd forgotten who it was she truly wanted. She bloomed beneath his hands, incandescent and addicting. She twined her arms around his neck and writhed against him as if she was as desperate as he was, as if she wanted nothing more than Pato deep inside of her.

But she wanted Lenz. She was in love with Lenz. Pato had seen it.

It was that unpalatable fact that he couldn't make himself ignore, no matter how hard he was and no matter what he would have given, in that moment, to simply drive into her and ride them both into an oblivion where Lenz did not exist. Could never exist.

Where there was only this heat. This need. This delicious electricity, intense and greedy, that made him want to taste every part of her, make her scream out in pleasure while he did, and then take her until she sobbed his name.

His name, not his brother's.

But he couldn't stop. He didn't *want* to stop. What was this woman doing to him? He'd never acted with so little thought before. He'd never forgot to hide himself. He'd certainly never opened his mouth and let some part of the truth come out. It was as if he'd lost the control that had defined him since he was eighteen....

That couldn't happen. He couldn't let it.

He spun around, walking them back to the bed with Adriana still wrapped around him, and then he tortured himself by bringing them down on the mattress—catching himself on one arm so he didn't crush her, but letting himself revel in the feel of her beneath him the way he wanted her, even for a moment.

Pato had never put much stock in the kingdom's insistence that Righetti women were akin to witches, temptresses and jezebels without equal, but pulling himself away from Adriana, from all that soft, hot fire, was the hardest thing he could remember doing.

He didn't understand this. He didn't understand himself.

"I can handle it, Adriana," he told her. "I can handle you. But I won't."

He stood over her, telling himself it didn't matter that she sprawled there before him, her lips swollen from his, her breasts spilling from her bra and crying out for his hands, her silken limbs spread out before him like a dessert he hungered for as if he was a starving man. It didn't matter because it couldn't.

He smirked, knowing it would hit her like a slap. "But I appreciate the offer."

Her face blazed red as he'd thought it would, and she looked tense and unhappy as she pushed herself up to a sitting position. Her lovely blond hair fell in a sexy tangle around her pretty face, making her look as if he'd already had her. He wished he had, with an edge of desperation that should have alarmed him. But she sat before him, with all that lust and wild need still stamped on her face, and the only thing he felt was that pounding desire.

She inclined her head at the clear evidence that he wanted her, badly and unmistakably, then looked up to hold his gaze with hers, her chocolate eyes dark and still too hot.

"I can see how much you appreciate it, Your Royal Highness," she said softly, but with that kick beneath that he couldn't help but enjoy. He didn't understand why he liked her edginess. Why he liked how unafraid she was of him, even now.

He could still taste her. He was so hard for her it hurt, and he wasn't used to denying himself anything. Much less women. He couldn't remember the last time he'd tried. Pato had slept with any number of women who had assumed he'd be a conduit to his brother, who had cold-bloodedly used him for that purpose. It had never bothered Pato before.

He didn't know why it bothered him now—why that look on her face in the shadows last night kept flashing in his head. He only knew he wouldn't—couldn't—be this woman's path to his brother, no matter her reasons, no matter how convoluted it all was. He wanted her head to be full of him, and nothing else.

"We can't always have what we want," he said quietly. He meant it more than she knew.

"You can. You do." She frowned at him. "You've made a career out of it."

Pato shook his head. "You're not going to win this argument with me. No matter how sweetly you pout, or how naked you get. Not that I don't enjoy both."

She made a small sound of frustration, mixed, he could tell from the color in her cheeks, with that embarrassment that he found himself entirely too obsessed with. When was the last time he'd met a woman who still blushed?

"Is there any woman alive you *haven't* slept with?" she demanded. "Or is it only me?"

"It's only you," Pato assured her, not knowing why he was doing this. Not understanding what there was to gain from it. Surely it would be better simply to have her. That was the time-honored approach to situations like this. Chemistry never lasted. Sex was white-hot for only a small while, and then it burned itself out. The only thing denial ever did—or so he'd heard—was make the wanting worse.

But he had never wanted someone like this. And having tasted her, he very much doubted that sex would be a cure. More like his doom.

He didn't know where that thought came from, and yet it clawed into him.

"You didn't even know the word *no* until today!" she snapped at him.

"If I were you," he said in a low voice that he could see got to her when she shivered again, as if he'd run his fingers down the line of her elegant neck, "I'd quit now, before tempers are lost and consequences become far greater. I'd put on some clothes and remember myself. My place. Just a suggestion."

She pulled in a breath, and her hands balled into fists, and then she shook her head slightly as if she really was remembering herself.

"I told you I'd resign," she said after a moment. Her mouth firmed. "And I will. Today, in fact."

"No, you will not."

She *should* resign. He should see to it she was sacked, barred from the palace, kept away for her own good. She should take her melting brown eyes and that impossibly tempting body of hers, her irritating martyr's love for the undeserving Lenz, and leave Kitzinia far behind. She should protect herself from her family's history, from the endless, vicious rumor mill that comprised the highest levels of Kitzinian society, and was even nastier than usual when it came to her.

He wished he could protect her himself.

He was, Pato realized then, in terrible trouble. But this was a game, he reminded himself, and Adriana was a part of it. His strange, protective urges didn't matter—they couldn't. She wasn't going anywhere. He needed her to stay right where she was.

"You won't help me help your brother, and you won't let me leave," Adriana said, her voice as stiff as her body had become, her brown eyes rapidly cooling, which he told himself was better. "What *will* you let me do?"

"I suggest you do your job." It came out harsher than he'd intended, and he saw her blink, as if it hurt. He tried to force his usual laughter into his voice, that devil-may-care attitude he'd perfected, but he couldn't quite do it. "If you can. I can't promise I'll cooperate, but then, you knew that going in."

"I don't want—"

"I am Prince Patricio of Kitzinia and you are a Kitzinian

subject," he said, more himself in that moment than he'd allowed himself to be in years, and that, too, was trouble. Big trouble. It was too soon to be anything but Pato the Playboy, even here—and still, he couldn't stop. "You serve at my pleasure, Adriana. Yours is irrelevant."

For a breath, she seemed to freeze there before him. Then she averted her eyes in appropriate deference to his rank, and there was no particular triumph in winning that little skirmish, Pato found. Not when it made him feel empty. Adriana shot to her feet then and started for the door, her spine straight and every inch of her obviously, silently, furious. It hummed in the air between them. He knew it should offend his royal dignity, had he been possessed of any, but it only made him want to taste her again. Taste her temper. Let it take them both on a ride.

"Thank you, Your Royal Highness, for reminding me of my duty. And my place. I won't forget it again."

She spoke as she moved, her words perfectly polite if not *quite* as respectful as they should have been. There was that edge beneath it, that slap, that was all Adriana. It made him hunger for her all over again.

He reached out and snagged her elbow as she passed, pulling her against him, her back to his front, cursing himself as he did it but completely unable to stop.

"I won't forget this," he said, directly into her ear, all of her soft skin smooth and warm and delicious against his chest, his aching sex. "As you march around to my brother's tune and make your doomed attempts to keep me in line, I'll remember all of this." He let his gaze drift down over her body, satisfaction moving hard in him when her nipples hardened, when another flush worked over her sensitive skin, when her eyes eased closed and her breath went shallow. "I'll remember those freckles between your breasts, for example, three in a line. I'll wonder how they taste. I'll be thinking about the way you look right now, kissed and wild and desperate, when you're ordering me around in your conservative little business suits. It will always be there, hanging in the air between us like a fog."

She shook her head in confusion, and he could feel the fine, delicate tremors that shook in her, the staccato beat of her pulse, all that need and fire and loss. It raged just as brightly in him.

"Then why...?"

Pato leaned closer, spurred on by demons he didn't recognize, needs he didn't understand at all. But their teeth were in him. Deep. And he wanted them in her, too.

"*My* pleasure, Adriana," he told her fiercely, as if it was some kind of promise. A dark threat. He couldn't tell the difference any longer. "Not yours."

CHAPTER FIVE

ADRIANA EYED PATO across the aisle of his royal jet as it winged its way into the night from the glittering shores of Monaco back to Kitzinia, cutting inward across the top of Italy toward Switzerland, Liechtenstein and home.

He was still wearing the formal black tie he'd worn to debonair effect earlier this evening, causing the usual deafening screams when he'd walked the red carpet into the star-studded charity event. Now he murmured into his mobile phone while he lounged on the leather sofa that stretched along one side of the luxury aircraft's lounge area. It had been a long night for him, she thought without a shred of sympathy, as he'd not only had to say a few words at the banquet dinner, but had fended off, at last count, three Hollywood actresses, the lusty wife of a French politician, a determined countess, two socialites and one extremely overconfident caterer.

Left to his own devices, Adriana was well aware, Pato would have stayed in Monaco through the night as he had in years past, partying much too hard with all the celebrities who had flocked to the grand charity event there, and running the risk of either appearing drunk at his engagement with the Kitzinian Red Cross the following morning, or missing it entirely.

She'd insisted they leave tonight. He'd eventually acquiesced.

But Adriana didn't kid herself. She didn't know why he'd pretended to listen to her more often than not in the weeks since that humiliating morning in his London flat. She only knew she found it suspicious.

And that certainly wasn't to suggest he'd *behaved*.

"Your schedule is full this week," she'd told him one morning not long after they'd returned from London, standing stiffly in his office in the palace. Wearing nothing but a pair of battered jeans, he'd been kicked back in the huge, red leather chair behind his massive desk, with his feet propped up on the glossy surface, looking more like a male model than a royal prince.

"I'm bored to tears already," he'd said, his hands stacked behind his head and his golden gaze trained on her in a way that made her want to squirm. She'd somehow managed to refrain. "I think I'd prefer to spend the week in the Maldives."

"Because you require a holiday, no doubt, after all of your hard work doing...what, exactly?"

Pato's mouth had curved, and he'd stretched back even farther in his chair, making his magnificent chest move in ways that only called attention to all those lean, fine muscles packed beneath his sun-kissed skin.

Adriana had kept her eyes trained on his face. Barely.

"Oh, I work hard," he'd told her in that soft, suggestive way that she'd wished she found disgusting. But since London, she'd been unable to dampen the fires he'd lit inside her, and she'd felt the burn of it then. Bright and hot.

"Perhaps if you dressed appropriately," she'd said briskly, forcing a calm smile she didn't feel, and telling herself there was no fire, nothing to burn but her shameful folly, "you might find you had more appropriate feelings about your actual duties, as well."

He'd grinned. "Are my clothes what make me, then?" he'd

asked silkily. "Because I feel confident I'm never more my-self than when I'm wearing nothing at all. Don't you think?"

Adriana hadn't wanted to touch that, and so she'd listed off his week's worth of engagements while his eyes laughed at her. Charities and foundations. Various events to support and promote Kitzinian commerce and businesses. Tours of war memorials on the anniversary of one of the kingdom's most famous battles from the Great War. A visit to a city in the southern part of the country that had been devastated by a recent fire. Balls, dinners, speeches. The usual.

"Not one of those things sounds like any fun at all," Pato had said, still lounging there lazily, as if he'd already men-tally excused himself to the Maldives.

Adriana didn't understand what had happened to her—what she'd done. She shouldn't have responded to him like that in London. She shouldn't have lost her head, surrendered herself to him so easily. So completely. If he hadn't stopped, she knew with a deep sense of shame, she wouldn't have.

And every day she had to stand there before him, both of them perfectly aware of that fact.

It made her hate him all the more. Almost as much as she hated herself. She'd worked closely with Lenz for three years. They'd traveled all over the world together. She'd adored him, admired him. And not once had she so much as brushed his hand inappropriately. Never had she worried that she couldn't control herself.

But Pato had touched her and it had been like cracking open a Pandora's box. Need, dark and wild. Lust and *want* and that fire she'd never felt before in all her life. Proof, at last, that she was a Righetti in more than simply name.

It had to be that tainted blood in her that had made her act so out of character she'd assured herself every day since London. It had to be that infamous Righetti nature taking hold of her, just as the entire kingdom had predicted since her birth, and just as the tabloids claimed daily, speculating madly about her relationship with Pato.

Because it couldn't be him. It couldn't be.

"Yours is a life of great sacrifice and terrible, terrible burdens, Your Royal Highness," she'd said then, without bothering to hide her sarcastic tone. Forgetting herself the way she did too often around him. "However do you cope?"

For a moment their eyes had locked across the wide expanse of his desk, and the look in his—a quiet, supremely male satisfaction she didn't understand at all, though it made something in her shiver—caused her heart to pound. Erratic and hard.

"Does your lingerie match today, Adriana?" he'd asked softly. Deliberately. Taunting her with the memory of that London morning. "I liked it. Next time, I'll taste it before I take it off you."

Adriana had flinched, then felt herself flush hot and red. She'd remembered—she'd *felt*—his hands on her, slipping into her panties to mold the curves of her backside to his palms, caressing her breasts through her bra. The heat of her embarrassment had flamed into a different kind of warmth altogether, pooling everywhere he'd touched her in London, and then starting to ache anew. And she'd been certain that she'd turned the very same cranberry color as the lingerie she'd worn then as she'd stood there before him in that office.

Pato, of course, had smiled.

She'd opened her mouth to say something, anything. To blister him with the force of all the anger and humiliation and dark despair that swirled in her. To save herself from the truths she didn't want to face, truths that moved in her like blood, like need, like all the rest of the things she didn't want to accept.

"I told you how I feel about challenges," he'd said before she could speak, dropping his hands from behind his head and shifting in his chair, his gaze intense. "Disrespect me all you like, I don't mind. But you should bear in mind that, first, it will reflect on you should you be foolish enough to do it in public, not on me. And second, you won't like the way I retaliate. Do you understand me?"

She'd understood him all too well. Adriana had fled his office as if he'd been chasing her, when all that had actually followed her out into the gleaming hall was the sound of his laughter.

And her own deep and abiding shame at her weakness. But then, she carried that with her wherever she went.

Adriana shifted in her seat now, flipping the pages in her book as if she was reading fiercely and quickly, when in fact she hadn't been able to make sense of a single word since the plane had left the airport in Nice, France. Pato was still on his mobile phone, speaking in Italian to one of his vast collection of equally disreputable friends, his low voice and wicked laughter curling through her, into her, despite her best efforts to simply ignore him.

But she couldn't seem to do it.

Her body remembered London too well, even all these weeks later. It thrilled to the memories. They were *right there* beneath her skin, dancing in her veins, pulsing hot and wild in her core. All it took was his voice, a dark look, that smile, and her body thundered for more. More heat, more flame. More of that darkly addictive kiss. More of Pato, God help her. Adriana was terribly afraid that he'd flipped some kind of switch in her and ruined her forever.

And that wasn't the only thing he'd ruined.

"You are clearly a miracle worker," Lenz had said as the young royals had stood together outside a ballroom in the capital city one evening with their various attendants, waiting to make their formal entrance into a foundation's gala event. "There hasn't been a single scandal since you took Pato in hand."

Adriana had wanted nothing more than to bask in his praise. Lenz had always been, if not precisely comfortable to be around, at least easy to work for. He'd never been as dangerously beautiful as Pato, but Adriana had always found him attractive in his own, far less flashy way. The sandy hair, the kind blue eyes. He was shorter than his brother, more solid than lean, but he'd looked every inch the king he'd become. It was the way he held himself, the way he spoke. It was who he was, and Adriana had always adored him for it.

Ordinarily, she would have hung on his every word and only allowed herself to think about the way it made her ache for him when she was alone. But that night she'd been much too aware of Pato standing on the other side of the great doorway, with Princess Lissette. Adriana had been too conscious of that golden gaze of his, mocking her. Reminding her.

He was grooming you to be his mistress.

And when she'd looked at Lenz—*really* looked at him, searching for the *man* and not the Crown Prince of Kitzinia she'd always been so awed by—she'd seen an awareness in his gaze, something darker and richer and clearly not platonic.

There had been no mistaking it. No unseeing it. And no denying it.

"I'm afraid I can't take credit for it, Your Royal Highness," she'd said, feeling sick to her stomach. Deeply ashamed of herself and of him, too, though she hadn't wanted to admit that. She'd been so sure Lenz was different. She'd been so *certain.* She hadn't been able to meet his eyes again. "He's been nothing but cooperative."

"Pato? Cooperative? You must be speaking of a different brother."

Lenz had laughed and Adriana had smiled automatically. But she'd been unable to ignore how close he stood to her, how familiar he was when he spoke to her. Too close. Too familiar. Just as her father had warned, and she'd been too blind to see it. Blind and ignorant, and it made her feel sicker.

Worse, she'd been grimly certain that Pato could see every single thought that crossed her mind. And the Princess Lissette had been watching her as well, her cool gaze sharp, her icy words from the ball in London ringing in Adriana's head.

She is widely regarded as something of a pariah.

Adriana had been relieved when it had been time for the royal entrance. They'd all swept inside to the usual fanfare, the other attendants had disappeared to find their own seats and she'd been left behind in the hall, finally alone. Finally away from all those censorious, amused, *aware* eyes on her. Away from Lenz, who wasn't at all who she'd imagined him to be. Away from Pato, who was far more than she could handle, just as he'd warned her.

Adriana had stood there for a very long time, holding on to the wall as if letting go of it might tip her off the side of the earth and away into nothing.

"You seemed so uncomfortable with my brother last night," Pato had taunted her the very next day, his golden gaze hard on her. She'd been trapped in the back of a car with him en route to another event, and she'd felt too raw, too broken, to contend with the man she'd glimpsed in London, so relentless and powerful. She'd decided she preferred him shiftless and lazy, hip deep in scandal. It was easier. "Or perhaps it's only that I expected to see more chemistry between you, given that you wish to make such a great and noble sacrifice to save him."

His tone had been so dry. He was talking about *her life* as if he hadn't punched huge holes right through the center of it. Adriana had learned long ago how to act tough even if she wasn't, how to shrug off the cruel things people said and did to her—but it had been too much that day.

He'd taken everything that had ever meant something to her. Her belief in Lenz. Her position in the palace. Her self-respect. *Everything.* And finally, something had simply cracked.

"I understand this is all a joke to you," she'd said in a low voice, staring out the window at the red-roofed city, historic houses and church spires, the wide blue lake in the distance, the Alps towering over everything. "And why shouldn't it be? It doesn't matter what you do—the people adore you. There are never any consequences. You never have to pay a price. You have the option to slide through life as pampered and as shallow as you please."

"Yes," he'd replied, sounding lazy as usual, but when she'd glanced back at him his gaze was dark. She might have thought he looked troubled, had he been someone else. Her stomach had twisted into a hard knot. "I'm a terrible disappointment. Sometimes even to myself."

Adriana hadn't understood the tension that had flared between them then, the odd edginess that had filled the interior of the car, fragile and heavy at once. She hadn't *wanted* to understand it. But she'd been afraid she did. That Pandora's box might have been opened, and there wasn't a thing she could do to change it after the fact. But that didn't mean that she needed to rummage around inside it, picking up things best left where they were.

"Your brother was the first man who was ever kind to me," she'd said, her voice sounding oddly soft in the confines of the car. "It changed everything. It made me believe—" But she hadn't been able to say it, not to Pato, who couldn't possibly have understood what it had meant to her to feel safe, at last. Who would mock her, she'd been sure. "I would have been perfectly happy to keep on believing that. You didn't have to tell me otherwise."

"Adriana." He'd said her name like a caress, a note she'd

never heard before in his voice, and she'd held up a hand to stop him from saying anything further. There had been tears pricking at the back of her eyes and it had already been far too painful.

He would take everything. She knew he would. She'd always known, and it was that, she'd acknowledged then, that scared her most of all.

"You did it deliberately," she'd said quietly, and she'd forced herself to look at him. "Because you could. Because you thought it was *funny*."

"Did you imagine he would love you back?" Pato had asked, an oddly gruff note in his voice then, his gleaming eyes unreadable, and it had hurt her almost more than she could bear. "Walk away from his betrothal, risk the throne he's prepared for all his life? Just as the Duke of Reinsmark did for your great-aunt Sandrine?"

"It wasn't about what Lenz would or wouldn't do," she'd whispered fiercely, fighting back the wild tilt and spin of her emotions, while Pato's words had dripped into her like poison, bitter and painful. "People protect those they care about. If you cared about anything in the world besides pleasuring yourself, you'd know that, and you wouldn't careen through your life destroy—"

He had reached over and silenced her with his finger on her lips, and she hadn't had time to analyze the way her heart slammed into her ribs, the way her whole body seemed to twist into a dark, sheer ripple of joy at even so small and furious a touch from him.

"Don't."

It had been a command, a low whisper, his voice a rough velvet, and that had hurt, too. The car had come to a stop, but Pato hadn't moved. He hadn't looked away from her, pinning her to her seat with too much darkness in his gaze and an expression she'd never seen before on his face, making him a different man all over again.

"You don't know what I care about," he'd told her in that low rasp. "And I never thought any of that was *funny*."

She'd felt that touch on her mouth for days.

"Ci vediamo," Pato said into his mobile with a laugh now, ending his call.

Adriana snapped back into the present to find him looking at her from where he lounged there across the plane's small aisle. She felt as deeply disconcerted as if the scene in the car had only just happened, as if it hadn't been days ago, and she was afraid he could take one look at her and know exactly what she was thinking. He'd done it before.

If he could, tonight he chose to keep that to himself.

"Good book?" he asked mildly, as if he cared.

"It's enthralling," she replied at once. "I can't bear to put it down for even a second."

"You haven't looked at it in at least five minutes."

"I doubt you were paying that much attention," she said coolly. "Certainly not while making juvenile plans to wreak havoc across Italy with your highly questionable race car driving friends who, last I checked the gossip columns, think the modeling industry exists purely to supply them with arm candy."

He laughed as if she delighted him, and she felt it everywhere, like the touch of the sun. He moved in her like light, she thought in despair, even when he wasn't touching her. She was lost. If she was honest, she'd been lost from the start, when he'd stood there before her with such unapologetic arrogance, naked beneath a bedsheet, and laughed at the idea that she could make him behave.

She should have listened to him. She certainly shouldn't have listened to Lenz, whose motivations for sending her to Pato in the first place, she'd realized at some point while standing in that hallway after seeing him again, couldn't possibly be what she'd imagined them to be when she'd raced off to do his bidding. And she couldn't listen to the tumult inside her, the fire and the need, the chaos that Pato stirred in her without even seeming to try, because that way lay nothing but madness. She was sure of it.

Adriana didn't know what she was going to do.

"Keep looking at me like that," Pato said then, making her realize that she'd been staring at him for far too long— and that he was staring back, his eyes gleaming with a dark fire she recognized, "and I won't be responsible for what happens next."

Pato expected her to throw that back in his face. He expected that cutting tongue of hers, the sweet slap of that smile she used like a razor and sharpened so often and so comprehensively on his skin. He liked both far more than he should.

But her eyes only darkened as they clung to his, and a hectic flush spread over those elegant cheekbones he wanted to taste. He was uncomfortably hard within the next breath, the wild, encompassing need he'd been trying to tell himself he'd imagined, or embellished, slamming into him again, sinking its claws deep, making him burn hot, and *want*.

How could he want her this much?

It had been weeks since London, and his fascination with her should have ebbed by now, as his little fascinations usually did in much less time. And most of *those* women had not fancied themselves tragically in love with his brother. But Adriana was always with him, always right there within his reach, prickly and unimpressed and severe. He spent his days studying her lovely face and its many masks, reading her every gesture, poking at her himself when he grew tired of the distance she tried to put between them.

This woman was his doom. He understood that on a primal level, and yet couldn't do the very thing he needed to do to avert it. He couldn't let her walk away. That was part of the game—but he found he couldn't bear the thought of it.

And he didn't like to think about the implications of that.

"Careful, Adriana," he said quietly. Her chest rose and fell too fast and her hands clenched almost fitfully at the thick paperback she held. If he asked, she would claim she didn't want him and never had—but he could see the truth written all over her. He recognized what burned in her, no matter what she claimed. It made him harder, wilder. Closer to desperate than he'd been in years. "I'm in a dangerous mood tonight."

She blinked then, looking down into her lap and smoothing her hands over the abused book, and he had rendered himself so ridiculous when it came to this woman that he felt it like loss.

"I don't know how you can tell the difference between that and any of your other moods," she said in her usual sharp way, which Pato told himself was better than that lost, hungry stare that could only lead to complications he knew he should avoid. "They're all dangerous, sooner or later, aren't they? And we both know who'll have to clean up the mess."

"I expected applause when we boarded the plane," he told her, smiling when her gaze came back to his, her brows arched over those warm, wary eyes that made him forget about the hollow places inside him. "A grateful speech or two, perhaps even a few thankful tears."

"You board planes all the time," she pointed out, her expression smooth, and that decidedly disrespectful glint in her dark eyes that he enjoyed far too much. "I was unaware that you required encouragement to continue doing so. I'll be sure to make a note of that for future reference. Perhaps the Royal Guard can break from their regular duties protecting our beloved sovereign, and perform a salute."

"I want only your applause, Adriana," he told her silkily.

"After all, you're the one who insisted I become chaste and pure, and so I have. At your command."

"I'm sorry," she murmured, something that looked like a smirk flashing across her mouth before she wisely bit it back. "Did you describe yourself as 'chaste and pure'? In an airplane, of all places, where we are that much closer to lightning, should you be struck down where you sit?"

She was a problem. A terrible problem, the ruin of everything he'd worked for all these years, but Pato couldn't seem to keep himself from enjoying her. He couldn't seem to do anything but bask in her. Tart and quick and the most fun he'd had in ages. With that sweet, hot fire beneath that would burn them both.

"Shall I tell you what I got up to at this particular benefit last year?" he asked.

"Unnecessary," she assured him. "The video of your ill-conceived spa adventure is still available on the internet. Never has the phrase 'the royal jewels' been so widely and hideously abused."

He laughed, and spread out his hands in front of him as if in surrender—noting the way her eyes narrowed in suspicion, as if she knew exactly how unlikely it was he might ever truly surrender anything.

"And look at me now," he invited her. "Not a single lascivious actress in sight, no spa tub in a hotel room that was meant to be private, and I'm not even drunk. You should be proud, Adriana."

She shifted in her chair, crossing her legs, and then frowning at him when his gaze drifted to trace the elegant line of them from the hem of her demure skirt down to the delicate heels she wore.

"Your transformation has been astonishing," she said in repressive tones when he grinned back at her. "But you'll forgive me if I can't quite figure out your angle. I only know you must have one."

"I prefer curves to angles, actually," he said, and laughed again at her expression of polite yet clear distaste at the innuendo. "And it has to be said, I've always found lingerie a particularly persuasive argument."

Adriana let out a breath, as if he'd hit her. Something terribly sad moved over her face then, surprising him and piercing into him. She ran her hands down the length of her skirt, smoothing out nonexistent wrinkles, betraying her anxiety.

Pato knew he was a bastard—he'd gone out of his way to make sure he was—but this woman made him feel it. Keenly. She made him wish he was a different man. A better one. The sort of good one she deserved.

"Perhaps you've managed to convince me of the error of my ways," he said quietly, hating himself further because he wasn't that man. He couldn't be that man, no matter how much she made him wish otherwise. "Just because it hasn't been done before doesn't mean it's impossible."

Her dark eyes met his and made something twist in him, sharp and serrated.

"We both know I did nothing of the kind," she said, her voice soft and matter-of-fact. She let out a small breath. "All I managed to do was make myself one among your many conquests, indistinguishable from the rest of the horde."

"I don't know why you'd think yourself indistinguishable," he said, keeping his tone light.

He could have sworn what he saw flash in her dark eyes then was despair, but she swallowed it back and forced a smile that made his chest hurt.

"I should have realized," she said, and he wondered if she knew how bitter she sounded then, how broken. "You've always been a trophy collector, haven't you? And what a prize you won in London. You get to brag that the Righetti whore propositioned you and you—*you,* of all people—turned her down. My congratulations, Your Royal Highness. That's quite a coup."

For a long moment a black temper pulsed in him, and Pato didn't dare speak. He only studied her face. She was pale now, and sat too straight, too stiff. Her eyes were dark again in exactly the same way they'd been that morning in the car, when he'd felt pushed to confront her about Lenz, and was fairly certain she'd broken his heart. Had he had one to break.

Pato hated this. He was perilously close to hating himself. For the first time since he was eighteen, he wished that he could do exactly what he wanted without having to worry about anyone else. Without having to play these deep, endless games. Adriana sat there and looked at him as if he was exactly the depraved degenerate he'd gone to great lengths to ensure he really was, when she was the first woman he'd ever met that he wanted to think better of him. The irony wasn't lost on him.

It stung. *Congratulations, indeed,* he thought ruefully. This was what doom looked like as it happened, and he was doing nothing at all to prevent it.

"Adriana," he said, trying to keep his temper from his voice. Trying to make sense of his determination to protect her not only from the things he shouldn't allow himself to want from her, but from herself. "You and I both know you're no whore. Why do you torture yourself over the lies that strangers tell? They're only stories. They're not even about you."

"On the contrary," she said after a moment, her voice thick and uneven. "Some of us are defined by the stories strangers tell."

"You're the only one who can define yourself," he countered gently. "All they can do is tell another story, and who cares if they do?"

Emotion moved through her then, raw and powerful. He saw it on her face, in the way her eyes went damp, in the faint tremor of her lips. Her hands balled into fists in her lap and she moved restlessly in her seat, stamping both feet into the floor as if she needed the balance.

"Easy for you to say," she stated, a raw edge to her voice. "Not all of us can be as beloved as you are no matter what you do, forgiven our trespasses the moment we make them."

"Fondness is hardly the same thing as forgiveness."

Her dark eyes seared into him. "You cheerfully admit each and every one of your transgressions," she said. "There are videos, photographs, whole tabloids devoted to your bacchanals. But you are still the most popular young royal in all of Europe. No one cares how dirty you get. It doesn't cling to you. It doesn't matter."

"I prefer 'adventurous' to 'dirty,' I think," he said mildly, watching her closely, seeing nothing but shadows in her beautiful eyes. "Especially in that tone."

"Meanwhile," she said, as if he hadn't spoken, "I happen to be related to three women who slept with Kitzinian royalty over a hundred and fifty years ago, and one woman who ruined a duke more recently. I'm the most notorious slut in the kingdom, thanks to them." She pulled in a breath. "It isn't even *my* dirt, but I'm covered in it, head to toe, and I'll never be clean. Ever." Her eyes held his for a long moment, fierce and dark. "It isn't just another story strangers tell. It's my life."

Pato was aware that he needed to shut this down now, before he forgot himself. But instead, he shook his head and continued talking, as if he was someone else. Someone with the freedom to have dangerous conversations with a woman he found far too fascinating, as if both of them weren't pawns in a game only he knew they were playing.

"You must know that almost all of that is jealousy," he said, letting out a small laugh at the idea that she didn't. "You're a legend, Adriana, whether you earned it or not. Women are envious of the attention you get, simply because you have a notorious name and the temerity to be beautiful. Men simply want you."

She let out a frustrated noise, and snatched up her book again, that smooth mask of hers descending once more. But he could see right through it now.

"I don't want to discuss this," she said, more to the book than to him. "You can't possibly understand. There's not a day of your life you've been envious of anyone, because why should you be? And you certainly don't *want* me. You made that perfectly clear in London."

Pato didn't know he meant to move. He shouldn't have. But one moment he was on the couch and the next he was looming over her, swiveling her chair around and leaning over her, into her, planting his hands on the armrests and caging her between his arms. Risking everything, and he didn't care.

"I never said I didn't want you," he growled down at her.

Pato felt unhinged and unpredictable, capable of anything. Especially a mistake of this magnitude—but he couldn't seem to stop himself. Adriana still smelled of jasmine and her eyes were that rich, deep brown, and he didn't have it in him to fight off this madness any longer.

"Not that I want to revisit the most humiliating morning of my life," she said from between her teeth, "but you did. If not in words, then in actions. And don't misunderstand me, I'm grateful. I wasn't myself."

"The question on the table that morning was not whether or not I wanted you." He moved even closer, watching in satisfaction as her pretty eyes widened with a shock of awareness he felt like hands on his skin. "The question was whether or not I wanted to sleep with you knowing full well you planned to shut your eyes and imagine Lenz in my place. They're not quite the same thing."

She paled, then burst into that bright red blush that Pato found intoxicating. He liked her cheeks rosy, her cool exterior cracked and all her masks useless, the truth of her emotions laid bare before him.

"What does it matter?" Her voice was barely a whisper. "It didn't happen. Crisis averted. There's no need to talk about it now."

"I told you I wouldn't forget," he said, intent and hungry, "and I haven't. I remember the noises you made in the back of your throat when I kissed you, when you rubbed against me like silk, hot and—"

"Please!" Her voice was low. Uncertain. "Stop."

"What do *you* want, Adriana? That's tonight's question."

He leaned in closer, so he could hear the tiny hitch in her breath, and so he could find the pulse in her neck that was drumming madly, giving her away, and tease it with his tongue.

She whispered something that came out more a moan, and he smiled against the delicate column of her throat. Her skin smelled of his favorite flowers and her hair smelled of holidays in the sun, and he wanted to be deep inside her more than he wanted his next breath.

"And when I talk about *want,* I don't mean something tame," he said, a growl against the side of her neck, directly into her satiny skin, so he could feel her tremble against his lips. "I mean hunger. Undeniable, unquenchable hunger. Not because you're drunk. Not because you want to martyr yourself to your great unrequited love. *Hunger,* Adriana. What do you want? What are you hungry for?"

"Please…" she whispered, desperation thick in her voice. She was right there on the edge, right where he wanted her.

He could feel it. He felt it flood through him, dark and thrilling and scorchingly hot.

"I don't think you love him, Adriana," he told her then, and she let out a small sound of distress. "Not really. I know you're not hungry for him. Not like this."

She trembled. She shook. But she didn't argue.

"I asked you a question," he urged her, his mouth at her jaw. "If it helps, I already know the answer. All you have to do is admit it."

CHAPTER SIX

ADRIANA'S BREATH CAME out like a sigh. A release.

Like surrender, Pato thought, satisfaction moving through him like another kind of need, dark and demanding, like all the ways he wanted her.

"I thought it would help your brother's reputation," she said almost too softly, her eyes bright with heat. "I really did."

He nipped at her jaw, and she shivered.

"But I never would have suggested—" She broke off, bit her lip in agitation, then tried again. "I mean, I wouldn't have thought of it if I didn't—"

Pato waited, but she only pulled in a ragged breath, then another. She could hardly sit still. She was flushed hot, shining with the same need he felt pulling at him. Coming apart, right there in the chair, and he'd hardly touched her.

She was going to be the end of him. He knew it.

He couldn't wait.

"Say it," he ordered her. "If you didn't…?"

He felt her give in to it before he saw it, a shift in that tension that tightened the air between them. And then her shoulders lowered, she let out a long breath, and what stormed in him then felt like much, much more than simple victory.

"If I didn't want you," she admitted hoarsely.

Pato kissed her, hard and long and deep, his fingers spearing into her sleek chignon and sending pins scattering to the floor.

And she met him, the feel of her mouth beneath his again—at last—like a revelation.

He couldn't get enough of her taste. He angled his jaw for a better fit and it got hotter, wilder, and then he thought he might explode when he felt her hands running along his arms, trailing over his chest, making him wish he could remove all the layers of his formal clothes simply by wishing them away.

He wanted her mindless. Now. He wanted her falling apart in his arms, lost to this passion that might very well destroy them both. He wanted to claim her.

Pato broke away from the glory of her mouth and sank to his knees before her, making room for himself between her legs. She made a small, dazed sort of sound. He grinned at her, then simply pulled her hips toward him, pushing her skirt up toward her waist and out of his way as he positioned her at the edge of her seat.

He ran his palms up her smooth, satiny thighs, grinning wider as she bit back a moan. He sank his hands underneath her, grasping her perfect bottom and ducking lower, arranging her so that her legs fell over his shoulders and hung down his back. Then he tilted her hips toward him.

"Oh, my God," she whispered, slumped down in her chair with her skirt around her waist and that delectable flush heating her face, making her dark chocolate eyes melt and shine as they met his.

She was delicious and shivering and his. All his, at last.

God help them both.

"Hold on," Pato advised her, hardly recognizing his own voice, so stark with desire was it. So focused. "You'll need it."

He lifted her to him, smiling at the pretty scrap of blue lace that covered the sweet heat of her, and then he leaned forward to suck her into his mouth.

* * *

The shock of his mouth against the very center of her need took Adriana's breath, so that the scream she let out sounded only inside her, ricocheting like a bullet against glass and shattering whatever it touched.

The heat. The fire. The terrible, wonderful ache.

His wicked, talented mouth, so hot and demanding, pressed against the tiny layer of lace that separated them. His hard shoulders felt massive and the fabric of his jacket rough against the tender skin behind her knees. His clever hands gripped her and held her fast, and his impossibly beautiful face was between her thighs so that all she could see when she looked down was that thick, wild hair of his, sunshine and chocolate and that delicious bit too long, and her own hands fisted in the mass of it as if they'd gone there of their own accord.

She thought she'd died. She wanted to die. She didn't know how anyone could take this much pleasure, this much scalding heat, and live through it—

And then he made a low noise of male pleasure, shoved her thong out of his way and licked deep into her molten core.

Adriana burst into a firestorm of white-hot heat and exploded over the edge of the world, lost in a shower of shivering flames.

When she was herself again, or whatever was left of her, she couldn't seem to catch her breath. And Pato was laughing in dark masculine delight, right there against the heat of her core, making the pleasure curl in her all over again, sweeter and hotter than before.

"Again, I think," he murmured, each syllable humming into her and making her press against him before she knew she meant to move, greedy and mindless and adrift in need.

And he took her all over again.

He used his tongue and the scrape of his teeth. His mouth

learned her, possessed her, commanding and effortless. His jaw moved against the tender skin of her thighs, the faint rasp of his beard making the fire in her reach higher, burn hotter. The hands that held her to him caressed her, a low roll of sensation that made her shudder and writhe against him, into him, wanting nothing in the world but this. Him.

And that coiling thing inside her that he knew exactly how to wind tight. Then tighter. Then even tighter still.

Adriana felt the fire surge into something almost unbearable, her whole body stretched taut and breathless, heard his growl of approval and her own high, keening noise—

And then, again, she was nothing more than the fire and the need, shattering into a thousand bright, hot pieces against his wicked, wicked mouth, and then falling in flames all around him.

When Adriana opened her eyes this time, reality slammed into her like a hammer at her temples.

What had she done?

Pato had moved to lounge on the floor, his back against the couch opposite her, with his long legs stretched out and nearly tangled with hers. He wasn't smiling. Those golden eyes were trained on her, brooding and dark, and she didn't know how long she stared back at him, too shaken and dazed to do anything else.

But that hammer kept at its relentless pounding, and she forced her gaze from his, looking down at herself as if he'd taken her body from her and replaced it with someone else's. That was certainly what it felt like.

She thought she might cry. Adriana struggled to sit upright, tugging her skirt back down toward her knees, aware as she did so that she could still feel him. That mouth of his all over the core of her, his hands wrapped so tightly over her bottom. It felt as if every place he'd touched her was a separate drum, and each beat in her with its own dark pulse.

Then something else hit her, and she froze. She didn't have much practical experience, but Adriana recognized that what had happened had been…unequal. She swallowed nervously, sneaked a glance at him and then away.

"You didn't—" She was still in pieces and wasn't sure she'd ever manage to reassemble herself. Not the way she'd been before. Not now that he'd demonstrated exactly how much she'd been lying to herself. She cleared her throat. "I mean, if you'd like…"

"How tempting," Pato said drily when she couldn't finish the sentence, his gaze harder when she met it, a darker shade of gold she'd never seen before. "But I prefer screams of passion to insincere sacrifices, thank you. To say nothing of enthusiastic participants."

And the worst part, she realized, as her heart kicked at her and made her feel dizzy, was that she couldn't run from him the way she had that morning in London. She couldn't find a far-off corner of his luxurious penthouse and hide herself away until she wrestled her reactions under control. They were on a plane. There was no hiding from what she'd done this time. No rationalizations, no excuses. And she hadn't had anything to drink but water all night long.

The silence between them stretched and held, nothing but the sound of the jet's engines humming all around them, and Adriana didn't have the slightest idea what to do. She was aware of him in ways she suspected would haunt her long after this flight was over, ways she should have recognized and avoided weeks ago. Why had she thought she could handle this—handle him? Why had she been so unpardonably arrogant?

He'd been leading her here all along, she understood. And she'd let him, telling herself that what was happening to her wasn't happening at all. Telling herself stories about tainted blood and Pandora's box. Thinking she could fight it with snappy lines and some attitude.

She'd known she was scraped raw by this, by the things that had happened between them. What he'd done and what he'd said. The brutal honesty, the impossible need. But it was her own appalling weakness that shamed her deep into her bones. That made her wonder if she'd ever known herself at all.

"Why did you do that?" she asked, when the silence outside her head and the noise within was too much.

His dark brows edged higher. There was the faintest twitch of that mouth of his, which she now knew so intimately she could still feel the aftershocks.

"I wanted to know how you tasted," he said.

So simple. So matter-of-fact. So Pato.

A helpless kind of misery surged through her, tangled up with that fire he'd set in her that never died out, and she wished she hadn't asked. She kept her eyes on the floor, where his feet were much too close to hers, and wondered how she could find something so innocuous so threatening—and yet so strangely comforting at the same time.

"Was that your first?" he asked, with no particular inflection in his voice. "Or should I say, your first two?"

"My first…?" she echoed, confused.

And then his meaning hit her, humiliation close behind, and she felt the scalding heat of shame climb up her chest and stain her cheeks. She wanted to curl into a ball and disappear, but instead she sat up straight, as if posture alone could erase what had happened. What she'd done. What she'd let him do to her without a single protest, as if she'd been waiting her whole life to play the whore for him.

Weren't you? that voice spat at her, and she flinched.

"I apologize if I was deficient, Your Royal Highness." She

threw the words at him, in an agony of embarrassment. "I neglected to sleep with the requisite seven thousand people necessary to match your level of—"

"There was only the one, I know," he interrupted, his even tone at odds with the storm in his eyes and that unusually straight line of his mouth. No crook, no curve. Serious, for once, and it made it all that much worse. "And I imagine all five seconds of unskilled fumbling did not lead to any wild heights of passion on your part."

Adriana couldn't believe this conversation was happening. She couldn't believe any of this had happened. If she could have thrown herself out the plane's window right then and there, she would have. A nice, quiet plummet from a great height into the cold embrace of the Alps sounded like blessed relief.

But Pato was still looking at her. There was no escape.

"Of course it wasn't my first," she managed to say, but she couldn't look at him while she said it. She couldn't believe she was answering such a personal question—but then, he'd had his mouth between her legs. What was the point of pretending she had any boundaries? Any shame? "I might not have cut a swathe across the planet like some, but I didn't take a vow of celibacy."

"With a man," he clarified, and there was the slightest hint of amusement in his eyes then, the faintest spark. "A private grope beneath the covers, just you and your hand in the dark, isn't the same thing at all. Is it?"

Adriana didn't understand how she could have forgotten how much she hated him. She remembered now. It roared through her, battling the treacherous, traitorous embers of that fire he'd licked into a consuming blaze, filling her with the force of it, the cleansing power—

But it burned itself out just as quickly, leaving behind the emptiness. That great abyss she'd been skirting her whole life, and there was nothing holding her back from it anymore, was there? She had spent three years with Lenz, thinking her dedication proved she wasn't what her surname said she was. And hardly more than a month with Pato, demonstrating exactly why Righetti women were notorious.

She had betrayed herself and her family in every possible way.

And he was still simply looking at her, still sitting there before her as if sprawling on the floor made him less threatening, less diabolical. Less *him*.

Worse, as if he expected an answer.

"Adriana," he began evenly, almost kindly, and she couldn't take it.

She was horrified when tears filled her eyes, that hopelessness washing over her and leaving her cruelly exposed. She shook her head, lifting her hands and then dropping them back into her lap.

He had destroyed her. He'd taken her apart and she'd let him, and she didn't have any idea how she would survive this. She didn't know what to *do*. If she wasn't who she'd always thought she was, if she was instead who she'd always feared she might become, then she had nothing.

Nothing to hold on to anymore. Nothing to fight for. Nothing at all.

"What do you want from me?" she asked him, and she didn't sound like herself, so broken and small. She felt the tears spill over, the heat of them on her cheeks, and she was too far gone to care. Though her eyes blurred, she focused on him, dark and male and still. "Is this it—to make me become everything I hate? Everything I spent my whole life fighting against? Are you happy now?"

He didn't answer, and she couldn't see him any longer, anyway, so she stopped pretending and covered her face with her hands, letting the tears flow unchecked into her palms, her humiliation complete.

She didn't hear him move. But she felt his hands on her, lifting her into the air and then bringing her down on his lap. Holding her, she realized when it finally penetrated. Prince Pato was *holding* her. She tried to push away, but he only pulled her closer, sliding her across his legs so that her face was nestled into the crook of his neck. There was the lightest of touches, as if he'd pressed a kiss to her hair.

He was warm and strong and deliciously solid, and it was so tempting to pretend that they were different people. That this meant something. That he cared.

That she was the kind of woman someone might care for in the first place.

It was shocking how easy it was to tell herself lies, she thought then, despairing of herself—and so very, very sad about how eager she was to believe them. Even now, when she knew better.

"We don't always get to play the versions of ourselves we prefer," Pato said after a long while, when Adriana's tears had faded away, and yet he still held her.

He smoothed a gentle hand over her hair as he spoke, and Adriana found that she didn't have the strength to fight it off the way she should. She couldn't seem to protect herself any longer. Not from him. Not from any of this. She could feel the rumble of his voice in his chest, and had to shut her eyes against the odd flood of emotion that rocked through her.

Too much sensation. Too many wild emotions, too huge and too dangerous. *Too much.*

"I don't think you understand," she whispered.

"The army was the only place I ever felt like a normal person," he replied. Did she imagine that his arms held her closer, more carefully, as if she really was something precious to him? And when had she started wanting him to think so? "None of the men in my unit cared that I was a prince. They cared if I did my job. They treated me the same way they treated each other. It was a revelation." He traced the same path over her hair, making her shiver again. "And if I like Pato the Playboy Prince less than I liked Pato the Soldier, well. One doesn't cancel out the other. They're both me."

There was nothing but his arms around her and the solid heat of him warming her from the inside out. Making her feel as if everything was somehow new. Maybe because he was holding her this way, maybe because he'd told her something about him she hadn't already read in a tabloid. Maybe because she didn't have the slightest idea what to do with his gentleness. Adriana felt hushed, out of time. As if nothing that happened here could hurt her.

It wasn't true, she knew. It never was. But she couldn't seem to keep herself from wanting, much too badly, to believe that just this once, it could be.

"Yes," she said, finding it easier to talk to that strong neck of his, much easier when she couldn't see that challenging golden gaze. She could fool herself into believing she was safe. And that he was. "But none of the versions of you—even the most scandalous and attention-seeking—are called a whore with quite the same amount of venom they use when it's me." He sighed, and she closed her eyes against the smooth, hot skin of his throat. "You know it's true."

She felt him swallow. "What they call you reflects far more on them than on you," he said gruffly.

"Perhaps it did when I wasn't exactly what they called me. But I can't cling to that anymore, can I?"

She pushed herself away from him then, sitting up with her arms braced against his chest so she could search his face, and the way he frowned at her, as if he was truly concerned, made her foolish heart swell.

"You said it yourself," she continued. "Kitzinian princes

and Righetti women. History repeating itself, right here on this plane." His frown deepened and she felt his body tighten beneath her, but she kept going. "I held my head up no matter what they said because I knew they were wrong. But now…" She shrugged, that emptiness yawning inside her again, black and deep. "Blood will tell, you said, and you were right."

Pato's gaze was so intense, meeting hers, that it very nearly hurt.

"What happened between us does not make you a whore."

"I think you'll find that it does. By definition."

His eyes moved over her face, dark and brooding, almost as if she'd insulted him with that simple truth.

"But," he said, his tone almost careful, "you were happy enough to risk that definition when it was your suggestion, and when you thought it would benefit Lenz."

There was no reason that should hurt her. She didn't know why it did. *I don't think you love him,* he'd told her in that low, sure voice.

"That was different," she whispered, shaken. "That was a plan hatched in desperation. This was…"

She couldn't finish. Pato looked at her for a long moment, and then his eyes warmed again to the gold she knew, his mouth hinted at that wicked curve she'd tasted and felt pressed against her very core, and she didn't know if it was joy or fear that twisted inside her, coiling tight and making it difficult to breathe.

"Passion, Adriana," he said with soft intent. "This was passion."

She told herself she didn't feel that ring inside her like a bell. That there was no *click* of recognition, no sudden swell of understanding. She didn't know what he was talking about, she told herself desperately, but she was quite certain she shouldn't have anything to do with either passion or princes. There was only one place that would lead her, and on this end of history she very much doubted she'd end up with her portrait in the Royal Gallery. Like her great-aunt Sandrine, she'd be no more than a footnote in a history book, quietly despised.

"Passion is nothing but an excuse weak people use to justify their terrible behavior," she told him, frowning.

"You sound like a very grim and humorless cleric," Pato said mildly, his palms smoothing down her back to land at her hips. "Did my mouth feel like a justification to you? Did the way you came apart in my hands feel like an excuse? Or were you more alive in those moments than ever before?"

Adriana pushed at his chest then, desperate to get away from him, and she was all too aware that she was able to climb out of his lap and scramble to her feet at last only because he chose to let her go.

"It doesn't matter what it felt like." She wished her voice didn't still have that telltale rasp. She wished Pato hadn't made it sound as if this was something more than the usual games he played with every female who crossed his path. More than that, she wished there wasn't that part of her that wanted so badly to believe him. "I know what it makes me."

Pato shoved his hair back from his face with one hand and muttered something she was happy she didn't catch. She wanted to make a break for the bathroom and bar herself inside, but her legs were too shaky beneath her, and she sat down on the chair instead, as far away from him as she could get. Which wasn't far at all. Not nearly far enough to recover.

"My mother was a very fragile woman," he said after a long moment, surprising Adriana.

She blinked, not following him. "Your mother?"

Queen Matilda had been an icon before her death from cancer some fifteen years ago. She was still an icon all these years later, beloved the world over. Her grave was still piled high with flowers and trinkets, as mourners continued to make pilgrimages to pay their respects. She had been graceful, regal, feminine and lovely. Her smile had once been called "Kitzinian sunshine" by the rhapsodic British press, while at home she'd been known as the kingdom's greatest weapon.

She had been anything but *fragile*.

"She was so beautiful," Pato said, his voice dark, skating over Adriana's skin and making her wrap her arms around herself. "From the time she was a girl, that was the only thing she knew. How beautiful she was and what that would get her. A king, a throne, adoring subjects. But my father married a pretty face he could add to his collection of lovely things and then ignore, and my mother didn't know what to do when the constant attention she lived for was taken away from her."

Pato's eyes were troubled when they met hers, and Adriana caught her breath. That same celebrated beauty his mother had been so famous for was stamped all over him, though somehow, he made it deeply masculine. He was gilded and perfect, just as she had been before him, and Adriana would never have called him the least bit fragile, either. Until this moment, when he almost looked…

But she couldn't let herself think it. There was too much at stake and she couldn't trust herself. She didn't dare. What he felt wasn't her concern. It couldn't be.

He smiled then, but it wasn't his usual smile. This one felt like nails digging into her, sharp and deep, and she wanted to hold him the way he'd held her, as if she could make him feel safe for a moment, however fleeting.

You're such a fool.

"You don't have to tell me this," she said hurriedly, suddenly afraid of where this was going. What it would do to her if he showed her things she knew he shouldn't. "It's your family's private, personal business."

She wanted him too much. She'd proved it in unmistakable

terms, with her legs flung over his shoulders and her body laid open for his touch. Somewhere inside of her, where she was afraid to look because she didn't want to admit it, Adriana knew what that meant. She knew.

He gave half the world his body. She would survive that; his women always did. But if he gave her his secrets, she would never recover.

"So she did the only thing she knew how to do," Pato said, his gaze never leaving Adriana's, once again that different, harder version of himself, every inch of him powerful. Determined. *Bleak,* Adriana thought, and ached for him. "She found the attention she needed."

Adriana stared at him, not wanting to understand what he was saying. Not wanting to make the connection. He nodded, as if he could see the question she didn't want to ask right there on her face.

"There were always men," he said, confirming it, and Adriana hugged herself that much tighter. "They kept her happy. They made her smile, laugh, dance in the palace corridors and pick flowers in the gardens. They made her *herself.* And my father didn't care how many lovers she took as long as she was discreet. He might not have wanted her the way she thought he should, the way she needed to be wanted, but he wanted her happy."

Adriana found it hard to swallow. She could only stare at Pato in shock. And hurt for him in ways she didn't understand. He leaned forward then, keeping his eyes on hers, hard and demanding. She felt that power of his fill the space between them, pressing at her like a command.

"Was my mother a whore, Adriana?" he asked, his voice a quiet lash. "Is that the word you'd use to describe her?"

She felt too hot, then too cold. Paralyzed.

"I can't— You shouldn't—"

Pato only watched her, his mouth in that serious line, and

she felt the ruthlessness he hid behind his easy smiles and his laughter pressing into her from all sides and sinking deep into her belly. How had she ever imagined this man was *careless*?

"Of course not," she said at last, feeling outside herself. Desperate. As if what she said would keep her from shaking apart from the inside out. "She was the queen. But that doesn't mean—"

"It's a word people use when they need a weapon," he said, very distinctly, and that look in his eyes made Adriana feel naked. Intensely vulnerable. As if he could see all the ugliness she hid there, the encroaching darkness. "It's a means of control. It's a prison they herd you into because they think you need to be contained."

She shook her head, unable to speak, unable to handle what was happening inside her. Some kind of earthquake, rolling long and hard and destroying foundations she hadn't known she'd built in the first place.

"That's all well and good," she whispered, hardly aware of what she was saying, seeing only Pato and that look on his face, "but there's no one here but you and me and what happened between us, the way I just—"

"Don't do it," he warned her, cutting her off, his eyes flashing. "Don't make it ugly simply because it was intense. There was nothing ugly about it. You taste like a dream and your responsiveness is a gift, not a curse."

What moved in her then was so overwhelming she thought for a long, panicked moment that she might actually be sick, right there on the floor. She was too hot again, then freezing cold, and she might have thought she'd come down with a fever if she hadn't seen the way he looked at her. If she hadn't felt it deep inside her, making so many things she'd taken for granted crumble into dust.

But she couldn't bring herself to look away. She was falling apart—he was making sure she did—and she didn't *want* to look away.

"Don't use their weapons on yourself," he told her then, very distinctly, the royal command and that brooding darkness making her shiver as his gaze devoured her, changed her, demanded she listen to him. "Don't lock yourself in their prison. And don't let me hear you use that word to describe yourself again, Adriana. As far as I'm concerned, it's a declaration of war."

But Adriana knew that the war had started the moment she'd been sent to work with this man, and despite what she'd told herself all these weeks, despite what she'd so desperately wanted to believe, she'd already lost.

Pato couldn't sleep, and he could *always* sleep.

This was one more thing that had never happened to him before Adriana had walked into his life and turned it inside out. He'd entertained a number of very detailed ideas about how he'd enjoy making her pay for that as he sprawled there in his decidedly empty bed—none of them particularly conducive to rest.

Damn her.

It was her insistence that she was, in fact, all the things the jackals called her that had him acting so outside his own parameters, he knew. It was maddening. Pato had handled any number of women over the years who had used their supposed fragility as a tool to try to manipulate him. He could have piloted a yacht across the sea of tears that had been cried on or near him, all by women angling for his affection, his protection, his money or his name—whatever they thought they could get.

He'd never been the slightest bit moved.

Adriana, by contrast, wanted nothing from him save his good behavior. She was appalled that he'd touched her, kissed her, made her forget herself. She'd now offered herself to him twice while making it perfectly clear that doing so was an act of great sacrifice on her part. A terrible sacrifice she would lower herself to suffer through, *even after* he'd brought her to a screaming, sobbing climax more than once.

She was killing him.

No wonder he was wide-awake in the middle of the night and storming through his rooms in a fury. If he'd been possessed of the ego of a lesser man, she might very well have deflated it by now. He'd even altered his behavior to please her. He, Pato, Playboy Prince, tabloid sensation and scandal magnet, hadn't even glanced at another woman unless it was specifically to annoy Adriana, since he didn't seem to be able to do without the way she took him to task.

He was like a lovesick puppy. He was disgusted with himself.

And he would never be able to fly on that plane again without being haunted by her. Her taste, her silken legs draped over his back, her gorgeous cries. He cursed into the dark room, but it didn't help.

The list of things he shouldn't have done grew longer every day, but tasting the heat of her, making her shatter around him, *twice,* was at the very top. It wasn't only that he'd tasted her at last and it had knocked him sideways, or that it had taken every shred of willpower he possessed to keep himself from driving into her and making her his in every possible way right there and then, again and again until they both collapsed. It wasn't only that he'd been unable to stop thinking about the fact that he was more than likely the first man to pleasure her, which made a wholly uncharacteristic barbarian stir to life inside him and beat at his chest in primitive masculine triumph. That was all bad enough.

But it went much deeper than that, and Pato knew it.

He'd known it while they were still in the air. He'd known

it when he'd started telling her things he never spoke about, ever. He'd known it when the plane had finally landed and he'd sent her off in a separate car and had found himself standing on the tarmac, staring at her disappearing taillights and wanting things he couldn't have.

He'd known for some time, if he was honest, but tonight it had all come into sharp and unmistakable focus.

Pato didn't simply want her in his bed.

He *liked* her. She made him laugh, she challenged him and she wasn't the least bit in awe of him. From the very start, she'd treated him as if she expected him to be the educated, intelligent, capable man he was supposed to be rather than the airy dilettante he played so well. He wanted to teach her every last sensual trick he'd ever learned, and bathe them both in that scalding heat of hers. He wanted to prove to her that the passion that flared between them was rare and good. He wanted to take away the pressure of all that family history she wore about her neck like an albatross.

Worst of all, most damning and most dangerous, he wanted to be that better man she deserved.

"It isn't even my dirt, but I'm covered in it," she'd said tonight, breaking the heart he didn't have all over again, and he'd wanted nothing more than to be the one who showed her that she had never been anything but beautiful and clean, all the way through. Pato never should have let himself get lost in the fantasy that he might be that man. He wasn't. There was no possibility that he could be anything to her, and couldn't allow himself to forget that again.

Not until the game he and Lenz had played for all these years reached its conclusion. He couldn't break the faith his brother had placed in him all those years ago. He couldn't break the vow he'd made. He wouldn't.

And he'd never been even remotely tempted to do so before.

Pato found himself on one of his balconies that looked out over the water to the mainland beyond and the city nestled there on the lakeshore. His eyes drifted toward the sparkling lights of the old city, the ancient quarter that had sprawled over the highest hill since the first thatched cottages were built there in medieval times. It was filled with museums and grand old houses, narrow little lanes dating back centuries and so many of Kitzinia's blue-blooded nobles in their luxurious, historic villas. And he knew precisely where the Righetti villa stood on the finest street in the quarter, one of the kingdom's most famous and most visited landmarks.

But tonight he didn't think about his murdered ancestor or Almado Righetti's plot to turn the kingdom over to foreign enemies, all in service to long-ago wars. It was only the house where she lived, where he imagined her as wide-awake as he was, as haunted by him as he was by her. He didn't care what her surname was. He didn't care if this was history repeating itself. He certainly didn't care about the malicious gossip of others.

The ways he wanted her almost scared him. Almost.

And of all the things he couldn't have while this game played on, he understood that she was going to hurt the worst. She already did.

Pato slammed his fist against the thick stone balustrade. Hard. As if that might wake him up, restore him to himself. It did nothing but make his knuckles ache, and it didn't make him any less alone.

He hated this game, but he couldn't lose his focus. There was one week left until the wedding, and she'd served her purpose. He had to let her go.

CHAPTER SEVEN

ADRIANA WALKED INTO the palace the following morning on shaky legs, trying with all her might to feel completely unaffected by what had happened the night before. And if she couldn't quite feel it, to *appear* as if she did. Cool. Calm. Professional. Not riddled with anxiety, her body still humming with leftover desire.

"I wanted to know how you tasted," she could hear him say, as if he whispered it into her ear. Her skin prickled at the memory.

Nothing had changed, she assured herself, save her understanding of her own weakness and her ability to tell herself lies. And nothing *would* change, because this was Pato. Careless, promiscuous, thoughtless, undependable for the whole of his adult life, and proud of it besides. No depth, she reminded herself. No conscience and no shame. Those hints she'd seen of another man—that ruthless power, that dark focus, that devastating gentleness—weren't him.

They couldn't be him.

And the things he'd said, which she could still feel running through her like something electric...well. She'd lost herself in a sensual storm. She'd never experienced anything like it before and she'd decided it was entirely possible she'd made it all seem much more intense than it had been. Pato had made her sob and writhe and fall to pieces. He'd made her body sing for him as if she were no more than an instrument—and well he should. *Passion,* he'd called it, and he would know. Sex was his occupation, his art. He was a master.

He'd mastered her without even trying very hard.

It was no wonder she'd concocted some fantasy around that, she told herself as she made her way down the gleaming marble hall that led to Pato's office. He did things like this—like *her*—all the time. The number of women who fantasized about him was no doubt astronomical, and none of them hung about the palace, clinging to his ankles. Nor would she.

She would be perfectly serene, she chanted to herself as she let herself into his office. Efficient and competent. And she wouldn't verbally spar with him anymore, as he obviously viewed it as a form of flirtation, and she found it far too easy to slip into, putting herself at risk. Last night was a mistake, never to be repeated. No conversation was necessary, no embarrassing postmortem. It was done. She marched around the quietly opulent office, turning on lights and arranging the papers he wouldn't read on his desk. The two of them would simply…move forward.

Or so Adriana told herself, over and over, as she waited for him to appear.

He didn't come. She waited, she lectured herself more sternly, and still he failed to saunter in, disheveled and lazy and wearing something that violated every possible palace protocol, the way he usually did. When Adriana realized he was going to miss his engagement with the Kitzinian Red Cross—after what she'd gone through to get him back into the country, specifically to meet with them—she braced herself, smoothed her hands over the very conservative suit she'd chosen this morning, which was in no way protective armor, and set off through the palace to find him.

Pato's bed, she was relieved to find when she made it to his bedroom, was empty.

It was only then, while she stared at the rumpled sheets and the indentation in the pillows where his head must have been at some point last night, that Adriana admitted to herself that maybe she was a little *too* relieved. That maybe it had hurt to imagine that he could have carried on with his usual depravity after she'd left him last night.

You are nothing but another instrument, she reminded herself harshly, amazed at her capacity for self-delusion. *And he happens to be a remarkably talented musician—no doubt because he practices so very, very often.*

If only she could make that sink in. If only she could make that traitorous part of her, the part that insisted on wild fantasies and childish hope no matter how many times it was crushed out of her, believe it.

"You look disappointed," Pato drawled from the doorway behind her. Adriana whirled around to face him, her heart leaping out of her chest. "Shall I ring a few bored socialites and have them fill up the bed? Just think of all the sanctimonious lectures you could deliver."

He sounded the way he looked this morning: dangerous. Edgy. Dark and something like grim. Adriana's breath tangled in her throat.

Pato was draped against the doorjamb, looking as boneless as he did rough around his gorgeous edges. His eyes glittered, too dark to shine like gold today, and he hadn't bothered to shave. His hair stood about his head in a careless mess, and he was wearing an open, button-down shirt over those ancient jeans he preferred, she'd often thought, because they molded so tightly to his perfectly formed body. He looked moody and formidable, that ruthless power he usually concealed a black cloud around him today, making it impossible for Adriana to pretend she'd imagined it.

And the way he was looking at her made her heart stutter.

She'd been so sure that she was prepared to see him again. She wasn't.

Her whole body simply shuddered into a blazing, embarrassing heat at the sight of him. She felt as if she'd been lit on fire. Her nipples hardened as her breasts swelled against her bra. Her belly tightened, while her core melted into that hot, needy ache. Her skin prickled with awareness, and she could feel the dark heat of his gaze all the way through her, from the nape of her neck to the soles of her feet. Not ten minutes ago she'd vowed she wouldn't spar with him anymore, but she understood in a flash of insight that it was that or simply surrender to this wildness inside her—and she wasn't that far gone, surely. Not yet.

"I'm relieved, actually," she managed to say, making her voice as brisk as she could. "The last thing I wanted to do today was troll about your usual dens of iniquity, looking for you in the dregs of last night's parties, especially when you are expected to charm the Red Cross in less than hour."

He looked at her for a long moment, his beautiful face hard and his eyes dark, and yet she had the strangest notion that he was in some kind of pain. She had to grit her teeth to keep herself from doing something stupid, like trying to reach out to him. Like imagining that she of all people could see beneath his surface to the far more complicated man beneath.

Such hubris, a voice inside her hissed, *and we all know what comes after pride like yours. Like night follows day.*

"It's amazing," Pato said in a low voice, something in it raising the fine hairs on the back of her neck. "It's as if you never wrapped your legs around my neck and let me taste you. You may not remember it, Adriana, but I do."

Adriana went utterly still.

She should have anticipated this. She should have known. It had been the same when she was seventeen. She could still remember with perfect clarity the faces of all her schoolmates who'd gathered around to point and stare and laugh as she'd walked out of that party alone. Used and humiliated. She could still remember the name they'd called her snaking along with her like a shadow, following her, connected to her, the truth of her as far as they'd been concerned. Inevitable.

The Righetti whore.

Pato was only one person, not a crowd of cruel teenagers, and yet she recognized that this was worse. Much, much worse. She could feel it deep inside, in parts of her that pack of kids had never touched.

But she'd be damned if he'd see her cry again, Adriana thought then with a sharp flash of defiance. She'd rather he executed her alongside Almado Righetti's ghost in the old castle keep than show him one more tear.

"Is this the part where you call me a whore?" she asked, her stomach in a hard knot but her voice crisp. Her head high. "You're not doing it right. It works much better when mixed with public humiliation, so you can get the satisfaction of watching me walk a little gauntlet of shame. Would you like me to assemble a crowd? We can start over when they arrive."

Pato didn't move, but his eyes went completely black. Frigid and furious at once. Adriana crossed her arms over her chest and refused to cower or cringe. That deep defiance felt like strength, sweeping through her, making her stand tall. She would never bow her head in shame again. Never. Not even for a prince.

"If you want to call me names, feel free to do it to my face," she told him. "But I should warn you, I won't fall to pieces. I've survived far worse than you."

It shouldn't have been possible for his eyes to flash even darker, but they did, and she could feel the pulse of his temper rolling off him in waves. She told herself it didn't bother her in the least, because it shouldn't. It couldn't.

"You think you're ready to go to war with me, Adriana?"

he asked, that mild tone sounding alarms inside her, sending a little chill racing down her back. "I told you what would happen if you used that word again."

"Here's a news flash, Your Royal Highness," she snapped, ignoring the alarms, the chill, that look on his face. "I've been at war since the day I was born. I'm hardly afraid of one more battle, especially with a man best known for the revealing cut of his swimming costume and his ability to consume so much alcohol it ought to put him in a coma." She eyed him while a muscle she'd never seen before flared in his jaw. "Is that what today's little display of temper is all about? You're drunk?"

Pato straightened from the door, and her heart kicked at her in a sudden panic, not quite as tough as she was trying to appear. Adriana almost took an instinctive step back, but forced herself to stop. To stand still. He looked nothing less than predatory and the last thing she wanted to do was encourage him to give chase. Because he would, she knew on some primal level. In this mood he might do anything.

"No," he growled in a voice like gravel, when she'd almost forgotten she'd asked him a question. "I'm not drunk. Not even a little."

She didn't like the way he watched her then. Panic and awareness twisted inside her, sending out a shower of sparks, but Adriana didn't let herself back down. She wasn't going to break. Not this time. Not here.

"Perhaps you should consider getting drunk, then," she suggested icily. "It might improve your disposition."

She didn't see him move, and then he was right there in front of her, his hand on her jaw and his eyes so tortured, so dark, as he gazed down at her. Adriana didn't understand what was happening. The things he was saying, that dangerous tone of voice, his dark demeanor—but then she looked in his eyes and she wanted to cry. And not for herself.

"What's wrong?" she whispered.

Something she didn't understand flashed through those eyes. Then he bent his head and brushed his lips across hers. It was soft and light, hardly a kiss at all, and even so, Adriana felt it as if he'd wrapped both hands around her heart and squeezed tight. Her eyes closed of their own accord, and she felt the sweetness of it work through her, warming her, making her feel as if she glowed.

And then he let go of her, though he didn't step back, and when she looked at him he was that dark, edgy stranger again. His mouth was severe as he gazed at her, a grim line without the faintest possibility of any curve. Much less anything sweet.

"For the first time since you walked through the door and started ordering me around," he said quietly, "I feel like myself."

Adriana stared at him for a long moment. He looked back at her, that wicked mouth unrecognizable, those beautiful eyes so terribly dark and filled with things she didn't understand—but she understood this. He didn't need to call her names. He didn't need to stoop to the level of seventeen-year-olds. He was a royal prince. He could do it with a glance, a single sentence.

She had to stop imagining that anything would ever be different.

"If you want to be rid of me, Pato," she said, fighting to keep her voice cool and her head high, "you don't have to play these cruel little games. All you have to do is dismiss me, and you could have done that with a text. No unpleasant scene required."

He reached over and ran the back of one hand along her cheek, his knuckles slightly swollen, and Adriana fought to keep from jerking her head away. His touch was confusingly tender. It slid through her like honey. And it was at complete odds with everything he was saying.

"That's the first time you've used my name," he said, as if it shook him. And Adriana wanted to lean into him, to turn her head and kiss his hand, as if this was about affection.

But she knew better. This was another game. It couldn't be anything else—and she was finished playing. No matter what she thought she saw in his eyes then, as if using his name had been some kind of invocation. As if it had changed something.

"I'll take that as a yes, I'm dismissed," she said somehow, and moved to step around him. The need to escape, to flee this place and him and never look back, was like a drumbeat inside her skin. "I'll leave my formal resignation letter on the desk in your office."

But he reached out and took her arm as he had once before in London, holding her against his side though they faced different directions.

"Adriana," he whispered, as if her name hurt him.

It hurt her.

But all this would pass. It would, it always did. All she had to do was walk out the door, and she'd never be allowed in his presence again. It wasn't as if she could work for Lenz again, not now. Her access to the palace would be revoked, and she'd never have to worry about her outsize reactions to Pato, her insatiable hunger for him. All that would fade away as if it had never happened, as if he'd never been anything more than a face on a glossy magazine. And she would move far away from Kitzinia, to a place where no one would recognize her name or her ancestors' faces in hers, and someday, she thought—*prayed*—she might even forget that she'd fallen in love with him without ever meaning to.

Everything inside her went still then. Quiet. The truth she'd been avoiding for much too long was like a hush, stealing through her, changing everything, making sure she would leave here, leave him, in tatters.

But then she supposed that, too, had always been inevitable. History had repeated itself, and he was right, it might kill her. But not where he could watch, she told herself fiercely. Not where he could see how far she'd fallen.

"Thank you, Your Royal Highness," she said, jerking her arm from his grasp, amazed that she sounded so calm. So controlled, as if her whole world hadn't shuddered to a halt and then altered forever. "This has been an educational experience. I particularly enjoyed your need to destroy the entire royal family, living and dead, in my esteem." She aimed a hard smile at him. "Rest assured, I now think as little of your family as you do of mine."

He met her gaze then, and what she saw on his face sliced into her, making her feel as if she might shake apart where she stood. Making her think she already had.

"Don't," he said, as he had in the car that day. That was all, and yet she felt it everywhere.

But his pain wasn't her problem, she told herself harshly. She couldn't let it matter.

"I didn't need to know any of that," she whispered fiercely. His secrets, that tempting glimpse of his inner self. As if any of it was real, or hers. She'd known it would lead nowhere good, and she was right. "And why would you risk telling me? I could walk out of here today and sell that story to the tabloids."

The way he looked at her didn't make any sense. It made her heart thud hard against her ribs. It made her eyes go blurry.

"You won't."

"You have no reason to think that. You don't know me. You don't even like me."

His smile was faint, like a ghost. "I trust you, Adriana."

It was sad how much she wished he did, despite everything. She was such a terrible, gullible fool. Such a deep and abiding disappointment to herself. Because he was still playing her. She knew it. She was one instrument among many, and he didn't know how to do anything else.

"Or," she said slowly, as the ugly truth of it penetrated even her thick skull, the misery crashing over her, into her, making her voice too thick, "you know perfectly well that the last person in the world anyone would believe when it came to accusations of promiscuity is me."

"Don't," he said again, his voice harsher.

And this time when he pulled her to him, he turned her so she came up hard against his chest, and then he held her face in his hands and kissed her. Ravenous and raw. Uncontrolled.

Dangerous.

And Adriana couldn't help herself. She kissed him back.

He slanted his head and she met him, kissing him with all the passion he'd showed her, all the love she hadn't wanted to admit she felt for him. The pain, the misery. Her foolish hopes. She held back nothing. She wrapped her arms around his neck and let him bend her backward, as if this was the happy ending to some kind of fairy tale instead of a sad goodbye at the close of a story even Adriana had known would end like this. Exactly like this, in dismissal and disgrace.

Pato kissed her again and again, as if he was as desperate, as torn, as she was. As if he felt what she did when she knew very well he didn't. He couldn't. He kissed her so thoroughly that she knew she would pretend he did, that it would be the fire she warmed herself near in all the lonely days to follow, and she kissed him back with the same ferocity so she could remember that, too.

But too soon he pulled away, still holding her face in his hands. He looked at her for a long moment, his eyes gleaming that darker gold that made her shiver deep inside, and then he stroked her cheeks with his thumbs, as if memorizing her.

Adriana didn't say a word. She couldn't. But she knew it was time to go, before she found she couldn't.

She pulled in a shuddering breath, and when she stepped back, Pato's gaze went stormy and his jaw flexed—but he dropped his hands and let her.

It was the hardest thing Adriana had ever had to do. It made her bones ache as if she was breaking them, but she did it. She wrenched herself away from him and turned toward the door.

And then stopped dead.

Because Lenz stood there, staring at them both in appalled disbelief.

Adriana made a small sound of distress, almost too low to hear, and Pato wanted nothing more than to put himself bodily between her and whatever attacked her—even if it was his brother. Even worse, if it was him.

But he couldn't. He certainly hadn't today. He didn't now, and he thought he loathed himself.

For a moment, they all stood there, frozen in place.

"Excuse me, Your Royal—" Adriana began, but Lenz interrupted her.

"I didn't give her to you so you could make her one of your bedmates, Pato." He threw the accusation into the room, his face a work of thunder. But Pato watched Adriana and the way she simply stood there, her spine achingly straight and her hands in fists at her sides. "What the hell are you thinking?"

Pato said nothing. He saw Adriana tremble slightly, and had to fight the need to pull her back against him, to protect her from this. He hated that she thought he was like those jackals who had hounded her all these years. He hated that she believed he thought so little of what had happened between them. He hated all of this.

And yet he had no choice, he reminded himself bitterly. It didn't matter that he had the taste of her in his mouth, that he would have held her there forever if she hadn't pulled away. He had to let her go.

"Enough," he snapped when Lenz opened his mouth again. Pato met his brother's eyes. Hard and unyielding. "This is not a conversation Adriana needs to take part in. Why don't you step aside and let her go?"

It appeared to dawn on Lenz that this was not a request. His eyes narrowed, but he walked stiffly into the room, leaving the exit clear.

Pato willed Adriana to look at him one last time—to let him study that beautiful face of hers once more—but he wasn't surprised that she didn't. The moment Lenz stopped moving, she left. She walked out of Pato's bedroom the way she'd walked into it, her head high and her back straight, and she didn't look back or break her stride.

And Pato stood there, listening to the sound of her heels against the polished floors until even that disappeared. And that was it. She was gone. He'd done his goddamned duty.

"You didn't have to sleep with her!" Lenz declared, sounding fierce and protective, which made Pato feel that much more hollow. "She deserves better than that!"

"By all means, brother, let's talk about what Adriana deserves," Pato murmured dangerously. "The crown prince installs her in the position usually allocated to his mistresses, and keeps her there for years. And then his dirty playboy brother takes his sordid turn. And we planned it that way, because we knew exactly what would happen if we brought the last Righetti girl into this game. Does she deserve any of that?"

Lenz stared at him. "What is she to you?" he asked after a long moment.

"She is nothing to me," Pato replied, his voice harsh. "Because *nothing* is the only thing I am allowed. *Nothing* is my stock in trade. I am useless, faithless, untrustworthy, and most of all, a great and continuing disgrace to my royal blood." He held Lenz's gaze for a taut breath. "Don't worry, brother. I know who I am."

Lenz looked pale then.

"Pato," he said carefully, as if he was afraid of what Pato's response might be. "We are finally in the endgame. We've worked too hard to get here. Didn't you tell me this yourself only weeks ago?"

Pato scraped his hands over his face as if that could change the growing hollowness inside him. As if anything could.

"I know what I promised." But he didn't look at Lenz. He felt unbalanced, half-drunk, and he knew it was Adriana. She'd crippled him, and she thought he didn't care. It was almost funny. "I have no intention of breaking my vow. I haven't yet, have I?"

Lenz stared at him, lifting one hand to stroke his mouth, clearly mulling over the right approach to a thorny problem he hadn't seen coming. Pato almost laughed then. This was why Lenz would make the perfect king. He could detach, step back, consider all outcomes. Pato, by contrast, couldn't seem to do anything but seethe and rage. Especially today.

"We picked Adriana because of her name, yes," Lenz said after several moments passed, his voice carefully diplomatic once again. "But she's special. I know it. I—"

Pato laughed then, a rusty blade of a sound that stopped his brother flat.

"We're not going to stand about like pimpled schoolboys and compare notes," he said in a tone that brooked no argument. "We'll be the only people in this petty kingdom who do not find it necessary to pick over her body like so many carrion crows."

For a moment, that simply hung there. Then Lenz blinked.

"Oh," he said in a curious voice, a new light in his eyes as he looked at Pato. "I didn't realize."

"She's out of this," Pato said, ignoring that. "She isn't coming back."

Lenz studied him. "Is that wise?" he asked quietly. "Can we afford a deviation from the plan at this point? The wedding—"

"Is in a week, I know." Pato couldn't hide the bleakness that washed over him then. He didn't try. "And she's out of this. She's free. If she deserves anything, it's that."

Lenz's brows rose, but he only nodded. "Fair enough."

Pato smiled then, though it was too sharp, and he understood that he was not himself. That he might never be himself again. That Adriana was gone and he was emptier than he'd been before, and he wasn't sure he could live with it the way he knew he must. But he smiled anyway.

"How is the king's health?" he asked, because Lenz was right. This was the end of this game, and he'd agreed years ago to play it. There was no changing that now, even if he'd changed the plan.

"The same," Lenz said. He didn't smile. He only looked tired. "The ministers are beginning to press him. It might happen sooner than we thought."

Pato nodded. It was exactly as they'd planned. It turned out they were good at this, this dance of high-stakes deception and royal intrigue.

He sickened himself.

"Then I suppose we play on," he said wearily.

Lenz's gaze was sad. "We always do."

Adriana walked through her family's villa slowly, taking the time to really look around her as she did. She couldn't remember the last time she'd paid attention to all the familiar things in front of her, which she'd somehow stopped seeing over the years. The graceful rooms, the antique furniture. The art still on the walls and the places where art had been removed and sold in the leaner years. All the *things* that made up a Kitzinian pedigree, a certain station in Kitzinian society, even a tarnished one. Collections of china in carved wood cabinets. Beautiful rugs, hand-tiled floors, mosaics lining the fountain in the center courtyard. Coats of arms, priceless statues and pieces of pottery handed down across centuries.

And in the small parlor in the farthest corner of the villa, the one no one talked about and never visited by accident, were the trio of portraits. The faces of the women whose choices hundreds of years ago had sentenced Adriana to infamy in the present.

"What they call you reflects far more on them than on you," Pato had said. She couldn't get his words out of her head.

Her father might hate their family history, Adriana thought as she stood in the musty room, but he still felt called upon to preserve it. And so the portraits hung on the walls of the villa instead of being packed away in the attic or burned in the back gardens. This was his duty to the Righetti legacy, however shameful he found it.

Adriana pulled open the heavy drapes to let the light in, and then stared up at the three great temptresses of old Kitzinia sitting there so prettily in their frames. The Righetti whores, lined up in chronological order. The harlots Carolina, Maria and Francesca.

And, of course, Adriana herself, though she, like her great-aunt Sandrine, could not expect to be rendered in oils and hung in museums. Times had changed.

She couldn't help the small laugh that escaped her. *She* didn't feel much like a notorious whore in the comfortable jeans and soft magenta sweater she'd tugged on when she'd arrived home from the palace. She studied the faces of the women before her, seeing herself in the shape of Carolina's brow, the color of Maria's hair and the curve of Francesca's lips. None of them looked particularly like slinking sexpots, either. They simply looked like young women somewhere around Adriana's age, all smiling, all bright-eyed, all pretty.

Don't lock yourself in their prison, Pato had said.

Maybe, Adriana thought, staring at the portraits but remembering the way he'd held her when she cried, they'd simply fallen in love.

She sat down heavily in the nearest chair, her own heart beating hard in her chest as if she'd run up a hill. How had that possibility never occurred to her before? Why had she always believed that she was descended from a line of women who were, for all intents and purposes, callous prostitutes?

Maybe they were in love.

It rang in her like a revolution.

The Righetti family had always kept their own copies of these portraits, and Adriana remembered being herded into this room by her grandmother after church on Sundays, as her aunts had been before her. Her grandmother had droned on about purity and morals, while Adriana had stood there feeling increasingly cross that her brothers were allowed to entertain themselves elsewhere.

The lecture had been repeated with increasing frequency throughout her adolescence, which was when Adriana had discovered the truth about her grandfather's younger sister, the lovely old woman with sparkling eyes who lived in France and whose name was only ever spoken in distaste. And Adriana had internalized every word of her grandmother's lecture. She'd accepted the fact that she was dirty, tainted. Ruined before she began. She'd never questioned a word of it.

"Don't use their weapons on yourself," Pato had said so fiercely, as if it had angered him to hear her talk about herself like that. As if the casual way she hated herself, her easy ac-

ceptance of the idea that she was the dirty thing others called her, was what was upsetting.

Not her. Not her name. Not what had happened between them.

And she realized then, as she sat in the presence of the women who'd supposedly ruined her, that she couldn't do it anymore. That well of ugliness she'd spent her whole life drawing from simply wasn't there in her gut the way it always had been. In its place, she thought in some astonishment, was that defiance she'd called on at the palace—that strength she hadn't known she had.

She looked at the Righetti women, at their mysterious smiles and the sparkle in their eyes, and she knew something else, too. These women hadn't been ashamed. They hadn't torn themselves apart in penance for their sins. Adriana knew for a fact that each and every one of them had died of old age, in their beds. These were not meek, placating women. They'd been the favorite lovers of kings and princes in times when that meant they'd wielded great power and political influence. They'd made their own rules.

And so, by God, would Adriana.

At some point she realized that tears were flowing down her cheeks. Was this joy? Heartbreak? Despair? How could she keep track of the wild emotions that clamored inside of her? Adriana knew only that she loved him. She loved Pato, and she wasn't ashamed of it, either. She didn't know how she would tell her father what had happened, or what she'd do next, but she couldn't hate herself for this.

She *wouldn't* hate herself for this.

Adriana had thought for a moment that she might have a heart attack when she'd turned to see Lenz standing there in Pato's doorway, when she'd seen that shocked look on his face. But seeing him there, standing next to his brother, had made everything very clear. *"I don't think you love him,"* Pato had told her, and he was right. Lenz had been kind to her, no matter what his ulterior motives, and she'd been so desperate to prove to him that she wasn't *that kind* of Righetti. She'd mistaken her gratitude for something more.

But Pato had changed her, she realized now, gazing at that trinity of women before her as she wiped at her cheeks. What had happened on that plane had altered everything. He had wanted her, and he'd encouraged her to want him back. He hadn't used her; if anything, she'd used him. Twice. And the things he'd said to her had knocked down walls inside her she'd never known were there.

It didn't matter what came after that. It didn't matter if he regretted opening up to her the way he had. It didn't matter that he'd rejected her today, or that it had hurt her terribly.

It didn't even matter if she never saw him again, though that possibility broke her heart. He'd given her a gift she could never repay, she understood now. She wasn't sure she ever would have got there on her own. He'd showed her how.

He'd set her free.

Later, Adriana sat on the wide sill at her open bedroom windows, looking out at the stretch of the kingdom below her, gleaming in the crisp afternoon light.

She watched the ferries cutting through the crystal blue lake toward the cities on the far shore, racing the pleasure boats with their white sails taut in the breeze. She let her eyes trace the graceful lines of the palace, the gentle bow of the causeway that connected it to the mainland, and the towering Alps all around. There was nothing keeping her here besides sentiment. She could go back to university, collect another degree. She could travel abroad the way she'd always meant to do. There was no reason she had to stay here. None at all.

And even so, even now, she found it hard to imagine leaving.

Adriana heard the motorcycle long before she saw it. It was brash and loud, shouting its way through the streets of the old city. Louder and louder it roared, until it whipped around the corner at the end of the lane, charged down her street in an obnoxious cloud of noise and then stopped directly below her windows.

Her heart slammed against her chest.

Pato tilted back his head and glanced up, pulling off his helmet and piercing her with a long, hard look. Adriana couldn't seem to move. His expression was serious, unsmiling, and he paused there, one foot on the ground, handling the sleek black machine beneath him with an easy, unconscious grace.

And his eyes gleamed gold for all that they were grave.

She didn't know how long they stared at each other. The whole city could have gathered around, jeering and pointing, and it wouldn't have registered. There was only Pato. Here, beneath her window. *Here.*

And then he smiled, and she felt it everywhere, like that hungry mouth of his, demanding and hot. *So hot.* She felt herself flush red.

Pato crooked his finger at her, arrogant and sure. He looked anything but careless. He was impossibly powerful, decidedly male, every inch of him a prince though he wore jeans and a black T-shirt that made love to his lean and chiseled body, and held that lethally beautiful machine between his legs.

Adriana scowled at him, because she wanted to melt, and saw his eyes heat in response. He crooked his finger again, with even more lazy command this time, and she shook her head.

"You dismissed me for a reason, or so I assume," she said, in a reasonable attempt at her usual brisk tone, as if she didn't care that he was here. That he'd come when she'd thought she'd never see him again. "You can't change your mind back and forth on a whim and expect—"

"Adriana," he said, and the sound of her name in his mouth like that, so quiet and so serious in the narrow, cobblestone street, made her fall silent. Pato didn't smile or laugh; he didn't show her that grin of his, though his golden gaze was bright. "Come here."

CHAPTER EIGHT

ADRIANA STEPPED INTO the street, pulling the door to the villa shut behind her, and felt Pato's eyes on her long before she turned to face him. His golden gaze seared into her, brighter than the afternoon around them, making her heart pick up speed.

"That machine is much too loud," she told him, the stern tone surprising her even as she used it. His mouth curved in the corner. "It's noise pollution and you are a—"

"Get on the bike." His voice was as commanding as that crook of his finger had been, and that gleam in his gaze had gone hotter, more challenging.

"I no longer serve you, Your Royal Highness," she said primly, though her heart was beating too fast, too hard, and she could see the way he studied the color on her cheeks in that lazy way of his. "At your pleasure or otherwise."

He still didn't smile, though the gleam in his eyes suggested it, and then he reached out and hooked his fingers in the waistband of her jeans. Her skin ignited at his touch, making her forget what she'd been saying. The burn of it went deep when he tugged her close, so close her head fell back and all she could see was him.

"I was cruel," Pato said, his voice dark. "Chastising me won't change that, though perhaps it makes you feel better. But you can admit you want me anyway." His gaze was steady. He wasn't toying with her. He knew. "There's no shame in it."

Adriana went white, then red. Shock. Embarrassment. Fury.

"I don't know what makes you think—"

Her breath left her in a rush when his fingers moved gently over the soft skin just beneath her waistband, teasing her. Tormenting her. Making whatever she was about to say a lie.

"Adriana." His voice was pure velvet now, wrapped around steel. "Get on the bike." He held out a helmet.

And she'd known she would, since the moment he'd appeared outside her windows, hadn't she? Why had she pretended otherwise? It wasn't as if Pato was fooled. It wasn't as if she'd fooled herself.

But there was admitting she loved him in the privacy of her own head, and then there was proving it beyond any doubt—announcing it out loud. And she was fairly certain that climbing up on the back of that motorcycle mere hours after he'd ripped out her heart, sacked her and undone three years of attempted rehabilitation to the Righetti reputation by kissing her like that in front of his brother constituted shouting it at the top of her lungs. *To* him.

She either loved him or she was a masochistic fool, Adriana thought then. Perhaps both.

But she donned the helmet and got on the bike.

Pato headed away from the palace, out of the city and up into the foothills.

Adriana clung to his back, luxuriating in the feel of all his corded, lean strength so close to her and the wind rushing around them. She was pressed into him, her arms wrapped around his waist, her breasts against his back, her legs on either side of his astride the motorcycle he operated as if it was an extension of himself. She felt surrounded by him, connected to him, a part of him.

It was either heaven or hell, she wasn't sure which. But she wanted it to never end.

Eventually he turned off the main roads and followed smaller, less-traveled ones around the far side of the lake, winding his way to a small cottage nestled in a hollow, looking out over a secluded cove. Adriana climbed off the motorcycle when he brought it to a roaring stop, her legs shaky beneath her. Her body felt too big suddenly, as if she'd outgrown her skin. As if it hurt to sever herself from him. She pulled off her helmet and handed it over, feeling somewhat shy. Overwhelmed.

Pato's gaze met hers as he removed his helmet. His mouth moved into a small curve, and she flushed. Again. She felt restless. Hectic and hot, and the way he looked at her didn't help. There might not be shame in wanting him, but there was too much need, and all of it too obvious now that she'd admitted it. Now that she'd stopped pretending.

And all she could seem to do was ache.

Adriana turned to look at the water instead, breathing in the peaceful, fragrant air. Pine and sun, summer flowers and the deep, quiet woods. It was still in ways the city never was. She watched the water lap gently at the rocks at the bottom of the sloping yard, blue and clear and pretty.

It made the odd tension inside her ease. Shift. Turn into something else entirely. They could have been worlds away from the city, the palace, she thought. They could have been anyone, anywhere. Anonymous and free.

"What is this place?" she asked, her voice sounding strange in the quiet, odd in her own mouth.

"It's my best kept secret." Pato stepped away from the motorcycle and shoved his thick hair back from his forehead. The movement made his T-shirt pull tight over that marvelous torso of his, and Adriana's mouth went dry. The gleam in his gaze when she met it again told her he could tell. "I come here to be alone."

She couldn't let herself think about that too closely. She wanted it to mean much, much more than it did.

"More secrets," she murmured instead. His gaze seemed to burn hotter the longer he looked at her, more intense. She tried to shake off the strangeness, the shakiness. All that want and need, and no barriers to contain them. It made her feel off-kilter. Vulnerable. *Alive.* "Private stories, secret cottages. Who knew the overexposed prince had so much to hide? Or that you were capable of hiding anything in the first place?"

He moved closer, and she felt that sizzling current leap between them and then work its way through her, lighting her up the way it always did. The way *he* always did. Fire upon fire, a chain reaction, sweeping over her unchecked until she was molten all the way through. As needy and as desperate as if he was already touching her. As if this morning had never happened.

But it had, and Adriana understood, even through the sweet ache of all that fire between them, that it would again. He wasn't hers. He could never be hers.

And yet she'd come with him, anyway. She'd barely hesitated.

Maybe, like the Righetti women who came before her, it was time she loved what she had for as long as she had it, instead of mourning what she might have had, were she braver. Pato had told her this was passion, this thing that flared between them. She wanted to explore it. She wanted to know what he meant. She wanted *him.*

It didn't feel like surrender to admit that. There was no shame. It felt like a hard-won victory.

"You weren't what I expected," Pato said, as if the words were pulled from him, urgent and dark. Serious. "I've been hiding in plain sight for fifteen years and no one's ever seen me, any hint of me at all, until—"

Adriana turned to him and put her hand over his mouth, that beautiful mouth of his she'd felt devouring her very core, wicked and insinuating and warm to the touch. She felt his lips against her palm now, and the familiar punch of heat that roared through her and connected with that pulsing fire low in her belly.

She didn't want his secrets. Secrets came at too high a price, and she knew she'd pay a hefty one already. She wanted *him*. She wanted to throw herself in this fire at last, and who cared what burned?

"Don't," she whispered, and smiled at him. His gaze was dark on hers for a breath, and another. Then his lips curved against her palm.

Adriana pushed up on her toes, pressed her body flush against his *at last,* and took his mouth with hers. Claiming him here, now. While she could.

Pato met her instantly. He buried one hand in her hair and hauled her against him, and this time she was ready for him. She wrapped herself around him, shameless and abandoned, and let herself glory in it. He let out a sound that was halfway between a laugh and a curse, and then he was sweeping her up into his arms and heading toward the cottage.

"But—" she protested, though she went quiet when he looked down at her, his golden eyes hot and wild, making her shiver in anticipation as she hooked an arm around his hard shoulders.

"Rule number six," he growled, leaning down to nip at her nose. "Don't ever put on a sex show in the yard. Unless it's planned." He shifted her against his chest, holding her with one arm while he worked the door of the cottage with his free hand. "And if it's planned, there should be paparazzi at the ready, not horrified tourists out for a bit of pleasure boating."

Adriana frowned at him as he ducked into the cottage, barely taking notice of the place as he kicked the door closed behind him and carried her inside. She saw high beams and white walls, cozy furniture in bold colors. But she was far more interested in what he'd said.

"Exactly how many 'sex shows' have you participated in?" she demanded. "Planned or unplanned?"

"I don't think you really want me to answer that," he replied, laughter gleaming in those eyes of his now, mixing with all the fire and coiling inside her, tighter and tighter.

"More than five?" she asked, pushing it. Poking at him. *Flirting,* she understood now. She'd been flirting all this time. From the moment he'd opened his eyes and offered her a space in his crowded bed. "Ten? I imagine there would have to be quite a few to justify the making of rules and regulations."

Pato only laughed, and set her down on her feet slowly, letting her body slide down the length of his. Adriana melted against him, almost unable to stand on her own when he let go of her. She swayed slightly, and she didn't care that he could see how he affected her. She wanted him to see it.

"A gentleman doesn't count such things," he said, with a wicked quirk of his mouth. "That would be indelicate."

"Happily, you are no gentleman," she pointed out. "A prince, yes. But never a gentleman."

"Lucky you," he murmured, and then slid his hands under the hem of her whisper-soft sweater, directly onto the bare skin beneath.

Adriana's breath left her in a rush. Pato moved one hand around to the small of her back, and left the other where it was, big and delicious on her abdomen. Then he simply held her there, as if basking in the feel of her skin against his palms, her body between in his grasp.

"Listen to me," he said, and it took her a moment to pull

herself out of her feverish little haze and focus on him again. When she did, his expression was serious. "I can't seem to resist you. But I don't think you're a whore, Adriana. I never did."

She felt gloriously free with his hands on her, with that fire burning so bright in her. With need lighting her up, making her pulse and glow.

"I don't care."

Pato shook his head impatiently. "I care. There are things you need to understand, things that are bigger than—"

"Later," she interrupted.

He frowned at her. So she reached down and grabbed the hem of her sweater herself, then pulled it up and off. She met his gaze as she tossed it aside, smiling slightly at the instant flash of heat there, and the way his hands tightened on her skin, as if he wasn't so controlled himself.

"Pato," she whispered. "I don't want to talk anymore."

He looked torn for a split second. Then that mouth of his curved into pure, male wickedness, and she knew the fire won. She felt it burn ever higher inside her, the flames licking all over her skin.

Pato stepped away from her and then reached back with one arm to tug that tight black T-shirt off his chest, throwing it on the floor near her sweater. This time, she could touch. Taste. This time she could lose herself in the sheer masculine perfection of that lean torso. She couldn't wait.

"Keep your eyes on me," he ordered when she reached for him, his golden gaze amused as it seared into her. "And no touching until I say otherwise."

The air inside the cottage seemed too tight, too hot. How could she keep from touching him? And why—? Pato only smiled.

"Surely," she managed to say, "the *point* is to touch. I feel certain that one of your ninety thousand supermodel lovers must have taught you that in all these years of your celebrated promiscuity."

"If there were ninety thousand supermodels," he said, grinning lazily at her, "they couldn't all be super, could they? I do have standards."

He laughed when she rolled her eyes. But when he looked at her, everything got gold and hot and desperate, and that ache in her bloomed into an open flame.

"The point," he murmured in that silken voice of his, making that flame reach higher and higher, "is to want this so badly you think you might die from it."

"Pato…"

She didn't know she'd said his name again until she saw the way his eyes darkened, then tracked over her body, resting on her breasts and the lilac bra she wore. She felt heavy. Desperate for his touch. Any touch at all.

"I want to know if you match again. I want you to show me." Slowly, so slowly, he lifted his gaze back to hers, and what she saw there made her pulse heat. "And then I want you naked, and if I do it myself I'll be inside you before I get those jeans over your hips and then we'll be done and Adriana?" She stared at him, so wild with heat she thought she might explode. Or die. Or both. His smile was dark and dangerous and she felt it in her toes. "We want this to last a little while."

Her throat was dry. Her heart was pounding. The things she wanted whirled inside her, making her skin pull tight as if she might burst out of it.

"But what if I want to undress you?" she asked. Because she did. Almost more than she could bear. Because if she never had him again, she wanted to have this. As much of him as she could.

He touched her then, and she shuddered at the sheer joy of it. He ran his hand over her cheek, into her hair, and then held her there. Simply held her, and it made the need inside her turn into a white-hot surge of lightning.

"I told you this a long time ago," he said in that same darkly thrilling tone. "But I meant it. I like things my way."

He leaned closer then and brushed his mouth over hers, making goose bumps rise all over her body. She whispered a soft curse and Pato laughed against her mouth.

"And so will you," he promised.

She believed him.

He released her, then raised a dark, imperious brow.

Adriana hurriedly kicked off her shoes, grinning when he did the same. Then she unbuttoned her jeans and peeled them down her legs, feeling awkward until she saw the way he watched her, as if every millimeter of skin she revealed was a revelation.

And then she stood there before him, once again in nothing but her bra and panties. In matching lilac-colored lace.

Pato's smile had a dangerous edge to it. It worked its way into her pulse, making her shift restlessly from foot to foot. He stripped off his own jeans with a minimum of fuss, leaving him in nothing but another pair of those tight briefs that made him look edible.

And she wanted to taste him so badly it began to hurt.

Need made her clumsy. She forgot to be shy. She forgot she was inexperienced. She forgot everything but the man watching her, his gaze getting harder and more intense by the second.

Adriana unhooked her bra. When she pulled it away from her breasts, her nipples were already taut, and she heard Pato let out a sigh. Then she bent and tugged off her panties, and she heard him mutter something beneath his breath. And when she straightened she was naked, and he was looking at her as if she was something holy.

She felt beautiful. She felt like the temptress, the wanton

she'd always been called, and when he looked at her like that, she was glad. Bold women lived in her blood, she knew that now, and watching the way his eyes moved over her, bathing her in golden fire, she finally felt as bold as they were. As free as he'd made her.

He took off his briefs, studied her for another long moment, as if committing the sight of her to memory, and then crooked his finger once more, that wicked smile taking over his mouth.

Adriana walked to him immediately, too desperate to mind his high-handedness. She sighed happily when his hands went to her waist, then smoothed down to her hips—and then he pulled her to him, tumbling them both down on the sofa and arranging her over his lap so she sat astride him.

"Be still," he told her when she squirmed against him, and it very nearly hurt her to stop, but she did it. Her heart beat so hard she could feel it in her temples.

For a moment, he only stared up at her.

She felt his hard thighs beneath her, and the hardest part of him pressed against her, making her hotter, wilder. Needier by the second. She saw the blazing heat in his eyes, the dark passion, and thought she could drown in that alone. He waited. He watched.

"Do you feel like you might die?" he asked, his voice a low whisper, teasing at her skin, moving through her body and making her tremble.

"I think I already did," she confessed.

His mouth curved. And then he leaned forward and sucked her nipple into his mouth without the slightest hesitation, all of that wet heat against the tender peak, and she was lost.

Pato didn't ask, she discovered quickly. He took.

He used his mouth and his tongue against the weight of her breasts, used the hint of his teeth, until Adriana writhed against him, the intense sensations somehow arrowing straight to her core.

She explored that glorious torso of his, sun-kissed and hot beneath her hands, her mouth. And all the while she rocked against his hard, proud length, rubbing all of her heat against him helplessly. Wantonly. And he encouraged it, a big hand against the small of her back to hold her against him, keeping her right where he wanted her.

The more she moved the closer he held her, driving her higher and higher, keeping them close but not yet joined, making her whimper with need. Making her die, she thought, over and over and over again.

And then, when she was out of her mind, he kissed her.

Again and again, taking her mouth and making it his, making *her* his, with that devastating mastery that made her feel deliciously weak, made her shake and rock into him and forget her own name. And then at last he was lifting her, arranging her, reaching between them to test her heat with his fingers.

Once. Then again. Then he grinned at her, wicked and knowing, and did something else, a glorious twist of his clever hand—

Adriana shattered around him, a clenching, rolling burst of fire and light.

But Pato wasn't done.

He laughed, she thought, and then the smooth, hot length of him was pressing against her entrance. He wrapped his hands around her hips, held her fast between them, then thrust deep inside.

And she shattered again, instantly, the second explosion building from the first and tearing her into a million brilliant pieces. It went on and on. She gasped and she sobbed and then, when she started to breathe again, he flipped them around on the sofa, so she was lying on her back and he was cradled between her thighs.

"My turn," he whispered, grinning down at her, his eyes lazy and dark, and focused on her as if nothing else existed but this. Her. The two of them together, finally.

At last, Adriana thought.

And then he began to move.

She was exquisite. *Perfect.* Soft and trembling all around him, clinging to him, wild for him, hot cream and soft silk and *his.*

Finally his, and who cared about the consequences.

Pato set a slow, steady pace, watching her as he took her, watching every shimmer of ecstasy, every hint of joy, that crossed her expressive face. Her hips met his with each thrust, moving in a sinuous rhythm that nearly made him lose his mind. And his control.

Slowly, carefully, he built up the fire in her all over again, leaning down to worship her perfect breasts, her lush mouth. He pulled her knees up to cradle his hips, tasted the salt and sweet of her elegant neck. And then, when he couldn't take any more, he reached between them to find the core of her, and pressed there, rocking against her, into her, until she stiffened against him once more.

Then, at last, he let himself go.

And this time, when she shot over the edge he followed her, listening to her scream out his name as they fell.

It's not enough, he thought then, even as he held her to him, their hearts thundering in concert. *It will never be enough.*

And afterward, he let her crawl over him and drive him wild with her sweet kisses, her delighted exploration of his body. He had her again in the shower, losing himself in the heat and the steam and the slick perfection of her skin beneath his hands. He picked her up and pressed her against the glass, her head tipped back and her mouth open in a kind of silent scream as he rode them both straight back into the heart of that shattering fire.

He wouldn't let her dry herself. Succumbing to an urge he chose not to examine, he did it himself, drying every millimeter of her lovely skin with a soft towel, kissing those three distracting freckles below her breasts, then squeezing the water from her hair. He combed through it slowly, holding her captive between his legs as he sat on the bed in the adjoining bedroom. He noted the colors that sifted through his fingers, testing the heavy silk in his hands.

When he was finished he turned her around, and lost himself for a while in the heaven of her lush, hot mouth, its perfect fit against his, that taste of her that flooded into him and made him crazy, and the sheer poetry of her warm, naked curves beneath his hands.

Pato didn't know how he was going to do what he had to do. He shouldn't have indulged himself. He shouldn't have let her distract him. And yet he didn't regret a single moment of it.

Finally, he set her away from him, as hard again as if he'd never had her, and tempted almost past endurance by the soft invitation on her face, the flush he could see everywhere, from her cheeks to the rosy tips of her breasts.

He had never wanted anything more than this woman. He understood he never would.

And then he wrapped her in a cashmere throw that matched her beautiful eyes, sat her back on the sofa in the living room, where the bed didn't tempt him, and broke the only vow he'd ever made.

"My mother died when I was eighteen," he told her, because he didn't know how else to begin.

Adriana's blond hair was still damp and hung around her face in dark waves, making her look younger than she was. Innocent, despite all the ways he'd touched her, tasted her.

He didn't know why that pulled at him, why it made his chest feel tight.

"I know," she said, sitting with her feet tucked beneath her and the cashmere throw wrapped all around her. She looked delicate. *Perfect,* he thought again, and he couldn't have her. Why couldn't he keep that in mind? "I remember."

"Lenz was twenty-five." Pato shoved his hands in the pockets of the jeans he'd yanked back on when they left the bedroom. He roamed the cottage's small living space restlessly as he talked. "He had completed his military service and had taken his place at the king's side. He'd trained his whole life for it, as befits the heir to the throne." Adriana's gaze tracked Pato as he moved, and he smiled slightly. "I was the spare, and had far fewer expectations placed on me. I'd just started university. I paid some attention to my studies, but I was more interested in the girls."

"Shocking," Adriana said drily, but she was smiling.

"I didn't have to be serious," Pato said darkly. "That was Lenz's job. His duty. I always got to be the favorite, the happy disaster, but he was meant to be king."

For a moment, Pato only gazed at her. He'd let her walk out of the palace today thinking he'd turned on her like all the others, like the people who had called her names and made her feel dirty. He'd seen the look on her face, the crushed betrayal she'd tried to hide, and he'd done it anyway.

He couldn't stand it. He couldn't live with it.

And there was only one way to apologize: he had to explain. His life. His choices. Why he couldn't have her no matter how much he wanted her. She'd cried in his arms and he'd meant what he'd said to her, and he didn't have it in him to let her down. Not Adriana. Not this time. The whole world could think he was waste of space, as pointless as he was promiscuous, but he'd found he couldn't handle it if she did, too. He simply couldn't bear it.

"Pato." She was frowning again, deeper this time, and she stood then, the throw draping around her like a cape. "You don't have to tell me anything. You don't have to do this, whatever this is."

"I do," he said, surprised to hear how rough his voice was. "I need you to understand."

He didn't tell her why. He wasn't entirely sure he knew.

She shook her head, smiling slightly. "I don't expect anything from you," she said. "I know who you are and I know who I am. I'm at peace with it."

He blinked, then scowled at her. "What?"

"I love you," she said, so softly he almost thought he'd imagined it. But she was gazing at him, those melting brown eyes warm and glowing, and he knew she'd said it. That she meant it. "And that has nothing to do with what happens here, or after we leave. You don't owe me anything." She held up a hand when he started to talk. "I don't expect or need you to say it back."

Pato stared at her until she grew visibly uncomfortable under the weight of it. Until her sweet expression started to creep back toward a frown.

"The only thing less attractive than watching you attempt to martyr yourself for my brother in my bed," he growled, his temper kicking in as he spoke, like a black band tight around his chest, his gut, "is watching you martyr yourself for me so soon after I've been inside you, listening to you scream out my name." She sucked in an appalled breath, but he didn't stop, couldn't stop, and he stalked toward her until he stood within arm's reach. "I have no desire whatsoever to be quietly and distantly loved by some selfless, bloodless saint locked away in her self-imposed nunnery, prostrating herself daily to whatever it is she thinks she can't have or doesn't deserve. No hairshirt, no mortification of the flesh. No, thank you."

That telltale tide of red swept over her, but this time, he

thought, it wasn't so simple as embarrassment. Her eyes narrowed and she drew herself up, pulling the throw tighter around her as if it could protect her from him.

"What an ugly thing to say," she breathed, and he had the impression she was afraid to truly voice the words—as if she thought she might start yelling if she did. He wished she would. "Even for you."

He crossed his arms over his chest and glared at her.

"You want to love me, Adriana?" he demanded, his voice rough and hot and impatient, welling up from that place inside he'd thought he'd excised long ago, that heart it seemed only she could reach. He'd be damned if he'd let her hide. Not if *he* couldn't. He angled himself closer. "Then love me. Make it hurt. Make it jealous and possessive and painful. Make demands. Make it real or don't bother."

CHAPTER NINE

THERE WERE STAINS of red high on Adriana's cheeks, a dazed look on her pretty face, and Pato gave in to his driving need to be closer to her. Closer, always closer, no matter how irritated he might be with her and her proclamation of so-called love, as tepid as whatever she'd imagined she felt for Lenz.

Pato reached over and sat her down on the sofa, then gripped the back of it, pinning her there with an arm on either side of her. Caging her. Putting his face too close to hers. He couldn't read the way she looked at him then, didn't understand the darkness in her gaze, that sheen that suggested emotions she'd prefer to conceal from him.

"I know all about hiding, Adriana," he said quietly, though he could still hear that edge in his voice. He could feel it inside him. "I can see it when it's right in front of me."

"I don't know why you want to tell me anything." There was a raggedness in her voice, and he could see it in her face. "I don't know why you hunted me down at the villa, why you brought me here. It would have been easier to simply let me go this morning. Isn't that why you did it?"

"You know why." He wanted to touch her. Taste that lovely mouth. Take her again and again until neither of them could speak. But he didn't. He couldn't. "I can't have you, Adriana, but it's not because I don't want you."

She didn't say a word, but she was breathing high and hard,

as if climbing a steep hill. He could see that same darkness in her eyes, deeper now. Her confusion. He pushed away from the sofa but continued to stand over her, looking down at this woman who might, in fact, be the death of him. She'd already ruined him; that much was certain.

"My mother left behind some personal papers," he said then. It was time to finish this, before he forgot why he wanted that, too. "She left them to my father, which seemed an odd choice, given his profound disinterest in her personal affairs while she was alive. But eventually, he read them. And discovered that Lenz was not, in fact, his biological son."

It was Pato's greatest secret, it wasn't only *his* secret, and she could use it to topple his brother's kingdom if she chose. And there it lay, huge and ugly between them, taking up all the air in the cottage.

Adriana made a small, shocked noise, and covered her mouth with her hands. Pato let her simply stare at him, let all the implications sink in. For long moments she seemed frozen. But eventually, she blinked.

"Did Lenz know?" she asked in a whisper.

"We were both called before the king." Pato could hear the grimness in his voice. He'd never told this story before—he'd never imagined he would tell it to anyone. It certainly wasn't part of the plan. "He informed us that a great crime had been perpetrated against the throne of Kitzinia, and that it must be rectified. That was how Lenz found out."

Adriana's eyes closed, as if that was too horrible to imagine. Pato had been there, and he felt much the same. He and Lenz had been ordered before the king, commanded to appear, even though Pato had been in England and Lenz in South Africa at the time. Pato remembered how baffled they'd been, jet-lagged and even somewhat concerned about their father. Until the nasty, furious way he had delivered the news, as if Lenz had engineered his paternity himself for the sole purpose of deception.

"You have no brother from this day forward," the king had intoned into the stunned, sick silence, glaring at Pato as if Lenz had disappeared into thin air. "You are my heir, and your mother's bastard is nothing to you."

"But," Pato had begun, his head spinning. "Father—"

"I have one son," the king had snarled. "One heir to this throne, Patricio, and God have mercy on this kingdom, but it's you."

Pato had never cared much for his father before that day. He'd always been a distant, disapproving presence who had rarely lowered himself to interact much with his second son, which had always suited Pato well enough, as he'd seen what it was like for Lenz to have all that critical attention focused on him. But after that day, Pato had loathed him.

"My father cannot bear scandal," he said now. "He is obsessed with even the slightest speck of dirt anywhere near his spotless reputation. And I had recently landed myself in the tabloids for the first time with an extremely inappropriate British pop star. The king was not pleased about it when I was merely the ornamental second son, or so I heard through the usual channels, but when it turned out I was his heir, he went apoplectic."

Adriana was still sitting there, so straight and shocked, her eyes still wide. "Did he plan to simply toss Lenz out on the street?"

"He did." Pato moved to the nearby armchair and lowered himself into it. "He thought he'd wait until my pop star scandal faded, exile Lenz from Kitzinia and force me to take on the duties of a crown prince in a sober and serious manner that would indicate my brush with the tabloids was no more than a regrettable, youthful indiscretion, never to be repeated."

Adriana only stared at him, shaking her head slightly as if she couldn't take it in. Or perhaps she was attempting to imagine him in the role of dutiful crown prince—a stretch for anyone, he was well aware. Even him.

"Lenz's exile was to be presented as an abdication well before he was to take the throne." Pato smiled slightly. Darkly. "But I never let the scandal die down. From that day forward, I made it my job to be an embarrassment. To make it abundantly clear that I was and am unfit for any kind of throne."

"Pato." She shifted then, moving forward in her seat as if she wanted to reach over and touch him. Her hands moved, but then she held them together in her lap. "You know I admire your brother. But if you're the heir to the throne...?" She searched his face. "Isn't it your birthright?"

"You sound like Lenz," Pato said roughly. He had to get up again then, had to move, and found himself staring out the windows that looked down to the peaceful water. "I never envied Lenz his position. I never wished for his responsibilities. And when they were handed to me, I didn't want them. Can you imagine if it was announced I was supposed to be king? The people would take up arms and riot in the streets."

"They might object to the Playboy Prince, yes," Adriana said after a long moment. "You've made sure of that. But that's not who you are."

His breath left him. He ignored the ache in his chest.

"My choice was a throne or a brother," he said quietly. He turned to face her. "I chose my brother. And I don't regret it."

"Pato..." she whispered, and the look in her eyes nearly undid him.

"Since then," he said gruffly, pushing forward because he couldn't stay in this moment, couldn't let himself explore the way she gazed at him, "my father has had to pretend to keep Lenz in his good graces, because his pride won't allow him to explain the situation to his ministers. Especially when, as you say, I've made certain the alternative is so unacceptable."

For a moment there was nothing in the room but the sound of his own pounding heart.

"You're a good man, Pato," Adriana said then. There was a scratchy undertone to her voice that made him think she was holding back tears. For him. And he thought it might undo him. "And a very good brother."

Pato looked at her, then away, before he forgot what he could and couldn't have. Before he forgot he'd chosen to be a hollow man, with an empty life. Before he was tempted to believe her.

"My father is also unwell," he said instead, bitterly. "It is, ironically enough, his heart."

Adriana was worried about her own.

She hardly knew where to look, what to think. Nothing he was telling her could possibly be true—and yet it all made a horrible sense. It explained the chilliness she'd always sensed between Lenz and the king. It explained Lenz's extraordinary patience with Pato's messy escapades. More, it explained how Pato could do all the scandalous things he'd done and yet also be the man who'd held her on the plane, then quietly rid her of a lifetime of shame. It explained everything.

He stood there at the window so calmly, half-naked as ever, all sun-kissed skin and masculine grace, talking with such seeming nonchalance about things that would over-throw their government. He had given up a throne. He loved his brother more than he wanted what was his by birthright. He had deliberately crafted his own mythology to serve his own ends and to force his father, the king, into doing what he wanted him to do. He'd even hinted at this once before, in London, when he'd said his reputation was his life's work.

He was truly remarkable, she thought then. And he was hers.

It didn't matter for how long. It didn't matter if he couldn't have her, as he'd said. It didn't matter if all she ever had of him was the distance and the unrequited love that he'd mocked. He'd given her his secrets. He'd stepped out of hiding and shown her who he really was, because he believed she deserved to know. Because he hadn't wanted to let her leave him the way she had this morning, thinking the worst of him.

He would rather have her know the dangerous truth than have her think he didn't care.

That he cared, that he must or he would never have shared any of this with her, that he really must trust her, dawned inside her like the sun.

He was hers.

"His health is deteriorating, he is not a candidate for surgery and he is an unacceptable risk to the kingdom," Pato was saying. "He should have stepped down already. He will have no choice when Lenz marries Lissette, as she was betrothed at birth to the heir to the Kitzinian throne." Pato shrugged at Adriana's quizzical look. "If Lenz marries her, it is an assertion that he is, in fact, that heir. There can be no going back unless my father wants an international incident that could well become a war. He will have no choice but to face the inevitable." Pato's mouth moved into a curve that was far darker than usual. "He has grown more desperate by the day for another option."

"You," Adriana said.

"Me," Pato agreed, "even though I've gone to great lengths to keep myself out of the running." He sighed, and then leveled a look at her that made something twist in her stomach, made a sense of foreboding trickle down her back. "He had convinced himself that the kingdom would excuse me as a young man sowing his oats, who could in time settle down, as men do. But now he believes I am skulking about with one of Lenz's cast-off mistresses, which he finds truly distasteful. Worse, he is superstitious enough to believe that Righetti women possess some kind of witchcraft, and that I am weak enough to be under your spell."

Adriana couldn't breathe, as if he'd slammed that straight into her gut. But she couldn't look away from him, either.

"Bewitched by a woman descended from traitors and temptresses," Pato said softly, his golden eyes darker, more intense. "Crafted by the ages to be my downfall."

"You want him to think that," she managed to say, despite feeling as if the room were drawing tight on all sides. "That's why you decided to behave these last weeks. You wanted him to think I was influencing you."

"Yes."

His gaze was dark. Demanding. Without apology, and Adriana felt so brittle, suddenly. So close to breaking, and that wave of misery she'd thought she was rid of waited there for her, she knew. In the next breath. Or the one following. And it would crash over her and take her to her knees if she let it.

But she still couldn't look away from him.

"Was it all a game?" she whispered, that familiar emptiness opening again inside her, reminding her how easy it was to be sucked back in. "Was any of it real?"

"You know that it was both." His gaze bored into her, challenging her. "Almost from the very beginning."

She shook her head, aware that it felt too full, too fragile. That she did. There was too much noise in her ears and that dark pit in her stomach, and all she wanted was to get to her feet and run—but she couldn't seem to move.

"I don't know that."

"You do."

He pushed away from the wall and came toward her then, imposing and beautiful, and she knew the truth about him now. She knew his indolence was an act, that the powerful, ruthless man she'd glimpsed was who Pato was. Now she couldn't pretend she didn't see it. She couldn't pretend he was lazy, pointless, careless—any of the things he'd pretended he was. He'd manipulated her every step of the way and would no doubt do it again. He'd given up a throne for this. What was one woman next to that? She was nothing but collateral damage.

And still, she didn't move. Still, her heart ached for him. No matter what this meant for her, what it said about the last years of her life.

"This is why you have to leave the palace, Adriana," he said, that dark urgency in his voice and stamped across his face. "You deserve better than these games. No one comes out of them without being compromised. No one wins."

She struggled with the tears that pricked suddenly at the back of her eyes, and then he was right there, sinking down in front of her to kneel on the floor and take her face between his hands.

"I don't want to let you go," he whispered fiercely. "But I will. Somehow, I will. I promise."

The same old voices snaked through her then, crawling out of that darkness inside her to whisper the same old poison. *He wanted the Righetti whore and he got her, didn't he?* She'd been a means to an end for him, a tool. *Another instrument.* Something he could use and then toss aside. *"Remember who you are, Adriana,"* her father had said when she'd first got the job at the palace. *"Remember that your disgrace is already assumed—they only seek confirmation."* She was nothing but her surname, her face, her family's everlasting shame, another headline in another tabloid paper. Temptresses and a traitor, marking her as surely as if she wore their sins tattooed across her cheeks.

But Pato had trusted her. He'd come for her when he could have simply let her leave, none the wiser. He'd brought her here, and she'd been the one to insist they give in to the wild passion between them, not Pato. He'd wanted to talk and she hadn't let him. And now he'd told her everything, and yes, it hurt. But he'd told her a story that could rock the whole kingdom, and he wanted to set her free. Again.

And all *she* wanted to do, all she could think to do, was run away and hide—which was just what she'd done when she was seventeen. It was what she always did.

No wonder he'd mocked her declaration of love, she thought then, a different kind of shame winding through her. It wasn't love at all. It was safe and removed. It was loving the idea of him, not loving the man. The complicated, dangerous man, who wasn't safe at all and had never pretended otherwise—he only made her feel that she might be safe when she was with him.

Make it hurt, he'd challenged her, scowling at her, refusing to accept her half measures. *Make it real or don't bother.*

And this was her chance to step out of hiding, just as he'd done. She wanted to be bold. She wanted to feel *alive.* For once in her life, she wanted to use her infamous name and her notoriety instead of sitting back and letting others use it against her.

Not as a sacrifice. Pato deserved better than that. He deserved a gift.

"It sounds like I'm an excellent weapon," she said. She wrapped her hands around his wrists, tilted her face to his and lost herself in all that dark gold. "Why don't you use me? I'm sure your father isn't the only one who assumes that I'm your mistress as well as Lenz's. Why not make it public and damn yourself in his eyes forever?"

"I'm not going to use you that way, Adriana." Pato's voice was harsh. "I didn't accept the offer when it was for Lenz, and I won't do it now. You are not a whore. You do not wield dark magic that turns unsuspecting men into your slaves. You're better than this fairy-tale villain they've made you, that I've helped them make you, and I refuse to take part in it any longer. I won't."

She couldn't help herself then. She leaned in and kissed him, feeling the electric charge that shuddered through him, then sizzled in her, making what she'd intended to be sweet turn into something else entirely. When she pulled away, his eyes were still dark, but gleamed gold.

"I'm genetically predisposed to be the mistress of a Kitzinian prince," she told him, and smiled at him. She could do this. In truth, she already had. "And I'm already notorious. You may not want to accept your birthright, Pato, but I do."

He looked at her for what felt like a very long time. His hands still cupped her cheeks, and she was sure he could see through her, all the way down to the deepest part of her soul.

"I won't let you sacrifice yourself for this kingdom," he said finally, his gaze more gold than grim, though his mouth remained serious. "It has never done anything for you but make your life a misery."

"It's no sacrifice," she said, her hands tightening around his wrists. "I don't want to martyr myself, I want to help."

Another long moment, taut and electric, and then he shook his head.

"We have a week until the wedding." Pato stood, drawing her to her feet and into his arms. As he gazed down at her, his mouth began to curve into that wicked quirk she recognized. "Lenz will marry his ice princess, the poor bastard. The spectacle will bring in hordes of tourists, just as my parents' wedding did a generation ago. My father will finally cede the throne, and will spend the rest of his miserable life faced with the knowledge that the son he raised and then rejected is his king. And life will carry on, Adriana, without a single mention of the Righetti family, traitors and temptresses, or you."

"But—"

"I promise," he whispered against her mouth.

And then he kissed her, igniting fire and need and that searing joy, and she decided there were far better things to do with the man she loved than argue.

For now.

Adriana woke the morning before the royal wedding with a smile on her face. She turned off her alarm and settled back against her pillow, smiling at the light pouring in through her windows as if the sun shone only for her. As if it was simply another gift Pato had given her.

They hadn't spoken again of his letting her go.

Pato was not considered a legendary lover by accident, she'd learned. His reputed skills were no tabloid exaggeration. He'd had her twice more before they'd left the cottage that day, reducing her to a sobbing, writhing mess again and again, until she was deliciously limp, content simply to cling to him on the drive back into the city, thinking not of thrones and notoriety but him. Only him.

"Come to the palace tomorrow," he'd told her, letting her off on a deserted corner some distance from her family's villa, out of the circle of light thrown by the nearest streetlamp, safe from prying eyes and gossiping tongues.

"You sacked me," she'd reminded him primly. He'd grinned at her, sitting on that lethal-looking motorcycle and holding fast to one of her hands.

"I changed my mind. I do that." His wicked brows rose. "It is my great royal privilege."

"I'm not sure I want the job," she'd teased. "My employer is embarrassing and often inappropriately dressed. And the hours are terrible."

He'd tugged her to him then, kissing her as slowly and as thoroughly as if he hadn't done so already that day, too many times to count. He kissed her until she was boneless against him, and only then did he let her go.

"Don't be late," he'd said, his eyes gleaming in the dark. "And I do hope you can behave yourself. I can't have my assistant throwing herself at me at every opportunity. I take my position as the royal ornament and national disaster very seriously."

He'd roared off, splitting the night with the noise his motorcycle made, and Adriana had fairly danced all the way back to the villa.

And then, the following morning, he'd sauntered into his office wearing nothing but a pair of dark trousers low on his narrow hips. He'd shut the door behind him and had her over his desk before he'd even said good-morning. She'd had to bite her own hand to make sure she stayed quiet while Pato moved inside her, whispering dark and thrilling things in her ear, pushing them both straight over the edge.

He'd started as he meant to go on, Adriana thought now, rolling out of her bed and padding into her bath. They'd followed his usual schedule, packed this week with extra wedding requirements. The difference was, every time they were alone they'd been unable to keep their hands off each other. The car, his office, even a blazingly hot encounter all of three steps away from a corporate luncheon. He'd simply glanced into what was probably a coatroom, pulled her inside and braced her against a chair that sat near the far wall.

"Hang on," he'd murmured, leaning over her back and wrapping his hands around her hips. And then he'd thrust into her, hot and hard and devastatingly talented, and she'd stopped caring about the speech he'd been meant to give. She'd cared about nothing at all but the wild blaze between them and the way they both burned in it, together.

Adriana left her bedroom then, twisting her hair up into a knot as she walked through the villa in search of her morning coffee. She felt lighter than she had in years. She smiled down the hallways toward that closed-off parlor, and took her time descending the grand stairs.

Last night Pato had been called upon to entertain visiting dignitaries and royals from across Europe, all in town for the wedding. When the long evening was over and they were alone in his car, he'd pulled Adriana to him. He'd tucked her beneath his arm, arranged her legs over his lap and rested his chin on the top of her head. Then he'd simply held her. When his driver started up the hill toward the Righetti villa, he'd hit the intercom and told him to simply keep driving.

They'd driven for a long time, circling around and around the city. Pato had played with her hair idly. She'd closed her eyes and let herself enjoy the luxury of time to bask in him. He'd held her close against his heart while the city bled light and noise all around them.

Inside the car, it had been quiet. Soft. Perfect. And Adriana had never felt more cherished. More loved.

She didn't notice the strained silence in the kitchen until she was pouring herself a cup of coffee. She turned to find her father staring at her, an arrested expression on his face she'd never seen before. Even her mother looked pale, one hand clutching at her heart as if it were broken, her eyes cast down toward the table.

"What's happened?" Adriana asked, terrified. She left her coffee on the counter and took a step toward the table, looking back and forth between her parents. Was it one of her brothers? "Has there been an accident?"

Her mother only shook her head as if she couldn't bear to speak, squeezing her eyes shut, and Adriana went cold.

"You know what you've done," her father stated in a hard voice. "And now, Adriana, so does the world."

It took her a moment to understand what he was saying— and that he really was speaking to her with all that chilly animosity. And when she did understand it, she shook her head in confusion.

"I don't know what you mean," she said.

"I blame myself." Her father pushed back his chair and climbed to his feet, looking far older than he had the day before. Adriana felt a deep pang of fear. Then he stood there for a moment, his hard gaze raking over her as if she was something dirty.

And she knew, then.

That familiar, panicked cold bloomed deep inside her, spreading out and turning black, ripping open that same old wound and letting the emptiness back in.

He knew about Pato.

"Papa," she said softly, reaching out a hand toward him, but he recoiled. Her throat constricted when she tried to swallow, and she slowly dropped her arm back to her side.

"I knew you were too beautiful," he told her in that terrible voice, and Adriana felt it like a knife, sinking deep into her belly. "I knew it would ruin us. Beauty like that is only the surface, Adriana, and everything beneath it is corrupt. Sinful. Twisted. I saw it myself in Sandrine, in her contempt for propriety. It runs in this family like a disease. I knew it was in you since the day you were born a girl."

She felt unsteady on her feet, as if he'd actually cut her open. Perhaps it would have been better—less painful—if he had. And she was too aware of her mother's continued silence in place of her usual unspoken support, weighing on Adriana like an indictment.

"There's no Righetti family disease," she said when she could speak. It was hard to keep her voice calm, her gaze steady as she faced her father. "There never was. We're only people, Papa, and we all make our own choices."

His lip curled, and he stared at her as if he'd never seen her before now. As if she'd worn a mask her whole life, until today, and what he saw beneath it disgusted him. It made her feel sick.

"Tell me he forced you. Coerced you. Tell me, daughter, that you did not betray your family's trust in you willingly. That you did not follow in the footsteps of all the whores who sullied the Righetti name before you and take *Prince Pato*—" he spat out the name as if it was the foulest of curses "—as your lover. Tell me you are not so stupid as to open your legs for that degenerate. *Tell me.*"

Adriana didn't understand how this was happening. Her head pounded and her heart felt like lead in her chest, and she didn't know what to do, how to make this better. How to explain what it was like to be free of her chains to the man who'd helped fashion them, because he wore so many of his own.

"He's not a degenerate," she whispered, and it was a mistake.

Her father let out a kind of roar—enraged and humiliated and broken. It made her mother jerk in her chair. It made Adriana want to cry. But instead, she wrapped her arms around her middle and watched him, waiting for his eyes to meet hers again.

When they did, she thought the look in them might leave marks.

"You don't understand," she said quickly, desperately.

"I cannot bear to look at you." He sounded deeply, irreversibly disgusted. It made her eyes fill with tears. "All I see are his fingerprints, sullying you. Ruining you. Making you nothing more than one more Righetti whore, like all the rest." He shook his head. "You have proved to the world that we are tainted. Dirty. You have destroyed us all over again, Adriana, and for what? The chance to be one more conquest in an endless line? The opportunity to warm a bed that has never gone cold? How could you?"

She shook, but she didn't move, not even when he turned and slammed out of the room, the silence he left behind heavy and loud, pressing into her, making her want to slide into a ball on the floor. But she didn't do it. She forced herself to look at her mother instead.

"Mama—" she began, but her mother shook her head hard, her lips pressed together in a tight line.

"You knew better," she said in a harsh whisper. "From the time you were small, you knew better than this. Righettis can't put a single foot wrong. Righettis must be above reproach—especially a girl who looks like you, as if you stepped out of one of those paintings. I took you to meet Sandrine myself—living out her days in a foreign country with a man who should have been a duke, cast out from her home forever. *You knew better.*"

It was such an unexpected slap that Adriana took a step back from the table, as if her mother really had hit her.

"I never did anything to be ashamed of," she blurted out, something reckless moving in her then, impossible to contain, as if she'd waited all her life for this conversation. "And yet the first thing you taught me was shame. Why do we punish ourselves before anyone else does?" Her voice cracked. "Why did you?"

But that made it worse. Her mother stood then, straight and sorrowful, both hands at her heart and her eyes like nails, staring at Adriana as if she was a stranger.

"You've made your bed, Adriana," she said coldly. "We'll all have to lie in it, won't we? I certainly hope it was worth it. Sandrine always thought so, but then, she died alone and far away, in a cloud of disgrace. And so will you."

Her mother didn't slam the door when she left. She simply walked away and didn't look back, which was worse. Worse than a slap.

And Adriana stood there in all that silence, awful and simmering and ugly, and tried to keep herself from falling apart.

She looked around desperately, as if a solution might rise up from the tiled floor, and that was when she saw the paper spread out in the middle of the wooden table as if her parents had pored over it together.

The paper.

For a moment she couldn't bring herself to look, because she could imagine what she'd see. She'd been imagining it, in one form or another, since she was a girl. She'd had nightmares about it more than once. She stared at the paper as if it were a serpent coiled up in the middle of the kitchen, fangs extended.

But in the end, she couldn't help herself.

Playboy Pato Succumbs to Witchy Righetti's Spell! Well known for her notorious wiles, Adriana Righetti—very much an heir to her family's storied charms—has made a shocking play for the kingdom's favorite bachelor—

She couldn't do it, she told herself, squeezing her eyes shut, her hand at her throat as if her pulse might leap out from beneath her skin.

But there was more. She had to look.

There was the helpful sidebar that ran down all the infamous members of the Righetti family, complete with pictures and a few snide lines detailing their sins. Carolina, shameless mistress to Crown Prince and later King Philip. Maria, rumored to have slept with all three royal princes and some assorted cousins with dukedoms in an effort to trade upward, until she reached Eduardo, the future king. Francesca, lifelong consort of Prince Vidal. Sandrine, who'd disrupted the Reinsmark dukedom. And Almado the traitor, who had assassinated King Oktav. And somehow it managed to suggest, without ever doing so directly, that Adriana herself had been mistress to all those Kitzinian royals before going on to personally betray the country, before taking her position in the palace and turning her attention to the easily seduced and obviously beguiled Pato.

And then there were the pictures.

They'd been taken the day before yesterday, she saw at once. She reached out to run a shaky finger over the series of photos before her, smudging the newspaper ink. She'd thought they were alone. Pato had spent the morning at an event, and they had been waiting in the antechamber of the hall for his driver to pull around. She'd been *certain* they were alone.

And that was why she hadn't protested when he'd turned to her with that wild and hungry look in his eyes. Why she'd leaned into him when he'd taken her mouth in a lush promise of a kiss. It had been devastating and quick, a mere appetizer to what he'd do once they climbed into the car, he'd informed her with that gleam of gold in his eyes. And he'd kept his word.

It had been a single kiss. Hot and private. *Theirs.*

But the pictures looked openly carnal. The very number of photographs made it seem they'd kissed for a long time, so focused on each other that they were reckless, careless. The paper tutted about the locale and the fact that neither of them had apparently noticed or cared that they'd been in public—"par for the course for Pato, but can Adriana's history make her anything but a terrible influence on the kingdom's bad boy?"

She had no idea how long she stood there in the kitchen, all alone with the newspaper and its malicious recounting and reshaping of her life into nasty little innuendos and silly nicknames. At first she didn't know what snapped her out of it—but then she heard the banging at the door, harsh and loud. And the shouting.

Her stomach sank to her feet. Paparazzi.

She should have expected them. She'd dealt with them a thousand times before—but never when *she* was the target. Adriana took a deep breath, and then pulled all the curtains shut without letting them get a glimpse of her, took the landline telephone off its hook, making it as difficult as possible for the cockroaches swarming in her street to get what they were after.

She didn't seek out her parents. They would expect an apology—an apology Adriana doubted they would accept. And she might feel sick to her stomach, she might feel battered and attacked, exposed and alone, but she wasn't sorry.

When she finally climbed back up to her room, her mobile was lit up with messages. Reporters. Supposed "friends" she hadn't spoken to in years. Her few actual friends, quietly wondering how she was. More reporters. And then the clipped and frigid tones of the king's private secretary, a man Adriana had seen from afar but had certainly never met, informing her that her services to the royal household were no longer required.

She was cut off. Dismissed. The Righetti contamination had been officially removed from the palace.

It was not until dusk began to creep through the streets that Adriana admitted to herself that she'd expected Pato to appear again—to race to the villa and save her, somehow, from this public disgrace. Make it better, even if this public stoning via newspaper was exactly what she'd volunteered for. Twice.

Because it turned out that being called a whore her whole life had not, in fact, prepared her for what it was like to see it printed in the newspapers and all across the internet, not as speculation this time, but fact. It hadn't prepared her for that scene in the kitchen with her parents. It hadn't prepared her at all.

And when she'd wanted to do this, she understood as she sat there, barricaded in her childhood bedroom, she'd thought only about how Lenz or Pato might benefit from this kind of media attention. She hadn't thought about her family at all, and the guilt of that grew heavier as the day wore on. This wasn't only about her. It never had been. This was her family's nightmare, and she'd made it real.

Pato had been right. She'd been so busy rushing to martyr herself that she hadn't stopped to consider precisely what that might entail. Or just how many people it would hurt besides her.

Eventually, she had to accept the fact that Pato wasn't coming.

And with it, a wave of other things she didn't want to think about. Such as how ruthless he really was, how manipulative. He'd told her so himself. How he'd promised this wouldn't happen, and yet it had. And what his silence today suggested that meant.

She couldn't cry. She could hardly move. It simply hurt too much.

Late that night, Adriana found herself in the parlor with the other harlots. She curled up in the chair below their portraits and stared at them until her eyes went blurry.

This was inevitable from the start, she told herself. *You walked right into it anyway, talking about love and imagining you were better than your past.*

Adriana had no one to blame for this but herself.

CHAPTER TEN

ADRIANA WOKE WITH a start, her heart pounding.

For a moment she didn't know where she was, but even as she uncurled herself from the chair she found herself in, she remembered, and a glance at the wall before her, and the three portraits hanging there, confirmed it.

Adriana stretched out the kink in her neck, the events of the previous day flooding back to her, one after the next, as she stood. Her father's face. Her mother's harsh words. The newspapers, the paparazzi. Pato's obvious betrayal. She shut her eyes against it, as if that might make it all vanish.

Last night she hadn't been able to cry. This morning, she refused to let herself indulge the urge. If the women hanging on the wall could smile, she told herself, then so could she.

She squared her shoulders, told herself she was ready to face the next battle—and that was when she heard the shouting. *Her father.*

Adriana threw open the door and stepped into the hall, moving toward the angry sound. Her stomach twisted into a hard knot as she tried to imagine what could be worse than yesterday's newspaper spread, which hadn't sent him into this kind of temper—

"You've done enough damage—you can want nothing more! Will you take the house down, brick by brick? Demand our blood from the stones?" Her father sounded upset and furious in a way that scared her, it was so much worse than yesterday. She picked up her speed. "How many of your sick, twisted little games—"

Adriana reached the stair, looked down and froze solid.

Pato stood there in the lower hall.

She didn't know what poured through her then, so intense it was like an acute flash of pain, and she couldn't tear her eyes away from him.

Pato wore the ceremonial military regalia that tradition dictated served as formal wear to a grand state occasion like his brother's wedding, a dark navy uniform accented in deep scarlet at the cuffs, the neck, and in lines down each leg, then liberally adorned with golden epaulets and brocades that trumpeted his rank. He'd even tamed his hair from its usual wildness, making him look utterly, heartbreakingly respectable. He stood tall and forbidding, staring at Adriana's father impassively, a trio of guards arranged behind him.

He looked every inch the royal prince he was. Like the king he could have been. He looked dangerously beautiful and completely inaccessible, and it ripped at her heart.

Adriana sucked in a breath, and his gaze snapped to hers, finding her there on the landing.

His gaze was the darkest she'd ever seen it, hard and intense, and she didn't know how long they stood there, eyes locked together. Her father was blocking the stairs, his voice louder by the second, and yet while Pato looked at her like that, she hardly heard him.

Pato jerked his gaze away abruptly, leaving Adriana feeling simultaneously relieved and bereft.

"No more," he said curtly, cutting into her father's diatribe with a tone of sheer command. He seemed taller, more formidable, and yet he didn't change expression as he stared at her father. "You forget yourself."

The air in the villa went taut. Thin. Adriana's father fell silent. Pato waited.

One breath. Another.

"Step aside," Pato ordered, his voice even, but there was no mistaking the crack of power in it. The expectation of obedience. The guards behind him stood straighter. "I won't ask again."

Adriana's father moved out of his way, and even as he did, Pato brushed past him, taking the steps with a controlled ferocity that made something inside Adriana turn over and start to heat. She couldn't seem to look away from him as he bore down on her, or even catch her breath, and then he was there. Prince Patricio of Kitzinia, in all his stately splendor, looking at her with the same hard intensity as before, nothing the least bit gold in his gaze.

"You brought guards?" she asked. Of all the things she might have said to him.

"I dislike the paparazzi blocking my movements," he said in that same even tone. Then his head tilted slightly. Regally. "Is there a private room?"

It was another command, demanding instant compliance.

Adriana didn't hesitate any more than her father had. She waved her hand down the hall she'd come from, and Pato inclined his head, indicating she should precede him.

She did—but not without looking back.

Her father stood in the lower hall, watching her with the same tortured expression he'd worn yesterday, and the guilt swept through her again, almost choking her. She opened her mouth, as if there was something she could say to take away his horror at what was his worst nightmare come to life, right before his eyes.

But Pato's hand was on the small of her back, urging her ahead of him. There was nothing she could say to make this better. Her father wouldn't forgive her, and on some level, she didn't blame him. She'd known better than to do this, and she'd done it anyway.

Adriana couldn't stand Pato touching her—it was too much to bear, and her body only wanted him the way it always did—so she broke away as she led him back into the parlor, moving all the way across the room before facing him, her back to the far wall.

Pato stepped inside, closed the door behind him, and his gaze cut immediately to the trio of paintings on the wall. He went still, his mouth flattening into a grim line.

It took him a long time to look at her again, but when he did, Adriana had recovered herself. Maybe it was the women on the wall, reminding her that she could do this, whatever this was. It took a lot of strength to survive being as hated as they'd been—as she was. She remembered that Sandrine's eyes had sparkled merrily when she'd met her, that the older woman had looked anything but cowed.

Adriana could survive these final, painful scenes with Pato. *She could.*

"I would have preferred to sacrifice myself, I think," she said coolly, pulling the familiar defense around her gratefully. She crossed her arms and ignored that flash in his gaze. "Rather than wake up yesterday to find myself burned to a crisp on your little pyre with no warning whatsoever. Call me controlling if you must."

He eyed her from across the room in a way that unnerved her, but she refused to back down.

"You believe I did this?" he asked mildly. But she knew him too well to be fooled by that tone.

"I don't know why you didn't ask for assistance," she continued, as if this was any other conversation she'd ever had with him. As if it was easy to pretend there was no emotion beneath this, no dark whirling thing that threatened to suck her under. "I've been handling your paparazzi encounters for a long time, Pato. At the very least, I might have suggested a better nickname for myself than 'Witchy Righetti.'"

Again, he gave her a long look, and it occurred to her belatedly that he was fighting for calm and control as much as she was. It made her heart kick in a kind of panic.

"I promised you I wouldn't use you that way," he reminded her, almost politely. As if he thought she might have forgotten.

And it was too much. He was here, and the way he was dressed made the difference in their situations painfully clear to her. He would walk away from this a prince. She would crawl away from this the disgraced daughter of a despised family, personally responsible for this new helping of shame and recrimination heaped on her family's name.

She used the only weapon she had.

"You also promised your brother that you wouldn't reveal his secret, I assume," she said, very distinctly, and told herself she was pleased when she saw something dark and raw in his gaze. "And yet you did. Why would I think you'd keep a relatively small promise to someone like me?"

A muscle worked in his jaw. His hands curled into fists. And he looked at her as if she'd torn him wide-open.

Adriana told herself she was glad. He wasn't here to save her. He couldn't undo what she'd done to her family. But if she could make him feel a little bit of what she did, all the better—even if that look on his face clawed into her, shredding her from within.

He laughed, but it was short. Bitter.

"This, then, is what you mean when you say you love me," he said quietly, his dark eyes pinning her to the wall behind her. "Is it better this way, Adriana? If you succeed in running me off—if you take that knife and bury it deep enough, twist it hard enough—will that get you what you want?"

He was moving toward her—one step, then another—dark and furious and something more than that. Something that made him look as destroyed as she felt, and there was nothing good about that at all.

"I don't want—" she began, but he laughed again, and this time, it made her shudder.

"I think you do," he said, low and intense. Damning her where she stood. "I think you want to hole up in this mausoleum and paint your own portrait to hang on that wall." He pointed at the trinity of pictures, but he didn't take his eyes off her. "That's what Righettis have been doing in this place for the last hundred years, wafting through the kingdom like ghosts, subjecting themselves to whatever punishment is thrown their way—"

"You don't have any idea what you're talking about!" she cried, aware that she was shouting. But there was something hard and itchy and hot inside her, and she had to get it out or it would kill her, she knew. "It's not as if you have any idea what it's like to be the most reviled family in the kingdom. And why would you? It wasn't *your* ancestor who murdered the king!" She swept her hand toward the portraits. "Or slept with several branches of the royal family tree!"

His eyes blazed at her, and she realized only belatedly that he'd come much too close to her, as if he'd stalked her without her noticing.

"Do you imagine that my family took control of the throne of Kitzinia because we asked nicely?" he demanded, sounding as incredulous as he did angry. "Is that how you remember the history of Europe? Because to my recollection, every kingdom that ever was came about in blood and treachery." He shook his head, and then somehow his hands were on her upper arms and he was even closer, and she knew she should push him away. She knew she should extricate herself—but she couldn't seem to move. "Your family isn't the only one in the kingdom with blood on its hands, Adriana.

But it is certainly the only one I can think of that's created a cult out of its guilt!"

She hung there, unable to breathe, unable to think, suspended between his hands as surely as she was caught in that dark, ferocious glare he kept trained on her.

"What do mean by that?" she asked in a whisper, and then shivered when he pulled her so close to him that his lips almost touched her as he spoke.

"You didn't kill any Kitzinian kings," he snapped. "And last I checked, the only prince you've slept with is me. Stop accepting the blame for history you can't change." Something flashed in his gaze then, and she felt the echo deep inside her, deep and threatening, as if might tear her in two. "For God's sake," he growled at her. "*You* are not a painting on the wall, Adriana. You don't have to shoulder this. *Fight back.*"

Pato let go of her and stepped away.

He couldn't remember the last time he'd lost his temper. Not like this, so that it hummed in him still. And certainly not with that rough edge of need running through it, making him want nothing more than to continue this conversation while naked and deep inside her.

Even after she'd thrown what he'd told her in his face, he wanted her, with the same desperation as before. More, perhaps. He didn't know whether to laugh at that or simply despair of himself.

Adriana was breathing hard, and looking very little like the brazen harlot he'd read so much about yesterday. He could see the smudges of exhaustion beneath her beautiful eyes, the vulnerable cast to her sweet mouth, the flush in her cheeks that failed to disguise the paleness of her face. He let his gaze fall over her, from the blond waves in a messy knot on the back of her head, to a face scrubbed free of cosmetics, to the loose cotton clothes she wore that might very well be her pajamas. And her bare feet.

For some reason, the fact that he could see her toes made his chest hurt.

"I didn't plant that story," he told her then, biting out the words he shouldn't have to say. She raised a hand to her mouth as if she thought she might cry, then lowered it again, as if she was still trying to put on a front for him. He hated it. "It was Lissette."

"What?" Adriana shook her head. "Why?"

"Lenz told her the truth." Adriana's eyes flew to his, shocked. "He felt she deserved to make an informed decision about whether or not to marry him. She, in turn, felt that my father couldn't be trusted not to pull a last-minute stunt at the wedding, so she decided to make it clear that he was without options."

Adriana swallowed. "Lenz must be happy that she wants him anyway."

"That, or she very much wants to be queen of Kitzinia," Pato retorted. His voice lowered. "But I'm certainly pleased to learn that your opinion of me is as poor today as it ever was. And why is that, do you suppose?"

She blinked, and when she looked at him again, there was an anguish in her eyes that tore at him.

"You've been working toward this for a very long time," she said in a hushed tone. "You've given up so much. I thought that if you needed to do it, you would. And I'd volunteered, hadn't I?" He only watched her, until she shifted uncomfortably, her expression pure misery. "It seemed like the kind of thing you'd do."

"Why?" he asked quietly, though his voice was like a blade. He could see it cut at her. "What makes me so untrustworthy, Adriana?"

"I never said that," she whispered, but she was trembling.

"I know why," he told her. "And so do you. At the end of the day, I'm nothing more than a whore myself, and in my case, a real one. And who could possibly trust a whore?"

She flinched, and then she simply collapsed. Her hands flew up to cover her face and she bent over her knees, and for a simmering moment, Pato thought she was sick. But then he saw the sobs shake her body, silent and racking.

Pato couldn't stay away from her, not when she was falling apart right in front of him. Not when he'd pushed her there himself.

He moved toward her, but she held up a hand to ward him off, and straightened, tears streaming down her face. He considered that for a brief moment and then he simply took hold of her hand and pulled her into his arms.

"Listen to me," he said, his voice raw. "I can't give you what you deserve. I can't give you anything except tabloid gossip and innuendo, and I hate that. *I hate it.*" He shifted her against him, taking her chin in his hand and gently bringing her eyes to his, those melting chocolate eyes, wet and hurt and still the most beautiful he'd ever seen. "But you have to know that I love you, Adriana. I love you and I would never deliberately hurt you. You can trust that, if nothing else. I swear it."

"Pato…" she said, as if his name was a prayer.

"I can't fix this," he told her, the same fury that had ignited in him when he'd seen the papers yesterday surging in him again. That same dark, encompassing rage that had nearly taken him apart. "I can't protect you the way I should. The only thing I can do is let you go." She was shaking her head and he slid his hand from her chin to her soft cheek, holding her there. "You deserve better."

He watched her struggle to take a breath, and she didn't seem to care that her face was wet with tears. She frowned at him.

"And what will you do while I'm out there somewhere, finding whatever it is I deserve?" she asked. She shook her head again, decisively. "Martyr yourself?"

"It's not the same thing."

"It's exactly the same thing," she retorted.

"I don't have a choice," he exclaimed. "This doesn't end simply because Lenz marries today. I told you. Thrones are won by treachery. My father will be a threat until he's dead—or until Lenz produces his own heir. Pato the Playboy isn't going anywhere."

Adriana watched him for a moment, then angled herself back to wipe at her eyes. His hand dropped away, and he missed touching her immediately, so much his fingers twitched.

"The Princess Lissette strikes me as highly motivated," she said, a hint of that dryness in her voice that he adored, that he knew would haunt him forever. "I give her ten months, maybe a year, before she kicks off the next generation."

"You have to live better than this," he told her softly. "Please."

Adriana looked at him for a long time. He thought she might simply agree, and it would kill him, but he would let her leave him. He had no choice. But then she sighed.

"I thought you told me love was meant to hurt if it mattered," she said, her gaze on his, hard and warm at the same time. "And who's the martyr now? If you order me out of the country, does that mean you can wallow on your own crucifix?"

That dug beneath his skin, straight on into the center of him, making it hard to breathe for a moment. He said her name softly—a warning, or his own version of a prayer? He wasn't sure he could tell.

"Make it real or don't bother calling it love, Pato," she declared, slicing into him with his own words. Daring him.

"It *already* hurts. It's *already* painful. What's another year of the same?"

"You don't know what you're saying."

"I'm the one they picked apart the most in those papers," she reminded him, her eyes gleaming wet again. "I know exactly what I'm saying."

"This has been *one day* of tabloid coverage," he pointed out, determined to make her see reason. "Are you really prepared for the endless onslaught? Day after day after day, until sometimes you wonder if the story they're telling is the truth and you're the lie?"

She moved to him then and put her hands on his chest, leaning into him, making him want nothing more than to hold her close and keep her there forever.

"I have to think that it's better if there's someone else around to tell you which is which," she whispered. "And yesterday was a bad day in the tabloids, but it wasn't the first. I've been a favorite target since I turned sixteen."

Pato couldn't help himself. She was the only one who'd ever seen him, who'd looked straight through all the masks he wore and found him. And she thought he was a good man.

He wanted that. He wanted her. He wanted *this,* however he could have it.

"If you don't go now, Adriana," he warned her, even as he pulled her closer, "I will never let you try again. I will order you to stay with me, and it will ruin you. You will be the most infamous of all the Righettis, worse even than your great-aunt and her disgraced duke. The papers will never let it go. The people will be worse."

She shrugged, but her eyes were tight on his. "Let them say what they want. They do anyway."

"Your friends and family will think you've turned to the dark side," he said, his tone serious, though he could feel his mouth begin to curve, and saw an instant answering spark in her warm gaze. "They will despair of you. They will stage interventions, cut you off, sell secrets and lies to the tabloids and claim you brought it upon yourself."

"I think I love you most of all when you're romantic," she teased, and he could see the smile she tried to hide, even as he soaked in the words he'd wanted to hear again, ever since he'd thrown them back in her face at the cottage. "When you paint me such beautiful pictures of our future. Be still my heart."

But he wasn't done.

"It will be hard and lonely," he promised her. "But when it's done, my brother will sit on that throne, his heir will be hale and hearty and *his*, and I will make you a princess." Pato moved his hands to her head, smoothed back her pretty hair, then tilted her face up. "I will marry you in the great cathedral and make every single one of these Kitzinian hypocrites bow down before you. Our babies will be fat and happy, and know as little as possible of palace life. None of this intrigue. None of these games. And I will make you happy or die trying, I promise you."

"I love you, Pato," she told him, fierce and sure, the truth of it a wild light in her gaze. There was nothing tepid or lukewarm about it, and it burned into him like fire. "I'm not going to give you up." Her mouth curved. "And that means your famous debauchery starts and ends with me. No ambassador's daughters. No nameless former lovers. No *energetic* threesomes."

He grinned. "You think you can handle me all by yourself?"

"Try me," she whispered. "I know how much you like a challenge."

He took her mouth then, hot and hard, making them both shudder. And when he pulled back again, her eyes were shining, and he knew. She was his, at last.

His. For good.

When he let her go again she was smiling, until she glanced at the portraits on the wall and a shadow moved over her face.

"I have to think that someday my family will forgive me for this," she said quietly. "It will hurt them worst of all."

He kissed her again, bringing her attention back to him.

"I suspect they'll find a way to work past the shame," he said, amused, "when their daughter is a princess and the Righetti lands and fortunes are restored to their former glory by an eternally grateful monarch. I suspect they will discover that, secretly, they supported you all along."

Her smile then was like the sun, warm and bright, lighting up all the dark places inside him. Filling in the hollows. He would do the same for her, he vowed. He would take away the darkness. He would bathe her in light until she had no shadows left to haunt her.

He would spend the rest of his life chasing them away, one by one. She was right—he loved a challenge.

"I've never been scandalous *on purpose,*" she said then, as if the idea thrilled her.

Pato laughed. "I've never been anything else. You'll catch on. We can practice at my brother's wedding. I believe we're already late."

"It shouldn't be too hard," she told him, in that way of hers that made him want to lock the door and indulge himself in the perfect taste of her, especially when she looked at him as if she saw nothing but forever in his gaze. Then she smiled. "Rule number seven. I'm a Righetti. Scandal is in my blood."

* * * * *

ONE NIGHT WITH
PRINCE CHARMING

ANNA DePALO

For Olivia and Nicholas. Mommy loves you!

One

She'd just witnessed a train wreck.

Oh, no, not a literal one, Pia shook her head now at the wedding reception. But a figurative one was just as bad.

It was funny what a train wreck looked like from one end of a church aisle, with yards of ivory satin on display and the mingled scents of lilies and roses in the June air. As a wedding planner, she'd dealt with plenty of disasters. Grooms with cold feet. Brides who'd outsized their wedding dress. Even, once, a ringbearer who'd swallowed one of the rings. But surely Pia's always-practical close friend would have no such problems at her wedding. Or so Pia had thought up until about two hours ago.

Of course, the passengers in their pews had all been agape as the Marquess of Easterbridge had stridden purposely up the aisle and announced that, in fact, there *was* an objection to Belinda Wentworth marrying Tod Dillingham. That, in fact, Belinda's hasty and secret marriage to Colin Granville, current Marquess of Easterbridge, had never been annulled.

Collectively, the cream of New York City society had blinked. Eyes had widened and eyebrows had shot up in the pews of St. Bart's, but no one had been so gauche as to actually faint—or pretend to.

And for that, Pia was grateful. There was only so much a wedding planner could do once the dog ate the cake, or the cab splattered mud on the bride's dress, or, as in this case, *the legal husband,* for God's sake, decided to show up at the wedding!

Pia had sat frozen in her position off the center aisle. Angels, she'd thought absently, were in short supply today.

And on the heels of *that* thought had come another. *Oh, Belinda, why, oh, why didn't you ever tell me about your Las Vegas wedding to, of all people, your family's sworn enemy?*

But in her gut, Pia had already known why. It was an act Belinda regretted. Pia's brow puckered, thinking of what Belinda was dealing with right now. Belinda was one of her two closest friends in New York—along with Tamara Kincaid, one of Belinda's bridesmaids.

And then, Pia heaped some of the blame on herself. Why hadn't she spotted and intercepted Colin, like a good little wedding planner? Why hadn't she stayed at the entrance to the church?

People would wonder why she, the bridal consultant, hadn't known enough to keep the Marquess of Easterbridge away, or why she hadn't been able to stop him before a very public debacle ruined her friend's wedding and Pia's own professional reputation.

Pia felt the urge to cry as she thought of the hit that her young business, Pia Lumley Wedding Productions, would take. The Wentworth-Dillingham nuptials—or more accurately now, *almost*-nuptials—were to have been her most high-profile affair to date. She'd only struck out on her own a little over two years ago, after a few years as an assistant in a large event planning company.

Oh, this was horrendous. A nightmare, really. For Belinda *and* herself.

She'd come to New York City from a small town in Pennsylvania five years ago, right after college. This wasn't the way her dream to make it in New York was supposed to end.

As if in confirmation of her worst fears, right after the bride and both her groom *and* her husband had disappeared at the church, presumably to resolve the irresolvable, Pia had been standing in the aisle when a formidable society matron had steamed toward her.

Mrs. Knox had leaned close and said in a stage whisper, "Pia, dear, didn't you see the marquess approaching?"

Pia had smiled tightly. She'd wanted to say she'd had no idea that the marquess had been married to Belinda, and that, in any case, it wouldn't have done any good to intercept His Lordship if, in fact, he'd still been married to Belinda. But loyalty to her friend had kept her silent.

Mrs. Knox's eyes had gleamed. "You might have avoided a public spectacle."

True. But, Pia thought, even if she had known enough to try to stop him, the marquess had been a man on a mission, and one who had at least sixty pounds and more than six inches on her.

So Pia had done what she *could do* after the fact in order to try to save the day. After a quick consultation with assorted Wentworth family members, she'd encouraged everyone to repair to a show-must-go-on reception at The Plaza.

Now, as Pia looked around at the guests and at the waiters passing to and fro with platters of hors d'oeuvres, the low and steady murmur of conversation allowed her to relax her shoulders even as her mind continued to buzz.

She concentrated on her breathing, a relaxation technique

she'd learned long ago in order to help her deal with stressed-out brides and even more stressful wedding days.

Surely, Belinda and Colin would resolve this issue. *Somehow.* A statement could be issued to the press. With any luck something that began with *Due to an unfortunate misunderstanding...*

Yes, that's right. Everything would be okay.

She shifted her focus outward again and, right then, she spotted a tall, sandy-haired man across the room.

Even though he was turned away from her, the hair at the back of her neck prickled as a sense of familiarity and foreboding hit her. When he turned to speak to a man who'd approached him, she saw his face and sucked in a breath.

And that's when her world *really* came to a screeching halt. In her head, engines collided, the sound of crunching metal mixing with the smell of smoke. Or was the smoke coming out of her ears?

Could this day get any worse?

Him. James Fielding...aka Mr. Wrong.

What was James doing here?

It had been three long years since she'd last seen him, when he'd abruptly entered—and then promptly exited—her life, but there was no mistaking those seduce-you, golden Adonis looks.

He was nearly a decade older than her twenty-seven, but he hardly looked it, damn him. The sandy hair was clipped shorter than she remembered, but he was just as broad, just as muscular and just as impressive at over six feet tall.

His expression was studied rather than the fun-loving and carefree one she'd memorized. Still, a woman never forgot her first lover—especially when he'd vanished without explanation.

Unknowingly, Pia started toward him.

She didn't know what she would say, but her feet impelled her forward, as anger sang in her veins.

Her hands clenched at her sides.

As she approached, she noted that James was speaking with a well-known Wall Street hedge fund manager—Oliver Smithson.

"...Your Grace," the older and graying man said.

Pia's stride faltered. *Your Grace?*

Why would James be addressed as *Your Grace?* The reception room held its share of British aristocrats, but even marquesses were addressed as *My Lord.* As far as she knew, *Your Grace* was a form of address reserved for...dukes.

Unless Oliver Smithson was joking?

Unlikely.

The thought flashed through her mind, and then it was too late.

She was upon them, and James spotted her.

Pia noted with satisfaction the flicker of recognition in his hazel eyes.

He looked debonair in a tuxedo that showcased a fit physique. His facial features were even, though his nose wasn't perfectly sloped, and his jaw was square and firm. Eyebrows that were just a shade darker than his hair winged over eyes that had fascinated her in their changeable hue during their one night together.

If she wasn't so fired up, the impact of all that masculine perfection might have knocked the air from her lungs. As it was, she felt a sizzle skate along her nerve endings.

She could be excused for being a fool three years ago, she told herself. James Fielding was sex poured into civilized attire.

Though his rakish air, so undeniable when she'd first met him, had been tamed, both by his clothes and his demeanor, she sensed that it was still there. She was *intimately* acquainted with it.

"Ah, our lovely wedding planner," Oliver Smithson said, seemingly oblivious to the tension in the air, and then laughed heartily. "Couldn't have predicted this turn of events, could we?"

Pia knew the comment was a reference to the drama at the church, but she couldn't help thinking grimly that it applied just as well to the current situation. She would *never* have expected to run into James here.

As if following her line of thought, James raised an eyebrow.

Before either of them could say anything, however, Smithson went on, addressing her, "Have you made the acquaintance of His Grace, the Duke of Hawkshire?"

The Duke of...?

Pia's eyes went wide, and she stared in mute fury. *So he really was a duke?* Was his name even James?

No, wait—she knew the answer to that question. She had, of course, reviewed the guest list for the wedding. She'd had no idea, however, that her Mr. Wrong and James Carsdale, Ninth Duke of Hawkshire, were one and the same.

She felt suddenly light-headed.

James glanced at Oliver Smithson. "Thank you for attempting to affect an introduction, but Ms. Lumley and I have met before," he said before turning back to her. "And please address me as Hawk. Most people do these days."

Yes, they were more acquainted than anyone could guess, Pia thought acerbically. And how dare Hawk stand there so haughty and self-possessed?

Her gaze clashed with that of the man who was an intimate stranger to her. Angling her chin up, she said, "Y-yes, I-I've had the pleasure."

Immediately, her cheeks flamed. She'd meant to make a sophisticated double entendre, but she'd undermined herself by sounding unsure and naive.

Damn her stutter for making an appearance now. It just showed how flustered she was. She'd worked a long time with a therapist to suppress her childhood speech impediment.

Still, Hawk's eyes narrowed. Without a doubt, he'd understood her intended dig, and he didn't like it. But then his expression turned intense and sensual, before changing again to a perplexing flash of tenderness.

Beneath her sleeveless brown sheath, Pia felt a frisson of awareness, her breasts and abdomen tightening. Surely she was mistaken about that fleeting look that appeared almost tender?

Was he feeling sorry for her? Was he looking down at her, the naive virgin whom he'd left after one night? The thought made her spine stiffen.

"Pia."

As her name fell from his chiseled lips—the first time she'd heard it from him in three years—she was swamped by thoughts of a night of blistering sex between her white embroidered sheets.

Damn him. She rallied her resolve.

"What an unexpected...pleasure," Hawk said, his lips quirking, as if he, too, knew how to play at a game of hidden meaning.

Before she could reply, a waiter stopped beside them and presented them with a platter of canapés with baba ghanoush purée.

Staring down at the appetizers, Pia's first thought was that she and Belinda had spent an entire afternoon choosing the hors d'oeuvres for today.

Then, as another thought quickly followed, she decided to go for broke.

"Thank you," she acknowledged the waiter.

Turning back to the duke, she smiled sweetly. "It's a pleasure to savor. Bon appétit."

Without pausing a beat, she plastered his face with a fistful of eggplant.

Then she turned on her heel and stalked toward the hotel kitchen.

Dimly, she recorded the astonished gazes of the hedge fund manager and a few nearby guests before she slapped open the kitchen's swinging doors. If her professional reputation hadn't already been ruined, it was surely going down in flames now. *But it was worth it.*

Hawk accepted the cloth napkin from the waiter who came scurrying over.

"Thank you," he said with appropriate aristocratic sang-froid.

He carefully wiped baba ghanoush from his face.

Oliver Smithson eyed him. "Well…"

Hawk wiped his lips against each other. "Delicious, though a bit on the tart side."

Both the appetizer and the petite bombshell who'd delivered it.

The hedge fund manager laughed uneasily and cast a look around them. "If I'd known the Wentworth wedding would be this exciting, I'd have shorted it."

"Really?" Hawk drawled. "This is one stock that I'm betting won't fall in price. In fact, isn't notoriety the route to fame and fortune these days? Perhaps the bride will have the last laugh yet."

Hawk knew he had to do what he could to dampen today's firestorm. Despite the affront to his person, he thought of the pixie wedding planner who moments ago had stormed away.

He also wondered where his friend Sawyer Langsford, Earl of Melton, had gone, because right now he could use some help in putting out the blazes that were burning. He was sure Melton could be recruited despite being one of Dillingham's groomsmen. Sawyer was a distant relative and acquaintance of the groom's, but he was an even better friend of Easterbridge's.

Hawk realized that Smithson was looking at him curiously,

obviously debating what, if anything, to say at an awkward moment.

"Excuse me, won't you?" he asked, and then without waiting for an answer, stepped in the direction in which Pia had gone.

He supposed he shouldn't be so dismissive of a valuable business contact, but he had a more pressing matter to attend to.

He flattened his hand against the swinging kitchen door and pushed his way inside.

As he strode in, Pia swung around to face him.

She was unintentionally sexy, just like the first—and last—time they had met. A compact but curvy body was bound in a satin dress that hugged everywhere. Her smooth dark blond hair was caught up in a practical, working-glam chignon. And then there was the smooth-as-satin skin, as well as the bow lips and the eyes that still reminded him of clear amber.

Her eyes flashed at him now, just as Hawk was doing a quick recovery from being hit with all that stop-and-go sexy at once.

"C-come to find me?" Pia demanded. "Well, you're three years too late!"

Hawk had to admire her feistiness, much as it came at his expense at the moment. "I came to check on how you're doing. I assure you that if I'd known you'd be here—"

Her eyes widened dangerously. "You would have what? Run in the opposite direction? Never have accepted the wedding invitation?"

"This meeting comes as much of a surprise to me as it does to you."

A little surprisingly, he hadn't caught a glimpse of her until she'd come upon him at the reception. Of course, he'd been among the throng of four hundred invited guests—and one decidedly *uninvited* one—at the church. And then everyone, including him, had been transfixed by the appearance of

Easterbridge. Who the hell would have known the bride had a husband stashed away—who was none other than London's most famous landowning marquess? But that shock had been nothing compared to the surprise of seeing Pia again...and seeing the mingled astonishment and hurt on her face.

"An unfortunate surprise, I'm sure, *Your Grace*," Pia retorted. "I don't recall you mentioning your title the last time we met."

A direct hit, but he tried to deflect it. "I hadn't succeeded to the dukedom at the time."

"But you weren't simple Mr. James Fielding, either, were you?" she countered.

He couldn't argue with her point there, so he judiciously chose to remain silent.

"I thought so!" she snapped.

Hell. "My full name is James Fielding Carsdale. I am now the Ninth Duke of Hawkshire. I was formerly entitled to be addressed as Lord James Fielding Carsdale or simply—" his lips twisted in a self-deprecating smile "—Your Lordship, though I usually preferred to dispense with the title and the formality that came with it."

The truth was that, back in his playboy days, he had grown used to moving around incognito simply as Mr. James Fielding—thereby avoiding tiresome gold diggers and shaking off the trappings of his position in life—until someone, Pia, had gotten hurt by his charade and his dropping out of sight without a word.

He hadn't even been the heir apparent to his father's ducal title until William, his older brother, had died in a tragic accident, Hawk thought with a twist of the gut. Instead, he'd been Lord James Carsdale, the devil-may-care gadabout younger son who'd dodged the bullet that was the responsibilities of the dukedom—or so he'd thought.

It had taken three years of shouldering those very responsibilities to understand just how thoughtless, how careless, he had been before, and how much damage he might have done. Especially to Pia. But she was wrong if she thought he'd avoid her. He was glad to see her again—glad to have a chance to make amends.

Pia's face drew into a frown. "Are you suggesting that your behavior can somehow be excused because the name you gave me wasn't a total lie?"

Hawk gave an inward sigh. "No, but I am trying, belatedly, to come clean, for what it's worth."

"Well, it's worth nothing," she informed him. "I'd actually forgotten all about you until this opportunity presented itself to confront you about your disappearing act."

They were drawing curious stares from the kitchen staff and even some of the waiters, who were, however, too busy to linger and ogle the latest wedding spectacle.

"Pia, can we take this conversation elsewhere?" Hawk pointedly glanced around them. "We're adding to the events of a day that only needs a little push to tip it over into melodrama."

"Believe me," she retorted, "I've been to enough weddings to know we're nowhere near melodrama. Melodrama is the bride fainting at the altar. Melodrama is the groom flying to the honeymoon by himself. Melodrama is not the bridal consultant confronting her loutish one-night stand!"

Hawk said nothing. He was more concerned for her sake than his, anyway. And she was probably right. What was another scene in a day full of them? Besides, it was clear that Pia was very upset. The wedding disruption had to be troubling her more than she cared to admit, and then there was *his* presence.

Pia folded her arms and tapped her foot. "Do you run out on every woman the morning after?"

No, only on the one and only woman who'd turned out to be a virgin—her. He'd been attracted to her heart-shaped face and compact but shapely body, and the next morning, he'd known he was in too deep.

Hawk wasn't proud of his behavior. But his former self seemed aeons removed from his present situation.

Though even now, he itched to get close to her...to touch her...

He pushed the thought aside. He reminded himself sternly of his course in life ever since he'd become the duke, and that destiny didn't involve messing up Pia's life again. This time, he wanted to make up for what he'd done, for the gift he'd taken from her without realizing...the one she hadn't bothered to warn him about in advance.

Hawk bent toward Pia. "You want to talk about secrets?" he said in a low voice. "When had you been planning to tell me you were a virgin?"

Pia's chest rose and fell with outrage. Under other circumstances, Hawk thought with the back of his mind, he might have been able to enjoy the show.

"So I'm somehow responsible for your vanishing act?" Pia demanded.

He quirked a brow. "No, but let's agree that we were both putting on an act that night, shall we?"

Heat stained Pia's cheeks. "I turned out to be exactly who I said I was!"

"Hmm," he said, studying her upturned face. "As I recall, you disclosed that you'd never had unprotected sex—now who was shading the truth?"

After he'd accompanied her back to her apartment—a little studio on Manhattan's Upper East Side—they'd done the responsible thing before being intimate. He'd wanted to assure her that he was clean and, in return, she'd...lulled him into unintentionally taking her virginity.

Damn it. Even in his irresponsible younger days, he'd vowed never to be a woman's first lover. *He didn't want to be remembered. He didn't want to remember.* It didn't mesh with his carefree lifestyle.

But she'd claimed to have forgotten him. Was it pride alone

that had made her toss out that put down—or was it true? Because he hadn't succeeded in getting her out of his mind, much as he'd tried.

As if in answer to his question, Pia stared at him in mute fury, and then turned on her heel. "Th-this time, I'm the one walking away. Goodbye, Your Grace."

She strode away from him and deeper into the recesses of the kitchen, leaving Hawk to brood alone about their chance encounter—the perfect cap to a perfectly awful day. Pia had been nonplussed, to say the least, by his unexpected appearance and her discovery of who he really was.

But it was also clear that Pia was worried—Belinda's almost-wedding couldn't have good consequences for Pia's wedding planning business. And the fact that Pia herself had given him an unexpected taste of baba ghanoush before some stupefied guests couldn't have helped matters, either.

Pia obviously needed help. For, despite tasting eggplant and their angry confrontation, he still felt an overriding and overdue obligation to make amends.

And with that thought, Hawk contemplated a burgeoning idea.

Two

When Pia got home from the reception at The Plaza, she did *not* conduct an exorcism to banish Hawk from her life again. She did not create a likeness of him with ice cream sticks to ceremonially take apart.

Instead, after picking up and removing Mr. Darcy from her computer chair, she went straight to Google and typed in Hawk's name and title. She told herself it was so she could find a photo to make an Old West sheriff's poster: WANTED: RENEGADE DUKE MASQUERADING AS MR. RIGHT. In reality, she was thirsty for information now that she had Mr. Wrong's real name.

James Fielding Carsdale, Ninth Duke of Hawkshire.

The internet did not disappoint her. It offered up a bounty of hits in a few seconds.

Hawk had started Sunhill Investments, a hedge fund, three years ago, shortly after he'd—she let herself think it—taken her virginity and run. The company had done very well, making Hawk and his partners multimillionaires many times over.

Drat. It was hard to accept that after his dumping of her, he'd been visited with good fortune rather than feeling the wrath of cosmic justice.

Sunhill Investments was based in London, but had recently opened an office in New York—so Hawk's presence on this side of the Atlantic might be for more than the Wentworth-Dillingham wedding that wasn't.

As Pia delved beyond the first few hits, she absently scratched Mr. Darcy's ears as he stroked by her legs. She'd adopted the cat from a shelter close to three years ago and taken him back to the two-bedroom apartment that she'd just moved into—still, however, on the less fashionable edge of Manhattan's Upper East Side.

The fact that the apartment was rent-stabilized and also served as a tax-deductible office permitted her to afford a place that was on the outer fringes of the world that she wanted to tap into—that of Upper East Side prep school girls and future debutantes with well-heeled parents and with living quarters in cloistered prewar buildings guarded by uniformed and capped doormen standing under ubiquitous green awnings.

She'd decorated the apartment as a showcase for her creativity and style because she had the occasional visit from a potential client. Mostly, however, she traveled to see brides in their well-appointed and luxurious homes.

Now, she clicked on her computer mouse. After a few minutes, she brought up a link with an old article about Hawk from the *New York Social Diary.* He was pictured standing between two blond models, a drink in hand and a devilish glint in his eye. The article made it clear that Hawk had been a regular on the social circuit, mostly in London and somewhat in New York.

Pia's lips tightened. Well, at least the article served as some confirmation that she was his physical type—he appeared to have an affinity for blondes. However, at five-foot-four, she was a few inches shorter—not to mention a bit fleshier—than the leggy, skinny catwalkers he'd been photographed with.

The only saving grace in the whole situation was that Hawk's detestable behavior three years ago had given her the courage to embark on her own and start her namesake wedding planning business. She'd realized it was time to stop waiting for Prince Charming and take charge of her life. How pathetic would it have been if he'd been scaling the heights of the financial world while she'd been pining away for him, cocooned to this day in the studio apartment where she'd lived three years ago?

She'd moved on and up, just as he had. And Hawk—the duke or His Grace or however he liked to be referred to—could take a flying leap with his millions.

Still, she couldn't help digging for further information online. It was an exercise in self-flagellation to understand the extent to which she'd been a naive virgin who'd given away the goods to a smooth-talking playboy.

After a half hour of searching, she discovered that Hawk's reputation didn't disappoint. He'd dated models, actresses and even a chanteuse or two. He'd been part of the social whirl of people with money to spare even before his recent incarnation as a top financier.

How unworldly she'd been to expect more than one night with him. How stupidly trusting.

And yet, she reminded herself, it hadn't only been naiveté. She'd been tricked—duped—and used by a practiced player.

She pushed away from the computer screen and padded into her bedroom. Her mind on autopilot, she removed her brown satin dress and slipped into cotton striped pajama bottoms and a peach-colored sleeveless top. In the bathroom, she removed her makeup, moisturized her face and brushed her teeth.

Walking back into the bedroom again, she began to take the pins from her hair as she moved to her dressing table—bought used at a flea market—and sat down. When her hair was loose, she ran a brush through it and stared at herself in the mirror.

She'd never been glamorously beautiful, but she'd been able to lay some claim—if the occasional comments she'd received since high school were to be believed—to being a sort of *cute pretty*. Now, though, she forced herself to be more critical.

Was there something about her that screamed *Take advantage of me?* Did her face sing *I'm a pushover?*

She sighed as she stood, switched off the bedside lamp and slid into bed. She felt Mr. Darcy spring onto the bed and curl his warm weight next to her leg.

Pia turned her face to the window, where rain had begun to pelt the glass, blurring the illumination cast by the city lights outside.

It had been a long, too eventful day, and she was bone-tired. But instead of weariness overtaking her, she found herself awake.

In the privacy of her bedroom, in her own bed and covered by the shadows of the night, she was surprised by the sudden moisture of tears on her face—a reflection of the rain outside. She hadn't cried over Hawk in a long time.

Since she'd switched apartments, Hawk had never invaded this sanctum. But he'd slept in this bed.

Drat Hawk.

With any luck, she'd never have to see him again. She was over him, and this would be the absolute last time that she'd shed tears about him.

Déjà vu. Hawk looked around him at Melton's picturesque Gloucestershire estate, which wasn't so different from his own family seat in Oxford. The centuries-old limestone estate was surrounded by acres of pastoral countryside, which was in full greenery in the August warmth. They could and did set period movies in places like this.

Except his friend Sawyer Langsford, Earl of Melton, was going to have a very real wedding to The Honorable Tamara Kincaid, a woman who could barely be persuaded to dance with him at the Wentworth-Dillingham near-miss of a wedding two months ago.

At the thought of weddings, Hawk admitted to himself that he'd reached a point in his life when his professional life had quieted down a bit, and at age thirty-six, the responsibility to beget an heir for the dukedom had begun to weigh on him.

In his younger, more carefree days, he'd dated a lot of women. In fact, he'd reveled in distinguishing himself as the bon vivant younger son—in spite of his steady job in finance—in contrast to his more responsible older brother, the heir.

And now one of his closest friends was getting married. Hawk had come at Sawyer's request for what was to be a small wedding in the presence of family and close friends. Easterbridge would also be present, and heaven help them, at the bride's invitation, so would his wife, Belinda Wentworth—without, however, her almost-husband, Tod Dillingham.

And Hawk had it on good authority that none other than Pia Lumley would be the wedding planner today. He'd been forewarned by Sawyer. For, as circumstances would have it, Tamara Kincaid was another good friend of Pia's.

As if conjured by his thoughts, Pia walked out from the French doors leading to the stone terrace at the back of the house, and then down to the grassy lawn where Hawk stood.

She looked young, fresh and innocent, and Hawk felt a sudden pang. She'd been all those things three years ago when he'd first met her—and left her.

She was wearing a white shirt with cuffs rolled back beyond her elbows and lime-green cotton pants paired with pink ballet flats. The pants hugged her curves, and just a hint of cleavage was visible at the open collar of her shirt. Her smooth blond hair was caught in a ponytail, and her lips looked shiny and full.

Hawk felt a tightening in his gut.

Despite having been plastered with eggplant at their last meeting, he felt drawn to her. She had sex appeal without being contrived—so different from many of the women in his social circle.

She was everything he wanted, and everything he couldn't have. It would throw him off track from the life that he was supposed to be living now if he got involved with her again. He had put his playboy days behind him.

He was thirty-six, and he'd never been more aware of his responsibilities than since he'd succeeded to the dukedom. Among other things, he had a duty to produce an heir to secure a centuries-old title. And in the normal course of events, he would be expected to marry someone of his class and social station—certainly his mother expected that of him.

In the past year, his mother had taken it upon herself to bring him into contact with eligible women, including, particularly, Michelene Ward-Fombley—a woman whom some had speculated would have made a wonderful duchess for his older brother, before William's untimely death.

He pushed aside thoughts about his most recent transatlantic phone conversation with his mother, and the unspoken expectations that had been alluded to...

Instead, Hawk couldn't help noting now that Pia resembled an enticing wood sprite. She was clearly unafraid to wear flats with her petite frame for a working casual look on a tepidly warm August day typical for this part of England. In his own nod to the weather, he had dispensed with anything but a white shirt and tan pants.

Pia looked up and spotted him as she walked across the lawn.

He watched as she hesitated.

After a moment, she continued to move toward him, but

with obvious reluctance. He was clearly standing in the direct path of her intended destination—very likely, the pavilion on the property that would serve as one of the backdrops for the wedding.

He tried to break the ice. "I know what you're thinking."

She gave him a haughty, disbelieving look.

"We don't see each other for three years," he pressed on, "and now we somehow run into each other for the second time in two months."

"Believe me, it's no more pleasant for me than it is for you," she responded, coming to a stop before him.

He scanned her face, angling his head to the side.

He pretended to make his perusal casual, joking even. Still, he caught the way a stray strand of sun-kissed honey-blond hair caressed her cheek gently. He stopped himself from reaching out to touch her soft skin and run his thumb over the outline of her jaw.

Then he made the mistake of picking up the light scent of lavender that he'd associated with her ever since their first night together. He couldn't help being attracted to her—he just couldn't act on that attraction.

"Wh-what are you doing?" she demanded.

"I'm checking to see if you're hiding hors d'oeuvres or canapés somewhere. I wanted to be prepared for another missile attack."

His attempt at a jest was met with a frosty look.

Pia raised her chin. "I'm here to make sure this wedding proceeds without a hitch."

"Ah, trying to rehabilitate your image?"

He'd meant to tease and test, and at her momentarily arrested look, he realized he'd guessed correctly.

Pia was still worried about her business. Belinda Wentworth's almost-wedding had likely blemished Pia's professional reputation.

In a moment, however, Pia recovered herself, and her

eyes sparked. "My only concern is that you and your two compatriots, Easterbridge and Melton, are in attendance. I have no idea why another friend of mine would get mixed up with a friend of yours. Look at what Easterbridge did to Belinda!"

"What Colin did to Belinda?" Hawk asked rhetorically. "You mean speaking up as *her husband?*"

Pia narrowed her eyes and pressed her lips together.

Hawk had started out this conversation trying to put Pia at ease, but ruffling her feathers was proving to be irresistible. "I defer to your superior experience with wedding etiquette. Are husbands even allowed to speak?"

"The marquess needn't have done so at the wedding. A nice, private communication from his attorney to hers would have sufficed."

"Perhaps Easterbridge had little notice of Belinda's impending wedding to Dillingham. Perhaps he did what he could to prevent a crime from occurring." Hawk arched a brow. "Bigamy is a crime in many places, including New York, you know."

"I'm well aware of that!"

"I'm relieved to hear it."

Pia gave him a repressive look, and then eyed him suspiciously. "How much notice did you have of Easterbridge's actions?"

"I wasn't even aware that Easterbridge was married to Belinda."

Hawk was glad he could set the record straight because Pia obviously suspected him of double-dealing as a wedding guest of Dillingham's but a friend of Easterbridge's. Not only hadn't he known about Easterbridge's past marriage, but he suspected that the only reason he'd been invited to the wedding in June was because Dillingham wanted to cement important social ties, however tenuous up to that point.

"And *I* have no idea what would have made Belinda wed

a friend of yours two years ago, in Las Vegas, of all places," Pia countered.

"Perhaps my friends and I are irresistible," he replied mockingly.

"Oh, I'm well aware that you're irresistible to women."

Hawk raised his brows and wondered whether Pia was admitting to her own past susceptibility to him. Had *she* found him not merely attractive but irresistible? Had she fallen into bed with him because she'd been swept up in the moment and carried away by passion?

"Once I had your real name, a little internet search revealed a good deal of information," Pia elaborated, dashing his hopes that she'd been referring to herself when she'd called him irresistible.

Hawk had no doubt as to what an internet search had revealed. He mentally winced at the thought of the news reports and gossip that must have come up about his younger, more spirited days. The women...the carousing...

"You know, I suppose I should have been wary three years ago when my Google search on James Fielding turned up nothing in particular, but then I supposed *Fielding* was such a common name..."

He quirked his lips. "My ancestors are no doubt rolling in their graves at being labeled *common*."

"Oh, yes, pardon me, *Your Grace*," Pia returned bitingly. "You can rest assured that I'm no longer ignorant of the protocol due to your rank."

Damn protocol to hell, he wanted to respond. It was one of the reasons he'd preferred flying under the radar as plain James Fielding. Except these days, of course, having succeeded to the ducal title, he could no longer afford such a luxury. Then, too, he was all too cognizant of his responsibilities.

The irony wasn't lost on him that having succeeded to the title of Duke of Hawkshire, he'd gained all manner of wealth—and responsibilities—that most men coveted, but had lost the things he craved most: anonymity, a certain freedom and being valued for himself.

"Tell me about your wedding business," he said abruptly, turning the conversation back in the direction he wanted. "Three years ago, I recall you were still working at a large event planning firm and had big dreams of setting out on your own."

Pia looked guarded and then defiant. "I did manage to start my own business, as you can tell. It was shortly after your abrupt disappearance, in fact."

"Are you saying you have me to thank?" Hawk asked with exaggerated aristocratic hauteur and faint mockery.

Pia's hand curled at her side. "*Thanks,* I think, would be going too far. But I believe it was your abrupt exit that provided me with the impetus to strike out on my own. After all, there's nothing like a momentary disappointment to fuel the drive to succeed in another area of life."

Hawk gave a weak imitation of a smile. He very much regretted his actions in the past, but he wondered what she'd say if she knew the extent of his responsibilities, ducal and otherwise, these days.

"You were very creative with the décor at Belinda's wedding," he said, ignoring her jab in an effort to be more conciliatory. "The gold and lime-green color scheme was certainly unusual."

At Pia's look of momentary surprise, he added, "You needn't look so taken aback that I noticed the detail. After savoring baba ghanoush, I believe contemplating the scenery became a much more engaging pastime."

He had let himself study the décor because he had been curious about any detail that would reveal anything about *her*—and it had beat deflecting curious looks and probing questions from the other wedding guests.

"I'm glad my excellent aim had at least one beneficial consequence," Pia responded dryly.

"Ah, I assume the consequences to your wedding business weren't so satisfactory?" he probed, taking advantage of his opening.

Pia's expression turned defensive, but not before Hawk saw the fleeting distress there.

"What sort of wedding would you have for yourself, Pia?" Hawk asked, his voice suddenly low and inviting. "Surely you must have envisioned it many times."

He knew he was playing with fire, but he didn't care.

"I'm in the wedding business," Pia responded frostily. "Not the romance business."

Their eyes held for moments…until a voice called out Pia's name.

He and Pia turned at the same time to look back in the direction of the house, where Tamara was descending the terrace steps.

"Pia," Tamara announced, coming toward them across the lawn. "I've been looking for you everywhere."

"I was just walking over to the pavilion," Pia responded. "I wanted to see what can be done with it."

Hawk watched as Tamara glanced curiously from Pia to him and back.

"Well, I'm glad I found you," Tamara said, and then hooked her arm through Pia's.

Tamara spared Hawk a cursory look. "You don't mind if I commandeer Pia, do you, Hawk…I mean, Your Grace?" And then not waiting for an answer, she turned Pia toward the pavilion. "I thought not."

Hawk's lips quirked. Tamara wasn't one to stand on ceremony. Though she was the daughter of a British viscount, she'd been raised mostly in the United States and had the decidedly democratic tendencies of the bohemian jewelry designer she was.

She'd also obviously sailed in like a mother hen to rescue Pia.

"Not at all," Hawk murmured to Tamara's retreating back.

He watched the two women cross the lawn.

When Pia turned back briefly to glance at him, he returned her gaze solemnly.

He'd gleaned a lot from their conversation. He'd guessed correctly—as evidenced by her momentary distress just now—that Pia's wedding business needed help in the wake of Belinda's wedding. The fact that Pia's firm had managed to survive for more than two years said something, however.

Pia obviously had talent, and she'd nurtured it since their one night together.

With that thought, as he turned back to the house, Hawk realized that a conversation with his sister, a prospective bride, was in order.

Three

As she and Tamara walked toward the pavilion, Pia noticed her friend glance at her.

"I hope I wasn't interrupting anything," Tamara remarked, and then paused at Pia's continued silence. "On second thought, perhaps I hope I did."

As Tamara suddenly stopped to speak with one of the staff who hailed her, Pia stood nearby and soon found herself lost in thought about the night that she and Hawk had first met.

The beat of the music could be felt in the bar stools, on the tables and along the walls. In fact, everything vibrated. It was loud and packed, bodies brushing past each other in the confines of the tavern.

A bar wasn't her preferred scene, Pia thought, but she'd come here with a coworker from the event-planning business she worked for in order to rub shoulders with bright young things and their beaus.

People who liked a party—and needed event organizers—

usually attended parties prodigiously. And it had almost been a job directive from her boss to be social after work hours, making connections and trying to bring in business.

Except Pia's interest wasn't in anniversary parties or coming-of-age celebrations.

Instead, she liked weddings.

Someday, she promised herself, her dream of having her own wedding planning business would become a reality.

In the meantime, she shouldered her way past other patrons and reached the bar. But at her height, she could barely see above those sitting at the bar stools, let alone signal the bartender.

A man next to her gestured to the bartender and called out an order for a martini.

She glanced up at him and, a second later, sucked in a breath as he looked down at her with an easygoing grin.

"Drink?" he offered.

He was one of the most attractive men she'd ever seen. He was tall, certainly over six feet, his sandy hair slightly tousled, and his hazel eyes, flecked with interesting bits of gold and green, dancing. His nose was less than perfect—had it been broken once?—but that added to his magnetism. His grin revealed a dimple to the right of his mouth.

Most importantly, he was looking at *her* with warm, lazy interest.

He was the closest thing to her fantasy man as she'd ever seen—not that she'd ever admit to anyone that, at twenty-four, she'd had a fantasy lover and no other kind.

Pia parted her lips—*please, please let me sound sophisticated.* "Cosmopolitan, thank you."

He gave the briefest nod of acknowledgment, and then looked away to signal the bartender and order her drink. Within seconds, he effortlessly accomplished what to her had been blocked by multiple obstacles.

When he looked back at her, he was smiling again.

"Are you?" he asked, his low and smooth voice inviting intimacy.

She stalled. "Am I...?"

His eyes crinkled. "Are you a Cosmo girl?"

She pretended to consider the question for a moment. "It depends. Are you a pickup artist?"

He laughed, his expression saying he was respectful of her parry even as his interest sharpened. "I don't suppose you'd give a hint as to what the right answer is supposed to be?"

Pia played along. "Do you need a hint? Doesn't charm get you the answer you want?"

His accent wasn't easy to pinpoint—he appeared to be from here, there and anywhere—but she thought she detected a faint British enunciation.

"Hmm, it depends," he mused, rubbing his chin and showing his dimple again. "Are you here with anyone?"

She knew he meant a man—a date. "I'm here with a coworker, but I seem to have lost track of Cornelia in the crowd."

He looked momentarily intent and seductive beneath his easygoing veneer, but then his casual appeal took over again. "Great, then I can be as charming as I'm able. Let's start with names. No woman as lovely and enchanting as you can be called anything but—?"

He quirked a brow.

She couldn't help smiling. "Pia Lumley."

"Pia," he repeated.

The sound of her name falling from his chiseled lips sent shivers chasing over her skin. He'd called her *lovely* and *enchanting*. Her fantasy man had a voice, and it was dreamy.

"James Fielding," he volunteered.

Just then, the bartender leaned in their direction and slid two drinks across the bar between seated patrons.

James handed the cosmopolitan to her, and then picked up his martini.

"Cheers," he said, clinking his glass against hers.

She took a small sip of her drink. It was stronger than her usual party libation—a light beer or a fruity beach drink was more her style—but then again, she'd wanted to appear sophisticated.

She suspected that James was used to chic women. And she'd grown used to projecting a polished and stylish image when trying to drum up business for work. Potential clients expected it—people didn't want an inexperienced girl from small-town Pennsylvania running their six-figure party.

After sipping from his drink, James nodded at a couple departing from a corner table near them. "Would you like to sit?"

"Thank you," she said, and then turned and slid into a padded booth seat.

As she watched James sit down to her left, a little thrill went through her. So he meant to continue their conversation and further their acquaintance? She was happy she'd held his interest.

She hadn't had many men hit on her. She didn't think she was bad-looking, but she was short and more understated than bold, and therefore easily overlooked. She was cute, rather than one to inspire lust or overwhelming passion.

He looked at her with a smile hovering at his lips. "Are you new to New York?"

"It depends on what you mean by new," she replied. "I've been here a couple of years."

"And you were transported here from a fairy tale called—?"

She laughed. "Cinderella, of course. I'm a blonde."

His smile widened. "Of course."

He rested an arm along the back of the booth seat and reached out to finger a tendril of her hair.

She drew in a breath—hard.

"And a beautiful shade of blond, it is," he murmured. "It's gold spun with wheat and sunshine."

She looked into his eyes. She could, she thought, spend hours studying the fascinating mix of hues there.

James cocked his head, his eyes crinkling. "Okay, Pia," he continued in his smooth, deep voice, "Broadway, Wall Street, fashion, advertising or *The Devil Wears Prada?*"

"None of the above?"

His eyebrows rose. "I've never struck out before."

"Never?" she asked with feigned astonishment. "I'm sorry I ruined your track record."

"Never mind. I trust your discretion will spare my reputation."

They were flirting—or rather *he* was flirting with *her*—and she was, amazingly, holding her own.

It was all exhilarating. She'd never had a man flirt with her this way, and certainly no one of James's caliber.

In fact, though, she wasn't an actress, a banker, a model, or in advertising or publishing. "I'm an event planner," she said. "I organize parties."

"Ah." His eyes gleamed. "A party girl. Splendid."

There were party girls and then there were *party girls,* she wanted to say, but she didn't correct him.

"What about you?" she asked instead. "What are you doing here in New York?"

He straightened, dropping his arm from the back of the seat. "I'm just an ordinary Joe with a boring finance job, I'm afraid."

"There's nothing ordinary about you," she blurted, and then clamped her mouth shut.

He smiled again, his dimple appearing. "I'm flattered you think so."

She lifted her drink for another sip because he and his

smile—and, yes, that dimple—were doing funny things to her insides.

He was studying her, and she tried to remain casual, though he sat mere inches away.

She was very aware of his muscular thigh encased in beige pants on the seat beside her. He wore no tie, and the strong, corded lines of his neck stood in relief against the open collar of his light blue shirt.

He nodded, his eyes fixed at a spot near her collarbone. "That's an interesting necklace you're wearing."

She glanced down, though she knew what he'd be seeing. She wore a sterling silver necklace with a flying fish pendant. In deference to the July heat, she'd worn a sleeveless turquoise blue sheath dress. The pendant was one of her usual accessories.

She'd come directly to the bar from work, and she figured he'd done the same from the way he was dressed. Though he wasn't wearing a suit, his attire qualified as business casual. Work dress code was more relaxed in the summer in the city, especially on a dress-down Friday.

She flushed now, however, at the thought that between the color of her dress and the symbol on her pendant, she resembled nothing so much as a pond with a solitary fish swimming in it.

Drat. Why hadn't she thought of that when she'd dressed this morning?

But James's face held no hint of amusement at her expense—just simple curiosity.

She fingered her pendant. "The necklace was a gift from my friend Tamara, who is a wonderful jewelry designer here in the city. I like to fish."

"A woman after my own heart then."

Pia checked her surprise. Of course, he would be interested in fishing. He was her fantasy man—how could he not be?

"Do you fish?" she asked unnecessarily.

"Since I was three or four," he said solemnly. "What kind of fishing do you do?"

She laughed with a tinge of self-consciousness. "Oh, anything. Bass, trout… There are plenty of lakes where I grew up in western Pennsylvania. My father and grandfather taught me how to bait and cast a line—as well as ride a horse and, uh, m-milk a cow."

She couldn't believe she'd admitted to milking cows. How would he ever think of her as an urban sophisticate now? She ought to have quit while she was ahead.

James looked nothing but fascinated, however. "Horseback riding—even better. I've been riding since I could walk." His eyes glinted. "I can't say the same about milking cows, on the other hand."

She flushed.

"But I sheered a few sheep during a stay at an Australian sheep station."

Pia felt her lips twitch. "Well, then, you've bested me. I concede."

"Good of you," he deadpanned. "I knew sheep would win out."

"I've done some fly-fishing," she asserted.

He smiled. "Point to you. There are not many women who are willing to stand around in muck all day, wearing waders and waiting to get a bite." His smile broadened into a grin. "As petite as you are, I imagine you couldn't wade in very far."

She struck a look of mock offense. "I'll have you know I stood as still as a chameleon on a branch."

"Then I'd have been tempted to drop a frog down the back of your waders," he teased.

"Oh, you would! Don't tell me you have sisters whom you tormented."

"No such luck," he mourned. "I have one sister, but she's

several years younger than I am, and my mother wouldn't have looked well on any pranks."

"I wouldn't have expected she would," she said with mock indignation. "And if you'd attempted to foist a frog on me, I'd have—"

"Yes?"

He was enjoying this.

"I'd have thrown you for a loop!"

"Don't fairy-tale heroines need to get to know a few frogs?" he asked innocently.

"I believe the expression is *kiss a few frogs*," she replied. "And, no, the requirements have been updated for the twenty-first century. And anyway, I'd know when I kissed a frog."

"Mmm…do you want to put it to the test?"

"I—I—"

What a time for her stammer to make another appearance.

Not waiting for a clearer sign of encouragement, he leaned in, and as her eyelids lowered, gently pressed his lips to her. She felt the momentary zing of electricity, and her lips parted on an indrawn breath. And then his mouth moved over hers, tasting and sampling, giving and receiving.

His lips were soft, and she tasted the faint lingering flavor of his drink as they kissed. The crowd around them receded as she focused on every warm stroke of his mouth against hers.

Just as their kiss threatened to become more heated, he drew back, his expression thoughtful and bemused. "There, how was that?"

She searched his eyes. "Y-you are in no way related to Kermit the Frog."

He grinned. "How about my fishing? Am I reeling you in?"

"A-am I on the hook or are you?"

"James."

The moment was interrupted as he was hailed by someone and turned in the direction of a man coming toward them.

Pia straightened and sat back in her seat, belatedly realizing with some embarrassment that she was still leaning forward.

"The CEO of MetaSky Investments is here, James," the man announced, sparing her a cursory look. "I'll introduce you."

Pia judged the man to be a contemporary of James's. Perhaps he was a friend or a business colleague.

At the same time, she sensed James hesitate beside her. She could tell that whoever this CEO was, it would be valuable for James to meet him. After all, he was important enough for a friend to have sought James out in the crowded bar.

James turned toward her. "Will you—"

"There you are, Pia! I've been searching for you."

Cornelia materialized out of the crowd.

Pia pasted a bright smile on her face as she glanced at James. "As you can see, you no longer need to worry about leaving me alone."

James nodded. "Will you excuse me?"

"Of course."

Pia tamed her disappointment as James rose to depart. She noticed that he didn't say he'd be back. And she knew better than to expect that he would return. She understood—sort of— that these flirtations in bars were fleeting and transient.

On the other hand, the romantic in her believed in kismet. He was the most magnificent man she'd ever met.

And if that had been the last she'd seen of him, she probably would have remembered him as nothing more than a handsome, charming fantasy—a brief glimpse of a fairy-tale prince to brighten her disappointing night. Certainly, the evening began to show few signs of success once they went their separate ways.

Two hours afterward, however, it was hard to keep

disappointment at bay. She hadn't glimpsed James since he'd departed, nor had she had any luck in making potential contacts, aside from handing her business card out to a couple of women who'd expressed a casual interest in retaining an event planner.

Pia sighed as she slid off a bar stool, having settled her tab. Cornelia had departed twenty minutes ago while Pia had still been conversing with a potential client. The woman who'd just vacated the bar stool next to Pia was an office manager at a small real estate firm, and though she'd had someone whom she used to help plan the firm's annual holiday party, she'd been willing to listen to Pia's pitch.

Business development was the part of her job that Pia found most challenging. Coming from Pennsylvania, she didn't have an extensive social network in the city. And it was so disheartening to get the brush-off from strangers. She supposed that telemarketing could be worse, but then again, at least telemarketers only had to deal with rejection by phone rather than face-to-face.

There was no doubt about the high point of the evening. James had shown real interest in *her*—however briefly.

Pia felt her heart squeeze. *Definitely time to leave.*

She'd head home to a rent-stabilized apartment on the unfashionable edge of the Upper East Side. She decided she'd pop in a DVD and lose herself in one of her favorite Jane Austen flicks, spending the rest of the evening forgetting what would never be.

It was a decent feel-good plan. Except as soon as she stepped out of the bar, she realized that it was pouring rain.

Oh, great.

She huddled under the bar's awning and looked down at herself. Even with the platform heels on her beige sandals, she knew her feet—and likely more—were going to get soaked. She'd tucked a small umbrella into her handbag this morning, just in case, but she'd been betting it wouldn't rain when she'd chosen what to wear. The weather report had said showers weren't in the forecast until the wee hours of the morning.

Her one hope was hailing a cab, but she knew one would be scarce in this kind of weather, and in any case, on her salary, taxis were a luxury she tried to avoid. The only alternative was walking to the subway and then making the long hike from the train station to her apartment.

As she stood there, hugging herself for warmth and debating her options, the tavern door behind her opened.

"Need a ride?"

She turned and glanced up. *James.*

Paradoxically, she felt embarrassed—as if she were the one running out on *him,* when in reality he hadn't sought her out again.

"I thought you'd already left," she blurted.

A slow smile spread across his face. "I did, but I came back in. I was conversing with the CEO of MetaSky outside, where we could hear each other and speak with more privacy." He looked around them. "It wasn't raining then."

She blinked. "Oh."

"Do you need a ride?" he asked again, glancing down at her.

She tried for some belated dignity, even as a gust of wind pelted her with raindrops. "I'm f-fine. I'm just debating whether to walk, row or swim home."

His smile spread. "What about a car instead?"

She raised her eyebrows. "How are we ever going to catch an empty cab in this weather?"

She knew that rain made New York City taxis disappear.

"Leave it to me."

She watched as James scanned the street. Two cabs passed them but their lit signs indicated that they were occupied. As the two of them waited, they made idle chitchat.

Close to fifteen minutes later, by a stroke of luck, James spotted a cab letting out a passenger beyond the nearest intersection. He moved swiftly from the shelter of the awning and into the street when the empty cab started to make its way down their block. He raised his arm, a commanding presence, and hailed the cab.

As the rain continued to assault him, he opened the taxi's door and motioned for her to step in.

"What's your address?" he called as she hurried toward him. "I'll tell the driver."

She called it out to him, realizing that he had an excuse to find out where she lived. He made everything appear smooth, charming and effortless.

"Are you leaving? Do you want to share a cab?" she asked as she reached him. "You're getting drenched! I should have offered you the umbrella in my bag but you stepped out so suddenly."

She couldn't stop the flow of words, though she knew she was nearly babbling. She had no idea what direction was home for him, but it seemed churlish not to offer to share the cab that he'd hailed for her. Yet again, he'd handily managed to accomplish something she herself often found difficult, being petite and certainly less imposing.

James looked at her and his lips quirked. Even with his hair getting matted by the rain and his face wet, he looked unbelievably handsome.

"Thanks for the offer," he said.

She wasn't sure if he meant to accept her offer, but once she entered the confines of the cab, she slid across the seat so he would have room to join her.

A moment later, he slid in beside her, folding his tall frame onto the bench seat and answering her unvoiced question.

She felt relief and a happy flutter, even as she also experienced a sense of nervous awareness. She had never left a bar with a man before—she was cautious. But then again, no man had attempted to pick her up in a bar before.

"I live on First Avenue in the high Eighties," she cautioned

James belatedly as he closed the car door. "I don't want to put you out. I don't know in what direction you need to head."

"It's no problem," he said easily. "I'll see you home first."

She noticed that he didn't divulge whether she was taking him out of his way or not.

He leaned forward to the partition separating the front from the backseat and told the cab driver her address. And in no time at all, they were speeding through Manhattan's wet and half-empty streets.

They were content to make some more desultory chitchat as the car ate up the distance to her apartment. She discovered that he was thirty-three to her twenty-four—not ancient by any means, but older and more worldly than the boys she'd dated back in high school and college in Pennsylvania.

Perhaps in order to make the gulf between them seem less so, she shared her dream of opening her own wedding planning business. Surely, he wouldn't think of her as so young and inexperienced if he knew she had plans to be a business owner.

He showed enthusiasm for her plans and encouraged her to proceed with them.

All the while, as thoughts raced through her mind, she wondered if he felt the sexual tension, too. Would she ever see him again?

In no time at all, however, they arrived outside her building.

James turned toward her, searching her eyes in the silence drawing out between them. "Here we are."

"W-would you like to come up?" she asked, surprising herself.

It was a daring move. But she felt as if their evening had been cut short when he'd had to meet with the CEO of MetaSky.

He paused and looked at her meaningfully for a moment. "Sure…I'd love to."

He settled the cab fare, and then they raced up the front stoop of her building, sharing her small umbrella.

She managed to fish out her keys in record time and let them inside. They stumbled into the vestibule and out of the cold and wet.

She lived in a studio on the top floor of a four-story brownstone. At least, however, the rental was hers alone. On a night like tonight, she didn't have to worry about the awkwardly timed arrival of a roommate or two. She'd made the best of her situation by putting up a partition wall to create a separate bedroom, though she couldn't do anything to alter the fact that her windows were the small ones beneath the roof.

As she heard and felt the tread of James's feet behind her on the stairs, she couldn't help feeling nervous about having him step into her little world.

Fortunately, she didn't have much time to dwell on the matter. Within a few minutes, they reached the uppermost floor, and she inserted her key in her door and let them inside.

She dropped her handbag on a chair and turned around in time to see him scanning her apartment.

He dominated the small space even more than she'd anticipated. Here there were no fellow bar patrons to defuse the full force of the magnetism that he exuded. There was no crowd to mitigate the sexual attraction between them.

James's eyes came back to hers. "It's cute."

She'd tried to make the apartment cheerful, as much to lift her own mood as anything else. A tiny table flanked by two chairs and sporting a vase of pink peonies and tulips sat near the door. The kitchen lined one wall, and a love seat guarded the space on the opposite side. Facing the entry, a small entertainment center stood in front of the partition that separated her bedroom from the rest of the space.

Pia knew what lay beyond the partition that shielded what remained of her apartment from James's gaze. A white croquet coverlet covered the full-size bed that occupied most of her sleeping area.

Nervously, she wet her lips. She couldn't keep her eyes from straying to the rain-soaked spots of his shirt. Some of those wet areas clung to the muscles of his arms and shoulders.

She'd never done this before.

"Pia."

Pia found herself jerked from her memories as Tamara closed the space on the lawn between them. Over Tamara's shoulder, she noticed the member of the household staff with whom Tamara had been speaking was heading back toward the stone terrace and French doors at the back of the house.

Hawk was nowhere to be seen. He, too, must have gone indoors.

"I'm sorry to have left you stranded here."

Pia pasted a bright smile on her face. "Not at all. It's all part of the prerogatives of the bride."

And one of her prerogatives, Pia thought, was to stay away from Hawk for the rest of this wedding...

Four

Pia walked along East 79th Street on Manhattan's Upper East Side looking for the correct house number. She'd received a call from Lucy Montgomery yesterday about being hired as a bridal consultant. She hadn't paid much attention to the particulars, but had jumped at the chance for new business because it had been a slow summer.

She hadn't liked to dwell on how much her silent phone was due to the Wentworth-Dillingham wedding being, well, both *more* and *less* than expected. She hadn't been directly to blame for the first part of the debacle. But the hard truth was that if the wedding had been a resounding success, her phone might have been ringing with more interested brides.

True, she'd been called on to help with Tamara's wedding last month. But that had been a small wedding—mainly family—and had transpired in England, so her involvement hadn't counted for much in the eyes of New York society. And while she'd also worked on a wedding in Atlanta over the summer, she'd been retained for that function *before* Belinda's nuptial debacle.

Now, though, on a breezy day in late September, with clouds overhead and the threat of rain in the air, she walked along one of Manhattan's tonier side streets, glad she'd worn her belted trench to ward off the threatening elements and even happier for the possibility of a new client.

Finding the house number she was looking for, she stopped and surveyed the impressive double-width, four-story limestone town house. A tall, black, wrought-iron fence guarded the façade, and flower boxes and black shutters framed tall, plate-glass windows. In the center of the building, stone steps ascended to the double-door front entrance at the parlor level. But instead of windows, the parlor floor boasted French doors embraced by tiny balconies.

There was no doubt that Lucy Montgomery came from money. This house was a well-preserved example of Manhattan's Gilded Age.

Pia ascended the steps and knocked before ringing the doorbell.

Within moments, an older gentleman, dressed in somber black and white rather than a clear uniform, responded. After Pia introduced herself, the butler took her coat and directed her to the parlor.

Pia soon discovered that the parlor was a spectacular room with a high, molded ceiling and a marble mantel. It was decorated in gold and rose and outfitted with antique furniture upholstered in stripes and prints.

She knew she should recognize the furniture style, but for the life of her, she could never remember how to separate Louis XIV style from its successors, Louis XV and Louis XVI. In any case, expensive was expensive.

She sat on one of the couches flanking the fireplace and contemplated her surroundings, taking several deep breaths to calm her nerves. *She'd never needed an account more.*

She hoped she would sufficiently impress Lucy Montgomery. She'd dressed with care, donning a chic and timeless short-sleeved peach dress and beige pumps, and keeping her jewelry to a minimum. She'd chosen wedding colors, even on an overcast day, because they were cheery and they resonated with brides.

At that moment, the parlor door opened, and with surprising promptness, Lucy appeared, a smile on her face.

Her hostess was a slim, attractive blonde of medium height with hazel eyes. She looked crisp in a salmon-colored shirt and knee-length tan skirt cinched by a wide black belt. Her legs stretched down to strappy sandals and showed off a tan that was courtesy, no doubt, of time spent at one of the sand-dusted retreats favored by the rich or famous or both.

Pia guessed that Lucy was around her own age or younger.

She rose from her seat in time to shake her hostess's outstretched hand.

"Thank you for scheduling this appointment on such short notice," Lucy exclaimed, her inflection British. "I was just about to come down the stairs when Ned told me you were here."

"It was no inconvenience, Ms. Montgomery," Pia responded with a smile of her own. "Client service is what my business is all about."

"It's Lucy, please."

"Pia, then."

"Good," Lucy responded happily, and then glanced at the clock. "I'll have tea brought in, if that meets with your approval." She smiled. "We British consider late afternoon to be teatime, I'm afraid."

"Yes, please. Tea would be wonderful."

After Lucy had gone to the door and spoken in low tones with a member of the household staff, she returned to sit on the sofa with Pia.

"Now then," she said. "I'm rather in desperate need of help, I'm afraid."

Pia tilted her head and smiled. "Many brides come to that conclusion at some point during their engagements. May I offer my congratulations, by the way?"

Lucy lit up. "Thank you, yes. My fiancé is American. I met him while working on an off-Broadway play."

Pia's eyebrows rose. "You're an actress?"

"Shakespearean trained, yes," Lucy replied without a hint of boast, and then leaned forward conspiratorially and winked. "He was one of the producers."

Money married money, Pia thought, if only because the people involved tended to move in the same social circles. She'd seen it many times before. And yet, it was clear from the way Lucy lit up that she was in love with her fiancé.

"You see," Lucy explained, "Derek and I were planning to marry next summer, but I've just landed a new role and we need to move up the wedding. Suddenly, everything seems upon us at once. Since I'm currently working in another production—" Lucy spread out her hands helplessly "—I have no time to organize things myself."

"How quickly would you like to wed?"

Lucy gave her an apologetic smile. "I'm hoping for a New Year's Eve wedding."

Pia kept her expression steady. "Three months. Perfect."

"I should say that the church has been booked and that, quite astonishingly, the Puck Building is available for a reception."

Pia's shoulders relaxed. The most important details had been taken care of. Since the church and the reception hall were set for the new date, she wouldn't have to scout locations.

She and Lucy discussed some other details for a few minutes, until Lucy glanced at the door.

"Ah, tea. Perfect," Lucy said as a middle-aged woman,

obviously one of the household help, appeared with a tray of tea.

Pia felt she was going to like Lucy. Her hostess had a sunny disposition, and there was already a lot to suggest that she would be easy to work with.

Lucy leaned forward as the tray was set down on a table in front of them. "Thank you, Celia."

"How do you take your tea?" Lucy inquired as Celia departed, and then shot Pia a teasing, self-deprecating look. "No matter how long I've been in New York, this is teatime for me. You can imagine the problems it causes when I'm giving a matinee performance!"

Before Pia could respond, Lucy glanced toward the door again. "Hawk," Lucy acknowledged with a smile. "How nice of you to join us."

Pia followed the direction that Lucy was looking, and froze.

Hawk. Him.

It wasn't possible.

What was he doing here?

Pia felt a sensation like emotional vertigo.

Hawk looked relaxed and at home in a green T-shirt and khakis, as casual as she'd ever seen him. He looked, in fact, as if he might have sauntered in after watching some television or grabbing a bite to eat in another part of the house.

Pia glanced at Lucy, bewildered.

"Have you met my brother, James Carsdale?" Lucy said with an inviting smile, seemingly unaware of anything untoward happening.

Lucy cast her brother an impish grin. "Do I need to recite all your titles, or will it suffice to enlighten Pia that you're also known as His Grace, the Duke of Hawkshire?"

"Carsdale?" Pia repeated, still forcing herself to focus on Lucy. "I thought your surname was Montgomery."

"Pia knows I have a title," Hawk said at the same time.

It was Lucy's turn to look perplexed. She glanced between her brother and Pia. "I feel as if I've walked in during the middle of the second act. Is there something I should know?"

Pia swung to look at Lucy. "Your brother and I are—" she spared Hawk a withering look "—acquainted."

Hawk arched a brow. "Well-acquainted."

"Past tense," Pia retorted.

"Obviously—on all counts," Lucy put in before turning to look at her brother. "You didn't tell me that you knew Pia. You suggested only that, on good authority, you had the name of an excellent wedding planner whom you wanted to recommend to me."

"The truth," Hawk responded.

Lucy arched a brow. "I take it *the good authority* was none other than yourself?"

Hawk inclined his head in silent acknowledgment, a mocking look in his eyes as they met Pia's.

"Yes," Pia put in acidly, "your brother is practiced in making the artful omission."

Lucy looked with interest from her brother to Pia and back. "On the stage, this would be called a moment of high drama," she quipped. "And here I thought, Hawk, that I had a lock on the thespian skills in the family."

Pia stood and reached for her handbag. "Thank you for the offer of tea, Lucy, but I won't be staying."

As Pia tried to step by Hawk on the way to the door, he took hold of her elbow, and she froze.

It was the first time he had touched her in three years—since the night they had first met. And despite herself, she couldn't help feeling Hawk's casual touch on her elbow to the tips of her toes. Her skin prickled at his nearness.

Why, oh why, did she have to remain so responsive to him?

Pia forced herself to look up. It was at a moment such as

this that she rued her lack of stature. And Hawk bested her on all counts…physical height, bearing and consequence in the world.

"I see you have the knack of anticipating requests," he said smoothly. "It's a useful skill in a wedding planner. And, as it happens, I was going to ask for a private word."

Fortunately, she regained some of her combativeness at his words, and she fumed silently even as she let Hawk guide her out the door to the parlor without protest. She was headed in that direction anyway and there was no use making a scene in front of his sister.

Once in the hall, however, she pulled away from Hawk's loose hold. "If you would summon your butler or majordomo, or whatever you call him, for my coat, I'll be on my way and we'll put an end to this charade of an interview."

"No," Hawk responded, pulling shut the parlor door.

"No?" *The gall…the utter nerve.*

Hawk smiled grimly. "Why pass up the chance to tell me, again, what you think of me? Or better yet, say it with finger food?" He nodded toward the room they'd just exited. "I noticed at least a few good scones in there."

"I'll permit Lucy to enjoy them."

"What a relief."

Her gaze clashed with his.

"It seems we're at an impasse," Hawk said dryly. "I refuse to let you leave with your coat until we've spoken, and you're—" he looked at a nearby window and the steady drizzle coming down "—determined to get wet."

"You're all wet," she retorted. "And for your information, I have a compact umbrella with me in my handbag."

Hawk sighed. "We can do this the hard way, and perhaps make a scene that Lucy will overhear, or we can retire to somewhere with a bit more privacy."

"You leave me little choice," Pia tossed back, her chin set at a mutinous angle.

Without waiting for a further invitation, Hawk steered her into a room across the hall.

As Hawk shut the door behind them, Pia noted that this room was unmistakably a library or study. It had built-in bookshelves, a marble mantel as impressive as the one in the parlor, and a large desk set in front of high windows. With plenty of dark, leather-upholstered furniture, the room was clearly Hawk's domain.

Pia turned back to confront Hawk. "I had no idea Lucy was related to you. She gave her name as Lucy Montgomery. Otherwise—"

"—you'd never have come?" he finished for her, his tone sardonic.

"Naturally."

"Montgomery is the stage name that Lucy adopted. It is, however, also a surname that appears in our family tree."

Pia raised her eyebrows. "Do all you Carsdales operate under a variety of names?"

"When it suits."

"And I suppose it suits when you're intent on seduction?"

She'd intended the comment as a sharp riposte, but he had the audacity to give her a slow, sensuous smile.

"Is that what it was—seduction?" he murmured. "To which you fell victim?"

"Through foul means."

"But still you were seduced by the man…not the title."

Pia detected a note of naked honesty in Hawk's banter, but she didn't let herself dwell on it. She didn't let herself dwell on anything—including the fact that they were in his library alone together—except holding on to her outrage.

"You masterminded this," she accused, looking around them. "You arranged to have me come here when you knew I was not suspecting…not ex-expecting…"

Words deserted her.

"It's not a charade, however," Hawk countered. "How could

it be? My sister needs to move up her wedding date, and you're a wedding consultant, last I heard."

"You know what I mean!"

"Does it matter if you can use the business?" Hawk replied.

Pia's eyes widened. "I don't know what you mean. In any case, I'm not that desperate."

"Aren't you?" Hawk said. "You've dropped hints that you've been less than busy lately."

Pia's eyes widened further.

"Never play poker."

"Seeking to make amends?"

"In a sense."

Pia placed her hands on her hips, contemplating him and his vague response. It *couldn't be* that he was feeling guilty about his behavior toward her in the past. He was a seasoned player who had forgotten her easily. That much was clear from the *three years* it had taken for their paths to cross again.

There was only one other possibility, then, for his motivation in linking her to Lucy.

"I suppose you feel some sense of responsibility since it was your friend who torpedoed my professional standing by ruining Belinda's wedding?" she asked.

Hawk hesitated, and then inclined his head. "I suppose *responsibility* is as good a term as any."

Pia eyed him. He was holding out a lifeline to her business, and it was hard not to grasp hold of the opportunity that he was offering. What better way to signal to society that all was well than to be hired to organize the wedding of the sister of the man whom she'd bearded with baba ghanoush?

She was being foolhardy.

"Lucy isn't part of New York society, but her future husband's family is," Hawk cajoled, as if sensing her weakness. "This wedding could help establish you. And Lucy has many ties to the theater world. I'm betting you've never planned a wedding for an actress before?"

Pia shook her head.

"Then Lucy's wedding will let you tap into a whole new market for your services."

"Wh-who would be employing me?"

She hated herself for asking—and hated herself more for stammering—but the question came out of its own volition. Rather than appear satisfied, however, Hawk's expression turned into a study of harmlessness.

"I'd be employing you, but only as a minor, technical detail."

"Minor to you."

"I'm the head of the family, and Lucy is young—only twenty-four." Hawk's lips twitched. "It seems only fair that I support her bid to remove herself from under the imposing family umbrella. Lucy was an unexpected bonus for my parents more than a decade after my mother delivered the heir and the spare."

Pia noted that Hawk had deftly turned an act that might be viewed as generous and loving on his part into a statement of sardonic self-deprecation.

She started to waver. She *had* liked Hawk's sister even on the basis of a very brief acquaintance. She felt a natural affinity for Lucy. It had deepened on learning that Hawk's sister was only three years younger than she was. Lucy was, in fact, the same age that Pia had been when she'd first met Hawk.

If her own tale with Hawk wasn't destined to have a happy ending, then at least she could see to it that one Carsdale...

No, she wouldn't let herself think of matters in that vein.

"You'll be dealing with Lucy mostly, obviously," Hawk continued, his expression open and unmasked. "I'll try to make myself as unobtrusive as possible."

"H-how?" Pia asked. "Are you planning to sequester yourself at your country estate in England?"

"Nothing so drastic," Hawk replied with amusement, "but, rest assured, I have no interest in weddings."

"Obviously—judging from your past behavior."

"Ouch." He had the grace to look abashed. "I stepped right into that comment, and I suppose I deserved it."

She raised her eyebrows and said nothing.

"The town house belongs to me," Hawk went on unperturbed, "but Lucy has had the run of it since I haven't been in regular residence until recently. And though I'm based in New York, rather than London, for business at the moment, I expect that my corporate dealings will still mean I'm not much at home."

Pia knew all about Hawk's hedge fund, of course. She'd read about it online. The success of his company over the past three years had raised his reputation to that of a first-class financier.

Darn. He must have women throwing themselves at him.

Not that she was interested, of course.

Pia wondered why Hawk was at home now, actually. The thought had occurred to her earlier, too—the minute he'd walked into the parlor. It could only be that he'd chosen to come into her meeting with Lucy, possibly betting that once she said yes to his sister, it would be best to reveal his connection to Lucy sooner rather than later.

Hawk arched an eyebrow. "And so...?"

Pia regarded him.

"I make you nervous, don't I?"

"N-naturally. I have a fear of snakes."

He grinned, unabashed.

"The endearing hiccup in your speech tells me everything I need to know about how much I affect you," he said, his voice smooth as silk and doubly seductive.

Pia felt a shiver of awareness chase down her spine for a

moment, but then Hawk's face changed to one as innocuous as a Boy Scout's.

"Of course," he went on solemnly, "we'll say no more on that topic. I plan to be on my best behavior from now on."

"Promise? Really?" she parried.

Before Hawk could reply, the library door opened. Lucy stuck her head inside, and then walked in when it was clear that she'd found them.

"Ah, there you are," Lucy said. "I was wondering if you'd run off, Pia."

"Nothing so drastic," Hawk responded mildly. "Pia and I were just discussing the terms of her employment."

Lucy looked at Pia with some surprise, and then clasped her hands together in delight. "You've agreed? Splendid!"

"I—"

"The hot water has gotten cold, but I'll order another pot for tea," Lucy said. "Shall we all return to the parlor?"

"Yes, let's," Hawk responded, his lips twitching.

As Pia followed Lucy from the room, and Hawk fell into step behind her, she was left to wonder if all the Carsdales had the gift of polite and subtle railroading.

For despite everything, she was finding herself agreeing to be Lucy's bridal consultant.

When Hawk emerged from the elevator, he had no trouble locating Pia's place. She'd opened her front door and was standing in the entrance to her apartment.

She looked fresh as a daisy in a yellow-print knit dress that displayed her lithe, compact body to perfection. The cleavage visible at the V-neck was just enough to give a man interesting thoughts.

He wondered whether he would always experience a quick jolt of sexual awareness when he saw her.

"How did you find me?" she asked without preamble.

He gave a careless shrug. "A little digging on Pia Lumley Wedding Productions. It wasn't hard."

Pia, he'd discovered, now lived on the fifth floor of a modest white-brick doorman building. The older man downstairs—more guard than doorman—had glanced up from his small television set long enough to ring Pia and announce Hawk's arrival. Even though Hawk had been privy only to a brief one-sided conversation—and from the guard's end at that—he'd sensed Pia's hesitancy when she'd been informed of his unexpected arrival. Still, moments later, he'd been directed to the elevator, and then the guard had gone back to viewing his talk show.

"Naturally," Pia responded now with a touch of sarcasm. "I should have expected you'd do some digging of your own. With a business, I'm easy to find, whether I like it or not."

Despite her words, she stepped aside to let him into the apartment, and then shut the door once he'd entered.

"In a way, I'm glad you're here," she said as he turned back to face her. "It makes matters easier."

He quirked a brow. "Only *in a way?*" he queried with dry amusement. "I suppose I should be happy there is at least one way."

"I've been having second thoughts."

"Of course you have." He let his mouth tilt upward. "And that's why *I'm* glad I'm here."

Hawk watched as Pia sucked in a deep breath and squared her shoulders.

"I'm afraid it wouldn't be wise for me to accept the job as Lucy's wedding planner."

"She'll be devastated."

"I'll find a suitable replacement."

"A rival?" he questioned sardonically. "Are you sure you want to?"

"I have contacts—friends."

"And I'm not one of them, presumably."

Hawk glanced around. The apartment wasn't big, but nevertheless bigger than he expected.

The living room was dressed in a pastel theme, from the peach-colored couch to the rose-print armchair. *Wedding colors.*

Binders of various wedding vendors—for invitations, decorations, flowers and more—stood out on the cream-colored bookshelves.

He glanced down as a cat sauntered in from an adjoining room.

The animal stopped, returned his stare, still as a statue, and then blinked.

"Mr. Darcy," Pia announced.

But of course, Hawk thought. A wedding planner with a cat named after Jane Austen's most renowned hero.

Hawk's lips twisted. Pia had wound up with Mr. Darcy, so all should be right with the world. Except Mr. Darcy was a damn cat, and Hawk surmised that *he'd* been cast as the villainous Mr. Wickham in this drama.

Still, he bent and rubbed the cat behind the ears. The feline allowed the contact and then moved to rub himself against Hawk's leg, leaving behind a trail of stray animal hairs on Hawk's pants.

When Hawk straightened, he caught Pia's look of surprise.

"What?" he asked. "You look astonished that I'd cozy up to your cat."

"I thought you would be a dog person," Pia responded. "Aren't all of you aristocrats fond of canines? Fox hunting and such?"

Hawk smiled. "Afraid I'd feed Puss 'n Boots here to the dogs?"

"The possibility wouldn't bear thinking about except that you've already proven yourself to be a wolf in sheep's clothing," Pia retorted.

He gave a feral grin and then, just to annoy her, allowed his gaze to travel over her. "And are you Little Red Riding Hood? Is that the fairy tale you prefer these days?"

"I don't prefer any fairy tales," she shot back. "N-not anymore."

Hawk's smile faded. She didn't believe in fairy tales anymore, and he felt responsible for robbing her of her innocence in more ways than one.

Of course, all that made it even more imperative that he change her mind and get her to accept his help. He intended to make restitution of sorts.

He pulled some papers from the inside pocket of his blazer. "I suspected that you might have a change of heart once you had a chance to think about what you were getting into with Lucy."

"You were the one who wanted time to review the contract!" she accused. "I'm within my rights to change my mind, and if you don't have any recourse, you have only yourself to blame."

It was true that when Pia had handed Lucy her standard written wedding services contract on Monday, before she'd left Hawk's house, he'd taken the contract in hand and had asked to review it. But only because he'd thought it would give him another opportunity to interact with her when he brought it back to her.

He'd come here this afternoon directly from work, and was still wearing a navy business suit.

The discussion of the contract, he told himself, would afford him a chance to change her low opinion of him. Maybe he could begin to demonstrate that he wasn't quite the reprobate she thought he was. Not anymore.

"I did do as I said," he acknowledged, unfolding the paper in his hand. "I did review it."

Pia arched a brow. "One wonders why you don't bring

the same thoroughness and discrimination to your choice of dates."

Hawk stifled the dry chuckle that rose unbidden. "You've done some research on me, I take it."

Pia nodded. "The internet is a wonderful thing. I believe you were referred to on at least one occasion as Jolly Lord James, his Rollicking Rowdy Ruffianness?"

"Ruffian?" Hawk rubbed the bridge of his nose with his finger. "Ah, yes, I believe I had my nose broken at least once in a brawl. A useful thing once I became Hawkshire, as I was able to live up to the profile implied."

"Charming."

"And did your research also reveal how I succeeded to the title of Duke of Hawkshire?" he asked with deceptive casualness.

Pia shook her head. "I believe the tabloids were already fully occupied with your ne'er-do-well travails."

"So I've heard," he deadpanned. "Much to my regret, however, my sojourn as the rollicking younger son of the previous Duke of Hawkshire was cut short when my older brother died from injuries sustained in a boating accident."

He saw Pia hesitate.

"An early morning phone call awakened me from a pleasant slumber, as I recall," he went on, searching her gaze. "I still remember the view from your apartment window as the news reached me."

Pia looked momentarily bewildered. He knew he'd flummoxed her.

"So you departed without a word?"

He nodded. "On the first flight back to London."

The unexpected news about his brother had changed the trajectory of his life. He'd left Pia's apartment quietly, while she'd still slept. Then he'd rushed back to London for a bedside vigil that had ended days later when William had taken his last breath.

With the tumult in his life that had followed the tragedy, he'd been able to push Pia to the back of his mind. Then with the space of days and miles, and the weight of his newfound responsibilities as a ducal heir, he convinced himself that it would be better if he didn't get in touch with her again—if he let matters end as they were.

It had all been convenient, too, he admitted to himself now. Because the truth was that after sleeping with Pia and discovering that she'd been a virgin, he'd had the feeling of being in too deep. It had been a novel and uncomfortable sensation for him. His younger, inconsiderate self had simply been looking for a steamy fling. But he'd been spared the need to figure out how to handle it all by the news of his brother's tragic accident.

"I'm sorry, however belatedly, for your loss," Pia said, a look of openhearted feeling transforming her face.

"I'm not asking for your sympathy," he responded.

He didn't deserve it. As much as Pia had claimed to have developed a more cynical shell since they'd been lovers, she still, he could tell, possessed a soft-hearted fragility about her that showed how easily she could be hurt.

He was thankful for that sign that he hadn't changed her too deeply, even though it made her all that more dangerous. *To him.*

He was here to help, he reminded himself. He was going to make amends for past wrongs, however inadequately, and that's all.

"My father died months later," he elaborated, forcing himself to stay on topic. "Some would say brokenhearted, though he'd already been in poor health. So by two quirks of fate within a year, I became the duke."

"And then you started Sunhill Investments," Pia observed without inflection. "You've had a busy few years."

He inclined his head. "Again, some would say so. And yet it was all born of necessity, and nothing more so than the need to find a new cash flow for the maintenance of the ducal estates."

When his father had died, the full weight of the dukedom had been thrust upon his shoulders. He'd stepped up to take care of the family...become responsible...

He'd already started exploring his options for starting a hedge fund, but the costs associated with the ducal estates had added new urgency to matters.

And in the shuffle—in the crazy upheaval and burdensome work schedule that had been his life for the past three years—it had been easy to shut the door on his discomfort as far as Pia was concerned. He had, at many moments, been too busy to think about their one stupendous night, when he'd broken his vow and done what he said he'd never do, even in his careless playboy days—be remembered as a woman's first lover. And even in his younger days, he hadn't been the type to leave without a word—instead, he stuck around and made sure there were no hard feelings.

"You never got back in touch," Pia stated, though without rancor.

He searched her eyes—so unusual in their warm amber tone that he'd been arrested by them on their first meeting.

Now, he sensed in them that her adamancy from when he'd walked in the door was weakening, exactly as he'd wanted. Still, what he said next was the truth. "None of this explanation was intended as an excuse."

"Why go out of your way to arrange for me to be Lucy's wedding planner?" Pia asked. "To make amends?"

Hawk couldn't help but smile at her astute query. Pia might still be rather sweet and naive, despite her posturing to the contrary, but she was intelligent. He'd been drawn to her wit on the night they'd first met.

"If I said yes, would you let me?" he parried.

"I've found from past experience that letting you do anything is dangerous."

He gave a low laugh. "Even if it's a favor?"

"With no strings attached?"

He could sense her weakening toward him, so he gave her his most innocent look. "Would you let me wipe some of the dirt off my conscience?"

"So this is an act of mercy on my part?"

"Of sorts."

"So you're acting not only to make up for your friend Easterbridge's actions at Belinda's wedding but for yours in the past as well?"

"I don't believe I was ever motivated by Easterbridge's actions."

Then, not giving her a chance to backtrack, he withdrew a pen from his inner jacket pocket and using the nearby wall as support, he inked her contract with his signature.

"There, it's signed," he said, handing out the contract to her.

She looked at him with some wariness, but nevertheless took the contract from him and glanced at it.

"Hawkshire," she read, and then looked up, a sudden glimmer in her eyes. "How grand. Sh-should I receive it as a benediction of sorts?"

He shrugged, willing for her to be amused at his expense. "Am I being permitted to try to make restitution, however inadequately? Then please view this contract as a grant of clemency from you to me."

Deliberately, he held the pen out to her.

Pia seemed to understand his gesture for the meaning-laden act it was, and hesitated.

Hawk glanced down at Mr. Darcy for a moment, and then arched a brow. "Our one witness wants you to sign."

And indeed, Mr. Darcy was looking up at them, unmoving and unblinking. Hawk was starting to realize that it was a customary pose for the cat, and he got the uncomfortable feeling that Mr. Darcy understood too much for a feline.

"I'm not in the business of reforming rakes," Pia said as she reached for the pen.

Their fingers brushed, causing a sizzle of awareness to shoot through him.

Hawk schooled his expression. "Of course you are," he contradicted her. "I assume you adopted Mr. Darcy from a shelter?"

"That was saving a soul, not reforming a rake."

"Is there much difference?" he asked. "And anyway, who knows what dastardly deeds and reprobate behavior Mr. Darcy engaged in before you met him?"

"Better the devil you don't know," she responded, turning a well-known saying on its head.

He placed his hand over his heart. "And yet one could say we encountered each other under blind circumstances not so different from your first meeting with Mr. Darcy. Surely, if you can find it in your heart to take him…?"

"I am not taking you in like…a-a stray," she responded reprovingly.

"Much to my regret," he murmured.

Giving him a lingering cautionary look, she turned her back and, using the wall for support in imitation of his earlier action, signed the contract.

She turned back to him and handed him a copy of the contract.

"Splendid," he said with a grin. "I'd kiss you to seal the deal, but I'll venture to guess you wouldn't find it appropriate under the circumstances."

"Certainly not!"

"A handshake then?"

Pia eyed him, and he returned her regard with a bland look of his own.

Slowly, she extended her hand, and he grasped it in his.

He let himself feel the vibrant current coursing between

them. It was the same as when they'd met three years ago. It was the same as it always was.

Her hand was small and fine-boned. The fingers, he'd noticed, tapered to well-manicured nails that nevertheless showed not a hint of polish—so like her, delicate but practical.

When she tried to pull away, he tightened his hold, drawing out the contact for reasons he didn't bother to examine.

She looked up at him questioningly, and he read the turbulent sexual awareness in her amber eyes.

In a courtly gesture, he bent and gave her a very proper kiss on the hand.

He heard Pia suck in a breath, and as he straightened, he released her hand.

She swallowed. "Why did you do that?"

"I'm a duke," he said, the excuse falling easily from his lips. "It's a done thing."

In fact, Hawk admitted to himself, the context wasn't fitting even if the gesture might have been. He wasn't greeting a woman—one of higher social status—who'd offered him her hand. But he brushed aside those niceties, not least because it had been tempting to touch her.

"Of course," Pia acknowledged lightly, though a shadow crossed her face. "I know all about your world, even if I'm not part of it."

"You've agreed to be part of it now," he countered. "Attend the theater with me tomorrow night."

"Wh-what?" she asked, looking startled. "Why?"

He smiled. "It's Lucy's off-Broadway show. Seeing my sister on the stage, in her element, might give you useful insight into her personality."

Pia relaxed her shoulders.

He could tell she'd been wondering whether he was reneging on his promise even before the ink had dried on their contract. Was he trying to entice her back into his bed?

Yes—*no. No.* He corrected the response that had jumped unbidden into his head. Fortunately, he hadn't spoken aloud.

Nevertheless, Pia seemed ready to argue. "I don't think a show would be—"

"—the ticket?" he finished. "Don't worry about it. I've got two seats in the front orchestra." He winked. "I worked the family connection."

"You know what I mean!"

"Hardly. And that seems to be a recurring problem of mine."

Pia looked as if she wanted to continue to protest.

"I'll see you tomorrow night. I'll come by at seven." He glanced down at the cat. "I hope Mr. Darcy won't mind spending the evening at home alone."

"Why?" she jabbed, but lightly. "Is he an uncomfortable reminder that the role left to you might be that of villain?"

He felt the side of his mouth tease upward. "How did you guess?"

Pia raised her eyebrows, but the look she gave him was open and unguarded.

"I'm not too concerned."

"Oh?"

He glanced down at Mr. Darcy again. "I feel confident that only one of us can waltz."

"*Oh.*"

Pia looked startled and then, for a moment, dreamy—as if the idea of a waltz had called to the romantic in her.

Mr. Darcy just continued to stare at them unblinkingly, and Hawk realized that now was as good a time as any for him to leave, before he gave in to too much temptation.

He let the side of his mouth quirk up again. "Since I appear to have exhausted my options for acceptable salutations and social niceties, I'm afraid my goodbye will have to be rather dull."

"How reassuring," Pia answered, recovering.

He touched his finger to the tip of her pert nose in humorous salute of her impertinence.

And then, unable to stop himself, he let his finger wander down and smooth over her pink and inviting lips.

They both quieted.

"Tomorrow night," he repeated.

He turned away before he was tempted to touch her lips with his, and then let himself out the way he'd come in.

As he pulled shut the apartment door behind him, Hawk refused to let himself think about why he found it hard to leave Pia.

It was a vexing situation that could only mean no good for his best of intentions.

Five

Pia found herself staring at her apartment door after Hawk had left. Flooded with conflicting emotions, she hugged herself and sat down on her couch.

She touched her fingers to her lips, in imitation of Hawk's action moments ago. She could swear he'd wanted to kiss her. The last time he'd kissed her had been on the night that they'd first met....

Pia turned away and picked up the remote to her MP3 player because music relaxed her. Within a few moments, the dulcet tones of an orchestral ensemble drifted through the apartment from her small speakers.

"W-would you like a drink?" she asked.

James laughed close behind her. "What a question to ask, considering we've just been to a bar."

In truth, she felt light-headed herself. It must have been that last cocktail she'd had at the bar while trying to converse with the real estate office manager.

"Pia," James said quietly, laying his hands on her shoulders.

She froze at the contact, her nipples tightening.

"Relax," he murmured close to her ear.

Oh.

He removed his hands...but moments later, she felt his fingertips trail up her arms as he nuzzled the hair near her ear.

She shivered. "Really, I—"

He nipped her earlobe.

She gulped, and then forced herself to say, "D-don't you want to get to know each other better?"

"Much better," he agreed on a soft laugh.

His body brushed hers from behind, sending delicious shivers through her.

Slowly, he turned her to face him, and then searched her eyes. "I've been wanting to do this—" he bent and tasted her lips "—ever since we left the bar."

"Oh," she breathed.

This was her fantasy. *He was here now.*

He cupped her shoulders, his thumbs tracing a soothing circular pattern. "We won't do anything you don't want to do."

"Th-that's what I'm afraid of."

He smiled. "Ah, Pia. You really are special." Then his expression turned more intent and amorous. "Let me show you how much."

He cupped her cheek, laid his lips against hers and tasted her.

She sighed and gripped his shirt, fisting her hand into the material, as little shock waves of pleasure jolted her.

She felt his arousal grow between them as his mouth stroked hers. Within moments, they had fitted their bodies together, giving in to the desire that had been kindled in the bar and stoked on the cab ride to her apartment.

He cupped her face with both hands, his fingers delving into her hair as he sipped from her mouth.

She relaxed her grip on his shirt and flattened her hands against his chest, where she could feel the steady beat of his heart.

Around them, the sweet notes of string instruments sounded, the tune low and soulful.

Pia felt herself relax even as every inch of her skin tingled with awareness. She sighed against James's mouth, wanting the kiss to go on and on as his hunger matched her own.

Giving in to the urge to shed attire, she kicked off her sandals. In the next moment, she lowered a couple of inches, enough to break the contact of her lips with James's.

"My bed isn't very big." They were the first words to pop out of her mouth, her tone apologetic, and she flushed.

James looked indulgent, and then dimpled as he nodded beside them. "You've never made love on a love seat before?"

She'd never made love *period*. But she was afraid if she told him, he'd flee out the door. She knew he must be used to more experienced women.

She shrugged one shoulder. "Why bother when a bed is available?"

"Mmm," he said, and then bent and nuzzled her ear.

Oh. She gripped his upper arms for support, her fingers digging into his biceps, as his action did funny things to her insides.

She felt his hand go to the zipper at the back of her dress.

"Would it be okay if I did this?" he murmured.

"Yes, please," she breathed.

She heard the rasp of the zipper and felt her dress slither downward, exposing to his gaze that she wasn't wearing a bra.

James stepped back and looked at her with a hooded, rapt expression.

"Ah, Pia, you're so beautiful." He raised his hands to cup

and caress her. "You're just as pretty as I thought when my imagination was running rampant in the bar."

"Kiss me," she whispered.

He sat on the arm of the love seat beside them and, pulling her toward him, fastened his mouth over one pert breast.

Pia was lost. Her heart beat wildly, and she tangled her fingers in his hair.

He pushed the rest of the dress off her, and then peeled her panties away without lifting his mouth from her.

Pia moaned.

He shifted his focus to her other breast, but then paused, his lips hovering over her taut flesh, his breath fanning her erect nipple.

"And would it be okay if I kissed you here?" he said hoarsely.

Pia had never been so close to begging and pleading.

But instead of answering, she guided his head to her breast, her eyes fluttering shut on a sigh as his lips closed over her.

He soothed and aroused her with his tongue, fanning the fire of their desire.

Before she knew it, she was on his lap on the love seat, and they were kissing passionately but yet like longtime lovers who had all the time in the world. His arousal pressed against her flesh, and his hand caressed up and down her thigh.

When they finally broke away, he groaned softly. "Have mercy, Pia."

In response, she snuggled closer. He nuzzled her temple and his breath rasped in her ear. She shivered and rubbed against him.

She let her hand go to the buttons of his shirt, undoing one and then another. The strong, corded line of his neck came into view.

"Pia," he said from somewhere above her head, "please say you don't want to stop."

"Who said anything about stopping?" This was her

fantasy, and she found that she wanted to see it through to its conclusion. Her last drink at the bar had given her a delicious, unbound feeling, and James's seduction had lowered her inhibitions even more.

"Ah, Pia." He slipped his hand between her thighs and pressed, giving her a heady sensation. "I just want to assure you that I'm clean."

"I am, too," she answered, understanding what he was alluding to. "I've never had unprotected sex."

It was literally true, though it hid the truth—that she'd never had sex at all.

He kissed her neck. "Are you…? If not, I have something with me. Not that I walked in here with any expectations, of course, but I'd be lying if I said I wasn't attracted to you from the first moment I spotted you."

"Mmm…when did you first notice me? Are you saying our encounter in the bar wasn't by chance?"

"I saw you minutes before you tried to order a drink," he admitted. "When I spotted a damsel in distress, though, I saw my opening. I took a chance that Cinderella was looking for a Prince Charming to come rescue her, and that she'd mistake me for him if I tried to do her a favor."

Pia's heart gave a little squeeze. It was as if he knew her well already. Did he suspect that she was a romantic at heart? Did he know that she'd thrilled to stories of true love, though a part of her knew better?

She pulled his head down for a kiss as the music reached a low crescendo around them.

They kissed deeply, their mouths clinging, unable to get enough of each other.

When he finally broke their kiss, he stood up with her in his arms. "What's your preference, Cinderella?"

She glanced down at the love seat—next time.

"Bed," she said.

"My sentiments exactly," he said, and then strode with her

around the partition to where the bed was. "See, we have a lot in common."

"Besides riding and fishing?"

He paused in the act of placing her on the bed. "Oh, Pia, sweetheart," he said huskily, a wicked glimmer in his eye, "isn't that what tonight is all about—fishing and riding?"

Pia felt a full-body flush sweep over her. As she came down on the mattress, she propped herself up on her elbows to stop from lying completely on her back.

She swallowed, unable to say anything.

Holding her eyes, James undid the remaining buttons on his shirt and cuffs, and then pulled fabric from his waistband, stripping off his shirt and undershirt.

Pia soaked up the sight of him. Taut muscle rippled underneath the planes of smooth and lightly tanned skin.

She hadn't been mistaken. He was fit and in top shape.

He made short work of the rest of his clothes, working methodically until he was naked.

His arousal stood in imposing relief against his toned frame.

Pia sucked in a breath. "You're very beautiful."

James gave her a lopsided smile. "Isn't that my line?"

It occurred to her that while she'd viewed pictures of naked men, this was the first time she'd seen one in the flesh. And again, James was beyond her expectations. He was impressive—tall and built as well as fit. The flat planes of his abdomen tapered down to…a definite sign that he wanted to couple with her. *Right now.*

A tingle went through her, a tightening of anticipation.

As if in response, he pulled her toward him on the bed and began kissing his way down her body.

Pia looked up at the white plaster ceiling, her hands tangling in his hair, and thought she'd die of pleasure.

James kissed the jut of her hip and then worked his way down the soft skin of her inner thigh to the sensitive spot behind her knee. He lifted her other leg and turned his head to nip and brush the pliant flesh of her other thigh.

With one finger, he traced down the cleft at the juncture of her thighs, and she moaned, her head twisting until she pressed her face into the coverlet beside her.

James muttered sweet encouragement as he lowered her leg and caressed his hand down her thigh.

Then he bent, picked up his pants from the floor and fished out a packet of protection. He donned the sheath with economical moves. Stretching out beside her on the bed, he gathered her to him and soothed her with his lips and hands as he muttered soft endearments under his breath.

Pia was lost to the sensation and emotion sweeping her. She was petite and felt surrounded by him.

When James shifted over her, parting her thighs and settling against her, she worried about being able to accept him. But within seconds she was again consumed by the desire flaring between them.

"Touch me, Pia," he said hoarsely.

He sipped and feasted on her lips, his hands readying her with a gentle kneading. Pia responded in kind, meeting his mouth and trailing her fingertips over the corded muscles of his back.

This was the moment she'd waited a lifetime for. *He* was the man she'd waited for.

James nudged her, and Pia concentrated on relaxing as he sucked on her lower lip.

Lifting his head, he muttered, "Wrap your legs around me."

Oh, sweet heaven. She'd never been plastered, open and exposed, to an aroused male before.

She concentrated on what she'd imagined countless times in her fantasies, where her partner's features had always been indistinct but he'd carried an aura so very much like James's.

She did as he instructed, and James grasped her hips in his hands.

He looked deeply into her eyes and then gave her a quick, gentle kiss.

"Let me take you, Pia," he said throatily. "Let me bring you pleasure."

She arched toward him, and in response, he buried his head in her neck and penetrated her.

Pia gasped, and then bit down hard on her lip.

James froze.

Moments passed and they held still. The thumping of his heart sounded against hers.

He lifted his head, his expression puzzled, and also shocked and doubtful.

"You're a virgin."

He stated it with surprise.

She wet her lips. "W-was. I think past tense is appropriate."

She felt full and stretched, almost to the point of the unbearable, where pleasure met pain. It was a strange sensation that she tried to get used to.

"Why?"

She swallowed, and then whispered, "I wanted you. Is that so bad?"

James closed his eyes, his muscles remaining full of tension as he rested his forehead against hers and then muttered a self-deprecation. "You're so unbelievably tight and hot. Sweet like I've never experienced... Pia, I can't—"

Afraid he'd pull out, she clamped her legs around him. "D-don't."

After a moment, some of the tension eased out of him—almost as if he was reluctantly admitting defeat.

"I'll try to make it good for you from now on," he muttered, as if the words were torn from him.

"Yes."

He moved slowly then, his hands pressing the right spots and easing the tension in her body.

Pia focused on relaxing and concentrated on the sensation of his movements.

Slowly, slowly, she felt a small spark, and then a faint tingle. She was awakening, her body coming to life under his sure ministrations.

Eventually, as she relaxed further, tension built. She felt herself reaching for a release that she'd never experienced with a man before.

James stroked between their bodies, his fingers pressing on her most sensitive spot.

Within moments, she cried out with pleasure and then crested before she knew it. She was carried on a wave of sensation as feeling after feeling swamped her.

Her body undulated around James of its own accord, massaging him into his own frenzy of need.

"Have mercy, Pia," he groaned.

It was too late, however. With a hoarse oath, he grasped her hips and pumped into her.

She came for him again. And then with a final thrust, he took his own release.

As James slumped against her, Pia hugged him and suddenly became aware of tears in her eyes.

He'd taken her across the final barrier to realizing herself sexually as a woman. Their joining and her first time couldn't have been more wonderful.

Pia closed her eyes, and of their own accord, exhaustion and sleep claimed her.

The next time she blinked up at her ceiling, he was gone.

In a moment, Pia was brought back to the present. She realized she wasn't staring at her ceiling, but at her apartment wall.

Different apartments, three years apart.

Same man, though.

Hawk.

His presence was palpable still, and her body was awakened and aware as if they'd made love moments, not years, ago.

Pia shook her head. *No.*

She'd let him into her sanctuary—her apartment—again, but she resolved not to let him into her life one more time.

The night after Hawk signed the contract at her apartment, Pia discovered they had a couple of the best theater seats in the house—no doubt thanks to Hawk's personal connection.

Hawk had appeared at her apartment at seven and driven them so they could make the eight o'clock curtain call for Lucy's show, an off-Broadway production of the musical *Oklahoma,* in which Lucy had a supporting role.

Pia made a show of studying her program as they waited for the lights to dim. Tonight, she reminded herself, was all about business. She'd dressed in a short-sleeved, apricot-colored dress that she'd worn to work-related parties before and that she hoped sent the appropriate message. She'd avoided those items in her wardrobe that she considered purely off-hours attire.

She stole a quick sidelong glance at Hawk, who was looking at the stage. Even dressed casually in black pants and a light blue shirt, he managed to project an air of ducal self-possession.

She just wished she wasn't so aware of his thigh inches away from her own, and of his shoulder and arm within dangerously close brushing distance. If there was a petition right now for having individual armrests in places of public accommodations, she'd sign on the spot.

Determinedly, she pulled herself in, making it clear that she'd cede the shared armrest to him.

In the process, she absently tugged down the hem of her dress, and Hawk's gaze was drawn to her actions.

As Hawk surveyed her exposed thighs, his expression changing to one of alert but lazy amusement, Pia rued her involuntary action.

Hawk's eyes moved up to meet hers. "I have a proposition for you."

"I-I'm not surprised," she shot back, rallying and cursing her telltale stammer. "They do appear to be your forte."

He had the indecency to grin. "You bring out the best—" he waited a beat as her eyes widened "—urges in me."

She hated that he could bait her so successfully. "You give me too much credit. As far as I can tell, your urges don't need any help in being called forth. They appear of their own volition."

Hawk chuckled. "Aren't you at least curious about what I have to offer?"

She frowned, but forced herself to adopt a saccharine-sweet voice. "You forget that I already know. Unless your offer involves business, I'm not interested."

Was his facility with sexual innuendo boundless?

He shifted toward her, his leg brushing her own, and Pia tried to stifle her response of frozen awareness before he could discern it.

Hawk looked too knowing. "As it happens, it does. Involve business, that is."

This time, Pia didn't try to hide her reaction. "It does?"

Hawk nodded. "A friend of mine, Victoria, needs help with a wedding."

"A female friend? Ready to give up on you, is she, and move on?"

She couldn't stop herself from needling him, it seemed.

He flashed a grin. "We never dated. Her fiancé is an old classmate of mine. I introduced them to each other at a party last year."

"You do seem to know quite a few people who are getting

married." She raised her eyebrows. "Always the matchmaker, never the groom?"

"Not yet," he replied cryptically.

She fell silent at his vague response.

Once upon a time, *he* might have featured in *her* wedding fantasies, but they were well past that point, weren't they? Instead of the well-trod path, they'd veered down a detour from which there was no turning back.

"When is the wedding?" she heard herself ask.

"Next week. Saturday."

"Next week?"

She wasn't sure she'd heard correctly.

Hawk nodded. "The wedding planner is quarantined abroad."

Pia raised her eyebrows.

Hawk quirked his lips. "I'm not joking. She went on safari with her boyfriend, and they were both exposed to tuberculosis. She can't get back to New York until after the wedding date."

Pia shook her head in bemusement. "I suppose I should thank you…?"

"If you want to," he teased. "It might be appropriate under the circumstances."

Pia bit her lip, but Hawk looked down and pulled out a piece of paper from his pocket.

"Here's the bride's contact information," he said. "Will you do it? Will you call her?"

Pia took the paper from him, her fingers brushing his in a contact that was anything but casual for the two of them.

She noted the name and phone number that he'd written. *Victoria Elgemere.*

Just then the lights overhead blinked a few times, indicating that people should take their seats because the show was about to begin.

"I'll call her," she said quickly.

"Good girl," Hawk responded, and then mischievously patted her knee, his hand lingering. "I'll be a wedding guest, by the way."

"Then it'll be déjà vu."

He grinned. "I've developed a taste for baba ghanoush."

She threw him a stern look, and then picked up and returned his hand to him. Her actions belied the emotional tumult that he so effortlessly engendered in her.

Facing forward as the lights dimmed, she was left to reflect that her company had again received a desperate transfusion of new business thanks to Hawk.

She'd acted quickly in accepting the job—or, at least, agreeing to call—forced into an impulsive decision by the imminent start of the show, but she didn't want her feelings toward him to get murky.

She could start feeling gratitude or worse.

Six

Hawk emerged from an Aston Martin at the New York Botanical Garden—where Victoria's wedding would shortly be held at four o'clock on a Saturday afternoon—and looked up.

He saw nothing but clear blue skies. There was just the faint hint of a warm breeze. *Perfect.*

As the valet approached for his car keys, Hawk heard his cell phone ring and smiled as the notes of "Unforgettable" by Nat King Cole sounded. He'd assigned the ringtone to Pia's cell, whose number he'd acquired ostensibly for business reasons.

He'd thought of using the theme music from *Jaws* for her ringtone, but then he figured that while it might be appropriate, given the sparring nature of his relationship with her, she didn't need further encouragement, if she ever found out, to attempt to annihilate him.

With a grin, he took the call.

"Hawk, where are you?" Pia demanded without preamble.

"I'm about to hand my cars keys to the valet," he responded. "Should I be anywhere else?"

"I'll be right there! The bride left her veil in the back of a Lincoln Town Car that departed minutes ago. I need your help."

"What...?"

"You heard me." Pia's voice held an edge of crisis. "Oh, I can't be associated with another wedding disaster!"

"You won't." *Not if he could help it.* "What's the name of the car service?"

As Pia gave it to him, Hawk shook his head at the valet and jumped back into his car to start the ignition.

"Call the car company," he told Pia, "and tell them to contact the driver."

"I already have. They're trying to get in touch with him. He can't go too far. Otherwise, we'll never get the veil back in time for the ceremony."

"Don't worry, I'm on it." He started to steer back down the drive with one hand. "Do you think he's heading back to Manhattan?"

If he had some idea in which direction the car was heading, he'd know which way to go once he got out of the Botanical Garden. Then when contact was made with the driver, at least he'd be nearby and they could meet at a convenient exit or intersection.

"I think he is heading south, and I'm coming with you," Pia replied.

"No, you're needed here."

"Look to your left. I'm heading toward you. Stop and I'll hop in."

Hawk turned to look out the driver's-side window. Sure enough, there was Pia, hurrying toward him across the grass, a phone pressed to her ear.

"Good grief, Pia." He disconnected the call and stopped the car.

Moments later, she pulled open the passenger-side door and slid inside.

As he pulled away again, he observed with amusement, "I don't think I've ever seen a woman so anxious to get into a car with me."

"It's an Aston Martin," she said, breathing heavily from her jog. "You can really accelerate, and I'm desperate."

"The first time I think I've been praised for my ability to go fast."

"J-just drive." She breathed in deep, then, pressing a button, put her phone to her ear once more.

Hawk assumed she was calling the car service again.

He glanced at her. She was wearing a short-sleeved caramel-color satin dress with a gently-flared skirt and matching tan kitten heels. He'd already identified the outfit as she was racing toward him as another of what he'd come to think of as her working-party dresses—festive but not so eye-catching that they'd detract attention from where it was meant to be.

Now he listened to her half of the conversation with the car service. It seemed as if she was getting good news.

In fact, when the call was over, Pia slumped with relief.

"They got through to the driver," she said. "He's getting off the highway and meeting us three exits away at a gas station rest stop."

"Great." *On to more enchanting matters.* He nodded to her dress. "You look nice."

She threw him a startled look, as if not expecting the compliment. "Thanks."

He felt a smile pull at his lips as he tossed her a sidelong look. "Do you pick your wedding clothes with an eye toward being able to make a quick sprint? You made good time across the grass. Rather impressive in those shoes."

"Weddings can be full of the unexpected," she replied. "You should know that as well as anyone."

He arched a brow. "Still, I'm curious. You phoned me to come to your rescue. Am I your modern-day knight riding to the rescue in a black sports car?"

"Hardly," she replied tartly. "There are very few people I know at this wedding, and you got me into this mess—"

He laughed.

"—so the least you could do when you arrived at just the right moment was to lend a set of wheels."

"Ah, of course."

He let the discussion go at that, though he was tempted to tease her some more.

Moments later, he took the highway exit that she indicated and found the gas station.

The driver of the car service was waiting for them, a shopping bag in hand.

After Pia took the errant veil from the driver and thanked him quickly, she and Hawk hopped back into his car.

"The day has been saved," Hawk remarked as he put the key back in the ignition.

"Not yet," Pia responded. "The wedding isn't over. Trust me on this one. I've been to more weddings than there are lights in Times Square."

"Yes, but isn't this the moment when you thank your hero with a kiss?"

She jerked to look at him, her eyes widening.

Not giving her a chance to think it over, he leaned forward and touched his lips to hers.

Lord, he thought, her lips were as pillowy soft as they looked. *Just as he remembered.*

Even though he knew he should stop, when he heard and felt Pia's breath hitch, he deepened the kiss, settling his lips more firmly on hers.

She didn't pull away, and he drew out the kiss, molding her lips with his. With his hand, he stroked the soft skin of her jaw and throat.

She relaxed and sighed, and leaned toward him. And it was all he could do not to draw her into an embrace and feed the desire between them.

He finally forced himself to pull back and look at her. "There...recompense received."

"I—I—" Pia cleared her throat and frowned. "You're quite the expert at stealing kisses, aren't you?"

Solemnly, he placed his hand over his heart. "It's a rare occasion that I have the opportunity to act so gallantly."

She hesitated, and then gave him a stern look and faced forward. "We need to get back."

They made it back to the New York Botanical Garden in record time while Pia filled him in with desultory wedding details.

When he pulled up in front of the valet again, Pia rushed away to help the bride. As Hawk dealt with the car and the valet again, he reflected that he'd heard nothing but good things from Victoria and Timothy about Pia's eleventh-hour help with their wedding. He was impressed by how professionally Pia had handled herself with little time to prepare.

After leaving the valet, Hawk sauntered alone toward the other guests mingling on the grassy outdoor space where the ceremony was to take place, surrounded by the Botanical Garden's rich greenery. The bridal arch and bedecked chairs, arranged by the florist, stood at the ready.

He made idle chitchat with some fellow guests, but within twenty minutes, everyone was seated and the ceremony started.

The bride looked pretty and the groom beamed, but Hawk only had eyes for Pia, standing discreetly to one side, within a few feet of the seat he'd chosen for himself in one of the back rows.

Suddenly catching Pia's eye, he motioned for her to take the empty seat next to him.

She hesitated for a moment, but then slipped into the white folding chair next to him.

Hawk smiled to himself. But as he stared ahead, watching the bride and groom, more weighty thoughts eventually intruded.

He'd chosen long ago to attend this wedding alone. Victoria and her groom, Timothy, were longtime friends of his, and he'd found that for this occasion at least, he wanted to be free of expectations. At his age, society and the press were apt to view any date of his as a potential duchess.

Hawk reflected that Victoria and Timothy were going through a rite of passage that would soon be expected of him. Tim was an Old Etonian, like him, and Victoria was a baron's daughter who had attended all the right schools and now had a socially acceptable job as the assistant to an up-and-coming British designer.

Victoria, in fact, had precisely the pedigree and background that would be expected for the bride of a duke. She was the sort of woman of whom his mother would approve.

Hawk's mind went to his mother's attempt at matchmaking with Michelene Ward-Fombley in particular, but he pushed the thought aside.

He stole a look at Pia next to him. Her business had trained her in the etiquette of the elite, but that couldn't change her background or give her connections that she didn't possess. With the crowd here today, she'd always be the bridal consultant, never the bride.

At that moment, Pia's lips parted as she looked to the front, and her expression became rather emotional.

Pia cried at weddings.

The thought flashed through Hawk's mind like a news bulletin and was closely followed by the realization that Pia was doing what she loved to do. Weddings, he realized, were more than a job to her.

He'd meant to make things up to her, in a way, by arranging for her to coordinate this wedding and Lucy's. But he'd also, in the process, tested the limits of their relationship because he enjoyed teasing her.

It had been too tempting to spar with her and watch her eyes flash. He admitted to himself that any reaction from Pia was better than having her treat him with indifference. And her kiss…it was hard to imagine a better reaction than that.

But the last thing he wanted to do was to hurt Pia again, he reminded himself. A relationship wouldn't be possible for them, and he shouldn't tease either of them with kisses that couldn't lead to anything more. She deserved to be able to get on with her life, and so did he.

A dog started barking, recalling him from his thoughts.

Beside him, Pia sat up straighter.

Hawk had noted before that the only surprising touch to the ceremony was the bride's King Charles Spaniel, who'd been dressed with an ivory collar and bow and had been led down the aisle by an attendant.

Now, he spotted the dog up front near the bridal arch, playing with—or rather, tearing at—a flower arrangement on the ground.

"Not the dog, please," Pia said under her breath. "We haven't even taken photos with the bridal bouquet yet."

Hawk glanced at her. At the beginning of the ceremony, he'd seen the bride place her flowers on a small pedestal. The pooch-cum-bridal attendant had somehow gotten hold of them.

Hawk couldn't remember the name of Victoria's canine. Finola? Feefee? In any case, *Trouble* seemed appropriate at the moment.

He watched as the bride knelt down, and then her dog sprinted away, bouquet in mouth.

So much for asking if anyone had any objections to this marriage...

"I have to do something," Pia muttered as she started to rise.

Hawk wasn't sure if Pia was talking to herself or to him, and if it mattered. He rose, too, and laid a staying hand on Pia's wrist. "Forget it. In those heels, you'll never catch—"

"Finola."

"Full of trouble."

Hawk moved forward as the dog eluded a well-intentioned guest.

The wedding had truly been disrupted now. Everyone had turned to watch the wily four-legged perpetrator of chaos.

The dog headed toward the back of the gathering, as if sensing that with another few passes, she'd be home free, dashing away from the assembled guests.

Hawk shoved back his chair as he moved into the aisle. He knew he had one shot at catching Victoria's renegade pooch.

He tensed and then dove forward as the furry and furious fuzzball tried to whiz by.

In mid-lunge, he heard gasps, and someone called out a bit of encouragement. And in the next moment, he'd caught the excited Finola with his outstretched arms before landing hard on the ground.

The dog relinquished the bouquet as she was tackled and started yapping again.

A few guests began clapping, and a man called out, "Well done."

Hawk held on firmly to the squirming animal as he straightened and then stood upright. He held Finola away from him.

Victoria rushed forward. "Here, Finola."

Pia snatched the battered bouquet, her expression one of disbelief mixed with dismay.

Hawk watched her, and then murmured, "Just remember, bad luck comes in threes."

She looked up at him, eyes wide. "Please tell me this is number three."

Before he could reassure Pia, Victoria reached to take Finola from him and then snuggled the dog close.

The bride started to laugh and some of the guests joined in. Others broke out into smiles.

Hawk watched Pia relax and smile herself. He could practically read her mind. *If the bride and everyone else could see the humor in the situation, then everything was going to be okay.*

"Who's been the naughty pooch, hmm?" Victoria said.

Hawk resisted rolling his eyes. *Perhaps he did have a preference for women who owned cats rather than dogs.*

With a wave of the arm, he acknowledged the scattered praise from the wedding guests and righted his fallen chair.

Victoria looked at him. "Thank you so much, Hawk. You saved the day."

Hawk glanced at Pia, a smile pulling at his lips. "Not at all. I'm glad I was able to be of service."

Pia lifted her eyebrows.

Victoria walked back up the aisle so the ceremony could resume, and Pia returned the bouquet to its position on the pedestal. Someone kept a firm hold on Finola.

Everything proceeded without a hitch after that. Much to Hawk's regret, though, Pia did not retake her seat next to him but chose to remain positioned near the front of the assembled guests. He couldn't blame her, though, in light of all the recent excitement.

Once the ceremony was over, however, he was able to approach her at the indoor reception, where he spotted her standing with her back to him near the open bar.

"Drink?" he said as he came up behind her.

She turned around at his query, looking as if she was

amused in spite of herself. "For some reason, I'm experiencing a sensation of déjà vu."

Hawk grinned. "I thought so." He chucked her under the chin. "You acquitted yourself splendidly today."

"With your help. Victoria seems to think you went above and beyond the call of duty."

"It was the least I could do," he demurred with a touch of self-mockery. "I was the one who got you involved with the crazy bride."

She smiled. "Only with the best of intentions."

Hawk felt momentarily dazzled by Pia's smile. She could light up a room with it, he thought. Give her a wand and she could sprinkle some glittering fairy dust, no problem.

He pushed aside the whimsical thought, and for Pia's benefit, he shook his head in resigned amusement. "A doggy attendant dressed up to match the bride? Who'd ever have thought it?"

"You'd be surprised," Pia returned. "I've even seen a pet pig march up the aisle."

"Well, Finola is no match for Mr. Darcy."

Pia laughed. "Mr. Darcy would agree with you, I'm sure."

They discussed the wedding at that point, with Pia remarking on how beautiful Victoria had looked, and Hawk commenting on some of the faces he recognized among the guests.

"This is a working party for me," Pia said eventually, as if to remind herself as much as him.

"I suppose you'll have to stay until the very end then?" he remarked.

She nodded. "I'll have to make sure everything is wrapped up."

Hawk looked through the reception room's paned windows and noted it was already dark.

"How are you getting back home?" he asked, guessing that she hadn't come in her own car because she'd had to borrow the services of his earlier.

She lifted a shoulder, and said simply, "I'll order a car service."

His eyes met hers. "I'll stick around then."

"I...i-it's not necessary."

"I know." He smiled. "Nevertheless, I'm at your disposal."

It wasn't until a few hours later that he was able to make good on his offer. He noted that Pia still managed to look as edible as dessert by the end of the evening, even though she also seemed drained.

They drove back to Manhattan mostly in silence, content to observe the darkened world whizzing by after a long day—and comfortable enough in each other's company not to make forced conversation.

When Hawk pulled up in front of Pia's building, however, he glanced over, only to notice that she had fallen asleep.

Her head was leaning back against the headrest, her lips parted.

He turned off the ignition and then stopped, taking a moment to study her face. For once, she looked unguarded.

Her blond hair had a fine, wispy quality, and he knew from experience that it was as soft as a baby's. Her eyebrows were delicately arched over eyes that he knew were large and expressive and a fascinating, changeable mix of amber hues.

Hawk let his gaze roam down to her lips. They held the sheen of a shimmery pink lipstick, but they needed no embellishment for their natural charm as far as he was concerned. He'd tasted them earlier in the day, because the temptation had been too great.

He debated for a moment, and then, unable to help himself,

leaned over, tilted her chin toward him with a light touch and pressed his lips to hers.

He rubbed his lips against hers, feeling the tingle of sensation, and then gently worked her lower lip with a small suck.

Dessert hadn't been nearly as good.

Pia's eyelashes fluttered. She opened her eyes and lifted her head.

Hawk pulled back, and then gave her a lopsided smile.

"Wh-what?"

"I was awakening Sleeping Beauty with a kiss," he responded in a low voice. "Isn't that the fairy-tale heroine that you are today?"

She blinked, coming further awake. "Unintentionally. This isn't a good idea."

He glanced past her and then back down again, keeping his expression innocent. "Did you prefer not to be awakened when we arrived at your apartment? Should I have driven straight on to my place instead?"

"Absolutely not," she said, though in a halfhearted tone.

He smiled for a moment before turning to open the driver-side door.

He reached her side of the car in time to help her alight, though she hesitated for a second before placing her hand in his.

By now, he was used to the sizzle of any physical contact between them.

"Good night, Your Grace," she said when she'd gotten out of his car, her eyes meeting his.

He let his lips drift upward. "Good night, Pia."

He watched as she made her way into her building, the doorman looking up from his television set to acknowledge her.

Only after she'd disappeared from view did he get back into his car.

As he pulled into traffic, Hawk acknowledged that he was pushing the boundaries with Pia. But, he told himself, he knew what the limits were.

Or so he hoped.

Seven

"*Ducal Gofer.* Gazillionaire bridal assistant, the Duke of Hawkshire…"

Pia gritted her teeth as she read Mrs. Jane Hollings's gossip column in *The New York Intelligencer.*

"What's wrong?" Belinda asked.

Pia had just sat down at a table in Contadini, where she, Belinda Wentworth and Tamara Langsford—née Kincaid—were having one of their Sunday brunch dates.

"Mrs. Hollings has written about me and Hawk in her gossip column," Pia said as she scrolled down the article on her smartphone. "Apparently she received notice that Hawk helped me handle some wedding escapades last night."

"That was fast," Belinda commented.

"Well, it's in her online column," Pia responded, looking up. "Her regular print one will appear in Monday's paper, where no doubt I will be able to savor the joy of having my name appear in print with—" her lips pulled down "—the Duke of Hawkshire's."

Belinda looked at Tamara. "Doesn't your husband own this paper? Can't you do something about this awful woman?"

Tamara cleared her throat. "I have news."

"You already told us, remember?" Belinda quipped. "We know you're knocked up, and Sawyer is the daddy."

"Old news." Tamara looked from Pia to Belinda. "The new news is that Sawyer and I plan to stay together."

"For the sake of the baby?" Belinda shook her head. "Honey…"

Tamara shook her head. "No, because we love each other."

Belinda stared at her blankly for a moment. Then she waved to a passing waiter. "Another Bloody Mary, please."

Pia knew this was a sore point for Belinda, since her friend still needed to get an annulment from the Marquess of Easterbridge.

"I suppose I should be addressing you both as *My Lady*," Pia mused. "Sawyer is an earl, making Tamara a countess, and since Colin is a marquess, you're entitled to be called—"

"Don't you dare," Belinda retorted. "I'm planning to shed the title as soon as possible."

Pia sighed. "Oh, well."

Belinda turned to Tamara. "I can't believe you're abandoning our trio of girlfriends for the aristocratic cadre."

"I'm not. It's just…"

"What?" Belinda asked, her expression sardonic. "You moved in with Sawyer and made a marriage of convenience. And then—" she snapped her fingers "—next thing you know, you're pregnant with his child and declaring yourself in love."

Tamara smiled and shrugged. "It's the most exciting thing that's ever happened to me," she admitted. "I wasn't looking to fall in love, and if you'd asked me months ago, I'd have said Sawyer was the last man…"

Tamara got a faraway look as her words drifted off. "I realized Sawyer was the one I wanted all along," she eventually continued. "And the best part is he feels the same way about me."

Belinda accepted the Bloody Mary that the waiter was about to set down in front of her, and took a healthy swig. "Well, I'm happy for you, Tam. One of us deserves to find happiness."

Tamara gave a faint smile. "Thanks. I know you and Pia don't like Sawyer's friends—"

"You mean my husband?" Belinda asked archly.

"You mean Hawk?" Pia said at the same time.

"—but Sawyer and I are hoping you all will make nice enough to be in the same room together. In fact, we're hoping to have all of you over next Saturday night for a small postwedding celebration."

"A we're-staying-married party?" Belinda queried.

"Sort of," Tamara acknowledged before looking across at Pia, who'd taken the seat to Belinda's right. "Please come. You love anything having to do with weddings."

Pia sighed again. She did. And she hated to disappoint Tamara, though it wasn't wise for her to spend too much time in Hawk's company.

"How are you getting along with Hawk these days, Pia?" Tamara asked suddenly, as if reading her mind. "I know you're planning his sister's wedding. And you just noted that Mrs. Hollings is gossiping about how he helped you last night."

Pia hesitated. How much should she reveal? Certainly not the stolen kisses—and the fact that she'd enjoyed them.

He'd said he was trying to make amends. And so far, she'd let him. *More than let him.*

The kisses came back to her. The tingle of excitement, the remembered feeling of delicious passion—just like the first time, and just like in her dreams—and the sensation of melding with a kindred spirit.

Pia shook her head slightly as if to clear it. *No.*

She was playing with fire, and she'd be foolhardy to go down that road again.

And yet...

She'd felt an acute sadness for Hawk when she'd discovered what had precipitated his abrupt departure from her apartment after they'd slept together. Her parents were alive and well back in Pennsylvania, and while she didn't have any siblings, she imagined that Hawk had been understandably devastated by the unexpected loss of his brother.

None of this is intended as an excuse.

Hawk had still acted toward her as if he felt he was at fault and was feeling guilty. Of course, his brother's untimely death didn't explain why he hadn't sought her out after their night together. Had the abrupt severing of ties made it easy for him to forget her? The thought hurt. And yet what other explanation could there be? She hadn't meant enough to him.

And yet...

She knew even if she softened toward him, let their explosive chemistry play out to its natural conclusion, this time she would no longer be the naive virgin who was new in town. She could show Hawk that she could play in more sophisticated circles, too, these days.

He was flirting with her, and she could enjoy it and not become besotted.

Why couldn't she be one of those women who enjoyed a fling or a casual hookup? She'd already had a one-night stand. *With him.*

These thoughts and more flitted through her mind.

Pia became aware of Belinda and Tamara staring at her.

She cleared her throat. "Hawk has been...helpful," she hedged, and then shrugged. "I—I suppose I'm feeling ambivalent at best."

"Ambivalent?" Belinda questioned, and then rolled her eyes. "Isn't that one step away from infatuated these days? Pia, please tell me you're not falling for the guy again."

"Of course not!"

"Because you have a soft heart, and I'd hate to—"

"D-don't worry. Once burned, twice shy." She shrugged. "But I am planning his sister's wedding, and I do need to be on cordial terms with him."

"Great," Tamara commented. "I'm so glad you won't have any trouble being in Hawk's company next weekend."

Belinda frowned. "It's not Hawk I'm worried about."

Pia refused to admit that Hawk *was* the one *she* was worried about.

Hawk took another sip of his wine and his senses came fully alert.

Pia.

He spotted her immediately when she came into the parlor of the Earl and Countess of Melton's Upper East Side town house. But it was as if he'd been able to sense her presence even before seeing her.

She looked spectacular. Her high-waist sheath dress with its black bodice and white skirt flattered her curves, making her seem taller than she was and showing off her great legs in black patent peep-toe pumps.

He glimpsed the deep pink color of the nail polish on her toes, and his gut tightened.

Heaven help him, but she packed a wallop in a small package. It was almost as if she'd been sent to entice him—to test his best resolutions.

He started toward her, but was suddenly stopped by a staying hand on his arm.

He turned his head to look inquiringly at Colin, Marquess of Easterbridge.

Colin gave him a careless smile. "Careful there. Your lady-killer ways are showing."

Hawk let the side of his mouth quirk up. "The opposite is more likely the case. She looks harmless but—"

Colin laughed shortly. "They all do."

Hawk had no doubt the marquess was also referencing his own wife, Belinda Wentworth, who legally remained the Marchioness of Easterbridge. Hawk was curious about the exact state of affairs between Colin and Belinda these days, but he didn't want to pry. Colin was an enigma even to his friends at times.

"I have it covered," Hawk responded. "I'm proceeding only with the best reconnaissance."

Colin gave another knowing laugh. "I'll wager you are."

Hawk shrugged, and then started toward Pia again, leaving Colin standing where he was.

So what if the look he'd given Pia made it clear that he found her desirable, and everyone knew it?

Pia was looking at *him* expectantly right now, though there was also puzzlement in her eyes—as if she wondered about his brief exchange with Colin.

"I won't offer you a drink," he quipped as he reached her. "You look fabulous, by the way."

There was no *by the way* about it, he thought. Everything else was tangential.

Pia flushed. "Th-thank you. I wouldn't mind a glass of wine."

He snagged a couple from a waiter who happened by, and handed one to her.

"Cheers," he said as he clinked his glass to hers. "How is the wedding planning going? I understand from my sister that she's been to your apartment twice this week."

Pia took a sip of her drink. "Yes, we were discussing invitations and décor. Fortunately, she already had a dress picked out." She smiled as if sharing a joke. "Everything with this wedding is going smoothly, so far."

"I've only been to your apartment once. Can I express envy?"

Pia raised her eyebrows for a moment, and then laughed. She tapped him on the wrist. "Only if you play your cards right."

Hawk hesitated. If he'd heard her correctly, she'd just met his flirtation with a bit of her own. He was used to banter between them, but it wasn't usually so…receptive.

"How is Mr. Darcy?" he tried, testing. "Perhaps he's in need of a male role model?"

"If he is, would you be one?"

Ah. "I am more than willing to try."

Pia gave an exaggerated sigh. "Are you ever serious?"

In response, he banked his amusement.

"Would it matter if I said yes?"

Though he could lapse into well-practiced flirtation—he remembered his old self well—he felt the weight of his responsibilities too much these days to be anything other than what was expected of him. A duke.

Pia searched his eyes, and he held her amber ones solemnly.

"That comment was rather unfair of me," she said. "I've seen how you feel a responsibility to your sister as the head of the family. A-and you've certainly helped me."

"Lucy has been talking?" he queried, not answering her directly.

She nodded.

"Burnishing my image, that's my girl."

Over Pia's shoulder, Hawk glimpsed Colin approach Belinda before Pia's friend turned on her heel and stalked toward the door. Colin followed at a more leisurely pace, drink in hand.

Realizing that she no longer held his attention, Pia turned

in the direction of his gaze. "Oh, dear," she said in a low voice as she swung back to face him. "Was that a confrontation I just missed?"

Hawk looked down at her. "A near-miss. Belinda walked away before Easterbridge could approach her."

"In contrast to you and me."

He shot her a surprised look, and then gave her a game smile. "Some of us are lucky."

Pia sighed. "Easterbridge should give Belinda the annulment that she's looking for, and let her move on with her life. Instead, he seems to enjoy tormenting her."

"My friends are not unlikable, despite what you may believe."

"In a way, it's hard to believe that you and Easterbridge are friends. He can't get unmarried, while you—"

Hawk quirked a brow. "Yes?"

"—have never been married," she finished lamely.

He could tell from the look in Pia's eyes, however, that she had intended to label him a commitment-shy player. The fact that she hadn't said something, at least.

Had Lucy's words had a salutary effect on Pia's opinion of him? There was only one way to find out.

Hawk took a sip of his wine. "Let's turn back to a more soothing subject for my ego. Lucy has been singing my praises."

A small smile rose to Pia's lips, and she nodded. "Lucy mentioned that you've been working nonstop these past three years as you've moved into your role as duke, learned the running of the estates and started Sunhill Investments."

"Are you surprised?"

Pia hesitated, and then shook her head. "No. You've acted... differently than you did three years ago." She paused. "It must have been very hard for you after your father and brother died."

He didn't recollect stories about his father and his brother every day anymore—not like three years ago—but their joint passing had set his life on a new trajectory. "William and I were two years apart. We grew up as friends and playmates as well as brothers, though I always knew I got a free pass as the younger son while William had his life and responsibilities mapped out for him."

It was more personal information than he was accustomed to divulging.

Pia didn't look as if she was sitting in judgment, however. "And then one day the free pass disappeared..."

He nodded. "As fate would have it."

"You had a reputation as a player," she stated without inflection. "The stories—"

"Old news, but reports will hang around the internet forever." His mouth twisted. "I do have two jobs that often take up more time than one person can handle, believe it or not. I do need to be serious for those."

"I've hardly had an opportunity to see it," she protested.

He'd meant to tweak her nose about her earlier query about his lack of seriousness, and he could tell she understood it.

"Maybe you just bring out the devilish side of me." He tilted his head. "Perhaps with you, I can relax and tease."

She flushed. "I'm such an easy target."

"You hold your own," he offered, taken in by her blush.

She moistened her lips, and he watched longingly.

"Would you like to see a more intense and focused side of me?" he asked, suddenly going with an idea. "I'm going rock climbing at a gym in Brooklyn tomorrow. The gym keeps me in shape for the real thing."

Pia's eyes glinted. "Who ever heard of a duke rock climbing?"

He assumed a suitable hauteur. "I'm a modern-day duke. This is an outlet for all those go-forth-and-conquer genes that my ancestors bequeathed to me."

"All right."

Accepting her response, he didn't add that rock climbing was also a good pressure-release valve.

Because right now, he was feeling an ungodly urge to conquer and possess *her*.

Eight

He had his hands all over her.

At least that's how it felt to Pia.

Between teaching her how to use the equipment and instructing her on how to place her feet on the climbing wall, it felt as if Hawk had covered her body even more thoroughly this morning at the gym than he might have in bed.

Downing a flavored-water drink, her heart thumping with spent energy, and sweat soaking her sports bra and biker shorts, she eyed Hawk and tried not to think of jumping him.

She was petite and a featherweight, so she doubted that even if she launched herself at him, he'd do more than stagger a step—if that.

He looked all primal male standing in the middle of the cavernous gym in his own sweat-dampened shirt and shorts, his lean, muscular frame exposed to her avid gaze. It was a sign of how physically fit he was, however, that *he'd* only perspired a little.

Still, she could smell the sweat—and, yes, she could swear, even the male hormones on him—and her body reacted in response. She willed her nipples not to become more pronounced. With any luck, he'd think it was all due to a blast of cool air hitting her damp skin, anyway.

Finishing off a swallow of water, Hawk eyed her speculatively as he capped his bottle. "You're the first woman who has indulged my rock-climbing hobby. You're the only one who, astonishingly, agreed to come along for the ride."

"So I was hoodwinked by you?" she teased, though inside she felt a thrill at his admission.

"You did well," he said, sidestepping the question. "You made it to the top of the wall and down." His eyes gleamed with respect and admiration. "More than once, in fact. Congratulations."

"Thank you."

She didn't know why it should matter that she'd proven herself at one of Hawk's pastimes—aside from fishing and horseback riding—but it did.

Even though it was a Sunday morning, several other patrons moved around them in the open gym.

Pia realized that she was tagging along on one of Hawk's regular workouts, except it hadn't been the typical gym that they'd gone to when he'd picked her up at her apartment in his car this morning. She did not have a wedding to attend to this weekend, so she'd easily been able to rise early herself.

She capped her drink bottle. She realized that she'd slaked her thirst—for water, anyway.

"Have you ever encountered one of your namesakes on any of your rock-climbing adventures?" she asked to make conversation.

She tried to distract herself from what he looked like in his clingy gym clothes.

He looked amused. "Have I met a hawk?" He shook his head. "Only once. I don't think the bird was impressed."

She wet her lips. "Did you become known as Hawk upon assuming the title?"

He nodded. "My father was known as Hawkshire, in the customary way of addressing peers by their titles rather than their given names. It felt right to distinguish myself in some way when I assumed the title. But in the end, I didn't have a say in the matter. Easterbridge and Melton began calling me Hawk, and it caught on."

She contemplated him. "It suits you."

He rubbed the bridge of his nose, looking further amused. "You mean this?"

"How did you break your nose?" she asked, glad that he didn't look insulted.

"Ah…" He smiled, but then hesitated. "At the risk of highlighting my former raffish ways, I'll admit to getting into a barroom brawl during my university days."

"Through no fault of your own, of course."

"Naturally," he deadpanned, dimpling. "And all participants have been barred from speaking further about the matter."

"I'll bet Easterbridge or Melton would know."

Hawk laughed. "You're at liberty to attempt to unearth the information."

"Maybe I'll try," she responded lightly.

He glanced down at himself and then at her, his gaze seeming to linger on all her softest places. "In the meantime, why don't we get ourselves ready and get out of here?"

She nodded. "Okay."

"Don't you have an appointment to meet with Lucy this afternoon at the house?"

She nodded again. "Lucy's understudy is filling in for her for today's performances."

"Then why don't you come straight back with me?" he offered. "The house will be a more comfortable place for you to shower and change than the gym. We could have something to eat and kill some time before you need to take your meeting with Lucy."

Pia hesitated. Shower and change at his residence? *No, no, no.* She thought of her gym bag in her locker. In the ladies' room, she'd be safe and surrounded by other members of the female tribe—not by a descendant of conquerors.

Hawk smiled. "I promise I won't bite. There are a couple of guest bedrooms with en suite bathrooms where you'll feel comfortable. You choose."

Pia blushed because it seemed he'd read her mind.

But, then again, what could it hurt to accede to his suggestion? Lucy would most likely be at home or there soon, and then there would be the presence of the household help.

Except when they got back to Hawk's house, Pia discovered that Lucy was not home and not expected back until shortly before her afternoon appointment with Pia. The staff, typically discreet, was nowhere to be seen.

Nevertheless, she chose a guest bedroom with cheery yellow-and-blue-chintz upholstery and a white canopy bed. She showered in the adjoining marble bath, and then wrapped herself in a plush blue towel.

The house was clearly appointed with luxury throughout, she realized. Before now, she'd only been in Hawk's home to talk with Lucy, and she'd never been on the upper levels.

As she came out of the bathroom, Pia eyed the bed. It was tempting to allow herself to sink onto it and revel in its comfort. The mattress and the counterpane seemed soft and thick. In fact, the whole bedroom was decorated in a way she'd have aspired to in her apartment if she'd had the money. Instead, she'd contented herself with the budget version of many items.

Turning away from temptation, she dressed, pulling on an emerald top with a square neckline edged with red ribbon. She paired it with a full taupe skirt, wide black patent belt, black leggings and gold ballerina flats.

Today, the weather was a little cooler, the breeze having a little nip, so she'd pulled some of her fall attire from her wardrobe while packing her gym bag.

When she was done getting ready, she wandered out of the bedroom and down the hall. Stopping before the door of the bedroom that Hawk had pointed out to her as his, she hesitated just a moment before knocking.

When Hawk opened his door, however, she found herself swallowing and wetting her lips.

He wore a crisp white shirt and black pants, and his hair was still damp from his shower. He exuded a virile magnetism.

Why must he look so effortlessly but devastatingly attractive?

And then he looked at *her,* his eyes making a quick but thorough perusal.

He smiled, slow and sexy, and Pia felt her heart thump.

"A gorgeous woman knocking on my door. Under other circumstances, my next move would have been to invite you in and—" he winked "—allow my licentious nature free rein."

She heated. "I—I didn't want to wander around your house by myself, and I didn't know where we'd be having lunch." She decided to try to lighten the moment. "Heaven forbid someone spotted me and thought I was snooping."

His smile widened. "Which fairy-tale heroine goes around snooping? I can't recall."

"No one," she protested. "A-and I—I don't believe in fairy tales."

He took her hand. "Great, then we'll just have to make up our own story."

He stepped aside and tugged her into his room.

As Pia glanced around, Hawk made a sweeping motion with his arm.

"This is my bedroom." He shot her a devilish smile. "In case you were wondering what it looked like. Or should I say, in this tale, the heroine *wants to know* what it looks like."

And she wanted him to want her.

The thought flashed through her mind, and she couldn't deny its truth.

She made a visual sweep of the room. "V-very nice."

Dark, rich furniture contrasted with stripe and damask upholstery in varying shades of cream and green.

A four-poster bed was dominated by a scrolled wooden headboard.

She parted and then wet her lips.

Her eyes connected with Hawk's, and she realized that he'd caught every reaction.

She wanted to say something, and then stopped.

"I hate my speech impediment," she blurted inanely.

He gave a lopsided smile. "I love your verbal quirk." He leaned close, a twinkle in his eye. "It tells me just how much I'm affecting you."

She felt flustered because he was affecting her right now. "Mmm…y-you p-promised you wouldn't bite."

"Little Red Riding Hood and the Big, Bad Wolf?" he queried as he moved closer. "Okay, I can work with that story line."

Despite herself, she laughed. "You're incorrigible."

He reached out and caressed her arm. "I promised I wouldn't bite, but that leaves much unbargained territory."

"I am not Little Red Riding Hood."

"Of course," he agreed soothingly. "Not into role-play?"

She gave a helpless laugh.

He ducked his head and brushed his lips across hers.

He made to pull back almost immediately, but then his lips lowered to hers again—as if Hawk couldn't help himself—and this time the kiss lingered.

Hawk's arms came around her, and she slid her own up to his neck. They pressed close, hard planes meeting soft curves and fitting together without gap, despite their difference in height.

He tasted minty and fresh, and as his tongue invaded her mouth, she made a sound deep in her throat and met him eagerly.

The kiss was intense, but finally slowed.

"Pia," Hawk muttered against her mouth. "It's been too long. How could I ever forget?"

She didn't want him ever to forget. She wanted him to remember her in the way he'd similarly always be with her.

She'd always remember him. *Her first lover.*

Suddenly Hawk bent and hooked his arm under her knees, and laid her on the bed. He came down beside her and took her in his arms again.

"Pia." He brushed the hair away from her face. "You remind me of a nymph or a fairy."

"I suppose it doesn't help that I'm wearing ballerina flats today."

He gave a short laugh. "Even when you're not in flats, you're petite." He brushed her hair so that it fanned out over the coverlet. "I've never seen a wood nymph climb a rock wall before."

She wrinkled her nose at his words as his delicious weight pressed her into the mattress. "I can just imagine what I looked like from the ground."

"I had trouble stopping myself from reaching out and doing this," he said, caressing her leg.

"Oh."

Hawk shifted, his knee wedging between her legs as he leaned over her. He kissed her then, sipping at her lips and lazily tracing their outline with his tongue.

"L-lucy will come home," Pia breathed against his mouth.

"Not for a long time," he whispered back.

Pia felt his arousal press against her, evidence of his growing need. Mirroring his response, her nipples felt tight, and a moist heat had gathered between her thighs.

She shifted. "Why did I bother getting dressed?"

Her remark elicited a low chuckle from him, and she felt it reverberate through his chest.

He placed a moist kiss near her ear. "Don't worry. We can remedy the situation."

True to his word, he made quick work of her shoes and leggings, and then settled himself between her legs.

She felt his warm breath on her thigh, and her delicate skin was stroked by the slight abrasiveness of his jaw.

He squeezed her calf as his lips grazed her thigh. He let his lips trail down first one leg and then the other.

Pia quivered in response.

In the next moment, she moaned as he sucked on her tender flesh. She couldn't help herself, but it seemed to excite him to hear how he was making her feel.

Her hands tangled in his hair, and she urged him upward for an urgent kiss. She met him halfway, sitting up, and they kissed, his hands wandering her back urgently.

She was crazy to think she could be unforgettable to a man of his experience. She was loony to think she could match his level of sophistication in seduction.

But then he obliged her with a groan deep in his throat. "Ah, Pia...what you do to me."

She rubbed his arousal. "I can tell."

He grew in a sharp breath. "You're not as shy as I remembered."

She hoped not.

Since he'd left her, she'd made a point of studying romantic movies, reading a book or two and renting some videos—all in an attempt to overcome some of her naiveté and inexperience. She'd thought she'd never have fallen for Hawk's practiced skills if she'd been more knowledgeable. And at the same time, irrationally, she'd started to believe that Hawk wouldn't have left her if she'd been more of a seductress.

Still, she didn't think now was the time to mention to him that she'd been educating herself.

Instead, she tilted her head, and asked innocently, "You don't want me to be...uninhibited?"

"Of course I'd love it."

She gave him a smile.

"How am I going to get you out of these clothes?" he mused, his eyes sweeping over her.

She straightened, and then slid off the bed and turned to face him. "You won't have to. I-I'm going to strip for you."

He smiled, slow and sexy, doing funny things to her insides.

The room was cool and shadowed, the shades apparently still drawn from when he was dressing and undressing.

Pia pulled her top over her head and tossed it on a dresser.

Catching Hawk's hot gaze, she teased him by tracing the edges of her lacy pink bra with her fingertips.

Hawk continued avidly watching her with hooded eyes.

Pia wet her lips, running the tip of her tongue over the plump and swollen formation of her mouth.

She still felt the imprint of Hawk's kisses there. And judging from the look of him, Hawk was on a tight leash, stopping himself from giving her more and then some.

"This is going to be the shortest strip on record," he murmured thickly. "Need some help there?"

She knew her nipples were outlined against the nylon fabric of her bra, the coolness of the room adding to her arousal. Her breasts were a bit oversized for her frame, giving her the appearance of a busty fairy. However, since high school, she hadn't caught a guy eyeing them as lustily as Hawk was.

She shivered, and Hawk crooked his finger at her.

Her stomach did a somersault.

She came to him, and he caught her, leaning back to lie down on the bed as she straddled him.

Mouth met mouth in a voracious kiss. Then he was feasting

on her breasts, and she threw back her head and luxuriated in the sensation.

"Hawk."

He unclasped her bra and peeled away the offending barrier, his mouth barely leaving her in the process. He suckled her, his hands bunching her breasts together for his greedy lips.

Pia felt sweet and piercing-hot sensations shoot through her. In response, she rubbed against him.

Hawk lifted his mouth from her breast and sat up so they were face-to-face. "If we don't slow down," he muttered thickly, his mouth close to hers, "this is going to be over in two minutes."

"Th-three y-years is a long time to wait."

"Too long."

With one hand, she opened the first button of his shirt, and then the next and the next. All the while, she was aware of the rasp of his breath as her gaze focused on the strong column of his throat.

She finally undid his cuffs and tugged at his shirt.

He obliged her by sitting up and shrugging out of his white shirt and the undershirt below.

He quirked his lips. "Now what?"

"D-do you have a blindfold for yourself?"

He laughed helplessly.

"You're only half-naked," she protested.

"It's a situation I'm more than happy to rectify."

She moved aside, and he got off the bed.

But before he could make a further move, she stopped him, laying a hand on his arm.

"Let me."

Getting up herself, she worked slowly but surely, her hands brushing his arousal and causing his breathing to deepen.

She slid his belt free of its loops and then lowered his zipper.

He helped her then, and the room sounded with the thud of his shoes and the slither of his pants and boxers.

Pia caressed his arousal freely before bending and kneeling before him.

Hawk groaned. "Pia, Pia...ah, sweet."

Pia was lost in the experience of making love in a way she never had before. She felt the tension in Hawk's muscles and the throbbing heat of his flesh. And when she gave him the most intimate kiss she could imagine, he stiffened and groaned again, gripping the bedside table.

"Pia," Hawk said, his voice heavy and thick with arousal. "You've definitely...changed."

She'd had time over the past three years to replay the night she'd lost her innocence to Hawk. She'd had time to imagine different scenarios. She'd had time to see herself as the seductress instead of the one being seduced.

And now, unexpectedly, she had a chance to realize some of those fantasies. *With him.* Because he'd always been the lover whom she'd imagined.

She focused on giving pleasure and soaking in the sounds of how much Hawk was enjoying her ministrations.

She wanted to make him lose control.

Moments ticked by, and then, on an oath, Hawk disengaged her, pulling her up for a rough kiss.

"I'm not going to ask where you learned that," he said darkly.

If only he knew, Pia thought.

She thrilled at the tacit admission that she'd given him unexpected pleasure. She warmed to the tinge of jealousy in his voice.

"T-take me," she said, her request a plea and a demand. "H-Hawk, p-please."

He swept her up into his arms and laid her on the bed again. He rid her of her belted skirt, her last piece of clothing and of protection from his avid gaze.

He leaned over her and caressed her body. "You're so beautiful, you make me ache."

Pia felt her heart squeeze.

"Are you using any protection?" he asked.

She shook her head. "No."

He opened a nearby nightstand drawer and removed a packet.

"I don't think I can be near you without being prepared," he said with self-deprecation.

She gave a small smile. "S-sort of like leaving the house without your BlackBerry?"

He chuckled. "Sort of. But you make me lose my mind, whether I like it or not."

He sheathed himself, and Pia reached her arms up to him.

She wanted him to lose control right now. The need to be joined to him was overwhelming. She wanted to experience falling over the edge again with him into paradise. It had been so long…

Hawk settled his weight on her. "Ah, Pia, let me in…"

He entered her, and they both closed their eyes, savoring the sweet sensation of their joining.

Hawk started to move, and a delicious friction began to build in Pia.

They kissed and moaned, and he bit down gently on the tender skin at the side of her throat, while she let her hands roam over his hard muscles, urging him onward.

Pia convulsed gently, once and then twice.

"That's right," Hawk muttered. "Come for me, Pia. Come again."

He whispered sweet encouragement.

Pia felt herself tremble, her body on the cusp of deliverance. She tightened around Hawk, and her hands fell from his back to grasp the coverlet.

He was relentless in pursuit of her pleasure. "Pia," he breathed in her ear. "Sweetheart, tell me."

"H-Hawk, p-please, y-yes."

The sound of how much he affected her was his undoing.

Hawk groaned and stilled just as her body began to shake. He spilled himself inside her, wondrously joining her powerful climax with one of his own.

Pia cried out with her release, and Hawk clasped her to him, his skin hot and damp.

Their hearts racing, they came back down to earth—or some version of it.

This, she thought, was what dreams were made of.

Nine

In the normal course of things, lunch with Colin, Marquess of Easterbridge, and Sawyer Langsford, Earl of Melton, in the dining room of the historic Sherry-Netherland Hotel should have been a tame and relaxing affair.

Hawk knew better.

Lately, notoriety had come nipping at the heels of his trio of friends.

Colin looked up quizzically from his BlackBerry. "Well, Melton, it seems Mrs. Hollings has done it again."

Sawyer nodded at a waiter who then proceeded to fill his wineglass, and took his time addressing Colin. "What, pray tell, has she deemed worthy of acid ink this time?"

"The topic is us...again," Colin said, his tone bland. "Or, more exactly, the subject is Hawkshire."

"How very fair of you, Melton," Hawk commented dryly, "to include us in the *Intelligencer's* gossip column."

Sawyer's lips quirked. "So what does our Mrs. Hollings have to say today?"

"Apparently Hawkshire has a second career as a wedding planner's apprentice."

Sawyer raised his eyebrows and swiveled his head to look at Hawk, his expression droll. "And you kept this tidbit from us? How could you?"

Damnation. Hawk knew he was in for a ribbing from his two friends. Still, it was worth mounting a defense, however feeble. "My sister is getting married."

"'We've heard,'" Colin said, quoting the text from his BlackBerry, "'that a certain very wealthy duke has been keeping company with a lovely wedding planner. Could it be that wedding bells are in the air?'"

"Charming, our Mrs. Hollings," Sawyer said.

"A veritable fount of useful information."

Hawk remained steadfastly mum, refusing to add his two cents to his friends' comments.

Sawyer frowned. "How is your mother these days, Hawk? The last time I had the opportunity to be in her charming company, she talked of finding you a bride. In fact, I believe one name in particular crossed her lips."

"Michelene Ward-Fombley," Hawk said succinctly.

Sawyer nodded. "Ah, yes, that sounds—" he paused to give Hawk a shrewd look "—exactly right... A suitable choice."

Of course, Sawyer and Colin would have a passing acquaintance with Michelene, Hawk thought. She was from their aristocratic social circle. Her grandfather was a viscount, not someone from a small town in Pennsylvania...

He and Michelene had dated a few times, back when he was still trying to sort out what his role as the new duke should be. He'd gingerly tested the waters by stepping into William's shoes with one of the leading candidates to be a future duchess. But then his work with Sunhill Investments had consumed him, and still grieving, he'd allowed himself to stop calling Michelene. It had been easy to do, since she hadn't awakened any strong emotion in him. But then, in the past year, the idea of Michelene as the Duchess of Hawkshire had gained renewed life, thanks to his mother's prodding.

"What game are you playing, Hawk?" Sawyer asked, going straight to the point.

Hawk kept his expression steady. Ever since Sawyer's marriage of convenience to Tamara had turned into a real one, he'd been protective of her and her girlfriends, Pia and Belinda.

Pia.

Damn it, he was not going to discuss Pia with Melton or Easterbridge.

Yesterday had been the most passionate experience of his life—for the second time. Inexplicably, he felt a visceral connection to Pia. Maybe that explained why he'd never forgotten her...

She'd been a virgin, but if last night was anything to judge by, she'd learned a lot in the past three years.

He acknowledged as much with a punch to the gut. He'd been unprepared for the Pia of yesterday afternoon. She'd caught him by surprise—again. He'd intended to be the seducer, and instead had been seduced.

Yet...had he really intended to seduce her again? Despite all his noble intentions?

Certainly, by the time she'd entered his bedroom, his mind had turned toward kissing her and more. But the idea had been gaining steam well before then. Without a doubt, while she'd been giving him a tantalizing view of her luscious posterior all morning. And maybe even before then...when she'd been running across the grass toward him at the New York Botanical Garden, or when...

He wanted her. All he'd been able to think about for the past twenty-four hours was getting Pia in bed again. And now that they'd crossed the threshold to being lovers again, he admitted he also didn't want to turn back. He wanted to remain lovers—unlike the first time three years ago—even if his relatively newfound principles were in jeopardy as a result!

They'd been forced to end their afternoon tryst yesterday when Lucy had arrived home. Otherwise, Hawk was sure that he and Pia would have spent all day in bed.

Instead, Pia had descended the stairs as if nothing untoward had happened—such as Lucy's wedding planner having completely undone her brother—and had met with Lucy as if she'd arrived at the house only a little early and had been awaiting her.

Why was it so upsetting that their lovemaking left her so unaffected? He couldn't fall into a too serious entanglement with her—not with all his responsibilities to his title.

Hawk noted belatedly that Sawyer was waiting for an answer, and even Colin looked intent.

"There's no game," he said, choosing his words with care.

Blast it, even *he* didn't know what to make of his relationship with Pia. Not anymore. He had no compass.

Sawyer looked dubious. "Then you're not practically eng—"

"There is no game," he repeated.

Sawyer eyed him, his expression thoughtful. "You might want to make sure Pia doesn't get hurt, either."

Right. If anything, Hawk thought, *he* was the one in danger here.

Pia felt a quiver of anticipation when her doorman rang and announced that Hawk was downstairs.

"Tell him to come up," she said before replacing her receiver and turning away from the phone.

She hugged herself and glanced at Mr. Darcy, who was eyeing her like a friend resigned to watching her make the same mistake twice.

She could sense the feline's disapproval—almost read his thoughts, if that were possible.

Wickham. Him again. Have we learned nothing?

"Oh, don't look at me that way," Pia said. "His name is not Wickham, as you well know. And I'm sure he has a very good reason for being here."

Right. And a cat has nine lives. I wish.

"You're way too cynical for a feline. Why did I adopt you from the shelter?"

You know why. I'm the antidote to your trusting romantic nature.

I'm not as naive as I once was, Pia responded in her head.

Mr. Darcy turned and padded toward his basket, set against one wall of her living room space. He stepped in, made himself comfortable and closed his eyes.

Pia stood there and then blushed as she remembered her afternoon idyll with Hawk on Sunday.

It was shocking how easily she lost her inhibitions with him. She'd forgotten herself in the moment. But he'd seemed equally affected.

At least she hoped so.

She still couldn't quite believe her daring—or foolhardiness—in trying to play in Hawk's league of seduction. She'd met him and upped the ante. And though she hadn't been able to admit it to herself, perhaps she'd set out to prove that she could bind him, unlike their first time.

Careful, careful. She couldn't and wouldn't risk her heart again. She was beyond being the naive virgin who believed in fairy tales. Instead, she'd take what she wanted from Hawk for her pleasure and be prepared to say goodbye with no regrets when the time came.

She looked at the clock. It was just after five. He must have come directly uptown to see her after the close of the New York financial markets.

She hadn't seen him since they'd wound up in bed together, but that was about to change.

Hawk stepped out of the elevator and immediately spotted Pia at her door—waiting for him.

"H-Hawk," Pia said, her voice a touch breathless.

She was dressed in a casual, cinched blue dress, her hair loose and with just a touch of shine to her lips.

She looked good enough to eat.

Without hesitation, he strode to her, wrapped his arms around her and gave her a bone-melting kiss.

When he finally lifted his head, he searched her gaze. "Blast it, I get so aroused when I hear you stutter."

She blushed. "I don't know why. Th-that has to be one of the most unusual compliments a woman has ever received."

He kissed her nose. "Do you know it's the most erotic thing in bed when your adorable speech tick is on full display?"

"How embarrassing."

"How perfect."

"*Oh.*"

Over Pia's shoulder, Hawk noticed Mr. Darcy lift his head from his cushioned basket and eye him.

Hawk got the sense that the pet's opinion of him had soured since the first time he'd been in Pia's apartment. Perhaps the cat had figured out who he was: The Duke Formerly Known as Mr. Wickham. Or rather, Mr. Fielding—wicked and wrong—as the case might be.

He held the feline's stare, giving the cat a stern but reassuring look, until Mr. Darcy lowered his head, closed his eyes and went back to his nap.

"Is something wrong?" Pia asked, stepping back and letting him into the apartment.

He followed her in and waited while she shut the door behind him.

Then he slid an arm around her waist and pulled her close. "Nothing is wrong except that since Sunday I've been desperate to see you."

He'd left work early to come here, hoping his appearance would be a welcome surprise. And judging from Pia's reaction, he'd bet right.

Pia slid her arms around his neck. "Oh?"

"I had a storm of work this week, and by the time I flew back from Chicago last night, I knew phone calls were no longer enough to sustain me."

"Mmm—really?"

He nuzzled her ear. "Nothing but your presence would do."

"You know, Your Grace," she responded playfully, "this is rather irregular. A client could arrive at any moment, or the phone could ring. We're on work hours."

He lifted his head to look into her eyes. "Are you expecting anyone this late in the day?"

"No," she admitted.

"Then there's no problem, as far as I see."

"There *is* a problem," she teased. "This has all the trappings of the lord of the manor cornering the backstairs maid."

"Because you're on my payroll?" he murmured, grazing her temple with his lips.

She nodded. "Exactly right. W-we had sexual relations in your bedroom right before I was to meet with your sister about wedding plans."

He almost laughed at her mock prudish tone even as *every* part of him was coming to stimulating arousal. He was finding this interchange with Pia more erotic than any of the more blatant attempts at seduction he'd been the recipient of in the past. It appeared that, after all, Pia might be skilled at role-play…

"Perhaps I should ask directly," he said, playing along. "Will you nevertheless oblige me?"

Pia tilted her head, pretending to consider. "Mmm…"

Not waiting for a response, he stroked her leg, and then let his hand wander under the hem of her dress until it connected with her hip. Sliding her panties to one side, he caressed her intimately.

He watched as her eyes clouded with desire.

"I want to know every inch of you," he murmured. "I want to taste your flavor and learn your scent."

Pia's eyelids drooped, and she gripped his arm hard.

"Pia?" he murmured when she still hadn't said anything.

He scanned her face and watched her eyelashes flutter against her pale skin.

She wet her lips. "Oh, y-yes. I-I'll oblige you."

They were both so turned on, they could hardly speak.

"This is the most erotic exchange I've ever had," she said as if she'd read his mind.

He had to have her. He kissed her, and then, removing his hand from under her dress, he wrapped his arms around her and lifted her off her feet.

He headed with her toward the bedroom.

"Are we destined to make love in the afternoon?" she asked.

He glanced down at her, a smile hovering at his lips. "Anytime becomes you, princess."

He stepped into her bedroom and deposited her on the bed, on top of her feminine white coverlet.

Straightening, he took a moment to let his eyes travel over her.

She looked up at him with desire. Her golden hair was spread out over the cover, and her lips were pink and wet from his kisses.

She was beautiful.

Pia parted her lips. "Oh, H-Hawk."

He closed his eyes and drew in a deep breath.

When he opened them again, he said with helpless amusement, "Don't say another word. I may go up in flames."

He pulled off her shoes, raised the skirt of her dress and pulled down her panties.

Bending toward her again, he slid his hands up under her thighs to cup her buttocks and pull her toward him.

She was open for him as he leaned in and kissed first one inner thigh and then the other.

Pia quivered and then tensed as he finally laid his mouth against her. Moving at a leisurely pace, he darted and licked with his tongue, and in no time, the room was filled with the sounds of Pia's gasps and moans.

"H-H-Hawk...o-oh!"

Pia tensed and let out a long moan, coming for him.

Only then did Hawk raise his head. She was so unbelievably responsive, he was fighting for control.

Holding her gaze, he undid his shirt and opened his pants, bothering to take off only his shoes. He removed protection from his pocket, sheathed himself and then leaned over her.

It didn't get any more passionate than this, Hawk thought. Lovemaking immediately after work, and they were so randy, they couldn't be bothered to eliminate more than the minimum of clothing.

He couldn't remember being this turned on since he'd been a teenager just discovering sex.

For her part, it was clear that Pia could hardly wait. She slid her hands up his arms in a light caress and arched her body toward him.

They both sighed as he slid inside her.

Hawk fought for control as he felt it slipping. Pia was still as tight as the time he'd taken her virginity.

He could, Hawk thought, lose himself in her again and again.

And in the next moment, he did.

He slid in and out of her, bringing them both mindless pleasure. Coherent thought shut down, and his focus narrowed down to one goal.

He felt Pia gasp and spasm around him with a small climax.

"That's right," he urged hoarsely.

"Hawk, oh, p-please…"

She didn't have to beg. The moment she spoke, a mighty climax shook him. And, dimly but with satisfaction, he was aware of Pia claiming her own peak once again.

With a hoarse groan, he thrust into her one final time, and then slumped against her.

Afterward, they lay on her bed, spent and relaxed. As Pia lay tucked against his side, he caressed her arm.

Since she appeared completely content, he decided to press his advantage.

"Come fishing and riding with me," he said without preamble.

Pia stilled and then stifled a sudden laugh. "You do know how to approach a woman at the right moment." She paused. "Isn't that what we just did?"

He shook his head and responded drolly, "Not that kind."

"Oh?"

"Come fishing and riding with me at Silderly Park in Oxford," he said, naming his ancestral estate in England.

Pia tilted her head to glance up at him.

He knew what he was asking. This had nothing to do with Lucy's wedding anymore. By visiting Silderly Park, Pia would be coming into the heart of who he was as a duke.

He'd made the request unexpectedly, and only belatedly realized how much her answer mattered.

"Yes."

Her answer came out as a breathy whisper before she lowered her head back down to his shoulder.

He smiled slowly, relaxing. "Good."

Pia was his, and he was going to make sure things remained so.

Ten

"The wedding invitations will go out next week," Pia remarked, her comment meant to reassure in case it was necessary.

It was Monday afternoon, and she and Lucy were sitting in the parlor of Hawk's Upper East Side town house. They were meeting over afternoon tea to discuss wedding details.

Most professional shows did not have performances on Monday nights, explaining why it was possible for Lucy to meet with Pia over tea today. Any other day of the week, Lucy might already have been preparing to head to work at this hour.

"Splendid," Lucy said, smoothing her blond hair. "Derek will be happy to know that detail has been taken care of."

It had been a pleasure to work with Hawk's sister, Pia reflected, trying not to dwell on when Hawk might be arriving home.

Lucy and Derek had wanted a relatively simple wedding

ceremony and reception, but one that nevertheless incorporated some nods to Lucy's English ancestry and theater work.

Everything so far had gone smoothly. During previous consultations, the couple had settled on a photographer, band and florist with a minimum of fuss. And today she and Lucy had already discussed wedding music, readings and various ceremony logistics.

"Now the florist has a website," Pia continued, "which you should consult, but in order to give you more ideas, I have my own book of photos from weddings that I've been involved with."

She slid a scrapbook across the coffee table toward Lucy, and Hawk's sister leaned forward and reached for it.

"I'll leave it with you so you can take your time going through it," she added as Lucy opened the book. "You'll see that some brides like more elaborate floral arrangements, and others prefer a simpler concept. Next time we talk, let's discuss what you're looking for before we meet with the florist."

Lucy nodded as she flipped through the scrapbook. "This is helpful." She looked up. "You're so organized, Pia."

"Thank you."

Pia smiled to herself because wedding planners received few acknowledgments of their work. Many brides were too consumed by preparations for their big event to thank the paid help, at least until the wedding was over.

"The other item on our agenda that you should be thinking about now," Pia went on crisply, "is the music that you'd like to be played at the reception."

"Definitely Broadway show tunes," Lucy said with a laugh. "Can I enter on the theme song from *Phantom of the Opera?*"

"You can do whatever you like," Pia responded before a thought intruded that she decided to query about delicately. "Has your mother voiced any opinions?"

In her experience, weddings were fraught with family

negotiations, and often no one had more of an opinion than the mother of the bride. Pia had been called on to referee in more than one instance.

Lucy sighed at Pia's words and sat back, letting the book of photographs fall closed. "Mother means well, but she can be a bit of a dragon, unfortunately."

Pia raised her eyebrows.

"But Hawk doesn't let her have complete free rein." Lucy grinned suddenly. "Of course, it helps that the wedding is happening in New York, thousands of miles from Silderly Park and Mother's back lawn."

In the past, Pia had studiously avoided probing Lucy for more information than she volunteered about her brother. But Lucy had just reminded her of who Pia's de facto employer was, and, as the current duke and head of the family, Hawk undoubtedly had some say in keeping his mother from overriding Lucy's wishes.

In any case, it was a revealing remark on Lucy's part about Carsdale family dynamics.

"Well, it was a deft maneuver to have the wedding here," Pia conceded, "if your intention was to keep interference at a minimum."

Lucy looked sly. "Thank you. It was Derek's idea."

"Ah, right." Pia's lips curved. "He also had the idea of a New Year's wedding, didn't he?"

"Brilliant, isn't it?"

"It's certainly an unorthodox choice."

"I know." Lucy laughed. "I'm sure Mother went absolutely wild. I can picture her pruning her garden with a vengeance after she found out."

A picture popped into Pia's head from Lucy's description, though she'd never met Hawk's mother. She fought an involuntary smile.

"You do have a flair for the dramatic visual, Lucy," she teased. "Anyone would think you should be on the stage."

Lucy gave another laugh. "My first act of rebellion."

"Your family objected?" Pia asked, curiosity getting the better of her.

Lucy's eyes twinkled. "Of course! Mother is well aware that the only actresses in the family tree were all born on the wrong side of the blanket."

Pia was tempted to ask flippantly whether any Carsdale ancestor had kept a wedding planner as a mistress, but she clamped her mouth shut. She wondered, though, how much Lucy knew or suspected about her relationship with Hawk, and what the other woman would say if she knew she was talking to a current lover of the present Duke of Hawkshire.

"Hawk was supportive of me, however," Lucy went on, seemingly oblivious to Pia's reticence. "He's the reason I'm in New York, frankly."

Pia gave a small smile. Lucy clearly thought the world of her brother.

"Speaking of Hawk," Lucy said, "he mentioned you'll be in Oxford and visiting Silderly Park."

Pia hesitated. Just what had Hawk said to Lucy? Did Lucy believe she simply had an incidental interest in touring Silderly Park while she was visiting England, if only because she was planning the wedding of the Duke of Hawkshire's sister?

She had been careful not to discuss Hawk with Lucy because, at first, she hadn't trusted herself to be less than withering in her opinion. And afterward, well, it had become problematic to speak about Hawk...

And, of course, now... Pia heated to think of all the things she *couldn't* bring up with Lucy about how she and Hawk passed the time.

She bit her lip. "Yes, I'm, um, planning to stay at Silderly Park for a few days to fish and ride."

As the words left her mouth, Pia felt a flush crawl up her neck. Drat—would she ever be able to talk about fishing or riding again without blushing?

"Please say you'll stay in Oxford until the first of December then," Lucy pleaded. "It would be so wonderful if you could attend the small engagement party that my mother insisted on hosting at Silderly Park."

"I—"

Pia had never been invited as a guest to a client's wedding function.

"In fact, it would be so nice to have you there."

Pia searched the younger woman's expression, but all she saw there was pure, unguarded appeal.

"I—" Pia cleared her throat and gave a helpless smile. "Okay."

Lucy returned her smile with a grateful one of her own.

Pia wondered whether all the Carsdales were so adamantly persuasive.

Lucy either had no clue about the current state of affairs between her brother and her wedding planner, or, well, she was a very good actress.

In her gossip column, Mrs. Hollings had twice referenced her and Hawk—once right after Belinda's almost-wedding, and more recently, when she'd hinted at a warming of their relationship after Hawk had unexpectedly played her assistant. But Mrs. Hollings had stopped short of naming them as lovers.

And, what's more, Pia wasn't sure if Lucy even paid attention to Mrs. Hollings's column. True, the column included a fair amount of society gossip, but Lucy was immersed in the theater world rather than in the social whirl, and Mrs. Hollings's column focused on New York rather than Britain.

Pia pushed those thoughts aside. "Thank you for the invitation."

Lucy laughed. "Don't be silly. I should be thanking you because you'll be putting up with my mother and my brother."

Ah, yes. *Hawk*.

If Lucy only knew, Pia thought.

Even though her acquaintance with Hawk three years ago had been fleeting—a one-night stand, if she looked at the matter unflinchingly—Pia recognized that he'd changed a lot. He was shouldering a lot more responsibility, and could claim a lot of success through his own hard work. He was also considerate. Look at how he'd tried to help her with her business—insisting on making amends. And she had intimate knowledge that he was a terrific lover.

Still, she couldn't help wondering how Hawk viewed their current sexual interlude. They'd never attempted to attach labels to it. Whatever was the case, though, she insisted to herself, this time she would no longer be the naive and vulnerable young thing.

Lucy regarded her closely. "If you don't mind my saying so, I couldn't help noticing that you and my brother had a testy interaction when you arrived here for our first meeting."

Pia schooled her surprise—Hawk's sister had never brought up that first meeting in prior conversations.

Still, she couldn't deny the truth.

"We did," Pia confessed. "I…didn't form a good opinion of him when I first met him a few years ago."

Now that was a lie. She'd been so taken with him, she'd fallen into bed. It was after their romantic interlude had ended that her opinion of him had soured.

Lucy gave her a small smile. "I can understand why you might not have. I know my brother had his party years, though he never shared the details with me because I was so much younger." She paused, looking at Pia more closely. "But that phase of his life all came to end three years ago."

"Hawk told me," Pia said with sympathy.

Still, Pia got the distinct impression that Lucy meant more than she was saying. Was she trying to persuade Pia that Hawk wasn't so terrible anymore? And if so, why? Because she cared what her wedding planner thought of her brother?

Again, Pia wondered how much Lucy suspected, and what she would say if she knew Pia and Hawk knew each other intimately these days.

Lucy sighed. "I guess there's no going back, is there?" she asked rhetorically. "In any case, Hawk has taken over as head of the family remarkably well. And Sunhill Investments has reversed the state of the ducal finances in just a couple of years—it's remarkable."

Pia fixed a smile. She was reminded of how Hawk had spent his time while he was apparently forgetting her, and an element of doubt intruded again. She was crazy to think she could somehow become remarkable herself—let alone unforgettable—to a man like him. He was a duke and a multimultimillionaire. She was a wedding planner from Pennsylvania.

She pushed back the heart-in-the-throat feeling and convinced herself again that she was prepared for the eventual end of their fling.

Lucy reached out a hand and touched her on the arm. "All I'm saying, Pia, is that Hawk isn't the person that he was even three years ago. You should give him a chance."

Pia wondered what kind of chance Lucy thought she should be giving Hawk. Was she suggesting that Pia should like him enough to interact nicely with him…or more?

Pia opened and closed her mouth.

"All is forgiven," she said finally for Lucy's benefit. "You needn't worry that Hawk and I are unable to get along."

In fact, lately, they'd gotten along so well, they'd gotten into bed together.

"Good," Lucy said with a smile, seemingly accepting her vague answer. "Because I know he likes you. He sang your praises when he suggested you to me as a wedding coordinator."

Pia smiled uncertainly.

She wasn't sure upon what basis Hawk's sister was resting the observation that Hawk *liked* her, but she felt a flutter of happiness at the thought.

Her reaction was both wonderful *and* a cause for concern…

Pia walked beside Hawk in his impressive landscaped gardens.

Since arriving at Hawk's family estate near Oxford two days ago, she and Hawk had gone fishing and riding on his estate, as promised. She'd also been busy working long distance and taking in the many, many rooms that comprised Silderly Park.

She'd tried not to be overwhelmed by the medieval manor house itself. On a previous trip to Britain, she had toured nearby Blenheim Palace, the Duke of Marlborough's family seat. And she could say without a doubt that though Silderly Park didn't carry the identifier in its name, it was no less a palace.

Pia glanced momentarily at the windowed stories of Silderly Park as she and Hawk strolled along and he pointed out various plantings to her. They were both dressed in jackets for the nippy but nevertheless unseasonably warm November weather.

Hawk's principal residence had two wings, and its medieval core had been updated and added to over the centuries. The manor house boasted beautiful painted plaster ceilings, two rooms with magnificent oak paneling and a great hall that could seat 200 or 300 guests. The reception rooms displayed an impressive collection of eighteenth- and nineteenth-century artwork, from various artists, including Gainsborough and Sir Joshua Reynolds.

Even though the income was no longer necessary to him, Hawk had kept Silderly Park open to the public, so that the formal reception rooms could be visited by tourists.

Still, Pia couldn't help feeling as if *she* didn't belong here. Unlike Belinda and Tamara, she hadn't been born to wealth and social position. Maybe if she had, she would have recognized Hawk as more than a plain Mr. James Fielding on the first occasion she'd met him.

"The gardens were created in the late eighteenth century," Hawk said, calling her back from her thoughts. "We use at least five or six different types of rose plantings in the section we're in now."

Pia clasped her hands together in front of her. "This would be a wonderful place to consult for roses to use in weddings. Every bride is looking for something different and unique."

"If you're interested, the gardener could tell you more," Hawk said, sending her a sidelong look. "Or you could come back in the Spring."

Pia felt a shiver of awareness chase down her spine. Was Hawk thinking their relationship would continue at least until Spring—well past Lucy's wedding?

"Perhaps," she forced herself to equivocate, careful not to look at him. "Spring is my busy season for weddings, as you can well imagine."

"Of course, only if you can fit me into your schedule," Hawk teased.

She chanced a glance at him. He looked every inch the lord of the manor in a tweed jacket and wool trousers.

"I'm becoming quite busy these days thanks to you, as you well know," she returned lightly. "I received a call just before we left New York from another friend of yours seeking a wedding coordinator."

Hawk smiled. "I'm hurrying them all to the altar for your sake."

"I'm surprised that you didn't spring for the ring and stage the proposal in this case."

"If I could have, I would have," he said with mock solemnity, "but my expertise lies in locating wedding veils and saving flower bouquets from canine bridal attendants."

Pia laughed, even as she silently acknowledged all of Hawk's help.

With the exception of Tamara's, the weddings that she'd coordinated this past summer had been ones that she'd been contracted for before the Marquess of Easterbridge had crashed Belinda's ill-fated ceremony. Since then, new business had come to her thanks mainly to Hawk.

She had a lot to thank him for, including arranging and paying for both their first-class tickets on a commercial flight from New York to London—though she knew in reality *that* had nothing to do with Lucy's wedding.

She and Hawk came to a stop near some elaborately shaped hedges, and he turned to face her.

He reached out and caressed the line of her jaw, a smile touching his lips.

Pia's senses awakened at his touch, even as time slowed and space narrowed, and her brain turned sluggish.

"D-don't tell me," Pia said, her voice slightly breathless, "that romantic assignations in the gardens are de rigueur."

"If only it wasn't November," he murmured, his eyes crinkling. "Fortunately, there's a bed nearby."

Pia heated as Hawk ducked his head and touched his lips to hers.

She knew the bed to which he was referring. She'd slept in it last night.

Hawk's bedchamber at Silderly Park was in an enormous suite, bigger than her apartment in New York. The suite was fronted by a sitting room, and the bedroom itself boasted a large four-poster bed, red-and-white wallpaper, and gold leaf detail on the molded ceiling.

Everything was fit for a duke.

Everything in Hawk's house, in fact, was out of a fairy tale. Including its owner, Pia thought whimsically.

It was easy to be enthralled, especially for a romantic such as herself…and Pia reminded herself again to keep her feet planted on the ground.

Hawk linked his hand with hers, and Pia allowed him to turn them back in the direction of the house.

Though it was a good fifteen minutes before they arrived at his suite, they snuggled and exchanged the occasional kiss along the way, heedless of whom they might encounter.

In his bedroom, Hawk looked into her eyes as he undressed her, slowly and tenderly, bringing tears to Pia's eyes.

They made love languorously, as if they had not a care in the world, but all the time.

Afterward, Pia lay in Hawk's arms, and sighed with contentment.

"We really have to stop doing this," she remarked.

"What?" Hawk glanced down at her. "Making love in the afternoon?"

"Yes, it's decadent."

"It's the only indulgence I'm allowed these days," Hawk protested. "And my BlackBerry is beeping nearby."

Pia lifted her head and smiled at him. "I'm not used to it."

He raised an eyebrow. "This is beyond your realm of expertise?"

"Oh, Hawk, haven't you guessed?" she asked tentatively.

He stilled, searching her gaze.

"You're my first and only lover." She paused, and then added, "Th-there hasn't been anyone else in the past three years."

Hawk's brows drew together in puzzlement. "You're a desirable woman—"

Pia gave a small, self-conscious laugh, her heart bursting. "I-it wasn't for lack of opportunity, b-but by choice."

Hawk shifted so he was looking down at her as she lay

back. "I don't understand. You've taken the initiative...unlike what I remembered."

"Books and videos," she answered succinctly. "I wanted to educate myself."

So I'd never run the risk of losing you again to lack of experience.

Hawk said nothing for a moment, and Pia gave him a tentative smile.

Hawk's expression softened. "Ah, Pia." He gave her a gentle kiss. "I'm honored."

She arched into him, responding intuitively to his advance.

"So that's why you weren't on any protection when we were first intimate again that day after rock climbing," he murmured.

Pia nodded. "There hadn't been any need."

"That day, you said three years was a long time," Hawk mused. "I thought you were referring to how long it had been since we'd last been together. But you meant since the last time you'd had sex, too, didn't you?"

Pia nodded again, and then her eyes crinkled. "Care to shorten the time between sex?"

Hawk gave a half groan, half laugh. "Ah, Pia. It's going to be difficult to keep up with you."

She gave him a quick kiss, her look mischievous. "Your performance has been off the charts so far. I thought—"

"Minx." He silenced her with a kiss.

And after that, neither of them got out of bed for a long while.

Hawk knew he was in too deep.

It was déjà vu. Except the first time he hadn't suspected that Pia was a virgin, and this time, he hadn't divined that she'd only ever had one lover. *Him*.

He felt a rush of possessiveness. He hadn't liked thinking

of Pia with other men—learning things…things that *he* could teach her.

Blast it.

"What do you think, Hawk?"

Hawk met three pairs of expectant female eyes. His mother, his sister and Pia were sitting in the Green Room at Silderly Park discussing assorted wedding details. He'd assumed a position by the mantel, at a safe remove.

"What do you think about seating Baron Worling next to Princess Adelaide of Meznia at dinner?" his mother asked, repeating and elaborating her question.

Hawk knew there was some nuance that he should understand, otherwise his mother wouldn't have bothered asking. But for the life of him, he couldn't think what it was.

Was Baron Worling a poor conversationalist? Did Princess Adelaide believe the baron was beneath her notice? Or perhaps one of the baron's poor ancestors had dueled to the death with a member of Princess Adelaide's royal family?

Hawk shrugged and punted. "I'm sure whatever you decide will be fine."

His mother looked nonplussed.

"What about placing the Crown Prince of Belagia on Princess Adelaide's left?" Pia suggested.

His mother brightened. "Splendid idea."

Hawk shot Pia a grateful look.

She looked superb in a navy polka-dot dress and heels. The dress accentuated her bust without being over the top, so that she looked demure but professional.

Whether Pia knew it or not, Hawk reflected, she'd chosen exactly an outfit of which his mother, the Dowager Duchess of Hawkshire, would approve.

As the wedding conversation resumed, Hawk started idly plotting ways to be alone again with Pia.

Could he invent a phone call that required her immediate

attention and called her away? Or perhaps he could feign a pressing need for her to consult on his attire for the wedding day? He stifled a grin.

Yesterday they had gone horseback riding and he'd shown her the various natural and architectural wonders on his estate. He couldn't remember when he'd enjoyed playing tour guide more, though he had an understandable bit of pride in his ancestral estate and childhood home.

His mother glanced up and caught his eye, and Hawk returned her look blandly.

He wondered whether his mother suspected that there was more than a business relationship between him and Lucy's wedding planner, and decided to leave her to speculate. He and Pia had separate bedrooms, and they'd been discreet about their late-night rendezvous, even though Silderly Park was so large that it was unlikely they'd have attracted the attention of anyone while slipping in and out of each other's rooms.

The truth was, he was still trying to sort out his feelings and next steps as far as Pia was concerned. How could he articulate them for someone else when he himself didn't understand them?

He'd started out trying to make amends, true, but matters had gotten more complicated from there. He bore a large share of the responsibility for his current circumstances—mostly because he couldn't seem to help himself as far as Pia was concerned. He must have been absent that day in grade school when they taught everyone about keeping their hands to themselves.

He was Pia's first and *only* lover.

It was astounding. It was wonderful.

It also made him freeze, not knowing what to do.

For years, his code of conduct with respect to women was never to get too involved. It was the reason why he'd never been or wanted to be a woman's first lover—until Pia.

And while he still wasn't sure about many things, he did know that he didn't want to see Pia hurt again.

The butler entered, followed by a familiar-looking brunette.

Hawk watched as his mother brightened, and as recognition set in, he was struck with an impending sense of doom, even before the butler spoke.

"Miss Michelene Ward-Fombley has arrived."

Eleven

Pia looked up as an attractive brunette walked into the room, and immediately and inexplicably sensed that something was wrong.

The Dowager Duchess of Hawkshire, however, rose gracefully from her seat on the settee, a smile wreathing her face. "Michelene, darling, how lovely of you to join us here."

Michelene stepped forward, and the two women exchanged air kisses.

Pia glanced around the room, noticing that Lucy had a worried expression while Hawk was still as a rock by the mantel.

Following Lucy's lead, Pia rose from her seat as introductions were made.

"...and this is Miss Pia Lumley, who has been ever so helpful as Lucy's wedding coordinator," the duchess said with a smile.

Pia shook hands with Michelene, whom she pegged as a

cool self-possessed blueblood. Though the other woman had said only a few words, Pia could tell that Michelene spoke Queen's English with a distinctive upper-class inflection.

Michelene looked over at the mantel.

"Hawk," Michelene murmured, her voice low and sultry.

Hawk? *Not Your Grace?* Pia frowned. Exactly what was the status of the relationship between Michelene and Hawk?

Pia knew that never in a million years—not even in the shower—could she imitate Michelene's smoky tone. She even stuttered during sex—for which she was self-conscious, though Hawk claimed to like it.

"Michelene," Hawk acknowledged, remaining at his spot by the mantel. "How nice to see you. I wasn't made aware that you were coming today."

Pia watched as Hawk threw his mother a meaningful look, which the dowager duchess returned with one—Pia could swear—of the cat who ate the canary. Score one for the dowager, it seemed.

"Did I not mention that Michelene was arriving early for Lucy's engagement party tomorrow?" the duchess said, raising her brows. "Oh, dear."

Michelene gave a little laugh. "I hope it's no inconvenience."

"Not at all. You are more than welcome here," Hawk said smoothly, his eyes traveling from Michelene to his mother. "Silderly Park is large enough, of course, to accommodate the occasional unexpected guest."

Whoever Michelene was, Pia thought, it was clear that she was close to the Carsdales.

Was she, in fact, a former lover of Hawk's? Pia tamped down the well of jealousy.

"We were just finishing up our discussion of the wedding," the duchess said as she sat back down. "Won't you join us, Michelene?"

Pia and Lucy followed the duchess's lead in retaking their seats.

"Thank you," Michelene said as she sat down as well. "I believe I would find listening to be vastly informative." She smiled toward the side of the room where Hawk was standing. "There was a time when I imagined I'd enjoy becoming a wedding planner myself. Unfortunately, life had other plans, and I remained in the fashion business."

Pia shifted uncomfortably. She wondered whether Hawk and Michelene had not only been lovers, but had come close to a walk down the aisle. Or perhaps Michelene had hoped for a marriage proposal that had never materialized, and Hawk had ended the relationship instead?

Pia mentally braked. She knew she was letting her imagination run away with her. She had no proof that Hawk and Michelene had even dated, let alone come close to marriage. And she was making an assumption that Hawk had ended any relationship between the two.

"Wh-what type of fashion?" Pia blurted, disconcerted by her thoughts.

A second later, she clamped her mouth shut. She was embarrassed by the sudden and unexpected appearance of her stutter. She must be more rattled than she realized.

Michelene looked at her keenly. "I'm a buyer for Harvey Nichols."

Pia was familiar with the upmarket department store. She just wished she could afford more of their goods.

"It must be so interesting to be a wedding planner," Michelene continued, hitting the ball back into Pia's court. "You must have some entertaining stories."

This year more than others, Pia thought.

"I do enjoy the job very much," she nevertheless responded honestly. "I love being part of one of the most significant days in a couple's life."

Pia could feel Hawk's gaze on her, his expression thoughtful.

"Pia has been a great help," Lucy put in with an encouraging smile.

"I see," Michelene said. "I'll have to get your business card, Ms. Lumley—"

"It's Pia, please."

"—just in case anyone I know is in need of the services of a wedding coordinator."

Pia again got the sense there was a subtext to this conversation that she wasn't privy to.

Before she could say anything else, however, the butler appeared again to announce that Lucy's dressmaker—the one Pia knew had been commissioned to make a suitable confection for the engagement party—had arrived.

As the dressmaker was shown in, Pia cast a speculative look at Hawk's enigmatic expression.

She wondered if she'd be able to learn the subtext of today's conversation sooner rather than later. Because she *and* Hawk would no doubt be seeing Michelene again tomorrow at Lucy's engagement party.

Pia surveyed the glittering crowd from her position near one end of the long dining table, one of two that had been set up parallel to each other in the Great Hall.

There would be dinner and dancing for the engagement party tonight, as befitted a formal reception given by a dowager duchess, since Hawk's mother was playing hostess. The men wore tuxes, and the women gowns.

Lucy had dismissed all of tonight's pomp and circumstance as more of a to-do than the wedding itself would be. But she had conceded that her mother should have a free hand tonight if the dowager duchess was to have very little say over the wedding itself.

Pia had donned one of the two floor-length gowns that she

owned. The nature of her line of work required her to dress very formally on occasion.

She wore a lavender, one-shoulder, Grecian-style dress whose artfully draped fabric accentuated her bust and gave her the illusion of additional height. She'd bought the designer Marchesa gown at an Upper East Side consignment shop that was a favorite with the rich and fashionable who looked to retire their clothes at the end of the season.

As she cut into her remaining filet mignon—during a momentary lull in conversation with the guests seated to her right and left—she shot a surreptitious look down the middle of the table at Hawk.

He looked handsome and debonair as he chatted with the graying man to his left—a prince of some long-defunct kingdom, if she recalled correctly, who also happened to be distantly related to Derek, Lucy's fiancé.

She herself sat far away from Hawk, near one end of the table, as befitted her position as a less notable guest—an employee, really, and no more, in the dowager duchess's eyes.

She couldn't help but note that Michelene, on the other hand, had been seated diagonally across from Hawk—within speaking distance.

She wished she'd questioned Hawk about the other woman, but, truth be told, she'd been afraid of the answers. She hadn't wanted her suspicions confirmed that Michelene and Hawk had been more than friends at one point. And Hawk hadn't volunteered any information.

Pia patted her mouth with her napkin and took a sip of her wine.

As waiters began clearing plates from the table, Hawk rose and a hush fell over the room.

Pia kept her gaze on him, even though his own eyes traveled over the room, surveying the assembled guests.

Hawk said a few short words, thanking all the guests for

joining his family in tonight's celebration and regaling the crowd with a couple of amusing anecdotes about his sister and future brother-in-law. Then he toasted the happy couple and all the assembled guests joined in.

When he took his seat again, the dowager duchess rose from hers. She gave the engaged couple seated near her an indulgent smile. "I'm so very happy for Lucy and Derek."

Hawk's mother cleared her throat. "As many of you know, Lucy hasn't always followed my advice—" there was a scattering of laughter among the guests "—but in this case she has my unqualified approval." She raised her glass. "Well done, Lucy, and it is with great pleasure that I welcome you to the family, Derek."

"Hear, hear," chorused some of the guests.

The duchess lifted her glass higher. "I hope I shall have the opportunity to make another toast on a similarly happy occasion in the not-too-distant future." Her gaze shifted for a moment to Hawk before returning to her daughter and future son-in-law. "To Lucy and Derek."

As everyone raised their glasses in toast and sipped their champagne, Pia watched as the dowager duchess's gaze came to rest on Michelene. In turn, the younger woman glanced at Hawk, who was gazing at his mother, his expression inscrutable.

Pia felt her stomach plummet.

Sightlessly, she placed her glass back on the table without taking a sip.

Feeling suddenly ill, she experienced an overwhelming need to get away—to get some air.

Pia murmured an excuse in the general direction of her nearest dinner companions and rose from her seat.

Trying not to catch anyone's eye, she hurried from the room as fast as decorum would allow.

In the hall, she ran up the stairs. She was roiled by emotion that threatened to spill over into tears.

She'd been so naive yesterday. It was something that she'd

vowed to herself she'd never be again. And yet, she'd mistaken the situation entirely.

It wasn't that Michelene and Hawk had a *past* relationship that had been broken off. It was that they had a *current* tie that had an expectation of marriage.

Pia had gathered as much from the interchange that had just occurred during the dowager duchess's speech, and from the significant looks that had been exchanged.

She'd finally pieced together yesterday's puzzle, but in the process, she'd nearly humiliated herself in front of dozens of people.

At the top of the stairs, she turned left. Her bedroom was down the hallway.

"Pia, wait."

Hawk's voice came from behind her, more command than plea. He sounded as if he was taking the stairs two at a time.

She picked up her pace. She hoped to reach the sanctuary of her room and throw the lock before he caught up with her. It was her only hope. She didn't want to risk having him see her break down.

She could hear Hawk's rapid steps behind her. In her gown, she couldn't move as fast as he could, though she had the hem raised with one hand.

And in the next moment, it was too late.

Hawk caught up with her, grasping her arm and turning her to face him.

"Wh-what?" she demanded, her throat clogged. "It's not midnight yet and C-Cinderella isn't allowed to disappear, is that it?"

"Are you leaving behind a glass slipper?" he countered, dropping his staying hand.

She gave an emotional laugh. "No, and you're not Prince Charming."

His lips firmed into a thin line. "Let's go somewhere and discuss this."

At least he understood why she was upset, and he wasn't going to pretend otherwise.

Still. "I'm not going anywhere with you!"

Hawk sighed. "Will you let me explain?"

"D-damn you, Hawk," she said, her voice wobbly. "I—I was just starting to trust you again! Now I discover that all along you've more or less had a fiancée waiting in the wings."

Pia's jaw clenched. Did he know how fragile trust was? How could she ever trust him again?

He looked her in the eye. "That's what my mother would like to believe."

"Oh? And you were unaware of this expectation?"

He remained silent.

Obviously, he was refusing to incriminate himself, Pia thought acerbically. He knew anything he said could and would be used against him.

"It appears that your mother had more than an expectation."

Michelene herself obviously did, too. And Pia recalled Lucy's troubled expression yesterday in the Green Room. Had Hawk's sister realized that Michelene's unexpected appearance would present an awkward situation for her brother?

Hawk muttered something under his breath.

"You and Michelene seemed quite familiar yesterday!"

"You're mistaking matters or else deliberately mischaracterizing them," he responded in a clipped tone. "I recall remaining by the fireplace when Michelene appeared."

"You know what I mean," Pia said, feeling like stamping her foot—as childish as that might be. "And why should I believe anything that you tell me? You failed to mention Michelene's existence to begin with."

"I was involved with Michelene briefly after my brother's death. Michelene had been considered an eligible candidate to be my brother's future duchess." Hawk shrugged. "I was stepping into my brother's shoes, and Michelene was part of the package."

And Pia wasn't. She could hear the words as clearly as if they'd been spoken aloud.

As Hawk trailed off, Pia acknowledged the situation that he'd been in. He'd fallen into doing what had been expected of him. She could almost understand that.

And yet. "Your mother acts as if an engagement announcement is imminent. If I hadn't stayed for the party at Lucy's request, is that how I would have heard about Michelene? An engagement notice in the paper?"

Hawk's engagement to another woman. She couldn't help feeling hurt as well as betrayed. She'd told herself she'd be prepared for the end of their affair, but she hadn't foreseen *this*.

"I am not engaged, I assure you," Hawk shot back, looking frustrated. "I hadn't planned a proposal or bought a ring."

"Well, then, you're running late," she replied. "Michelene is waiting."

She glanced down the hall. Someone could come at any time, interrupting and witnessing their argument. And he had to get back downstairs to the party. His absence would be noticed soon.

"Pia, you are the damnedest fe—"

"That's right I—I am," she responded. "I happen to be cursed with rotten luck as far as men are concerned. So much for fairy tales!"

"If you'll just give me a chance—"

"That's the problem," Pia tossed back. "I have."

She turned and started down the hall. "I can't believe I was charmed a-and tricked by you again. How could I have let myself be such a fool?"

Hawk caught up with her and took hold of her arm again, forcing her to look up at him.

His face was set and implacable, and Pia got a glimpse of the part of him that had made a fortune in the span of a few short years.

"I did not trick you," he grated.

A moment later, his lips came down on hers. The kiss packed all the potency of their past ones and then some.

She tasted the champagne on his lips, and inhaled the male scent of him. It was a combination heady enough to make her head swim, despite her anger.

Still, summoning an effort of will, she pulled away as soon as the kiss tapered off.

"You didn't trick me?" she inquired, repeating his words as he raised his head. "Perhaps not. I suppose I tricked myself. All you did was let me."

Hawk looked at her, eyes glittering.

She read her own meaning in his silence.

"I didn't think you approached me again with the idea of a marriage proposal," she scoffed, though she was willing the tears away with all her might.

Hawk searched her eyes. "You know why I approached you..."

Yes, to make amends.

"Pia—"

"I-it's t-too late, Hawk," she said, her voice agonized. "The cat's out of the bag, and we're finished. Our affair was going to have to end sometime, so why not now? Except this time, I'm the one walking away."

Before Hawk could respond, someone called his name, and she and Hawk turned as one to glance down the hall.

Michelene was standing at the top of the stairs.

Not waiting for more, Pia turned and hurried down the hall in the opposite direction, leaving Hawk standing where he was.

Pia slipped inside her bedroom and closed and locked the

door behind her. Then she leaned back against the wall of the darkened room, grateful for reaching sanctuary.

When all of this had started, Hawk's motivation was to make amends. His motivation had never been, she reminded herself, swallowing hard, to love her or promise forever more.

She bit her lip to stop it from trembling, even as the tears welled.

The only question was how was she going to mend her heart when this was over and she'd truly gotten away—if she ever could?

Twelve

As it turned out, Pia managed to make her escape more expeditiously than she'd imagined possible. After collecting herself and drying her tears, she packed her few bags in a hurry and summoned one of Hawk's chauffeurs to drive her to nearby Oxford.

She knew Hawk would remain occupied tonight with the engagement party, whether he liked it or not. She also knew Oxford would afford her a host of inns and hotels in which to stay for the night while she booked a flight back to New York—and planned her next move.

During the night at a small inn, however she remembered that the Earl and Countess of Melton were staying at their home, Gantswood Hall, in nearby Gloucestershire. So the morning, after a quick ring to Tamara, Pia used a rental car to drive to Gantswood Hall.

When Pia arrived after midday, Tamara greeted her inside the front door with a quick hug.

Before she'd left New York, Pia had mentioned to Tamara

that she planned to be in England for Lucy Carsdale's engagement party, so her friend was aware that she would be in the country.

But Pia had said nothing on the phone about the reason for her sudden trip to Gantswood Hall. And if Tamara had been surprised at Pia's impromptu plan to visit, she hadn't given any indication.

Now, as she and Tamara drew apart from their hug, Pia couldn't help experiencing a pang. She'd noticed that her friend's pregnancy had started to show. And Tamara looked happy and relaxed, dressed in a cowl-neck cashmere sweater and black tights, her red hair pulled back in a knot.

Pia knew her own situation was in startling contrast. She couldn't be further away from Tamara's happily-ever-after. She was sad and depressed, and she hadn't slept well last night. No amount of makeup this morning had been able to disguise her pallor and the peaked look around her eyes.

Tamara searched her face, her brow puckering. "What's wrong? You gave no indication on the phone. But I can see from the look of you that something is amiss."

Pia parted her lips. *What was the use in hiding the truth?*

"L-last night was Lucy Carsdale's engagement party," she said without preamble.

Tamara's eyes widened. "Did something go wrong? Oh, Pia!"

Much to her horror, Pia felt her eyes well with tears.

Tamara looked at her with concern for a moment, and then wrapped her in a hug again.

"It's okay," Tamara said soothingly, patting her on the back. "I've been prone to tears myself, what with raging hormones during this pregnancy. I'm sure whatever happened is not as bad as it seems right now."

Pia hiccupped and straightened, taking a step back. "No, it's worse."

Tamara had obviously concluded that Pia was upset because something had gone wrong with Lucy's engagement party, Pia realized. Tamara had no idea about Hawk's role.

When she'd told Tamara and Belinda that she'd be traveling to England in order to help with Lucy's engagement party, she'd left out that Hawk himself had extended an invitation to visit Silderly Park.

Tamara put an arm around her shoulders. "Come into the drawing room with me. We can be cozy there, and you can tell me all about it. I was about to have a light snack brought in."

As a member of the household staff appeared from the back of the house, Tamara added, "Haines, could you please arrange to have Pia's bags moved from her car to the Green and Gold Bedroom? Thank you."

"Of course," Haines acknowledged with an inclination of the head as they passed him.

Pia let Tamara guide her through the palatial house, Sawyer's ancestral family seat, until they reached a large room with French doors overlooking the back lawn and gardens. Despite the masterpieces framed on the walls, the room was warm and inviting.

Pia sat with Tamara on a brocade settee in front of a large fireplace.

Tamara handed her a tissue, and Pia made use of it to compose herself.

"Now," Tamara said encouragingly, "I'm sure this is nothing that you can't put behind you."

Pia bit her lip. *If only Tamara knew.*

"I don't know," she said. "I've been trying to put Hawk behind me for three years."

Tamara's eyebrows lifted. "Then all this emotion isn't because something went wrong with Lucy's engagement party?"

"Oh, something went wrong, all right. I found out Hawk had a fiancée waiting in the wings."

"Oh, Pia."

With some effort, Pia outlined what had happened at Silderly Park—from Michelene's unexpected arrival to what had transpired the night before at Lucy's party.

When she finished, she looked at Tamara beseechingly.

"How could I have been so stupid again?" she asked in an agonized voice. "How could I let myself become vulnerable to him once more?"

"You let yourself become susceptible to Hawk's charms..."

Tamara trailed off, and though she'd spoken without inflection, she seemed to be trying to guess at what Pia was really saying.

Pia sighed. Why not come out with the whole bald-faced truth?

She hadn't divulged details to Tamara and Belinda of her recent and evolving relationship with Hawk. She knew they would have tried to dissuade her from any deeper involvement—and certainly from trying to turn the tables in a high-stakes game with a seasoned player like Hawk.

"It's worse," Pia said succinctly. "I slept with him."

Tamara looked surprised, though not as caught unawares as Pia would have expected. Still, her friend didn't say anything.

"After the first time I slept with him, he disappeared for three years," Pia said, the words tumbling out of her. "This time, we sleep together, and then I discover he's nearly engaged to another woman!"

"Oh, Pia," Tamara said. "I had no idea, believe me. If I'd known, of course I would have said something."

Tamara frowned. "I wonder why Sawyer didn't say anything. He and Hawk are friends. He must have had at least some inkling about an engagement—"

Pia shrugged. "Perhaps Sawyer had no idea that a warning

was necessary. I mean, Hawk and I had a past but no present. And now, we definitely have no future…"

Pia felt a wave of pain wash over her. Had she started hoping for a future with Hawk? How much of her hurt was due to the fact that she really hadn't wanted the relationship to end, and how much due to the way she'd shockingly found out that it was over—because there was another woman?

It shouldn't hurt this bad.

If she was honest with herself, she'd say she'd never completely gotten over Hawk. And now…now she was in love with him while he was going to marry another woman.

The realization hit like a body blow.

"Pia?" Tamara said. "Are you okay?"

Pia could only nod, her throat too constricted for words.

Tamara stroked her arm soothingly. "I know it hurts. You'll need time."

Pia nodded, and then took a deep breath.

"I was so naive," she announced when she could speak again. "When Michelene arrived, I thought perhaps she and Hawk had dated in the past. It never occurred to me that I should be concerned about the future!"

"Well, don't worry. I'll have Sawyer call Hawk out," Tamara stated, trying to lighten the mood. "Sawyer must have some centuries-old ceremonial swords lying around somewhere that they can duel with…"

Pia gave a choked laugh. "I don't know. Hawk is in good shape. He's a rock climber."

Pia was thankful for Tamara's understanding. She wasn't sure if Belinda would have managed to be quite so deft at a time like this. But then Tamara was happily married, while Belinda was trying her utmost to be happily *unmarried*.

Pia tried to compose herself, and gave Tamara a watery smile. "Thanks for trying to cheer me up."

Tamara gave a rueful little smile of her own. "I know what

you're going through, Pia, believe me. It's where I was just a few months ago."

"But everything worked out for you. Sawyer adores you."

"I didn't think it was possible at the time. There'll come a day when you'll be happy again—I promise."

Pia sighed. "Not any time soon. I'm committed to seeing through Lucy's big event. How will it look if I end this horrible year by dropping Lucy's wedding at the last moment? It will truly be a fatal blow to Pia Lumley Wedding Productions!"

Tamara grimaced. "I wish I could question Sawyer right now, but he flew back to New York yesterday, and I know he's in a business meeting right now."

"It's okay. It won't change anything."

Nothing could make this right.

"What is Michelene's full name?" Tamara queried suddenly.

"It's Ward-Fombley. Michelene Ward-Fombley."

Tamara nodded. "I've heard of her, though I can't put a face to the name at the moment."

"She's genteel and attractive."

"So are you."

"You're loyal."

Tamara tilted her head. "I'm sure I've heard the name in connection with one social function or another here in England…"

"I'm not surprised," Pia admitted, though it hurt. "She's from Hawk's social circle. In fact, I believe she was a leading candidate to be Hawk's older brother's bride until William passed away."

Tamara grimaced again. "Oh, Pia, are you sure Hawk isn't just feeling some lingering halfhearted sense of obligation?"

"Even if he is, it doesn't change matters. He engaged in some artful omissions, and I can only assume that his sense of obligation remains."

Hawk had assumed responsibilities in the past three years, Pia reflected, and she was suffering the consequences.

She recalled the look on the dowager duchess's face last night. Yes, Pia thought with a stab, Hawk had his life mapped out for him, and their paths were apparently fated to cross only briefly and casually, with no serious feelings or commitment—at least not on his part.

"I need to book a flight," Pia told Tamara. "With any luck, I can catch a plane back to New York by tomorrow."

Her friend looked troubled. "Oh, Pia, please stay longer. You're upset."

Pia was glad for the offer, but still she shook her head. "Thank you, Tamara—for everything." She pasted on a brave smile. "But I have business that needs attending to back in New York."

At the moment, she added silently, she needed to put as much space as possible between her and Hawk.

She also worried that if Sawyer returned home, he'd inform Hawk of her whereabouts. Pia had come to like Tamara's husband, but she knew he was also Hawk's friend.

And she wasn't ready to face Hawk again quite so soon.

Once she was back in New York, she only had to figure out how to avoid Hawk until Lucy's wedding was over. Because one thing was certain—they were over as a couple.

Hawk sat in his office in New York in a rare quiet moment and reflected on the royal mess he'd made.

Pia had run from him, and he no doubt ranked even lower than the fictional wicked Mr. Wickham in her estimation at the moment.

Mrs. Hollings, no doubt using her crystal ball and her contacts across the Atlantic, had published more or less the heart of the matter in her column: "Could a certain rakish, hawkish duke have resurrected his randy dandy ways before heading to the altar with a suitable marriageable miss?"

His painstakingly built reputation as a serious financier with hardly a remarkable social life was threatening to collapse. He'd merited three thinly-veiled references in Mrs. Hollings's gossip column in the past months.

Pia had laid dust to his resolve to appear—and to *be*— strictly proper and responsible. He'd thought he was reformed. She'd proved him wrong.

She thought he'd played her false, and the truth was, he'd been less than aboveboard and forthright. As a result, Pia had been crushed by the unexpected events at Lucy's engagement party.

And Mrs. Hollings, blast it, knew it all.

It would be easy, of course, for him to track down Pia. He knew where she lived, and she was still working on Lucy's wedding—or rather, he thought she was.

Lucy had become rather tight-lipped on the subject of Pia. His sister had seemed to intuit what had transpired at Silderly Park, based on Michelene's unexpected arrival and Pia's abrupt departure. It was clear that Lucy disapproved of his treatment of Pia, though she'd refrained from outright verbal censuring.

And then again, what would he say to Pia if he tracked her down?

He should have told her about Michelene and *explained*— but what exactly? Until Pia had unexpectedly reappeared in his life on Belinda's wedding day in June, he and everyone else had thought he'd marry someone suitable. It had been, in so many ways, the path of least resistance. It was time to marry, and with his reputation as a top-flight financier in place, a predictable marriage had been the final step toward burying his playboy past for good.

Yet how serious could he ever have been about Michelene if she'd barely even crossed his mind the whole time he'd been with Pia? He asked himself that question now. The idea of proposing to Michelene had never assumed concrete terms...

When the phone rang, he leaned forward and picked up the receiver on his desk. "Yes?"

"Sawyer Langsford is here to see you."

"Tell him to come in."

After replacing the phone, he rose from his chair, just in time to see Sawyer walk into his office.

As Hawk came around his desk, he was glad to see his friend, even though he had some suspicion as to what had precipitated this visit.

"If you're here to castigate me," he said without preamble, "I can assure you that I'm already doing a fine job of it myself."

Sawyer smiled wryly. "Tamara suggested a duel at dawn, but I set her straight that it wasn't quite the thing anymore among us aristocrats."

"Good Lord, I should hope not," Hawk muttered as he shook hands with Sawyer. "I don't think my mother would take kindly to the dukedom passing into the hands of a distant cousin for lack of male heirs."

Sawyer's eyes crinkled.

Hawk nodded at one of the chairs set before his desk. "Have a seat."

Sawyer sat down, and Hawk went back around his desk and reclaimed his chair.

Sawyer's lips twisted into a sardonic smile. "My impression actually was that you were doing your utmost to sire an heir."

Hawk wasn't sure if Sawyer was referring to his liaison with Pia or rumors of his prospective proposal to Michelene. In any case, it hardly mattered.

"Ah, yes, the heart of the matter," Hawk said, steepling his fingers. "This is what has gotten me into hot water. Even your Mrs. Hollings is apparently on to the story."

Sawyer shrugged. "What can I say? Mrs. Hollings's realm extends even beyond my reach."

"Obviously."

"Much as I hate to point out the obvious," Sawyer said, "Mrs. Hollings was reporting a story of your own creation."

Hawk sighed, acknowledging the truth of Sawyer's statement. "Much to my regret."

Sawyer smiled. "In any case, my pretext for coming here was to extend an apology in person for your name's appearance in the wrong section of one of my newspapers."

Hawk inclined his head in mock solemnity. "Thank you. Far better than a duel at dawn."

"Quite." Sawyer arched a brow. "I did caution you about Pia."

"Yes, I recall," Hawk replied. "And I proceeded heedlessly. Obviously, I'm an inconsiderate libertine of the first order. A debaucher of innocence."

In fact, these days he found himself questioning what his intentions had been all along. Had he been disingenuous? And even if his intentions had been good, they now lay like flotsam on the shore.

Sawyer inclined his head. "You can always be reformed."

"I thought I was."

Sawyer gave a hint of a smile. "Again, then. You're the only one who can fix this situation."

Hawk twisted his lips. "How? I've been racking my brain and have yet to come up with a solution."

"You will," Sawyer replied. "I was sitting where you are only a few months ago, thinking similar thoughts about Tamara. Except that you came into your title unexpectedly as a younger son, unlike me and Easterbridge. You had less time to get accustomed to it. All I'll say is, yes, the title is a responsibility, but don't let yourself get overburdened by it. Think about what makes you happy rather than what's suitable."

Hawk nodded, surprised by Sawyer's insight, though maybe he shouldn't have been.

Sawyer's lips tilted upward. "And lastly, women appreciate grand gestures." He checked his watch. "Now, if you're free, let's have lunch."

Hawk shook his head in amused disbelief as he and Sawyer both rose from their seats. He'd had enough of grand gestures. Look where they'd landed him.

Still, he would venture to guess that Sawyer was correct.

Thirteen

Pia had decided to lie low.

She wasn't sure where and how Mrs. Hollings was getting her information, but the columnist seemed to have sources in the most unlikely of places.

In fact, Pia wondered fancifully for a moment if Mrs. Hollings had been able to bribe information out of Mr. Darcy. Mr. Darcy was known to be a pushover for having his tummy rubbed or for a handful of kitty treats.

As she moved along Broadway from the subway to her destination—jostled occasionally on the crowded street by a passerby or tourist—she noted that it was an unusually bright December day. *So unlike her mood.*

She'd suggested to Lucy that they meet in her dressing room before her performance tonight. She didn't want to run the risk of encountering Hawk at his house.

She didn't want to face him until she was ready, which might be never.

Still, though it was nonsensical, at the same time she missed Hawk terribly.

He appeared to be giving her a wide berth—it was the only way to explain why she hadn't heard from him. He could have tracked her down. He knew where she lived.

She was almost annoyed with him for *not* tracking her down. If he cared, wouldn't he beat a path to her door to mount a defense, however feeble?

Pia sighed. She ought to have hardened her heart against Hawk since their last confrontation. Instead, she was a mass of incredibly conflicted feelings.

Perhaps she was a pushover and always would be. She'd learned nothing, clearly, about eradicating her trusting nature and protecting her too-easily-bruised feelings.

Arriving at the Drury Theater, she went in the front entrance and was directed to Lucy's dressing room.

When she knocked on Lucy's partially-open dressing room door and then entered, Hawk's sister swiveled in her chair to face her.

"Pia!" Lucy rose and came over to give her a quick squeeze. "You're right on time."

She might have had a falling-out with Hawk, but Pia continued to like Lucy. The other woman's enthusiasm was almost contagious. And though this wasn't usually the case with her clients, she believed that she and Lucy had become friends of sorts over the past few months.

"Hardly anyone is here, since it's hours until curtain time," Lucy said as she stepped back. "Can I offer you something to drink? Tea—" Lucy's eyes sparkled with humor "—or maybe coffee or hot chocolate?"

"No, please," she declined. "I'm fine at the moment."

She removed her hat and coat, and Lucy took them and her purse from her to place on a nearby coatrack.

As they both sat down in vacant chairs, Pia looked around the smallish room. It boasted a mirrored dressing table lit by naked bulbs and strewn with an array of makeup and hair preparation items. There was also the coatrack, a few chairs and plenty of discarded wardrobe items.

Pia let her gaze come back to Lucy, and she smiled encouragingly. "You are one of the calmest brides whom I have ever worked with."

Lucy laughed. "I suppose I'd be more nervous if work wasn't keeping me so busy. But then I'm used to performing in front of people, and isn't a wedding a type of performance?"

"I suppose that explains it."

Lucy looked at her thoughtfully. "I want to thank you for attending the engagement party at Silderly Park. You left so soon, I didn't have time to say anything."

"Yes, well..." Pia found it hard to hold Lucy's gaze. "It was my pleasure."

Lucy tilted her head. "I don't suppose your abrupt departure had anything to do with Hawk and Michelene?"

Pia was startled by the direct question, and for a moment, she wasn't sure she'd heard correctly.

"Wh-what makes you ask that?" she said, eyes wide.

She flushed to think about how many of the other guests at the engagement party had surmised what happened.

Lucy smiled understandingly. "When it's your brother, and you're on the verge of getting married yourself, you notice things."

"You needn't worry," she tried gamely. "I'm well-prepared to deal with Michelene and H-Hawk's w-wedding plans."

"Pia..."

She fought to hold on to her composure. How humiliating would it be to break down in front of Hawk's sister, and to have Lucy tell Hawk about it?

Lucy's smile flickered, comprehension in her eyes. "If it helps, I'm convinced Hawk cares about you. Very much."

If he cared, Pia thought, he would have told her about Michelene instead of having her discover the other woman's position in his life in such a public way. If he cared, he would have called or contacted her.

If he cared, he wouldn't be so charming and easy to fall in love with.

Good grief, she thought, was there no end to Hawk's ability to toy with her life?

Lucy sighed. "I believe Michelene's arrival caught Hawk by surprise as much as it did you."

Pia thinned her lips. "I'm sure it did. I can just imagine what an uncomfortable position Michelene put him in. He suddenly had his current lover and his future wife under the same roof, and they weren't the same woman!"

Then she belatedly clamped her mouth shut, afraid she'd said too much.

Lucy grimaced. "Hawk has an amazing ability to muck things up, sometimes."

"Sometimes?" Pia queried, regaining some of her aplomb. "You know the first time I met him he presented himself as plain Mr. James Fielding?"

"So the rumors are true," Lucy murmured, as if speaking to herself.

Pia had wondered how much Lucy realized or suspected about her relationship with Hawk. Now she had her answer.

Lucy searched Pia's face, her own reflecting worry. "I've never seen Hawk as happy as he is with you. Please take that for what it's worth."

There was a part of her that yearned to believe Lucy's words. She was already a mix of conflicted feelings.

"Do you know he spoke glowingly of you when he suggested I use you as my wedding coordinator?" Lucy went on. "I could see from his face that you weren't a mere acquaintance. I could tell there was more he wasn't telling me."

Pia felt herself flush. "H-he told me he wanted to make amends for the past…"

"And he mucked up the setting-to-right part, too," Lucy guessed, finishing for her.

Pia nodded. "He didn't mention Michelene." She swallowed against the sudden lump in her throat. "But I should have known there'd be someone like her waiting in the wings. There's an expectation he'll marry someone suitable to his rank."

Lucy sighed again. "Well, there's no getting around the unfortunate fact that Hawk is a duke. However, I'm not sure what Hawk's feelings are, and it's possible not even he knows. He probably has never allowed himself to examine them. I sometimes think he's been on autopilot since William and Father died—on a one-man mission, if you will, to put the dukedom back on sound footing."

Pia felt her lips pull up in a reluctant smile. "You're a good advocate for him."

Lucy nodded. "I'm biased, of course, since Hawk is my brother. But I'd also like to think I'm just returning a favor." She smiled. "After all, Hawk found me a wonderful wedding coordinator—one I didn't even know I needed. And now I'm trying to persuade you to forgive him for his mistakes—just a little, and even if it is for the second time."

Pia chewed her lip.

Lucy gave her another understanding look. "All I'm saying is give him a chance."

One part of her, Pia knew, desperately wanted to grasp the shred of hope that Lucy was giving her. Lucy had said nothing about Hawk offering love, marriage or forever more, of course. But then again, if Hawk cared...

As her conflicted feelings assailed her, Pia let herself contemplate a heretofore unthinkable possibility.

She knew she loved Hawk.

Could she remain his lover, knowing their relationship could lead nowhere? Could she let go of the fairy-tale ending that she'd always wanted?

* * *

"I'm considering keeping my relationship with Hawk…a-at least until he really is engaged to Michelene," Pia said.

Her statement fell into the conversational void like a wrecking ball crashing through the restaurant's ceiling. It was why she'd waited awhile to make her statement.

Shocked stillness was followed by commotion inside Contadini, where she, Tamara and Belinda were having one of their Sunday brunches—indoors this time in a nod to the December weather.

"What?"

"What?"

Belinda and Tamara spoke practically in unison as they stared at her from the other side of the table.

Tamara sighed. "Oh, Pia."

"Have you lost your mind?" Belinda followed up.

Pia knew Belinda's harsh judgment was made simply in hopes of jolting her from a bad decision. "I know it may be hard for you to understand."

"Try impossible."

"Belinda means well," Tamara said, jumping in.

"On second thought," Belinda continued, "maybe you have the right idea, Pia. You can always walk away from an affair."

Pia understood what Belinda meant. Ironically, Belinda couldn't manage to get *unmarried,* while she herself, the romantic, couldn't find a ticket for a trip down the aisle…

"I knew it," Belinda mused, resting one silk-sweater-clad arm on the table as they waited for their meal to be cleared. "I knew the minute that you said you were wavering in your negative opinion of Hawk that there was reason to worry. What has he done to you?"

He's turned me inside out. He makes me want to be with him no matter what.

"It makes me happy to be with him," she said simply.

Belinda rolled her eyes, and Tamara touched her arm as if to restrain her.

"That's how it starts," Belinda argued, her brows drawing together. "One minute you're having a good time, the next you're in bed thinking you're ready to gift him your body forever more…"

"Are we talking about Pia here?" Tamara asked as she and Pia stared at Belinda.

Belinda pressed her lips together. "Sorry, yes."

Tamara pulled a worried frown of her own and searched Pia's face. "Have you really considered what this would mean?"

Pia hesitated, and then nodded. She could tell, however, that Tamara had picked up on her short pause before answering.

Tamara sighed. "I wish I'd been able to warn you about Michelene. After you left Gantswood Hall, I questioned Sawyer about what he knew. It seems he had his suspicions but felt he'd received enough assurance on the matter." She pursed her lips and shook her head. "I just wish Sawyer had bothered to tell me!"

"It's okay, Tamara," Pia responded. "It's not your fault."

Belinda shook her head, her expression perplexed and disbelieving. "Have you thought this through, Pia? Because, you know, he's a duke with an obligation to produce a legitimate heir sooner rather than later. This would give you only a little more time with him. And he's misled you now *twice*."

Pia had followed the same train of thought a dozen times already, tormenting herself. She was hoping it would be a long while before Hawk was officially engaged. He'd asserted during their argument that he hadn't planned a proposal or bought a ring. Did she dare believe him?

She'd managed to leave Silderly Park with a shred of dignity and self-respect, but only by the barest of margins. Was she willing to throw her self-respect out the window now by going back to Hawk's bed with no strings attached after all that had happened?

"Perhaps Tamara and I aren't the ones to be talking to you about this," Belinda joked with dark humor. "We're the first wives club, after all."

"The first and only," Tamara modified.

"For you, I hope," Belinda said. "For me, I wouldn't mind if Colin found another wife." A look of pain flashed across her friend's face in contradiction of her belligerent tone. "But even if Tamara and I can't fully relate to the situation, we still know *you*. Do you really think you could do this—hold on to Hawk for now and then let him go?"

"It's fine for you and Tamara to be married to aristocrats," Pia replied. "But unlike the both of you, I wasn't born into a world of titles and money. I don't know much about—"

"Oh, Pia, that's nonsense!" Tamara broke in. "If I had a dollar for every bonhomie aristocrat who married in questionable taste, I wouldn't have needed Sawyer to bail out Pink Teddy Designs."

Despite herself, Pia smiled.

"Not that a marriage to you would be in questionable taste, of course," Tamara hastened to add.

"Of course not," Belinda joined in.

"Look at me, for example," Tamara went on as a waiter cleared their plates. "I always considered myself poor countess material."

Pia smiled uncertainly. It was true that, until a few months ago, Tamara had been a bohemian New York jewelry designer. But she was also the daughter of a British viscount. And she was now, in the space of a few short months, adapting well to straddling the line of what was expected of her as the Earl of Melton's wife and as a New York-based designer.

On top of it all, Tamara glowed with happiness from an adoring husband and a pregnancy that was starting to show.

Pia wasn't sure if, given the chance, she'd fare so well.

Not that she'd have that chance. Hawk had protested that he wasn't ready to marry Michelene yet, but he'd said nothing about having any serious interest in Pia.

She'd longed for a happy ending for herself since she was a little girl. Could she settle for less? Perhaps she was deluding herself into thinking a dead-end affair with Hawk was for the best.

Tamara reached across the table and touched her hand. "I don't want to hear more talk about not being qualified to be a duchess. You're more qualified than I am to be a countess, frankly, if qualifications even enter into it. You know how to throw brilliant parties and entertain impeccably."

Pia swallowed hard.

"And you are a pro at two of the most important aristocratic pastimes—fishing and riding," Tamara continued. "I find fishing deadly dull, and as for riding, I only ever do it occasionally."

Pia gave a tremulous smile, even as she flushed with embarrassment. She didn't dare tell Tamara and Belinda that Hawk was interested in different types of fishing and riding with her—ones that had nothing to do with fishes and horses and everything to do with a bed and a lazy afternoon or evening, or morning, for that matter.

Belinda looked at her too knowingly. "My advice is not to be Hawk's plaything, even if I do think an arrangement without a legally binding contract is easier. I know you, Pia, and this isn't you."

Pia looked down and fiddled with her napkin. The rational part of her knew Belinda was right. The other part didn't want to think about tomorrow and consequences. She just wanted Hawk.

She'd been young, naive and romantic once, but perhaps she was always destined to act emotionally as far as Hawk was concerned.

Michelene. Oh, God.

Pia swallowed and looked up.

Belinda and Tamara were looking at her with worried but expectant expressions.

Pia bit her lip and punted. "Mr. Darcy is waiting for me at home."

Belinda relaxed a little, obviously taking her comment as a reassuring sign. "Good girl. Learn who the good guys are."

If only, Pia thought, she wasn't still so tempted by a certain wicked duke that her stubborn heart kept insisting was her Prince Charming.

Fourteen

Hawk looked up from his desk, and then automatically rose. "What a surprise to see you on this side of the Atlantic, Mother."

It seemed as if everyone was destined to pay a visit to his office these days. Everyone, that was, except Pia.

Undoubtedly, his mother must have told his secretary not to bother announcing her arrival after obviously having taken her coat and handbag.

The dowager duchess gave him a fixed look. "I thought it would be nice if we had lunch."

Hawk's lips twisted. His mother had shown up unannounced—a clear sign that something important was weighing on her.

"What is this I hear about you and Lucy's wedding planner, Pia Lumley?" his mother asked, not disappointing by going straight to the point. "Some dreadful woman has been writing—"

"Mrs. Hollings."

His mother stopped abruptly. "Pardon?"

"The Pink Pages of Mrs. Jane Hollings. It's a column that appears in the Earl of Melton's newspapers. Specifically, *The New York Intelligencer.*"

"I don't know why Melton hasn't put a stop to it then," the dowager duchess huffed. "He's a friend of yours, isn't he?"

"Sawyer believes in freedom of the press," Hawk responded dryly, coming around his desk.

"Nonsense. This terrible woman is assailing your reputation. Something must be done."

"And what, precisely, is it you suggest I do, Mother?" Hawk queried.

The dowager duchess raised her brows and gathered herself into her full hauteur. "Quite obviously, it must be made apparent to all parties that you have no interest in Ms. Lumley."

"Don't I?"

"Certainly not. This Mrs. Hollings is suggesting that you are having the near equivalent of a liaison with the household help. The Duke of Hawkshire does not dally with those in his employ like…like—"

"Have a seat, Mother," Hawk said, pulling back a chair without breaking stride. "Would you like something to drink?"

He could use something strong and therapeutic himself.

"You are being rather obstinate, James. A simple denial will do."

"And what should I deny?"

The dowager duchess shot him a peremptory look as she sat down. "That you and Ms. Lumley are—"

"—liaising?"

His mother nodded.

"Ah, but you see, I cannot do that."

His mother stilled, and then closed her eyes briefly, as if in resignation. "Goodness. It's not just the resurrected image of you as a playboy that I need to contend with. It's the reality."

"Quite right."

He deserved every condemnation, Hawk thought. He'd dallied with Pia and hurt her. Again.

His mother fixed him with a stern look. "Well, you must put a stop to this at once. My grandfather was a renowned philanderer who left a mess in his wake—"

"You mean offspring born on the wrong side of the blanket?"

The dowager duchess straightened her spine. "We do not speak of it in this family. Kindly curb your blunt speaking. It isn't charming."

Hawk felt his lips quirk. "But, Mother, you like Great-Aunt Ethel."

"Precisely, and that is why we do not refer to the family peccadilloes. However, I still would not have the past repeat itself."

He arched a brow. "Then maybe it would be best if you did not press this matter of an engagement to Michelene. Perhaps the old earl's wandering eye could be traced to an unhappy arranged marriage."

"I had no idea I was pressing anything upon you, James," the dowager duchess huffed.

His mother had a disingenuous ability to parse the truth, but Hawk let the matter go. At the moment, there was a more important discussion to be had—perhaps one that was long overdue.

"Mother," he said with forced gentleness, "Michelene may be a lingering tie to William, but William is gone."

He'd done a lot of thinking since his return from Silderly Park, and especially after Sawyer's visit. One thing he'd realized was that he had to stop any expectations with respect to Michelene for good. He didn't love her—no matter how suitable she was—and he never would.

His mother looked at him for a moment—uncharacteristically without a ready response. And then, disconcertingly, her eyes became moist.

Hawk shifted. "I know this is difficult for you."

"William considered Michelene for his wife because she was a natural choice," the dowager duchess observed finally. "He was doing what was expected of him. He knew his responsibilities."

"Precisely, and I therefore wonder how enamored William really was of Michelene," Hawk replied. "There were times when I thought William enjoyed boating and flying so much because they were the rare moments when he could feel free. In any case, William was groomed for his responsibilities as duke from birth, and I wasn't."

His mother looked pained, but then gathered and composed herself. "Very well, but what do we know about this woman Pia Lumley?" she argued. "Where is she from? She will have no understanding of our ways and what will be expected of her as the Duchess of Hawkshire."

In the way that mattered most, Pia was well-equipped to fill the role of duchess, Hawk disagreed silently. She knew how to please him.

"She's from Pennsylvania," he said aloud. "She knows how to entertain because she's a well-regarded wedding coordinator to New York society—a respectable proving ground for women who marry well, you'll agree."

In Pia's defense, he cited the things that he knew would matter to his mother.

The dowager duchess said nothing, so Hawk pressed on.

"She knows how to ride and fish as well as any woman of my acquaintance," he said. "She is sweet and intelligent, and charmingly devoid of guile or pretense. A breath of fresh air."

"Well," his mother replied finally, "with all those sterling qualities, James, why ever would she have anything to do with you?"

Hawk laughed but it was filled with a note of self-derision. "I wonder that myself."

He was in love with Pia, and he was unworthy of her.

He'd been so intent on defending Pia to his mother that he'd stumbled upon an important realization.

He loved Pia.

Suddenly everything seemed so simple and clear.

"James?"

Hawk looked at his mother. "Yes?"

"You seem lost in thought."

"Or perhaps simply lost."

His mother stood. "Well, quite clearly I've misread matters."

"Never mind, Mother. It's nothing that can't be put to rights."

He hoped.

Hawk knew there were a few things he needed to clarify with Michelene.

And then he needed to find Pia.

If it wasn't too late, and he hadn't hopelessly botched things, this time for good...

Pia had every reason to believe that Lucy's wedding would be the worst day of her life—or near to it. In all likelihood, this day would be Michelene and Hawk's appearance as a couple, if not the announcement of their engagement.

Who else would Hawk take to his sister's wedding but his future bride? It made eminent sense.

One thing was certain: he would not be escorting her, Pia. She was working, and she supposed Hawk's days playing her gofer or man Friday were over.

Hawk's mother, the dowager duchess, would no doubt be eager to segue from seeing one of her children walk down the aisle to seeing the other married—especially when the *other* was the current Duke of Hawkshire.

But as the day progressed, it became clear that Michelene wouldn't materialize—Hawk had come alone to the wedding.

Still, Pia refused to read too much into that, and distracted herself with work.

Thankfully, Hawk didn't approach her. She wasn't sure what she would do if he did.

Instead, he remained busy at the reception, speaking with various guests and exchanging pleasantries with others.

Pia couldn't help wondering if he'd relegated her to being simply the hired help and no more these days. The thought hurt.

Nevertheless, she hungrily absorbed all her glimpses of him, storing them away for a time when she'd no longer see him.

He looked so handsome and attractive tonight that she ached.

Still, by the end of the evening, Pia was weary enough to want the night to end—if only so she wouldn't have to maintain appearances in front of Hawk and everyone else.

She had just walked out of the loftlike reception room when she heard her name called out behind her.

"Pia."

She turned around, but she already knew who it was.

Hawk.

He walked toward her, still looking impeccable in a navy suit and silver-gray tie as the evening was drawing to a close.

She looked at the clock. It was nearing midnight on New Year's Eve.

Too bad this Cinderella couldn't disappear quite yet. She'd worn a simple light blue strapless dress and matching heels.

But she didn't have a carriage, or even a car. And the wedding was slated to continue until one.

Still, she didn't think she could speak to Hawk right now.

She had to get away…get some air. *Anything.*

"I—I was just—"

He quirked a brow. "Leaving?"

Damn him. How dare he look so composed when he was the reason she was upset?

"I was taking a moment to compose myself," she replied with halfhearted honesty. "I was going to touch up my makeup."

Where was a ladies' room when one was needed? It was the only place where she knew Hawk *wouldn't* be following her.

"Why?" He surveyed her. "You look perfect."

Except for the fact that her heart was a wreck.

She sighed. "That's what women do, Hawk. They freshen up. Powder their nose…touch up their lipstick…"

"Why? Expecting someone to kiss you?"

She stared at him mutely. How could he be so heartless?

"Why disappear now?" he persisted. "It's almost midnight."

That was the point. She didn't want everyone to witness that she had no one to kiss—not even a frog. Okay, she had some excuse in that she was on the job, but still… With Hawk in the room—who knew the truth of her circumstances—that helped little.

"Isn't it customary for people to don boas and crowns and blow noisemakers? Why fix your hair when it'll get messed up anyway?" He moved a little, and Pia belatedly noticed that he was holding a small bag. "In fact, I brought some items for you."

"It was considerate of you to think of me," she said, wondering why they were having this inane conversation.

She had no plans to blow a horn or kiss anybody.

Hawk gave a little smile. "I thought it was considerate, too."

Pia thought it was too bad there wasn't another platter of hors d'oeuvres nearby.

How much would it cost her to precipitate another incident at a wedding?

Too much. She couldn't afford it.

Hawk reached into the bag he was holding and pulled out a jeweled headpiece.

It took Pia a moment to realize the tiara wasn't one of those plastic jewel concoctions that everyone wore on New Year's Eve, but the real thing.

Her brain slowed, her mind caught in a moment of disbelief.

The diamond tiara in Hawk's hand had a swirl pattern and was of equal thickness all around. Large diamonds also dangled within the swirls.

Hawk's smile was tender and thoughtful.

Her eyes, wide with shock, remained fastened on his as he moved to settle the tiara on her upswept hair.

It was the first time in Pia's life she'd ever worn a real tiara—though she'd donned plenty of make-believe ones, especially in her dreams.

"There," he murmured, easing back, his eyes meeting hers. "I have pins to anchor it in place. I've been told it's wise to do so, though I have no idea how to go about it."

Pia swallowed hard.

"I wasn't sure what color you'd be wearing," Hawk said, his voice low and deep. "So I decided to go with a sure bet. The Carsdale Diamond tiara."

She sucked in a breath, her brain refusing to function. "G-good choice."

Just inside the reception room, the guests continued their dancing and merriment, waiting for the countdown to the new year and heedless of the two people standing just outside one of the exits.

"It's the traditional tiara worn by Carsdale brides," Hawk said, his voice laden with meaning. "It was worn by my mother on her wedding day."

Pia felt her heart constrict. It pounded loudly.

She couldn't bear it if Hawk was toying with her. If this was a gambit to win her back into his bed even as he planned to marry Michelene or search for a properly-pedigreed duchess...

She bit her lip. "Why are you giving it to me to wear?"

"Why do you think?" he asked thickly, searching her face. "It's a new year and a new beginning...I hope."

"I—I don't need a tiara to ring in the n-new year."

Hawk touched her chin and rubbed his thumb over her lips.

"I know," he responded tenderly. "The question is do you need a duke who is very much in love? He comes with a big house that needs someone who can preside over large and boring parties."

Pia's eyes welled.

Hawk cleared his throat. "You once fell for plain Mr. James Fielding, and it was the greatest gift that anyone ever gave me."

Her shock turned into a crazy kind of hope as Hawk went down on bended knee. He fished a ring out of his pocket with one hand even as the other lifted one of hers.

Pia glanced down at Hawk and began to tremble with emotion. She reached up with her free hand to steady the tiara.

Hawk smiled up at her. "This is meant to match the tiara."

Pia could hardly breathe despite his attempt at levity.

Hawk's expression turned solemn, however. "Pia Lumley,

I love you with all my heart. Will you do me the very great honor of marrying me and becoming my wife? Please?"

Her first proposal. *Ever.*

She'd dreamt of receiving one—from him.

And yet…and yet…

"Wh-what about Michelene?" she couldn't resist asking.

Hawk's lips twitched. "Usually a man doesn't expect a marriage proposal to be met with a question of its own."

"Usually the woman concerned hasn't been expecting him to propose to someone else."

"Touché, but there isn't anyone else," he responded. "Michelene decided not to attend today after it became clear she could no longer have the expectation of becoming a Carsdale bride."

"Oh, Hawk." Pia's voice caught on a sob as she grasped the tiara and lowered it to her side. "I—I l-love you—" she watched as Hawk's face brightened "—and I want to marry you. B-but…"

"No buts." Hawk slid the ring on her finger, and then rose and, taking the tiara from her, placed it on a nearby table.

He took her in his arms and kissed her deeply, quieting her upset.

When he raised his head, Pia swallowed hard.

"I'm not fit to be a duchess."

"I disagree," he said tenderly. "Where else does the heroine of a fairy tale belong but in a palace?"

"Oh, Hawk," she said again. "I have lived a fairy tale. Not because you're proposing that I be your duchess, but because this was a test of character. After I found out about Michelene, I considered continuing an affair until you were officially engaged. But then I realized I couldn't do it. I loved you too much, and I wanted all of you."

His eyes sparked like brown and green flames. "You have all of me. My heart and soul."

"Your mother won't be pleased."

"My mother wants to see me happy," he contradicted. "She and my father had a happy marriage, unlike those of some of their ancestors."

"I'm not conventional duchess material."

He shook his head. "You are in character, if not background."

"But you're eminently responsible these days," she protested.

Hawk smiled. "Then I suppose it's time for me to follow Lucy in her rebellion. You know, as of today, my mother already has one American in-law."

"So far you've managed to shoot down every good reason I have for not getting married."

"That's because there are no good reasons." Hawk touched her cheek. "Pia, do you love me?"

She nodded. "I do."

"And I love you desperately. That's all that matters."

Their lips met, their bodies drawing together.

When they finally broke apart again, Hawk raised her hand. "This ring is one of the Carsdale family jewels. I didn't want to make a proposal empty-handed, but we can get you something you like better if you prefer."

Pia shook her head. "No, the ring's perfect."

"We got a second chance."

She smiled, though she remained misty-eyed. "I'm glad."

He grinned. "Your ringtone on my cell phone is the notes to the song 'Unforgettable.'"

"Really?" she inquired with a tremulous smile. "Then I succeeded. I never wanted you to forget me. It was one of the reasons—"

She stopped and blushed.

"Yes?"

"It's one of the reasons I went to bed with you again," she said in a rush. "I told myself that this time I'd leave you wanting more."

"You were unforgettable the first time."

"And yet you left."

He nodded. "Much to my regret."

"Because your brother died unexpectedly, and you needed to rush home."

"I left not because our night together meant too little," he said with a note of self-deprecation, "but because it meant too much."

"Why didn't you tell me you were Lord James Carsdale?"

"Because I'd grown used to moving around as James Fielding. It was liberating not to have to shake off women who were overly impressed by a title and money. And frankly, it was freeing for me to avoid some of the trappings of my life as a duke's younger son. Little did I know—"

"That one day you'd be the duke yourself?"

He nodded. "And that someone—someone I've come to care about very much—would be hurt by my charade."

"Oh, Hawk, we've lost so much time. I wanted to hate you—"

"But instead, deep down inside, you waited for me, didn't you, Pia?" he murmured, his voice low and intimate.

She nodded, caught by the sudden heat in his eyes.

"And I'll thank heaven every day for that," Hawk said as he lowered his head to hers again.

Pia opened her mouth under his, wanting more of him, wanting to feel their customary flare of desire.

"We can't do this here," she said eventually against his mouth between kisses. "We'll scandalize everyone."

"I hope so," he whispered back wickedly.

For he was her wicked duke.

Epilogue

"You look divine. I can't wait for the wedding night."

Pia turned from the mirror, her heart flipping over as she spotted Hawk in the doorway to the changing room.

He was dressed in a cutaway morning coat that displayed his masculine physique to perfection. She couldn't wait for the wedding night, either.

"You shouldn't be in here," she said, her words belying her feelings. "It's bad luck to see the bride…"

She'd chosen a wedding dress with an all-over lace overlay and a chapel-length train. The dress had a dreamy, fairy-talelike quality, with a straight neckline and fitted sleeves.

It was a dress fit for a princess—or a duchess.

Hawk smiled lazily. "You might feel differently about my appearance when you realize what I've come to deliver."

She surveyed him with mild suspicion. "I—I can't think what that would be," she responded, feeling the weight of the tiara that held her veil in place. "Isn't it customary to present the wedding ring during the ceremony?"

In over an hour, she and Hawk would be exchanging their vows in the chapel on Silderly Park.

"First, a kiss," Hawk said as he stopped in front of her and bent to press his lips to hers.

Pia swayed into him as she felt the warm and supple pressure of his mouth against hers.

When Hawk straightened, Pia wore a dreamy little smile. "I-if that's an indication of what you're here to deliver, then I feel compelled to warn you that we don't have the time or the appropriate easily-disposed-of attire."

Hawk chuckled, and then bent in close. "Later."

Pia felt a shiver chase down her spine at the promise in his voice. "Yes, well, first we have a major production to get through."

After the ceremony, there would be a wedding breakfast for several hundred, in a bow to the dowager duchess's wishes—and somewhat inevitable in light of Hawk's title and position. And in a few weeks' time, after a honeymoon around the Mediterranean, there would be an elegant reception in New York for those who had been unable to attend the wedding.

"After this," Hawk joked, as if reading her mind, "you'll have no end of prospective brides and hostesses seeking your event-planning services."

"I want to assure you that you'll always be at the head of the line," Pia teased back.

Hawk grinned. "How reassuring that I have first dibs on your talent as a party organizer in case I have any more friends who desire a wedding coordinator."

"I thought you exhausted all of those on your way to resurrecting Pia Lumley Wedding Productions!"

"I only called in a few favors," he disagreed modestly. "The lost veil and other capers were not my doing."

"I should hope not."

Hawk sobered a little. "This all brings me back to the reason for my sudden appearance here."

Pia arched a brow. "Yes?"

He reached over and opened a nearby dresser drawer. "I put them in here earlier," he said, withdrawing a velvet case. "I wanted to add the finishing touches to your ensemble."

"Oh, Hawk, no," Pia protested. "You've already given me enough."

"Well, that is true," Hawk conceded with a twinkle in his eyes. "The weight of my heart alone…"

She giggled.

"Nevertheless," he continued solemnly as he opened the jewelry case in his hands, "I hope you'll make an exception for heirloom earrings."

Pia gasped as she caught sight of a magnificent pair of diamond drop earrings.

"They were made for my paternal great-great-grandmother and presented to her on her wedding day," Hawk said as he gazed into her eyes. "Her marriage lasted sixty-one years."

Pia felt emotion clog her throat. "Oh, Hawk, what wonderful history and significance."

Of course, she'd replace the simple diamond studs that she wore—something borrowed from Tamara—with Hawk's gift to her.

Hawk quirked his lips. "Don't thank me just yet. My great-great-grandmother also had eight children."

"Oh!"

His smile widened as he leaned toward her. "Don't worry," he said in a low voice. "I'm already committed to raising the feline Mr. Darcy."

"Hawk?" Lucy's voice sounded from the corridor outside.

"If she finds you in here," Pia said, "she'll be sure to scold you."

Hawk stole a quick kiss. "I'll meet you at the altar."

Pia knew her heart was full to bursting. "And I'll write the fairy tale with you."

From the first day and for the rest of their lives.

* * * * *

A ROYAL BABY
SURPRISE

CAT SCHIELD

To the 2008 Ionian Islands Crew: Erik, Sonia,
Charie, Renee, Jean and Val

One

Above the sound of the breeze blowing through the cedar trees that dotted the island hillside, Nic Alessandro heard the scuff of a footstep on flagstone and knew he wasn't alone on the terrace.

"So this is where you've been hiding." Brooke Davis's voice was like his favorite vodka: smoky and smooth, with a sexy, implied bite. And she went to his head just as swiftly.

Already suffering from a well-deserved hangover, Nic was further jolted by her unexpected arrival on this out-of-the-way Greek island. But he couldn't let himself be glad to see her. The future he'd once planned to have with her was impossible. His older brother, Gabriel, had married a woman incapable of having children, meaning he would have no son to inherit the throne of Sherdana, the European nation their family had ruled for hundreds of years. Now, as next in line to the throne, it was up to Nic to find a wife that the laws of his country would accept as the future mother of the royal line. As an American, Brooke didn't fit the bill.

"Is this the rustic cabin on the side of a mountain you told me about?" she asked. "The one you said I'd hate because it had no running water and no indoor toilets?"

Nic detected the strain she tried to hide beneath her teasing tone. What was she doing here? Had her brother Glen sent her to talk Nic into returning to California? He couldn't believe she'd come on her own after the way he'd broken things off.

"Here I was picturing you suffering in some hovel in the middle of nowhere. Instead, I find you living in a luxurious villa above the most gorgeous harbor I've ever seen."

Her voice came from the side of the terrace that led down to the beach, so she must have arrived by boat. Walking up the hundred and fifty steps hadn't winded her a bit. She loved to work out. It was what kept her lithe body in perfect shape.

What had he been thinking when he'd finally surrendered to the powerful attraction he'd hidden from her for the past five years? He shouldn't have been so quick to assume that his royal duty to Sherdana ended the minute Gabriel had gotten engaged to Lady Olivia Darcy.

"You're probably wondering how I found you."

Nic opened his eyes and watched Brooke saunter across the terrace. She wore a white, high-waisted cotton blouse and faded denim shorts with a ragged hem. The gray scarf wound around her neck was one of her favorites.

Everything she passed she touched: the back of the lounge chair, the concrete wall that bordered the terrace, the terra-cotta pots and the herbs and flowers they held. As her fingertips drifted along the fuchsia petals of a bougainvillea, Nic envied the flower she caressed.

At this hour of the morning, the sun was behind the villa, warming the front garden. On winter days he would have taken coffee to the side patio and made the most of the sunshine. In late July, he preferred the back terrace where he could enjoy the view of the town of Kioni across the harbor. The wind off the Ionian Sea kept the humidity at bay, making this a pleasant spot to linger most of the morning.

"I'm guessing Glen sent you."

She looked pained by his assumption. "No, it was my idea to come."

A double blow. She hadn't accepted the end of their relationship, and Glen didn't want him back working on the rocket after the explosion that had killed a member of their team. An explosion caused when the fuel system Nic had been working on malfunctioned. When the *Griffin* had blown up, his dream of privatizing space travel had gone up in smoke with it. He'd retreated from California in defeat, only to discover that he was now facing royal obligations back in Sherdana.

"You brought him here two years ago for a boys' weekend after a successful test firing. He came back with horror stories of long hikes in the mountains and an abundance of wildlife. I realize now those hikes involved stairs leading down to a private beach and the wildlife was in the bars in town. Shame on you two. I actually felt sorry for him."

Nic rubbed his hand across the stubble around his mouth, hiding a brief smile. They'd certainly had her going.

"Now I see you two were living like kings."

Kings. Her word choice smothered Nic's amusement. Had she used the word deliberately? Had Glen given up all Nic's secrets?

"How can you afford a place like this? You guys were always looking for investors. It seems to me that anyone who had enough money to own this villa could have financed the entire project."

A little of his tension fell away, but only a little. She didn't know the truth yet. And when she did find out…

Tell her. Tell her who you are.

Wise words. Pity he couldn't bring himself to follow his own advice. He'd been hiding his true identity from her for too long. She'd be devastated when she learned how much he'd lied about. Yet, it was only a matter of a week before the media found out he was wife-hunting and he went from obscure scientist to international news item. She would know soon enough. And hopefully when that happened she would appreciate that they'd kept their brief relationship quiet.

She believed herself in love with a man who didn't exist. A man of duty, honor and integrity. They were principles that he'd been raised to embrace, but they'd been sadly lacking the moment he'd pulled Brooke into his arms and kissed her that first time.

"My brothers and I own it," he said, wishing so many things could be different.

Brooke's very stillness suggested the calm before the storm. "I see."

That was it? No explosion? No ranting? "What do you see?"

"That we have a lot to talk about."

He didn't want to talk. He wanted to pull her into his arms and make love to her until they were both too exhausted to speak. "I've already said everything I intend to." He shouldn't have phrased that like a challenge. She was as tenacious as a terrier when she got her teeth into something.

"Don't give me that. You owe me some answers."

"Fine." He owed her more than that. "What do you want to know?"

"You have brothers?"

"Two. We're triplets."

"You never talked about your family. Why is that?"

"There's not much to say."

"Here's where we disagree."

She stepped closer. Vanilla and honey enveloped him, overpowering the scent of cypress and the odor of brine carried on the light morning breeze. With her finger she eased his dark sunglasses down his nose and captured his gaze. Her delicate brows pulled together in a frown.

He braced himself against the pitch and roll of emotions as her green-gray eyes scoured his face. He should tell her to go away, but he was so damned glad to see her that the words wouldn't come. Instead, he growled like a cranky dog that wasn't sure whether to bite or beg to be petted.

"You look like hell."

"I'm fine." Disgusted by his suddenly hoarse voice, he knocked her hand aside and slid his sunglasses back into place.

She, on the other hand, looked gorgeous. Rambunctious red hair, streaked with dark honey, framed her oval face and cascaded over her shoulders. Her pale, unblemished skin, arresting dimples and gently curving cheekbones made for the sort of loveliness any man could lose his head over. A wayward curl tickled his skin as she leaned over him. Shifting his gaze, he took the strand between two fingers and toyed with it.

"What have you been doing all alone in your fancy villa?" she asked.

"If you must know, I'm working."

"On your tan maybe." She sniffed him and wrinkled her slender nose. "Or a hangover. Your eyes are bloodshot."

"I've been working late."

"Riiight." She drew the word out doubtfully. "I'll make some coffee. It looks like you could use some."

Safe behind his dark glasses, he watched her go, captivated by the gentle sway of her denim-clad rear and her long legs. Satin smooth skin stretched over lean muscles, honed by yoga and running. His pulse purred as he recalled those strong, shapely legs wrapped around his hips.

Despite the cool morning air, his body heated. An hour ago, he'd opened his eyes, feeling as he had most of the past few mornings: queasy, depressed and distraught over the accident that had occurred during a test firing of their prototype rocket ship.

Brooke's arrival on this sleepy, Greek island was like being awakened from a drugged sleep by an air horn.

"Someone must be taking care of you," she said a short time later, bringing the smell of bitter black coffee with her when she returned. "The coffeepot was filled with grounds and water. All I had to do was turn it on."

Nic's nostrils flared eagerly as he inhaled the robust aroma. The scent alone was enough to bring him back to life.

She sat down on the lounge beside his and cradled her mug between both hands. She took a tentative sip and made a face. "Ugh. I forgot how strong you like it."

He grunted and willed the liquid to cool a little more so he could drain his cup and start on a second. It crossed his mind that coping with Brooke while a strong jolt of stimulant rushed through his veins was foolhardy at best. She riled him up admirably all by herself, making the mix of caffeine and being alone with her a lethal combination.

"So, am I interrupting a romantic weekend?"

Luckily he hadn't taken another sip, or the stuff might have come straight out his nose. His fingers clenched around the mug. When they began to cramp, he ground his teeth and relaxed his grip.

"Probably not," she continued when he didn't answer. "Or you'd be working harder to get rid of me."

Damn her for showing up while his guard was down. Temptation rode him like a demon every time she was near.

But he couldn't have her. She mustn't know how much he wanted her. He'd barely summoned the strength to break things off a month ago. But now that he was alone with her on this island, her big misty-green eyes watching his every mood, would his willpower hold out?

Silence stretched between them. He heard the creak of wood as she settled back on the lounge. He set the empty cup on his chest and closed his eyes once more. Having her here brought him a sense of peace he had no right to feel. He wanted to reach out and lace his fingers with hers but didn't dare to.

"I can see why you and your brothers bought this place. I could sit here for days and stare at the view."

Nic snorted softly. Brooke had never been one to sit anywhere and stare at anything. She was a whirling dervish of energy and enthusiasm.

"I can't believe how blue the water is. And the town is so quaint. I can't wait to go exploring."

Exploring? Nic needed to figure out how to get her on a plane back to America as soon as possible before he gave in to temptation. Given her knack for leading with her emotions, reasoning with her wouldn't work. Threats wouldn't work, either. The best technique for dealing with Brooke was to let her have her way and that absolutely couldn't happen this time. Or ever again, for that matter.

When she broke the silence, the waver in her voice betrayed worry. "When are you coming back?"

"I'm not."

"You can't mean that." She paused, offering him the opportunity to take back what he'd said. When he didn't, her face took on a troubled expression. "You do mean that. What about *Griffin*? What about the team? You can't just give it all up."

"Someone died because of a flaw in a system I designed—"

She gripped his forearm. "Glen was the one pushing for the test. He didn't listen when you told him it wasn't ready. He's the one to blame."

"Walter died." He enunciated the words, letting her hear his grief. "It was my fault."

"So that's it? You are giving up because something went wrong? You expect me to accept that you're throwing away your life's work? To do what?"

He had no answer. What the hell was he going to do in Sherdana besides get married and produce an heir? He had no interest in helping run the country. That was Gabriel's job. And his other brother Christian had his businesses and investments to occupy him. All Nic wanted to do, all he'd ever wanted to do, was build rockets that would someday carry people into space. With that possibility extinguished, his life stretched before him, empty and filled with regret.

"There's something else going on." She tightened her grip on his arm. "Don't insult my intelligence by denying it."

Nic patted her hand. "I would never do that, Dr. Davis." A less intelligent woman wouldn't have captivated him so completely, no matter how beautiful. Brooke's combination of sex appeal and brains had delivered a fatal one-two punch. "How many doctorates do you have now, anyway?"

"Only two." She jerked her hand from beneath his, reacting to his placating tone. "And don't change the subject." Despite her annoyance, a huge yawn practically dislocated her jaw as she glared at him.

"You're tired." Showing concern for her welfare might encourage her, but he couldn't help it.

"I've been on planes since yesterday sometime. Do you know how long it takes to get here?" She closed her eyes. "About twenty hours. And I couldn't sleep on the flight over."

"Why?"

A deep breath pushed her small, pert breasts tight against her sleeveless white cotton blouse.

"Because I was worried about you, that's why."

The admission was a cop-out. It was fourth on her list of reasons why she'd flown six thousand miles to talk to him in person rather than breaking her news over the phone.

But she wasn't prepared to blurt out that she was eight weeks pregnant within the first ten minutes of arriving.

She had a lot of questions about why he'd broken off their relationship four weeks earlier. Questions she hadn't asked at first because she'd been too hurt to wonder why he'd dropped her when things between them had been so perfect. Then the fatal accident had happened with *Griffin*. Nic had left California and she'd never received closure.

"I don't need your concern," he said.

"Of course you don't." She crammed all the skepticism she could muster into her tone to keep from revealing how much his rebuff stung. "That's why you look like week-old roadkill."

Although his expression didn't change, his voice reflected amusement. "Nice image."

She surveyed his disheveled state, thought about the circles she'd seen beneath his eyes, their utter lack of vitality. The thick black stubble on his cheeks made her wonder how long it had been since he'd shaved. No matter how hard he worked, she'd never seen his golden-brown eyes so flat and lifeless. He really did look like death warmed over.

"Brooke, why did you really come here?"

Her ready excuse died on her lips. He'd believe that she'd come here to convince him to return to the project. It would be safe to argue on behalf of her brother. But where Nic was concerned, she hadn't played it safe for five years. He deserved the truth. So, she selected item number three on her list of why she'd chased after him.

"You disappeared without saying goodbye." Once she better understood what had spooked him, Brooke would confess the number one reason she'd followed him to Ithaca. "When you didn't answer any of my phone calls or respond to my emails, I decided to come find you." She gathered a fortifying breath before plunging into deep water. "I want to know the real reason why things ended between us."

Nic tunneled his fingers into his shaggy black hair, a sure sign he was disturbed. "I told you—"

"That I was too distracting." She glared at him. Nic was her polar opposite. Always so serious, he never let go like other people. He held himself apart from the fun. She'd treated his solemnity as a challenge. And after years of escalating flirtation, she'd discovered he wasn't as in control as he appeared. "You weren't getting enough work done."

She exhaled in exasperation. For five months he'd stopped working on the weekends she'd visited and spent that entire time focused on her. All that attention had been heady and addictive. Brooke hadn't anticipated that he might wake up one morning and go back to his workaholic ways. "I don't get it. We were fantastic together. You were happy."

Nic's mouth tightened into a grim line. "It was fun. But you were all in and I wasn't."

Brooke bit her lip and considered what he said for an awkward, silent minute. "You broke up with me because I told you I loved you?" At the time she hadn't worried about confessing her feelings. After all, she was pretty sure he suspected she'd been falling for him for five years. "Did you ever intend to give us a chance?"

"I thought it was better to end it rather than to let things drag out. I was wrong to let things get so involved between us."

"Why didn't you tell me this in the first place?"

"I thought it would be easier on you if you believed I'd chosen work over you."

"Instead of being truthful and admitting I wasn't the one."

This wasn't how she'd expected this conversation to go. Deep in her heart she'd believed Nic was comfortable with how fast their relationship had progressed. She'd been friends with him long enough to know he didn't squander his time away from the *Griffin* project. This led her to believe she mattered to him. How could she have been so wrong?

Conflicting evidence tugged her thoughts this way and that. Usually she considered less and acted more, but being pregnant meant her actions impacted more than just her. She needed a little time to figure out how to approach Nic about her situation.

"I guess my optimistic nature got the better of me again." She lightened her tone to hide the deep ache centered in her chest.

"Brooke—"

"Don't." She held up both hands to forestall whatever he'd planned to say. "Why don't we not talk about this anymore while you give me a tour of your palatial estate."

"It's not palatial." His thick black eyebrows drew together in a grim frown.

"It is to a girl who grew up in a three-bedroom, fifteen-hundred-square-foot house."

Nic's only reply was a grunt. He got to his feet and gestured for her to precede him. Before entering the house, Brooke kicked off her sandals. The cool limestone tile soothed her tired feet as she slipped past him. Little brush fires ignited along her bare arm where it came into contact with his hair-roughened skin.

"This is the combination living-dining room and

kitchen," he said, adopting the tour guide persona he used when escorting potential *Griffin* investors.

She took in the enormous abstract paintings of red, yellow, blue and green that occupied the wall behind the white slip-covered couches. To her left, in the L-shaped kitchen, there was a large glass table with eight black chairs, offering a contrast among the white cabinets and stainless appliances. The space had an informal feel that invited relaxation.

"The white furniture and walls are a little stark for my taste," she said. "But it works with the paintings. They're wonderful. Who did them?"

"My sister."

He had a sister, too? "I'd like to meet her." Even as Brooke spoke the words, she knew that would never happen. Nic had made it perfectly clear he didn't want her in his life. She had a decision to make in the next day or so. It was why she'd come here. She needed his help to determine how the rest of her life would play out. "Did Glen know about your family?"

"Yes."

That hurt. The two men had always been as tight as brothers, but she never expected that Glen would keep secrets from her.

"Tell me about your brothers." She didn't know what to make of all these revelations.

"We're triplets. I'm the middle one."

"Two brothers and a sister," she murmured.

Who was Nic Alessandro? At the moment he looked nothing like the overworked rocket scientist she'd known for years. Although a bit wrinkled and worse for wear, his khaki shorts and white short-sleeved shirt had turned him into an ad for Armani's summer collection. In fact, his expensive sunglasses and elegant clothes transformed him from an absentminded scientist into your basic, run-of-the-mill European playboy. The makeover shifted him further out of reach.

"Is there anyone else I should know about?" Despite her best efforts to keep her tone neutral, her voice had an edge. "Like a wife?"

"No wife."

Brooke almost smiled at his dark tone. Once upon a time she'd taken great delight in teasing him, and it should have been easy to fall back into that kind of interaction. Unfortunately, the first time he'd kissed her, she'd crossed into a deeply serious place where his rejection had the power to bruise and batter her heart.

"Who takes care of all this when you're not here?" Keeping the conversation casual was the only way to keep sadness from overwhelming her.

"We have a caretaker who lives in town. She comes in once a week to clean when we're not in residence, more often when we are. She also cooks for us, and her husband maintains the gardens and the boat, and fixes whatever needs repairing in the house."

Brooke looked over her shoulder at the outdoor terrace with its informal wood dining table and canvas chairs. A set of three steps led down to another terrace with more lounge chairs. Potted herbs lined the three-foot-high walls, softening all the concrete.

"What's upstairs?"

Nic stood in the middle of the living room, his arms crossed, a large, immovable object. "Bedrooms."

"One I can use?" she asked in a small voice.

A muscle twitched in his jaw. "There are a number of delightful hotels in town."

"You'd turn me out?" Something flared in his eyes that brought her hope back to life. Maybe she hadn't yet heard the complete explanation for why he'd broken off their relationship. She faked a sniffle. "You can't really be so mean as to send me in search of a hotel when you have so much room here."

Nic growled. "I'll show you where you can shower and grab some sleep before you head home."

Although it stung that he was so eager to get rid of her, she'd departed California suspecting he wouldn't welcome her intrusion.

"Then, I can stay?"

"For the moment."

Mutely, she followed him back out through the open French doors and onto the terrace. He made a beeline toward the duffel bag she'd dropped beside the stairs that lead up from the beach.

"I can't get over how beautiful it is here."

"Most people are probably more familiar with the islands in the Aegean," he said, picking up her bag. "Mykonos, Santorini, Rhodes."

"I imagine there's a lot more tourists there."

"Quite a few. Kioni attracts a number of sailors during the summer as well as some people wanting to hike and enjoy a quieter island experience, but we're not overrun. Come on, the guesthouse is over there." He led the way along the terrace to a separate building.

"You should take me sightseeing."

"No. You are going to rest and then we're going to find you a flight home."

Brooke rolled her eyes at Nic's words and decided to take the fact that he kept trying to be rid of her as a challenge. "My return ticket is for a flight a week from now."

"Don't you have a lot to do to prepare for your students at Berkeley?"

"I don't have the job yet." Though Brooke held a position at UC Santa Cruz, teaching Italian studies at Berkeley had been a dream of hers since her sophomore year in college. And then she and Nic had begun a relationship. Soon the distance from San Francisco to the Mojave Desert had become an impediment to what she wanted: a life with Nic.

He shot her a sharp look.

She shrugged. "The interview got postponed again."

"To when?"

"Not for a few weeks yet."

In truth she wasn't sure when it was. There'd been some scheduling conflicts with the head of the department. He'd already canceled two meetings with her in the past month. Not knowing how many people were up for the position she wanted gnawed at her confidence. Few shared her research credentials, but a great many had more experience in the classroom than she did.

And before Nic had abruptly dumped her, she'd begun thinking she wanted to be closer to where he lived and worked. Seeing him only on the weekends wasn't enough. So she'd interviewed for a position at UCLA and been offered a teaching job starting in the fall. The weekend Nic had come up to San Francisco to break up with her, she'd been preparing for a very different conversation. One where she told him she was moving to LA. Only he'd beaten her to the punch and she'd decided to put the Berkeley job back on the table.

"Are you sure?" Nic questioned. "It's July. I can't believe they want to put off their decision too much longer."

She frowned at him, butterflies hatching in her stomach as she realized the risk she'd taken by flying here when she should be waiting by the phone in California. "Yes, I'm sure."

"Because I couldn't live with myself if you lost your dream job because you stayed here imagining I'm going to change my mind about us."

Had she been wrong about his initial reaction to her arrival? Had she so badly wanted him to be glad to see her that she'd imagined the delight in his gaze? It wouldn't be the first time she'd jumped to the wrong conclusion where a man's behavior was concerned. And Nic was a master at keeping his thoughts and emotions hidden.

"Don't worry about my dream job," she countered. "It will still be there when I get back."

She hoped.

When they arrived at the small guesthouse, Nic pushed open the door and set her luggage inside. "There's a private bathroom and a great view of Kioni. You should be comfortable here." Neither his impassive expression nor his neutral tone gave anything away. "Relax. Sleep. I'm sure you're exhausted from your travels. Breakfast will be waiting when you're ready."

"I'm not really hungry." Between morning sickness and anxiety, her appetite had fled. "And no matter how tired I am, you know I can't sleep when the sun is up. Why don't we go into town and you can show me around."

"You should rest."

His tone warned her not to argue. The wall he'd erected between them upset her. She wanted to tear it down with kisses and tears and impassioned pleas for him to change his mind about breaking up. But a big emotional scene would only cause him to retreat. She needed to appeal to that big logical brain of his.

"I've come a long way to find you. And talk."

"Later." He scowled at her to forestall any further discussion.

The determined set of his mouth told her she would get nowhere until he was ready to listen. She nodded, reluctant to provoke Nic into further impatience. She wanted him in a calm, agreeable state of mind when she imparted her dramatic news.

Left alone, Brooke took a quick shower in the white, marble bathroom and dressed in a tribal-print maxi dress of cool cotton. There was enough of a breeze blowing in through the open windows to dry her hair, but she didn't want to give Nic too much time to plan his strategy for getting her to leave. She decided to braid the damp strands rather than leave them loose. The last time they'd made love a little over a month ago, he'd shown a great appreciation for the disarray of her long, curly tresses, but now it seemed better to approach him logically and for that she needed to be restrained, not flirty.

Unfortunately, the mirror over the dresser reflected a woman in love, with wide eyes and a slightly unfocused gaze. Her mouth had a rosy fullness and her cheeks were pink. She doubted that this would go over well with Nic.

And after what he'd told her about his reasons for breaking up, Brooke was certain her pregnancy news would be unwelcome, too.

She hadn't given much thought to what came after she told Nic the news. Maybe she was afraid to face more rejection. What if he wanted nothing further to do with her? He'd said he wasn't returning to California. Would the news that he was going to be a father change his plans?

Brooke slid her feet into sandals, but paused before leaving the room. Talking with Nic about her Berkeley interview reminded her she hadn't checked her messages since leaving San Francisco. She dug her cell phone out of the side pocket of her duffel bag and tried to turn it on, but the battery had died. Time ticked away as she dug out her charger and searched for the adapter she'd borrowed. Then there were the minutes it took for the phone to charge enough to come back to life. By the time the display lit up and showed she'd missed a dozen calls, Brooke crackled with impatience.

Her heart sank as she listened to the messages. Her Berkeley interview had been rescheduled for 10:00 a.m. three days from now. This considerably shortened the amount of time Brooke had to tell Nic she was pregnant and figure out what form her future relationship with him would take. A quick check of flight schedules revealed that it would be daunting, but doable.

Brooke tossed the phone onto the middle of the bed and took several deep breaths until the tightness in her throat eased. After a few more deep breaths, the urge to throw herself onto the mattress and scream into a pillow subsided, too. Everything would work out just fine. Somehow it always did.

Applying a bright smile to her face, she strolled along the terrace. But as she stepped into the living room of the main house, the absolute quiet told her something was awry. A quick check confirmed her suspicions, but what clinched it was the car missing from the driveway.

Nic had vanished.

Two

Nic had switched from Greek coffee to beer by the time Brooke showed up in Kioni, the village rising from the harbor to cling to the side of Ithaca's rocky hills. From the shade beneath the taverna's white awning, he squinted against the bright sunlight sparkling off the cerulean water and watched his thirty-four-foot cruiser pull alongside the quay. Three Greek men, each wearing broad smiles, converged to issue instructions and help Brooke settle the boat. Although the distance prevented Nic from hearing their conversation, from Brooke's animated gestures and the men's cheerful faces, he guessed she was chattering away and doing what she did best: charming men.

"You're not drinking them as fast today."

Nic switched his attention to the voluptuous, dark-haired, dark-eyed waitress standing at his side. Natasa had waited on him all but one of the past ten days he'd been on the island. She picked up his half-full bottle, which he'd been nursing for the past hour.

"I'm not as thirsty."

Since arriving on Ithaca, Nic had been keeping himself anesthetized with boredom and beer. The combination was barely enough to keep his demons at bay. Before Brooke's arrival he'd given himself a week or so before he had to make peace with his failures and accept his fate. Now it was all coming to a head faster than he could handle.

Natasa gave him a smoky look and set her hand on her hip. "Perhaps you need some company."

Nic hadn't seen her flirt with any of the other men that came to the taverna, only him. He figured she knew who he was and suspected that had prompted her offer. Acid churned in his gut. Being treated like a personality rather than a person was something he hadn't had to endure in America. He hadn't had to be on his guard and question everyone's motives.

"I get off in two hours," she continued. "I would be happy to join you then."

Natasa had made him a similar proposition last night at closing time. Nic had been moderately drunk, but not enough to wish to share the bed with this woman, no matter how attractive she was. His carefree bachelor days had ended a month ago with Gabriel's marriage. Soon every woman he glanced at twice would become fodder for news stories.

It was worse for him being in Europe than living in America. In California he was an anonymous scientist trying to build a rocket ship. On this side of the Atlantic, he was known as Prince Nicolas, second in line to the throne of Sherdana. Avoiding reporters and paparazzi and being wary of helpful strangers had become a routine part of his life. That's why he and his brothers had chosen Ithaca as a retreat. Homer had described the island as "good for goats" but it gave the Alessandro brothers an escape from their hectic world.

Not that Nic was a fool. He knew his "anonymity" on this sleepy island was tenuous at best. But he and his brothers maintained a low profile, and the locals generously pretended the Sherdanian royals were like any other part-time inhabitants.

"I'm afraid I'm already due for some company," Nic said, nodding toward the harbor.

When the boat was snugly tied, three tanned hands extended to help Brooke onto the quay. She seemed to hesitate before accepting the hands of the two men nearest to her and offering the third man an engaging smile.

Natasa shielded her eyes as she gazed in the same direction Nic was looking. "Isn't that your boat?" Her keen black eyes narrowed as she glanced at him for confirmation.

"Yes."

"And the girl?"

"She's staying with me for a few days." Until the words left his lips he hadn't realized he'd changed his mind about putting her on a plane home as soon as humanly possible. Keeping her around was a mistake, but he was feeling battered and raw. Her company was the balm his psyche needed. He just needed to keep her at arm's length.

Natasa sniffed and tossed her head. Then, without another word, she turned to go. Nic gave a mental shrug. He'd retreated to Ithaca to come to grips with his future, not to tumble into some local's bed. He liked his own company. In fact, most days, he preferred it. Why didn't people understand that and leave him alone?

Reality smacked Nic right between the eyes. Soon enough he'd never be left alone again. Returning to Sherdana meant not only a return to duty, but also a complete loss of privacy and peace. Long, solitary hours in his workshop would be a thing of the past. His father and brothers would ensure that his calendar was packed with meetings, speeches and public appearances. He'd been absent for ten years, five years of studying and another five working with Glen on the *Griffin* project.

Now that he was returning home for good, his family would expect him to get up to speed on a variety of political, economic and environmental issues affecting the country. He would be surrounded by advisers, besieged by demands for decisions and sought after for his opinions.

Balls and state dinners with visiting foreign dignitaries would replace basketball tournaments and pig roasts with the team of specialists that he'd assembled to help build the *Griffin* rocket ship. Then there would be the selection of his bride. Once his mother finished narrowing the field of marriage prospects—women his brother had already rejected—Nic would have to choose whom he would spend the rest of his life with. And he wouldn't be allowed to dawdle over his decision because the succession needed to be secured by the birth of a royal heir.

The burden of what lay ahead of him sat on Nic's shoulders like a sack of cement. Was it any wonder he'd kept Brooke in the dark about his true identity all these years? He would have liked to continue pretending that he was just an ordinary man instead of a royal prince in serious trouble of doing the wrong thing with the right woman. But she'd never agree to back off unless she knew his whole story.

In disgruntled admiration, Nic followed Brooke's progress as she made her way around the horseshoe-shaped harbor. Since he'd left the house, she'd changed into an earth-toned sundress and accessorized with chunky bracelets and a peace sign necklace. Her red hair lay in a braided rope across her left shoulder. The breeze that frolicked through the streets teased the strands around her face that weren't long enough to be restricted by the braid.

Gulls jeered as they swooped past her. She appeared

oblivious to their taunts, focused as she was on scanning the quay. The hem of the sundress brushed her calves as she walked. The thin spaghetti straps were too narrow to hide a bra so he knew she was at least partially bare beneath the dress. Speculating on just how bare renewed the pounding in his head despite the aspirin he'd taken earlier.

She neared the taverna. Nic wasn't sure she'd spotted him yet. Eight restaurants edged the water. This particular taverna was Nic's favorite. He'd sampled enough of the menu in the years since they'd bought the villa to be able to make recommendations. The waitstaff always kept the cold beer coming while he took in the view of the vivid blue harbor, a welcome change from the beige and russet California desert where he'd spent the past several years.

For entertainment he liked to watch the comings and goings of the sailboats chartered by vacationers. The captains often wrestled with the difficulties presented by Mediterranean mooring, the docking technique where the anchor was dropped forty feet into the harbor and then the boat was backed up against the cement quay. Only an hour ago he'd been witness to what could go wrong when you had twenty boats snugged in side by side. One departing boat had lifted its anchor, catching its neighbor's as it went, only to at last drop that anchor across the lines belonging to the boat on the other side, hopelessly tangling the two boats. To Nic's amusement, much shouting and gesturing had accompanied the maneuver.

His earlier question about whether Brooke had spotted him was answered as she wove through the tables, aiming straight for him.

"Where did you get the keys to the boat?" he quizzed as she plopped a big canvas purse on the table and sat down with a whoosh of breath.

"Elena showed up shortly after you left. She fed me breakfast and told me where to find them. She's very nice.

And had flattering things to say about you. I think you're her favorite triplet."

Nic wondered what else Elena had said. Had the housekeeper divulged the rest of his secret?

"I doubt that very much. She's always been partial to Christian. He's the youngest. And the one all the ladies love."

"Why is that?"

"He's not as serious as Gabriel or me."

"What does he do?"

"He buys companies and takes them apart so he can sell off the pieces."

"And Gabriel?"

"He runs the family business." Not the truth, but not exactly a lie.

"And your sister paints."

"Ariana."

"And you build rocket ships. Sounds like you're all successful."

Not all of them. With the failure of his life's work, he certainly wasn't feeling particularly successful at the moment.

"I hope you don't mind, but I used your computer to print out some forms I needed to sign."

Even while on vacation the Alessandro triplets were often working on a project or a deal and having a state-of-the-art computer as well as a combination printer and scanner often came in handy.

"You figured out how to turn it on?"

As brilliant as she was when it came to learning languages or analyzing Italian literature, Brooke was technically challenged. She'd handwritten most of her first thesis until Nic had taken her to buy a laptop. He'd then lost an entire weekend to teaching her the ins and outs of the word-processing software as well as an app that enabled her to organize her research for easy reference.

"Ha-ha. I'm not as inept as you think I am."

"That's not saying much."

She pulled a face at him. "You had about forty unopened emails from the team. Why haven't you answered any of their questions?"

Nic shifted his gaze to the harbor and watched an inbound sailboat. "As I explained to you earlier, I'm done."

"How can you walk away from your team and all the hard work they've put in on the project?"

Why didn't she understand? Even if it wasn't his duty to return to Sherdana, Nic couldn't let go of the fact that his faulty design had destroyed the rocket and resulted in a man's death. Besides, Glen was the heart of the project. He would carry on in Nic's absence.

"Glen will find a new engineer," Nic said. "Work will continue."

The rocket's destruction had hastened the inevitable. Nic had known he couldn't stay in California forever. It was only a matter of time before responsibility to his country would have forced him to return home.

"But you were the brains behind the new fuel delivery system."

And his life's work had resulted in a complete disaster. "They have my notes."

"But—"

"Leave it alone." He kept his voice low, but the sharp snap of the words silenced her. An uneasy tension descended between them. "Are you hungry? If you like eggplant, the moussaka is very good."

She pressed her lips together, but Nic could see she wanted to argue with him further. Instead, she asked, "So, what are you going to do?"

"My family is going through a hard time right now. I'm going home."

"For how long?"

"For good."

"Wow."

The shaky breath she released was a punch to his gut. A week ago he'd left California as soon as the initial investigation of the accident concluded. He hadn't spoken to her before getting on a plane. His emotions were too raw. And he'd had no idea how to say goodbye.

"I wish I could make you understand, but I can't."

"You're afraid."

Nic eyed Brooke. Her perceptiveness where he was concerned had always made him wary of letting her get too close. Maybe telling her the truth would be a mistake. Giving her access to his life would increase his connection to her, and keeping his distance would become that much harder.

"Of hurting more people, yes."

She would assume he meant another scientist like Walter Parry, the man who'd died. But Nic was thinking about his family and her brother. And most of all her. When Gabriel's engagement had been announced, Nic had felt a loosening of the ties that bound him to Sherdana. Gabriel and Olivia would get married and go on to produce the future monarchs of Sherdana, raising them with Gabriel's twin two-year-old daughters, Bethany and Karina, who'd come to live with Gabriel after their fashion model mother had died a month earlier. They were illegitimate and the only children Gabriel would ever have.

Lady Olivia's infertility—and Gabriel's decision to make her his wife—meant Nic and Christian were no longer free to marry whomever they wished. Or, in Christian's case, to continue enjoying his playboy lifestyle and never marry at all.

Nic cursed the circumstances that had turned his life upside down and sucked him back into a world that couldn't include Brooke. If he'd been a simple scientist, he wouldn't have to resist the invitation in her eyes. Nic shoved away the traitorous thought. It was pointless to dwell on what could never be.

"I can't believe you're really going to give it all up," she said. "You and my brother were excited about the future. The pair of you would get so caught up in a new discovery you wouldn't have noticed if a tornado swept the lab away. You love being a scientist."

"I do, but…" In the three weeks since the rocket had blown up, he'd lost confidence in his abilities. Yet his passion continued to burn. The opposing forces were slowly tearing him apart.

"What are you going to do when you go home?"

"My brothers are interested in luring technology-based companies into the country. They want me to be their technical consultant."

He tried to inject some enthusiasm into his voice and failed. While he agreed with Gabriel that Sherdana's economy would benefit from an influx of such businesses, he wasn't excited about his role in the process. His whole life he'd been actively engaged in creating technologies that would shape the future. The idea of promoting someone else's vision depressed him.

"Sooo," she dragged the word out, "you're never coming back to California?"

"No."

"If this is about the rocket…"

"It's not."

"I don't understand what's going on with you." She looked more than puzzled. She looked worried. "It's not like you to give up."

Nic knew she deserved a full explanation, but once she

found out he'd been keeping a huge secret from her all these years she was going to be furious. "There's a little something about me you don't know."

"Oh, I think there's more than a little something."

He ignored her sarcasm. "It's complicated."

"It's okay. As you pointed out earlier, I have two doctorates. I can understand complicated."

"Very well. I'm not an ordinary scientist." He lowered his voice, wishing he'd had this conversation with her at the villa. "I'm Prince Nicolas Alessandro, second in line to the throne of Sherdana."

"A prince? Like a real prince?" Her misty-green eyes blurred and she shook her head as if to rid her brain of his admission. "I don't get it. You sound as American as I do."

"I went to college in Boston. In order to fit in, I eliminated my accent." Nic leaned forward, glad that there was a table between them. He longed to pull her into his arms and kiss away her unhappiness. That was something he could never again do. "My country is Sherdana. It's a small kingdom tucked between France and Italy."

"How small?"

"A little less than two thousand square kilometers with a population of just over four hundred thousand. We're mostly known for our—"

"Wines." She slapped her palm on the table. His beer rattled against the hard surface. "Now I remember why the name is so familiar. Glen had bottles of Sherdanian wine at one of his recent parties."

Nic remembered that evening without pleasure. "It was his way of sending me a message. He wanted me to tell you the truth."

She stared at Nic with dawning horror. "You jerk. I've known you for five years. And you've kept this huge thing from me the whole time? What did you think I was going to do with the information? Sell you out to the press? Torment you with Disney references? Well, that I would have done, but you're a prince—you could have handled that."

Nic waited for her rant to wind down, but she was on a roll and wasn't going to be stopped until she had her say.

"I thought we were friends." Below the irritation in her voice, she sounded as if her heart was breaking. "Why didn't you tell me any of this?"

"I've concealed my identity for a lot of years. It's a hard habit to break."

"Concealed it from strangers, coworkers, acquaintances." The breath she needed to take wasn't available. "How long has my brother known? Probably since you met. You two are as close as brothers." She shut her eyes. "Imagine how I feel, Nic. You've been lying to me as long as I've known you."

"Glen said—"

"Glen?" She pinned him with a look of such fury that a lesser man would have thrown himself at her feet to grovel for forgiveness. "My brother did not tell you to lie to me."

No. Nic had decided to do that all on his own. "He told me you'd never leave it alone if you knew."

"Are you kidding me?" Her eyes widened in dismay. "You were worried that I'd come on even stronger if I knew you were a prince? Is that how low your opinion is of me?"

"No. That's not what I meant—"

"I came here looking for scientist Nic," she reminded him. "That's the man I thought I knew. Who I've—"

"Brooke, stop." Nic badly needed to cut off her declaration.

"—fallen in love with."

Pain, hot and bright, sliced into his chest. "Damn it. I never wanted that." Which was his greatest lie to date.

"Was that how you felt before or after we became intimate?"

"Both." Hoping to distract her, he said, "Do you have any idea how irresistible you are?"

"Is that supposed to make me feel better?"

"It's supposed to explain why I started a relationship with you six months ago after I'd successfully withstood the attraction between us for the last five years."

"Why did you fight it?" She frowned "What happened between us was amazing and real."

His breath exploded from his lungs in a curse. "A month ago we had this conversation. I thought you understood."

"A month ago you claimed your work was the most important thing in your life. Now I find out you never had deep feelings for me and didn't mean to mislead me about where our relationship was heading. But I've always been of the opinion that a woman should react to how a man behaves, not what he says, and you acted like a very happy man when we were together."

"I was happy. But I was wrong to give you the impression I could offer you any kind of future."

"Because you don't care about me?"

"Because I have to go home."

Her brows drew together. "You didn't think I would go with you?"

"You have a life in California. Family. Friends. A career."

"So instead of asking me what I wanted, you made the decision for me."

"Except I can't ask." His frustration was no less acute than hers. "A month ago my older brother made a decision that affects not only my life, but the future of Sherdana."

"What sort of decision?"

"He married a woman who can never have children."

Brooke stared at him in mystified silence for a long moment before saying, "That's very sad, but what does it have to do with you?"

"It's now up to me to get married and make sure the Alessandro royal blood line is continued."

"You're going to marry?" She sat back, her hands falling from the table onto her lap.

"So that I can produce an heir. I'm second in line to the throne. It's my duty."

Her expression flattened into blank shock for several seconds as she absorbed his declaration. He'd never seen her dumbfounded. Usually she had a snappy retort for everything. Her quick mind processed at speeds that constantly amazed him.

"Your younger brother can't do it?"

The grim smile he offered her conveyed every bit of his displeasure. "I'm quite certain mother intends to see that we are both married before the year is out."

"It is a truth universally acknowledged," she quoted, "that a single man in possession of a good fortune, must be in want of a wife." She stared at the taverna's logo printed in blue on the white place mat as if the answers to the universe were written there in code. "And I'm not the one you want."

"It isn't that simple." He gripped his beer in both hands to keep from reaching out and offering her comfort. "In order for my child to be eligible to ascend Sherdana's throne someday, the constitution requires that his mother has to be either a Sherdana citizen or a member of Europe's aristocracy."

"And I'm just an ordinary girl from California with two doctorates." The corners of her mouth quivered in a weak attempt at a smile. "I get it."

Three

Beneath the grapevines woven through the taverna's roof beams, the afternoon heat pressed in on Brooke. Light-headed and slightly ill, she didn't realize how much she'd set her hopes on Nic's returning to California and giving their relationship another try until he crushed her dreams with his confession. Her fingers fanned over her still-flat abdomen and the child that grew there. Not once since she'd learned she was pregnant had she considered raising this child utterly on her own. Nic had always been there for her. First as her brother's friend. Then her friend. And finally as her lover.

When she'd strayed from her topic during the writing of her second thesis he'd spent hours on the phone talking her through her research and her arguments. He'd gone with her to buy both her cars. He always shared his dessert with her when they went out to dinner even though she knew it drove him crazy that she never ordered her own. And in a dozen little ways, he stayed present in her life even though physically they lived miles apart.

For an instant she recalled the last time she and Nic had made love. She'd gazed deep into his eyes and glimpsed her future. During their time together, their lovemaking had been in turn fast, hot, slow and achingly sweet. But on their last night in particular, they'd both been swept away by urgent intensity. Yet there'd been a single look suspended between one breath and the next that held her transfixed. In that instant, an important connection had been made between them and she'd been forever changed.

But now...

A prince.

The conversion from distracted, overworked scientist to intense, sexy aristocrat had been apparent when she'd arrived this morning. At first she'd ascribed the change to his European-style clothing, but now she understood he'd been transformed in a far more elemental manner.

A month ago he'd given her a speech about how he needed to refocus on *Griffin*, and that meant he had to stop seeing her. She'd been frustrated by the setback, but figured it was only a matter of time until he figured out they were meant to be together. When he'd left California in the wake of the accident, the bond had stretched and thinned, but it had held. Awareness of Nic had hummed across that psychic filament. Although compelled to track him down and investigate if her instincts were correct, she'd decided to give him some space to process the accident before she followed him. Her pregnancy had made finding him much more urgent.

But what good was the bond between them when the reality was he was a prince who needed to find a wife so he could father children that would one day rule his country?

And what about her own child? This was no longer a simple matter of being pregnant with Nic's baby. She was carrying the illegitimate child of a prince. For a moment the taverna spun sickeningly around her. Telling Nic he was going to be a father had become that much more complicated.

Somehow she found the strength of will to summon a wry smile. "Besides, you and I both know I'm not princess material."

"You'd hate it," Nic told her in somber tones. To her relief he'd taken her self-deprecating humor at face value. "All the restrictions on how you dressed and behaved."

"Being polite to people instead of setting them straight." He was right. She'd hate it. "The endless parties to attend where I had to smile until my face hurt. I'm so not the type."

The litany leached away her optimism. With hope reaching dangerously low levels, she cursed the expansive hollowness inside her. Nothing had felt the same since she'd stepped onto this island. It wasn't just Nic's fancy clothes, expensive villa and the whole prince thing. He was different. And more unreachable than ever.

How am I supposed to live without you?

The question lodged in her throat. She concentrated on breathing evenly to keep the tears at bay.

"Are you okay?"

Her pulse spiked at his concerned frown. In moments like these he surprised her by being attuned to her mood. And keeping track of how she was feeling was no small task. Her family often teased her about being a drama girl. She enjoyed life to the fullest, reveling in each success and taking disappointments as world-ending. As she'd gotten older, she'd learned to temper her big emotions and act on impulse less frequently.

Except where Nic was concerned. Common sense told her if she'd behave more sensibly, Nic might be more receptive to her. But everything about him aroused her passion and sent her into sensory overload.

"Brooke?"

Unable to verbalize the emotions raging through her, she avoided looking at Nic and found the perfect distraction in a waitress's hard stare. The woman had been watching from the kitchen doorway ever since Brooke had sat down. "I don't think that waitress likes me," Brooke commented, indicating the curvaceous brunette. "Did I interrupt something between you two?"

"Natasa? Don't be ridiculous."

His impatient dismissal raised Brooke's spirits slightly. She already knew Nic wasn't the sort to engage in casual encounters. Her five-year pursuit of him had demonstrated that he wasn't ruled by his body's urges.

"She's awfully pretty and hasn't taken her eye off you since I sat down."

"Do you want something to eat?" Nic signaled Natasa and she came over.

"Another beer for me," he told the waitress. "What are you drinking?" He looked to Brooke.

"Water."

"And an order of *taramosalata*."

"What is that?" Brooke quizzed, her gaze following the generous sway of Natasa's hips as she wound her way back toward the kitchen.

"A spread made from fish roe. You'll like it."

You'll like it.

Did he realize the impact those words had on her nerve endings?

It was what he'd said to her their first night together. To her amazement, once he'd stopped resisting her flirtatious banter and taken the lead, she'd been overcome by his authoritative manner and had surrendered to his every whim. Her skin tingled, remembering the sweep of his fingers across the sensitized planes of her body. He'd made love to her with a thoroughness she'd never known. Not one inch of her body had gone unclaimed by him and she'd let it all happen. Her smile had blazed undiminished for five months until he'd driven up to San Francisco for *the talk*.

Natasa returned with their drinks. She gave Brooke a quick once-over, plunked two bottles on the table and shot Nic a hard look he didn't notice. Brooke grinned as Nic reached for her bottled water and broke the seal without being asked. He didn't know it, but this was just one of the things that had become a ritual with them. During the past five years, Brooke had repeatedly asked him to do her small favors and Nic had obliged, grumbling all the while about her inability to do the simplest tasks. He'd never figured out that each time he helped her, he became a little more invested in their relationship.

Six months ago all her subtle efforts had brought results. After a successful test firing of the *Griffin's* ignition system, the team had been celebrating in Glen's backyard. Nic had been animated, electrified. She'd been a moth to his flame, basking in his warm smiles and affectionate touches. At the end of the evening he'd meshed their fingers together and drawn her to the privacy of the front porch where he'd kissed her silly.

Lying sleepless in her bed that night she'd relived the mind-blowing kiss over and over and wondered what she'd done to finally break through Nic's resistance. She hadn't been able to pinpoint anything, nor did she think that day's success had been the trigger. The team had enjoyed several triumphs in the previous few months. In the end Brooke had decided her years of flirting had finally begun to reach him.

After that night, she'd noticed a subtle difference in the way Nic behaved toward her and began to hope that he might have finally figured out she was the one for him.

Brooke increased the frequency of her weekend visits to the Mojave Air and Space Port, where the *Griffin* team had their offices. Despite the increased urgency to finish the rocket and get it ready for a test launch, Nic had made time for quiet dinners. Afterward, they'd often talked late into the night. After two months, he'd taken things to the next level. He'd shared not just his body with her, but his dreams and desires, as well. At the time, she'd thought she was getting to know the real Nic. Now she realized how much he'd kept from her.

With fresh eyes, Brooke regarded her brother's best friend and saw only a stranger. In his stylish clothes and expensive shades he looked every inch a rich European. She contemplated the arrogant tilt of his head, the utter command of his presence as he watched her. Why had she never picked up on it earlier?

Because his English was flawlessly Americanized. Because he went to work every day in ordinary jeans and T-shirts. Granted, he filled out his commonplace clothes in an extraordinary manner, but nothing about his impressive pecs and washboard abs screamed aristocracy. She'd always assumed he rarely let off steam with his fellow scientists because he was preoccupied with work.

Now she realized he'd been brought up with different expectations placed upon him than people in her orbit. A picture formed in her mind. Nic, tall and proud, his broad shoulders filling out a formfitting tuxedo, a red sash across his chest from shoulder to hip. He looked regal. Larger than life. Completely out of reach.

Brooke had always believed that people didn't regret the things they did, only the things they didn't. She liked to believe she was richer for every experience she'd had, good or bad. Would she have given her heart to Nic if she'd known who he was from the beginning? Yes. Brief as it had been, she cherished every moment of their time together.

While logic enabled her to rationalize why she couldn't marry him, her heart prevented her from walking away without a backward glance. And she suspected he wasn't thrilled to be sacrificing himself so that his family could continue to reign. As devastating as it was to think she'd have to give up on a future with Nic, wanting to be with him was a yearning she couldn't shake off.

"I'm going to ask you a question," she announced abruptly, her gaze drilling through his bland expression. "And I expect the truth this time."

Nic's beer bottle hung between the table and his lips. "I suppose I owe you that."

"You're darned right you do." She ignored the brief flare of amusement in his eyes. "I want to know the real reason you broke up with me."

"I've already explained the reason. We have no future. I have to go home and I have to marry." He stared at the harbor behind her, his expression chiseled in granite.

She'd obviously phrased her question wrong. "And if your brother hadn't married someone who couldn't have children? Would you have broken things off?"

What she really wanted to know was if he loved her, but she wasn't sure he'd pondered how deep his feelings for her ran. Also, a month ago he'd apparently accepted that he had to marry someone else and it wasn't his nature to dwell on impossibilities.

"It's a simple question," she prompted as the silence stretched. He surely hated being put on the spot like this, but she couldn't move on until she knew.

His chest rose and fell on a huge sigh as he met her gaze with heavy-lidded eyes. Something flickered within those bronze-colored depths. Something that made her stomach contract and her spirits soar.

She'd journeyed to Ithaca to tell him about the baby, but also because she couldn't bear to let him go. Now she understood that she had to. But not yet. She had two days before she had to return to the States. Two days to say goodbye. All she needed was a sign from Nic that he hadn't wanted to give her up.

"No." He spoke the word like a curse. "We'd still be together."

The instant the words left his lips, Nic wished he'd maintained the lies. Brooke's eyes kindled with satisfaction and her body relaxed. She resembled a contented cat. He'd seen the look many times and knew it meant trouble.

"I think we should spend the time between now and when you leave *together*." She gave the last word a specific emphasis that he couldn't misinterpret.

Nic shook his head, vigorously rejecting her suggestion. "That's not fair to you." *Duty. Honor. Integrity.* He repeated the words like a prayer. "I won't take advantage of you that way."

Brooke leaned forward, her gaze sharpening. "Has it ever occurred to you that I like it when you take advantage of me?"

The world beyond their table blurred until it was only him and her and the intense emotional connection that had clicked into place the first time they'd made love, a connection that couldn't be severed.

"I never noticed." His attempt to banter with her so that she'd adopt a less serious mood fell flat.

Her determination gained momentum. "Tell me you don't want to spend your last days of freedom with me."

Every molecule that made up his body screamed at him to agree. "It's not that I don't want to. I shouldn't." He spoke quickly to prevent her from arguing with him. "Ever since finding out I had to return home and get married, I promised myself I wouldn't touch you again."

"That's just silly." She gave him a wicked smile. "You like touching me."

In the time he'd known her, he'd learned just how powerful that smile could be. It had whittled away at his willpower until he'd done the one thing he knew he shouldn't. He'd fallen hard.

Duty. Honor. Integrity. The lament filled his mind. If only Brooke didn't make it so damned hard to do the right thing.

She got up from her chair and stepped into his space.

He tipped his head back and assessed her determined expression. His heart shuddered as she put her palms flat on his shoulders and settled herself on his lap. Even though Nic had braced himself for the arousing pressure of her firm rear on his thighs, it took every bit of concentration he possessed to put his hands behind his back, safely out of range of her tempting curves. What sort of hell had he let himself fall into?

"What do you think you're doing?"

"Are you all right?" she asked, tracing her fingertips across his furrowed brow.

God, she was a tempting lapful.

"I'm fine."

"You don't look fine."

"I'm great, and you didn't answer my question." He pulled her spicy scent into his lungs and held it there. He longed to bury his face in her neck and imprint her upon his senses. "What are you doing on my lap?"

"Demonstrating that you want me as much as I want you."

He hated himself for hoping she'd continue the demonstration until he couldn't catch his breath. Making love to her was amazing. He'd never been with anyone who matched him the way she did. Anticipation gnawed on him like a puppy with a stolen shoe.

"I assure you I want you a great deal more." How he kept his voice so clinical, Nic would never know.

"Then you'll let me stay on the island for the next few days?"

She knew him better than anyone and once she'd discovered his weakness where she was concerned, she'd pressed her advantage at every opportunity. Before they'd made love, she'd slipped past his defenses like a ninja. Now they'd been intimate and he didn't doubt that she would exploit his passion to get her way.

"I left California without saying goodbye because leaving you was so damned hard." When he'd broken off things a month ago, he'd been lucky to escape before her shock at his announcement wore off. Ending their relationship was one of the hardest things he'd ever done. If she'd begged him to stay, he wasn't sure if he could have done the right thing by Sherdana. "Nothing good will come of putting off the inevitable."

"The way you disappeared left me feeling anxious and out of sorts. I understood that we'd broken up, but what I didn't get was how you could take off without saying anything. You should have explained your circumstances. I could have processed the situation and gotten closure. That's what I need now. A few days to say goodbye properly."

"And by properly you mean…?"

Her serious expression dissolved into one of unabashed mischief. "A few days of incredible sex and unbridled passion should do it."

How could any man resist such an offer? Visions of her flat on her back with his hands skimming along her soft, delectable curves rose to torture him. A smile and a frown played tug-of-war on his face. But this was not the time to stop listening to the voice inside his head that reminded him he had to give her up. The smartest thing would be to avoid making more memories that would haunt him the rest of his life.

"Don't you think it would be better if we didn't let ourselves indulge in something that has no future?"

"I'm not going to pretend we have a future. I'm going to cherish every moment of our time together with the knowledge that in the end we'll say goodbye forever." She slid her fingers into his hair. Her thumbs traced the outline of his ears. "I can see you need more convincing, so I'm going to kiss you."

He drank in the scent of honey and vanilla rising off her skin, knowing she tasted as good as she smelled. Her generous lips, rosy and bare of lipstick, parted in anticipation of the promised kiss. Nothing would make him happier than to spend the rest of his life enjoying the curve and texture of her lips. The way she sighed as he kissed her. The soft hitch in her breath as he grazed her lower lip with his teeth.

A tremor transmitted her agitation to him. He longed to inspire more such trembling. To revisit her most ticklish spots, the erogenous zones that made her moan. With erotic impulses twisting his nerves into knots, Nic snagged her gaze. Silver flecks ringed her irises, growing brighter as she stared at his mouth. His pulse thundered in his ears as the moment stretched without a kiss coming anywhere near his lips.

"Damn it, Brooke."

He would not scoop the wayward strand of hair behind her tiny ear and let his knuckles linger against her flushed cheek. He refused to tug on her braid and coax her lips close enough to drift over his.

"What's the matter, Nic?" Her fingers explored his eyebrows and tested his lashes.

Duty. Honor. Integrity. The litany was starting to lose its potency.

"In less than a week I'll never see you again." He locked his hands together behind his back. Tremors began in his arm muscles.

"I know." She switched her attention to his mouth. Her long, red lashes cast delicate shadows on her cheeks.

Heat surged into his face. Hell, heat filled every nook and cranny of his body. Especially where her heart-shaped rear end rested. How could she help but notice his aroused state?

"We'd only be prolonging the inevitable," he reminded her, unsure why he was holding out when he wanted so badly to agree to her mad scheme.

"I need this. I need you." She stroked her thumb against his lower lip. "An hour. A day. A week. I'll take whatever I can get."

Nic counted his heartbeats to avoid focusing on the emotions raging through him. The need to crush her in his arms would overwhelm him any second. Denying himself her compassion and understanding in the days following the accident hadn't been easy, but at the time he'd known that he had to return to Sherdana. Just because Brooke now knew what was going on didn't give him permission to stop acting honorably.

He wasn't prepared for the air she blew in his ear. His body jerked in surprise, and he sucked in a sharp breath. "Stop that."

"You didn't like it?" Laughter gave her voice a husky quality.

"You know perfectly well I did," he murmured hoarsely. "Our food is going to be here any second. Perhaps you should return to your own seat."

"I'm here for a kiss and a kiss is what I'm going to get." She was enjoying this far too much. And, damn it, so was he.

With a fatalistic sigh, Nic accepted that he'd let himself

be drawn too far into her game to turn back. As much as he wanted to savor the expressions flitting across her face, he stared at the fishing boats bobbing near the cement sea-wall. Alert to her slightest movement, he felt the tingle on his cheek an instant before her lips grazed his skin.

"Let's stop all the foreplay, shall we," he finally said.

"Oh, all right. Spoilsport. I was enjoying having you at my mercy. But if you insist."

Lightning danced in her eyes. She secured his face be-tween her hands and grazed her lips across his.

"Again." His voice was half demand, half plea. He hard-ened his will and inserted steel into his tone. "And this time put a little effort into it."

"Whatever you say."

He let his lashes drop as her mouth drifted over his again. This time she applied more pressure, a little more technique. As kisses went, it was pretty chaste, but her little hum of pleasure tipped his world on its axis. And when she nibbled on his lip, murmuring in Italian, desire incinerated his resistance.

"Benedette le voci tante ch'io chiamando il nome de mia donna ò sparte, e i sospiri, et le lagrime, e 'l desio."

How was he supposed to resist a woman with a PhD in Italian literature? Although he knew what she'd said, he wanted to hear her speak the words again.

"Translation?"

"And blessed be all of the poetry I scattered, calling out my lady's name, and all the sighs, and tears, and the passion."

"Italian love poetry?" he groused, amused in spite of the lust raking him with claws dipped in the sweetest aph-rodisiac.

"It seemed appropriate." Her fingers splaying over his rapidly beating heart, she swooped in for one last kiss before getting to her feet. "I think I made my point." With a satisfied smirk, she returned to her chair.

"What point?"

"That we both could use closure."

Over the course of the kiss he'd grasped what she wanted to do, but he'd worked diligently over the past month to come to grips with living without her and couldn't imagine reopening himself to the loss all over again. And she'd just demonstrated he'd never survive a few days let alone a week in her company. He'd be lucky if he made it past the next hours. No. She had to go. And go soon. Because if she didn't, he'd give in and make love to her. And that would be disastrous.

"I got my closure a month ago when I broke things off," he lied. "But I understand that I've sprung a lot of information on you today that you'll want to assimilate. Stay for a couple days."

"As friends?" She sounded defeated.

"It's for the best."

Four

The discussion before lunch dampened Brooke's spirits and left her in a thoughtful mood as she ate her way through a plate of moussaka, and followed that up with yogurt and honey for dessert. Nic, never one for small talk, seemed content with the silence, but he watched her through half-lidded eyes.

Telling him she was pregnant had just become a lot more complicated. As had her decision regarding the teaching position at Berkeley. Before Nic had broken it off with her a month ago she'd been confident that he was her future and she'd chosen him over her ideal job. When he left she should have returned to her original career path, but finding out that she was pregnant had created a whole new group of variables.

Gone was her fantasy that once Nic heard he was going to be a father, he would return to California and they would live happily ever after as a family. Since that wasn't going to happen, the Berkeley job was back on the table. Brooke wished she could summon up the enthusiasm she'd once felt at the possibility of teaching there.

And then there were the challenges that came with being a single mom. If she moved back to LA she would be close to her parents and they would be thrilled to help.

Thanks to Nic's revelations she was a bundle of indecisiveness. They returned to Nic's car for the ride back to the villa. He told her he would have Elena's husband, Thasos, return the boat later. As the car swept along the narrow road circling Kioni's tranquil bay, Brooke felt her anxiety rise and fall with each curve.

From this vantage point, halfway up the side of the scrubby hills that made up the island's landscape, she could see beyond the harbor to the azure water of the Ionian Sea. Glen had described Ithaca as a pile of rocks with scrubby brush growing here and there, but he'd done the picturesque landscape a disservice.

"We'll be to my house in ten minutes." Nic pointed toward a spot on the hill where a bit of white was visible among the green hillside.

In the short time she'd been here, Brooke had fallen in love with Nic's villa. It made her curious about the rest of his family and the life they lived in Sherdana. Did they live in a palace? She tried to picture Nic growing up in a fussy, formal place with hundreds of rooms and dozens of servants.

As the villa disappeared from view around another bend, Brooke glanced over her shoulder and estimated the distance back to the village. Two or three miles. The car turned off the main road and rolled down a long driveway that angled toward the edge of the cliff. When first the extensive gardens and then the house came into view, she caught her breath.

"This is beautiful," she murmured, certain her compliment wasn't effusive enough. "I didn't see this side of the house earlier."

"Gabriel found the place. We bought it for our eighteenth birthday. I'm afraid I haven't used it much."

Built on a hillside overlooking the bay, the home was actually a couple buildings connected together by terraces and paths. Surrounded by cypress and olive trees, the stucco buildings with the terra-cotta tile roofs sprawled on the hillside, their gardens spread around them like skirts.

The nearby hills had been planted with cosmos, heather and other native flowering plants to maintain a natural look. A cluster of small terra-cotta pots, containing bright pink and lavender flowers greeted visitors at the door. A large clay urn had been tipped on its side in the center of the grouping to give the display some height and contrast.

Nic stopped the car. Shutting off the engine, he turned to face her, one hand resting on the seat behind her head. The light breeze blew a strand of hair across her face. Before Brooke could deal with it, Nic's fingers drifted along her cheek and pushed it behind her ear. She half shut her eyes against the delight that surged in her. Her stomach turned a cartwheel as she spied the thoughtful half smile curving his lips. Nic's smile was like drinking brandy. It warmed her insides and stimulated her senses.

"Maybe tomorrow I can show you the windmills," he said, his gaze drifting over her face. The fondness in his eyes made her chest tighten.

"Sure." Her voice had developed a disconcerting croak. She cleared her throat. "I'd like that."

She let out an enormous yawn while Nic was unlocking the front door. He raised his eyebrows and she clapped her hand over her mouth.

"I see you didn't take my advice earlier about getting some sleep."

"I was too wound up. Now I'm having trouble keeping my eyes open. Feel like joining me for a nap?"

Only a minute widening of his eyes betrayed Nic's reaction to her offer. "From what you've told me I have a bunch of emails to answer. I'll catch up with you before dinner."

All too familiar with Nic's substantial willpower, Brooke retreated to the terrace where she'd first found him. In the harbor a hundred feet below, the water was an incredible cerulean blue, the color accentuated by the tile roofs of the houses that lined the wharf and scaled the steep verdant green hills cupping the horseshoe-shaped harbor.

She rested her hands on the stone wall and pondered the nature of fate. Before she'd met Nic, she'd been pursued by any number of men who were ready to do what it took to win her affection. But instead of falling for one of them, she'd chosen a man who was far more interested in his rocket ship than her. All the while, she'd hoped that maybe his enthusiasm for his work could somehow translate into passion for her.

The explosive chemistry between her and Nic had seemed like a foundation they could build a relationship on. The way he'd dropped his guard and given her a glimpse of his emotions had left her breathless with hope that maybe his big-brother act had been his way of protecting his heart. Thanks to all her previous romantic escapades that Glen was only too happy to bring up over and over, Nic had regarded her as a bit of a loose cannon when it came to love.

Brooke turned her back on the view. She had a lot to think about. Following Nic to this island had proved way more interesting and enlightening than she'd expected.

While she'd only been his best friend's little sister, it hurt that neither man trusted her with the truth. She didn't blame Glen for keeping Nic's confidences. Her brother wouldn't have been the amazing man he'd been without his honorable side. But she could, and did, blame Nic for keeping her in the dark.

For five years he'd kept some enormous secrets from her. That knowledge stung. But now she had a secret of her own. Given what she now knew about Nic, what was her best course of action?

Despite her exhaustion after being awake for twenty-four hours, she paced, the sound of her sandals slapping against the stone of the terrace breaking the tranquil silence. Seeing Nic, kissing him and finding out that he was not the hardworking scientist she'd always known but a prince of some country she'd only heard of in passing, had her thoughts in a frenetic whirl.

And then there was the big question of the day. The one she'd been avoiding for the past hour. Was she going to tell Nic about her pregnancy?

In the wake of all she'd learned, was it fair to tell him he was going to be a father? He couldn't marry her even if he'd wanted to. Nor would they be living on the same continent. Being the prince of a small European country meant he would be under the keenest scrutiny. Would he even want to acknowledge an illegitimate child? Yet was it fair to deny him the opportunity to make that decision?

Her best friend, Theresa, would help her answer some of these questions. She was the most sensible and grounded person in Brooke's life. Brooke went down to the guesthouse, retrieved her phone from the bed where she'd left it and dialed Theresa's number.

"Well, it's about time you called me back," Theresa started, sounding more like Brooke's mother than her best friend. "I've left you, like, four messages."

Brooke tried to shrug away the tension in her shoulders, but that was hard when she was braced against an onslaught of lecturing. "Five, actually. I'm sorry I didn't call sooner—"

"You know I'm just worried about you. The last time we talked, you were going to get your brother to tell you where Nic had gone."

"I did that."

"So where is he?"

"About two miles down the road from the most gorgeous Greek town you've ever seen."

"And you know this Greek town is so gorgeous because…?" Theresa's voice held a hint of alarm.

"I've seen it."

"Brooke, no."

"Yep."

A long pause followed. Brooke almost wished she was there to watch her best friend's expression fluctuate from annoyed to incredulous and back again.

"What about the Berkeley interview?"

"It's in three days."

"Are you going to make it back in time?"

In truth she wasn't sure she wanted to. The idea of raising a baby by herself scared her. She wanted to be close to family and that meant living in LA. "That's my intention."

"What was Nic's reaction when you showed up?"

"He was pretty surprised to see me."

"And when you told him about the baby?"

Panic and longing surged through her in confusing, conflicting waves. Twenty-four hours earlier, coming to find him had felt necessary instead of reckless or impulsive. And in hindsight, it had been foolishly optimistic. She'd been convinced Nic would return to California with her once he knew he was going to be a father.

"I haven't yet."

"What are you waiting for?"

Brooke fell back on the bed and stared at the ceiling. "Things got a little complicated after I got here."

"Did you sleep with him again?"

"No." She paused to smile. "Not yet."

"Brooke, you are my best friend and I want nothing but the best for you," Theresa began in overly patient tones. "But you need to realize if he wanted to be with you he would."

"It's not as simple as that." Or was it? Hadn't Nic chosen duty to his country over her? Once again Brooke pictured Nic in formal attire, standing between two other men who looked just like him. Beside them were two thrones where an older couple wearing crowns sat in regal splendor. "But he cares about me. It's just that he's in a complicated situation. And I couldn't tell him over the phone that I'm pregnant."

"Okay. I'll give you that." Theresa was making an effort to be positive and supportive, but clearly she didn't believe that Brooke's actions were wise. "But you chased him all the way to Greece. And now you haven't told him. So what's wrong?"

"What makes you think anything is wrong?"

"Gee, I don't know. We've been best friends since third grade. I think I can tell when something's bothering you. What's going on?" Theresa's voice softened. "Is he doing okay?"

As long as the two girls had known each other, Theresa never understood Brooke's restless longing for the drama of romance. The thrill of flirting. The heart-pounding excitement of falling in love. Married to a man she'd dated since college, Theresa was completely and happily settled. Safe with a reliable husband. And although Theresa would never say it out loud, Brooke always felt as if her friend judged her because she wanted more.

"Physically yes, unless you count hungover. He looked terrible when I showed up this morning."

"So, he's really taking the accident hard."

"Of course he is. He and Glen have been obsessed with

this dream of theirs for five long years. And as you said, he blames himself for what happened." Brooke's breath came out in a ragged sigh as her reaction to what she'd learned finally caught up with her. "He's not coming back."

"Sure he is. If anyone can convince him to not give up it's you."

"I can't. There's a bunch of other things going on."

"What kind of other things?"

"Turns out there are problems at home and he has to go back and marry someone."

"What?" Theresa screeched. "He's engaged?"

"Not yet, but he will be soon."

"Soon? How soon? Does he have a girlfriend he's going to propose to? Is that why he broke your heart?"

"No." Brooke knew she wasn't being clear, but was having a hard time explaining what she still struggled to grasp. "Nothing so simple. Theresa, he's a prince."

Silence. "I'm sorry, a what?"

"A prince." Her reaction was beginning to settle in. Brooke swiped away a sudden rush of tears as her ears picked up nothing but the hiss of air through the phone's speaker. "Are you still there?"

"Yes, I'm here, but this damned international call has gone wonky. Can you repeat what you said."

"Nic is a prince. He's second in line to the throne of a small European country called Sherdana."

Her breath evened out as she waited out her best friend's stupefaction. It wouldn't last long. Theresa was one of the most pragmatic people she knew. It was part of what kept them friends for so long. Opposites attract. Theresa needed Brooke's particular variety of crazy to shake up her life, and Brooke relied on Theresa's common sense to keep her grounded.

"You're kidding me, right? This whole phone call is some sort of setup for one of those wacky reality shows

where people get punked or filmed doing stupid things."
She paused and waited for Brooke to fill in an affirmative.
When Brooke remained silent Theresa sighed and said,
"Okay, you'd better give it to me from the top."

Nic sat in the small den off the living room, his laptop on the love seat beside him, his thoughts lingering on
Brooke and her crazy notion that they should say goodbye and gain closure by spending the next few days in bed
together. Had he done a good enough job convincing her
that wasn't going to happen when he desperately wanted
to make love to her again? During their five months together, she'd learned all she had to do was crook a finger
and he was happy to abandon his work in favor of spending hours in her arms. Nic growled as he pondered his
susceptibility to her abundant charms. He was fighting a
battle with himself and with her. In a few hours she would
return, refreshed and ready for the next skirmish and he'd
better have his defenses reinforced.

With a snort of disgust, Nic turned on the computer in
the den and cued up his email. She'd claimed there were
dozens of unanswered emails, but the inbox was empty. It
took him fifteen minutes to find them among the folders
where he shunted the messages he didn't wish to delete
and restore the settings to the way he liked them. Brooke
was a disaster when it came to anything involving technology. Glen had found his sister's deficiency funny and
endearing. Nic just found it exasperating. Like so many
other things about her.

She was always late. In fact, her sense of time was so
skewed that if he needed her to be somewhere, he usually
built in a cushion of thirty minutes. Then there was her inability to say no to anyone. This usually led to her getting
involved in something she needed to be bailed out of. Like
at *Griffin*'s annual team picnic when she'd agreed to take

all the kids for a nature hike and then got lost. It had taken Nic and Glen, plus a half dozen concerned parents, to find them. Of course, the kids all thought it was the best adventure they'd ever been on. Brooke had kept them calm and focused, never letting them know how much trouble they were in. Later, when he'd scolded her for worrying everyone, she'd simply shrugged her shoulders and pointed out that nothing bad had happened. She just didn't think about the consequences of her actions. And that drove him crazy.

As crazy as the way she leveraged her lean, toned body to incite his baser instincts. Whenever she took a weekend break from school and came to visit, he found it impossible to concentrate on the *Griffin* project. She hung out in his office, alternating between cajoling and pouting until he paid attention to her. Most days he held out because eventually she'd grow tired of the game and let him get back to work. Unfortunately before that happened, he had to endure her flirtatious hugs and seemingly innocent body brushes. Usually by the time she headed back to San Francisco on Sunday afternoon, he was aroused, off schedule and in a savage mood.

His phone rang. Gabriel. The first in line to the throne sounded relaxed and a touch smug as he passed along the message Nic had been dreading.

"Mother is sending the jet to pick you up the day after tomorrow and wants to know what time you can be at the airport."

"What's so urgent? I thought I had over a week until your wedding."

"She has a series of parties and events leading up to the big day that you and Christian will be expected to attend. From what I understand she has compiled quite a list of potential brides for you two to fight over."

And so it began. Nic's thoughts turned toward the woman napping in the guesthouse. His heart wrenched at the thought of being parted from her so soon after reconnecting. She would be disappointed to find out their time would be cut short, but he had warned her.

"Are any of these women…?" What was he trying to ask? Without meeting any of them, he'd already decided they were unacceptable. None of them were Brooke.

"Beautiful? Smart? Wealthy? What?"

"Am I going to *like* any of them?" As soon as the question was out Nic felt foolish.

"I'm sure you're going to like all of them. You just have to figure out which one you can see yourself spending the rest of your life with." Gabriel's words and tone were matter-of-fact.

"Is that how you felt when you first started poring over the candidates?"

Gabriel paused before answering. "Not exactly. I had Olivia in mind from the first."

"But you spent a year considering and meeting possible matches. Why do that if you already knew who you wanted?"

"Two reasons. Because Mother would not have accepted that I had already met the perfect girl and at the time only my subconscious realized Olivia was the one."

Nic wished he was having this conversation face-to-face because his brother's expression would provide clues mere words lacked. "You've lost me."

"As I worked my way through the list, I realized I compared each woman I met to Olivia."

"She was your ideal."

"She was the one I wanted."

The conviction throbbing in Gabriel's low voice spurred Nic to envy his brother for the first time since they were kids. Before Nic had discovered his passion for science and engineering, he'd wondered what contribution he could make to the country. Gabriel would rule. All Christian cared about was having fun and shirking responsibility. Nic had wanted to have a positive effect on the world. A lofty ambition for an eight-year-old.

Gabriel continued speaking, "Only I resented my duty to marry and didn't know how perfect Olivia was for me. Even when I proposed to her I was blind to my heart's true desire. Thank goodness my instincts weren't hampered by my hardheadedness."

"At what point did you figure out you'd selected the perfect woman?"

"The night my girls came to stay at the palace. Olivia took them under her wing and zealously guarded them from anyone she believed might upset them. Me included." He chuckled. "And she never wavered in her love for them, not even when she thought I was still in love with their mother."

"And speaking of Karina and Bethany, how are your girls?"

"Growing more beautiful and more terrifying by the week. Thank goodness they adore Olivia or they'd be terrorizing the palace staff a lot more than they do. Somehow she guides their energy into positive channels and makes the whole process look effortless. No one else can manage them without being ready to pull their hair out."

"Not even Mother?"

"At first, but now they realize she is too fond of them to scold. Father indulges their appetite for sweets and Ariana has shown them every good hiding place the palace has to offer."

"It's not called the terrible twos for nothing."

"You'll see soon enough. I'll have the plane pick you up tomorrow around noon."

"Fine." That should give him time to make sure Brooke was safely on a plane heading for home.

"See that you're there on time."

"Where else would I be? I have nowhere to go but home."

Nic ended the call with a weary sigh and mulled what Gabriel had said about his search for a wife. That his brother had settled on the perfect woman before his quest had even begun didn't lessen Nic's unease over what was to come. Already his mind and body had chosen the woman for him. She was currently stretched out on the bed in the guesthouse. If he was anything like Gabriel, he was going to have an impossible time finding anyone who could match her perfect imperfection.

Several hours later, he was opening a bottle of Sherdana's best Pinot Negro to let it breathe when Brooke sailed into the living room. She'd changed clothes again. The tail of her pastel tied-dyed kimono fluttered behind her as she walked, exposing a mint-green crocheted tank and the ruffled hem of her leg-baring floral shorts.

A light breeze swept in from the terrace and plucked at her dark copper curls. She'd loosened her hair from its braid and it flowed in rich waves over her shoulders and down her back. She stroked a lock away from her lips. He caught himself staring at her and shifted his attention back to the wine.

How often in the past five years had he longed to sink his fingers into her tempestuous red locks and lose himself in the chaotic tangle? He'd imagined the texture would feel like the finest Chinese silk sliding along his bare chest. He'd been right.

Nic extended a glass of wine toward her. She shook her head.

"Something nonalcoholic if you have it."

He found a container of orange juice and poured her a glass. She sipped at it, her eyes smiling at him over the edge of the glass. Expecting a whole new round of verbal fencing, Nic was surprised when she said, "You mentioned that your sister paints here. Could I see her studio?"

"Sure."

He led the way onto the terrace and around the villa in the opposite direction of the guesthouse. A small building with broad windows facing north sat on a little rise overlooking the harbor mouth. Nic unlocked the door and gestured for Brooke to go inside.

"Oh, these are all wonderful," she said the minute she walked in.

Though Brooke was always generous with her praise, Nic thought she was going a little overboard in talking about Ariana's work. Nic was proud of what his sister had accomplished with her paintings but didn't really get her modern style. She had often accused him of being stuck in the Middle Ages in terms of his taste. Brooke, on the other hand, seemed to get exactly what his sister was trying to do.

He enjoyed watching her stroll through his sister's art studio and study each canvas in turn, treating every painting like a masterpiece. By the time Brooke returned to where he stood just inside the door, her delighted grin had Nic smiling, as well. The next time he saw Ariana, he would be sure to tell her what an accomplished artist she was.

"I never looked at Ariana's art that way before," Nic said as he relocked the studio and escorted Brooke back toward the main house. "Thank you for opening my eyes."

She looked caught off guard by his compliment. "You're welcome."

At that moment Nic realized how rarely he'd ever offered Brooke any encouragement or a reason to believe he appreciated her. How had she stayed so relentlessly positive as he'd thrown one obstacle after another in her path? All she'd ever asked was for him to like her and treat her with civility. Was it her fault that she agitated his emotions and incited his hormones?

"What are you thinking about?" she asked as they stepped back into the main house. She gathered her hair into a twist and secured it into a topknot.

"Regrets. I spent so much time keeping you at bay."

Again he'd startled her. "You did, but to be fair, I am a little overwhelming."

"And very distracting. I had a hard time concentrating when you were around."

She narrowed her eyes. "Why are you being so nice to me all of a sudden?"

"I had a call from my brother while you were resting and I have to leave for Sherdana the day after tomorrow."

"So soon?" Her lips curved downward.

Nic wanted to put his arms around her, but it would do neither of them any good to deepen their connection when the time to part was so near. "Apparently my mother has planned several events she'd like me to attend in the next week, culminating in Gabriel and Olivia's wedding."

"But I thought they were already married."

"They are. Actually…" Nic stared out the window at Kioni in the distance. "He brought her to Ithaca for a surprise wedding ceremony."

"That's very romantic."

"And unlike Gabriel to put his desires before the needs of the country. But he's crazy about Olivia and couldn't bear to live without her."

Something about Brooke's silence caught his attention. She was staring at the floor lost in thought. "So why are they getting married again?"

"The crown prince's wedding is pretty momentous and my parents decided it was better to have a second ceremony than to rob the citizens of the celebration. There will be parties every night leading up to the big event, both at the palace and venues around our capital city of Carone."

"Tell me about the parties at the palace. They must be formal affairs." Brooke's smile bloomed. "Do you have to dance?"

"Only when I can't avoid it."

"So you know how."

"It's part of every prince's training," he intoned, mimicking his dance teacher's severe manner. "I don't have Gabriel's technique or Christian's flair, but I don't step on my partner's toes anymore."

"After dinner tonight you are going to dance with me." She held up a hand when he began to protest. "Don't argue. I remember on three separate occasions when you told me you had no idea how to dance."

"No," he corrected her. "I told you I don't dance. There's a difference."

"Semantics."

"Very well." He knew that taking her in his arms and swaying with her to soft music would lead to trouble. But he could teach her a Sherdanian country dance. The movements were energetic and the only touching required was hand to hand. "After dinner."

"So what are we having that smells so delicious?"

"Elena left us lamb stew and salad for dinner."

Brooke drifted to the stove where a pot simmered on a low flame. "I don't know how I can be hungry after all we ate for lunch, but suddenly I'm starved."

Something about the way she said the word made him grind his teeth. She was hungry for food, but the groan in her voice made him hungry for something else entirely. Directing her toward the refrigerator where Elena had put the salad, he spooned the stew into bowls and tried not to remember Brooke beneath him in bed, her red hair fanned across his pillow, lips curved in lazy satisfaction.

"Can I help?"

He handed her a bowl and a basket of bread, almost pushing it at her in an effort to keep her at bay.

She walked toward the table. "I love the bread here in Greece. That and the desserts. I could live on them."

"I hope you like the stew, as well. Elena is an excellent cook."

"I'm sure it's wonderful."

Nic's housekeeper had set the table earlier so there was little left to do but sit down and enjoy the meal. The patch of late-afternoon sunlight on the tile floor had advanced a good three feet by the time they finished eating. Following his example, Brooke had torn pieces of the fresh-baked bread and dipped them into the stew. He'd lost count how many times her tongue came out to catch a crumb on her lip or a spot of gravy at the corner of her mouth.

For dessert Elena had left baklava, a sticky, sweet concoction made of stacked sheets of phyllo dough spread with butter, sugar, nuts and honey. He couldn't wait to watch Brooke suck the sticky honey from her fingers.

And she didn't disappoint him.

"What's so funny?" she demanded, her tongue darting out to clean the corner of her mouth.

Nic banked a groan and sipped his wine. "I'm trying to remember the last time I enjoyed a pan of baklava this much."

"You haven't had any."

He imagined drizzling honey on her skin and following the trail with his tongue. The bees in Greece made thick sweet honey he couldn't get enough of. Against her skin it would be heaven. The arousal that had taunted him all through the meal now exploded with fierce determination. Nic sat back in his chair all too aware of the tightness in his pants and the need clawing at him.

"You've enjoyed it enough for both of us."

"It was delicious." Cutting another piece, she held it out. "Sure you don't want some?"

The question was innocent enough, but the light in her gray-green eyes as she peered at him from beneath her lashes was anything but. Avoiding her gaze, he shook his head.

"As much as I'm enjoying your attempt to seduce me, I'm afraid my intentions toward you haven't changed."

"We'll see." Resolve replaced flirtation in her eyes. She sat back and assessed him. "I still have two nights and a day to dishonor you."

Eager to avoid further banter, he cleared the plates from the table and busied himself putting away the remnants of the stew.

"I can hear what you're thinking," Brooke murmured, following him to the sink. "You're thinking it took me five years to wear you down the first time." She set the pan of baklava on the counter and swept a finger over a patch of honey. "But have you considered that I know a little bit more about what turns you on after all the nights we spent together?"

Out of the corner of his eye Nic watched, his mouth dry, as she stuck her finger into her mouth, closed her eyes in rapt delight and licked off the honey. She was killing him.

"Two nights and a day, Nic." She said again. "Hours and hours of glorious, delirious pleasure as we explore every inch of each other and get lost in deep slow kisses."

But he wasn't free to have the sort of fun Brooke suggested. And one way or another, he intended to make her understand.

"And then what?" he demanded, his voice more curt than he'd intended.

She blinked. "What do you mean?"

"What happens after the fun?" While hot water ran into the sink, he propped his hip against the counter and crossed his arms. "Have you thought about what happens when we leave this island and go our separate ways?"

Her shoulders sagged. "I head back to California and my dream job."

"And I start looking for a wife." To his surprise, he'd managed to get the last word in.

Deciding to capitalize on his advantage, he scrounged up the CD with Sherdanian folk music Ariana had given him for his birthday several years earlier. As the first notes filled the air, he extended his hand in Brooke's direction. "Get over here. It's time for you to learn a traditional Sherdanian country dance."

Five

Nic woke to the smell of coffee and tickle of something in his ear. He reached up to brush away the irritation and heard a soft chuckle. The mattress behind him dipped. His eyes flew open as a hand drifted over his shoulder and a pair of lips slid into the erogenous zone behind his earlobe.

"You sleep like the dead," Brooke murmured. "I have been taking advantage of you for the last fifteen minutes."

"I doubt that." But oh, the idea that she might have hastened his body's awakening.

"Don't be so sure." She sounded awfully damned confident as she snuggled onto the bed behind him, a thin sheet the only barrier between them as she traced the curve of his backside with her knee, running it down along the back of his thigh. As if this caress wasn't provocative enough, she wiggled her pelvis against his butt, aligning her delicious curves against his back from heel to shoulders. "I know you're not wearing any underwear."

"You're guessing."

"Am not." Her palm drifted along his arm, riding the curve of his biceps. Her touch wasn't sexual; she was more like a sculptor admiring a fine marble statue. "I peeked."

He couldn't even gather enough breath to object. What the hell was she doing to him? Reminded of her threat the night before, Nic knew that letting her get her fill of touching him would only lead to further frustration on his part and more boldness on hers. Yet, he couldn't prevent his curiosity from seeing how far she intended to go.

"How long have you been awake?" he asked as her fingers stole up his neck and into his hair. He closed his eyes and savored the soothing caress.

"A couple hours. I went for a swim, started the coffee and grew bored with my own company, so I decided it was time to wake you. How am I doing?"

Brat.

"I'm fully awake," he growled. "Thank you. Now, why don't you run along and fix breakfast while I take a shower."

"Want some company?"

Her mouth opened in a wet kiss on his shoulder. Nic bit back a curse. The swirl of her tongue on his skin caused his hips to twitch. The erection he'd been trying to ignore grew painfully hard.

"Didn't we come to an understanding last night about this being a bad idea?"

"That was your opinion," she corrected. "I think we wasted a perfectly lovely night dancing around your living room when we could have set fire to this big bed of yours."

"Set fire?" Amusement momentarily clouded his desire to roll her beneath him and make her come over and over. She had the damnedest knack for tickling his funny bone.

"Set fire. Tear up the sheets."

He shifted onto his back so he could see her face. Bare of makeup, lips soft with invitation, eyes shadowed by long reddish lashes, her beauty stopped his breath. He cupped her pale cheek in his palm while his heart contracted in remorse. For five months he'd savored the notion of spending the rest of his life with her. He'd claimed her body and given her his heart. At the time, with Gabriel's wedding to Olivia fast approaching and the future of Sherdana safely in their hands, Nic believed he could at last have the life he wanted with the woman who made him happy. It wasn't fair that circumstances had interfered with his plans for the future, but that's the way it was.

His hand fell away from her soft skin. "You know we can't do this."

"Damn it, Nic."

The next thing he knew, she'd straddled him. Astonished by her swift attack and trapped between her strong, supple thighs, Nic reached for the pillow behind his head and dug his fingers in. The challenge in her green-gray gaze helped him maintain control—barely. She settled her hot center firmly over his erection and smirked as his hips lifted off the mattress to meet her partway. She obviously intended to push him past his limits. To incite him to act. He clenched his teeth and held himself immobile.

She put her palms on his chest and leaned forward. "I'm sad and I hate feeling this way. I want to be blissfully happy for just a little while. To forget about the future and just live in the moment."

Where she touched him, he burned. The curtain of her hair swung forward. Still damp from her swim, it brushed against his cheek. He gathered a handful and gently tugged.

"It's not that I don't want that, too," he began and stopped. She couldn't know that what he felt for her went way beyond physical attraction. "I just can't see where that's going to be good for either of us."

Her hands stalked from his chest to his stomach. His muscles twitched in reaction to her touch, betraying him.

He grit his teeth and focused on something less tantalizing than the slender thighs bracketing his hips or the heat of her burning into him through layers of cotton. Unfortunately with her current position, she dominated his field of vision.

"Is that my shirt?"

The last time he'd seen the white button-down, she'd been driving away from his house after they spent the night together. In his eagerness to get her naked the evening before, he'd torn the delicate fabric of her blouse and rendered the garment unwearable. Today, where her damp hair touched the fabric, transparent patches bloomed on her shoulder and chest.

"It is. Every time I wear it I think about you and the nights we spent together."

Nic gripped the bedsheets, endeavoring to stay true to his word and keep his hands off her. Even if his position didn't lend itself to a series of casual affairs, leaving a trail of broken hearts in his wake was not his style. On the other hand, he didn't need the sort of complication a romance with Brooke would bring to his life right now. But since yesterday afternoon he'd become obsessed with all the ways he could touch her without using his hands, and since she'd arrived, he hadn't brooded over the accident for more than five minutes.

"Tell me about the women who are dying to become your princess," she said in a tone as dry as the California desert near the airport test facility. "Are they all beautiful and rich?"

"Do you really want to talk about this?"

"Not really." Her fingers tickled up his sides toward his armpits.

In an effort to stop her before she made him squirm, Nic snagged her wrists and rolled her over. She ended up beneath him, her legs tangled in the sheets. Now that she was trapped in a web of her own making, this was his chance to escape. He should have immediately shifted away from her and put a safe distance between them, but her expression took on a look of such vulnerability that he was transfixed. Pressed chest to groin, they stared at each other.

"Touch me," she whispered, digging her fingers into his biceps.

He flexed his spine, driving his hips tight into hers. She shifted beneath him, rubbing her body against his in a tension-filled rhythm. A groan ripped from his throat as her heat called to him. Today she smelled like pink grapefruit, stimulating with a sweet bitterness. His mouth watered.

"I promised I wouldn't."

"Then, kiss me. You didn't promise not to do that."

That would be following the letter of the law instead of the intent. "You should have been a lawyer," he groused, surrendering to what they both wanted.

His lips lowered to hers. She opened for him like a rose on a warm summer afternoon. He kept the pace slow, concentrating on her mouth while ruthlessly suppressing the urgent thrumming in his groin. Her heart beat in time with his until Nic wasn't sure where he left off and she began. Time was suspended. The room fell away. There was only the softness of her skin beneath his lips, her soft sighs and the growing tension in his body.

This deviation from his intention wouldn't benefit either of them, but he'd grown sick to death of thinking in terms of what he couldn't do, what didn't work, what he stood to lose. He wanted to take joy in this moment and put the future on hold. Brooke had offered him a gift with no strings attached. He would face a lifetime of limits and restrictions soon enough. Why not go wild for a few minutes? Enjoy this exhilarating, vivacious woman who brought joy and laughter into his stolid existence. Who confounded him with her sassy attitude and liberated his emotions. For five years he'd fought against falling for her, afraid if he let her in he might one day have to leave her.

And he'd been right. No sooner had he risked his heart than he'd been forced to make a terrible choice.

"See, that wasn't so hard," she murmured as he broke off the kiss to trail his lips down her neck to the madly beating pulse in her throat.

"I've never met anyone like you. No one knocks me off my game faster."

"It's my dazzling personality."

"It's your damned stubbornness. If Berkeley doesn't work out, you could always teach seminars to salesmen on the art of not taking no for an answer."

Her rock hard nipples burned his chest through the thin cloth, branding him with each impassioned breath she took.

"Unbutton your shirt."

She hesitated at his demand as if unsure what his change of mind might mean. After a long moment, she raised her hands and slipped the first button free. As the top curve of her breast came into view, he lowered his head and tasted her skin. Her gasp made him smile. What he intended to do next would render her breathless.

"Another."

She obliged. He nudged into the ever-widening V, grazing her sensitive skin with the stubble on his chin. A shudder captured her. Nic smiled.

"Keep going."

She unbuttoned the next two buttons in rapid succession, but held on to the edges of the shirt, keeping the material closed. Sensing what he wanted, she peered at him from beneath her lashes. Nic eyed the pink tone in her cheeks.

"Spread the shirt open. I want to look at you."

"Nic, this is—" She broke off as he nudged the material off one breast.

"Not what you had in mind?" His tongue circled her tight nipple.

"It's exactly what I want." She arched her back, her fingers tightening convulsively. "I feel…"

"Tell me," he urged, eager to hear what effect his mouth was having on her body. He flicked his tongue across her nipple. She jerked in surprise. "I want to know everything. What do you like? What drives you wild?"

At last she unclenched her fingers and spread the shirt wide. Now it was Nic's turn to suck in his breath. She was beautiful. Breathtaking. Perfect. Her small round breasts, topped with dark pink nipples, were a perfect fit in his palm. Pity his mouth would be the only part of him to enjoy all that silky skin. And yet, as he pulled one bud into his mouth and sucked, perhaps that wasn't so bad after all.

She was mewling with gratifying abandon by the time he finished with one breast and moved to the other.

The situation was swiftly disintegrating. Nic felt his control slipping. Heaving a sigh, he caught the edges of her shirt and pulled them together, hiding her gorgeous breasts from his greedy eyes.

"You're stopping?" She sounded appalled. "But things were just starting to get interesting."

His muscles clenched at her frustrated wail. He levered himself out of bed and kept his eyes averted from her. He'd survived temptation once. He wasn't sure he could do it twice.

"You still don't get it, do you? I can't offer you anything beyond this bed."

"I know."

She rolled onto her side, her gaze steady on him. Accusations darted like deer through her gray-green eyes. Anger surged in his chest. Damn her for coming here and littering the clear path to his future with enticement and regret. He retreated to the bathroom. Just before closing the door, he shot a last glance in her direction. She had propped her head on her hand and lay watching him through half-closed lids.

She'd left the edges of her shirt unfastened and the three-inch gap gave him an eye-popping view of the curve of her right breast, almost to the nipple. Aphrodite in all her glory could not have appealed to him more than Brooke's slim form in his bed.

Nic shut the bathroom door with more force than necessary and started the shower. A cold shower, he decided.

As she heard the water start, Brooke exhaled raggedly and rolled onto her back. The empty bed mocked her. Frustration bubbled in her chest and rose into her throat, building into a shriek. She clamped her teeth to prevent any sound from escaping, but it was an effort to hold so much emotion in. So she grabbed one of Nic's pillows and covered her face in it to prevent him from hearing her shrill curses.

Once the tantrum had passed, she lay with her nose buried in the cool cotton, absorbing Nic's scent and reliving the moment when his control had broken. Heat wafted off her skin in surging waves, the source the smoking hot place between her thighs that pulsed and throbbed with frustrated longing. The man had a gift for turning her world upside down.

He only had to give her the slightest bit of encouragement and she went all in. How many times since she'd first discovered she had feelings for him had he crushed her hopes by deflecting her overtures or chasing her away when she'd tried to get him to take a break from a problem so he could gain some perspective on it?

Not for the first time an ache built in her chest. What had started out as a whim, a crush, a foolish game had escalated into something she couldn't break free from.

Her mother, Theresa, even Glen, had warned her she was better off with a man who appreciated her. But she hadn't wanted to hear the good advice from her friends and family. And for a while things had been perfect.

The way she'd felt about him the first time he'd kissed her six months ago was nothing compared to the growing connection she felt now. Each day in his presence it grew stronger. How was she supposed to just let him go and move forward? To raise this child on her own? To spend the rest of her life without him? Panic assailed her, causing dark spots in her vision and making it hard to draw a full breath for several minutes.

She rode the paralyzing fear until her emotions calmed. Able to think rationally again, Brooke was mortified by how badly she wanted to cling to Nic and beg him to give up his responsibilities and be with her. Once upon a time she'd prided herself on being an independent woman, capable of living abroad for a year in Italy while she worked on her doctoral thesis on Italian literature. She might make decisions based on emotion rather than logic, but she ruled her finances with a miser's tight fist and had a knack for avoiding bad relationships.

These days she was a rickety ladder of vulnerability and loose screws. What else could explain why she'd charged a fifteen-hundred-dollar airplane ticket on her credit card to chase after a man who'd vanished from her life without even a goodbye? If she'd picked up the phone and delivered her news about the pregnancy she could have saved herself a bucketful of heartache and said to hell with closure.

Brooke sat up and buttoned Nic's shirt once more. A sudden bout of nausea caught her off guard. If the positive pregnancy test result had seemed surreal, here was tangible proof that her body was irrevocably changed. Brooke slipped off the bed and fled the room, afraid Nic would exit the bathroom and catch her looking green and out of sorts, then demand to know what was wrong with her.

On her way to the guesthouse, she snagged a bit of bread and a bottle of water. Once there, she nibbled at the crust, put the chilled bottle to her warm forehead and willed her stomach to settle down. As the nausea subsided, Brooke's confidence ebbed away, as well.

In twenty-four hours Nic was heading home to find a wife. He would be forever lost to her. Maybe she should give up this madness today and run back to California.

Because she still hadn't done what she'd come here to do: tell Nic she was pregnant.

And yet, on the heels of all she'd learned, did it make sense to burden him with the news that his illegitimate child would be living far from him in California? He was returning home to find a bride and start a family. His future wife wouldn't be happy to find out Nic had already gotten another woman pregnant.

Then, too, he'd proved himself an honorable man. It would tear him apart to know he wouldn't be a part of his child's life? What if he demanded partial custody? Was she going to spend the next eighteen years shuffling their child across the Atlantic Ocean so that he or she could know Nic? And what about the scandal this would mean for the royal family? Maybe in America no one thought twice when celebrities had children without being married, but that wouldn't sit well where European nobility were concerned.

Yet morally was it right to keep the information from him? It would certainly be easier on her. Nic had turned his back on Glen and their dream of getting *Griffin* off the ground. Brooke knew she could count on her brother to keep her secret. Her life going forward would be quiet and routine. She would teach at Berkeley or UCLA and throw herself into raising her child. No one would ever know that she'd had a brief affair with a European prince.

Both options had their positives and negatives. And it was early in her pregnancy. So many things could go wrong in the first trimester. She could take another month to decide. The discovery that she was pregnant was only a week old. Maybe if she gave the situation some more thought she could arrive at a decision that she could live with.

Knowing that avoiding a decision was not the best answer, she dressed in black shorts and a white T-shirt. Maybe she would take a hike to the windmills a little later. Although her stomach wasn't back to normal, she had to act as if nothing was wrong.

Half an hour after her encounter with Nic, she returned to the house and found him standing in the kitchen drinking coffee. He was staring out the window as Brooke drew near and when she saw the expression on his face, all the energy drained from her body.

"Don't." Her throat contracted before she could finish.

He swiveled his head in her direction. His gaze was hollow. "Don't what?"

Hearing his tight, unhappy tone, frustration replaced anxiety. Brooke stamped her foot. "Don't regret what just happened."

"Brooke, you don't understand—"

"Don't," she interrupted, despair clutching at her chest. She didn't need to be psychic to know what ran through Nic's mind. "Don't you dare spew platitudes at me. I've known you too long."

"You don't know me at all."

And whose fault was that? She sucked in a breath. Harsh words gathered in her head. She squeezed her eyes shut, moderated her tone. "I wish we had time to change that."

The umber eyes that turned in her direction were a

stark landscape of cynicism and regret. "But we don't."
Although he pushed her away with his words, the muscle
jumping in his jaw proclaimed he wasn't happy to do so.
His agonized expression matched the pain throbbing in
his voice. "My family needs me."

I need you. Your child needs you.

But all of a sudden she knew she wasn't going to put
that burden on him. What he felt for her wasn't casual. She
was finding it hard to let go. He was going through something similar. But they each had their ways of coping and
she should respect that.

Brooke retreated to the opposite side of the room and
picked up her sandals. The silence in the house went un-
broken for several moments while she reorganized her
emotions and set aside her disappointment.

"Are these okay for a hike up to the windmills?" she
asked, indicating the footwear. "I'm afraid I don't have
anything more sturdy."

"They should be fine." He assessed her feet. "There's
a well-defined path up to get there."

"Great."

His brow creased at her flat tone. "Are you okay?"

"Fine. Just feeling a little off all of a sudden. Nothing
breakfast won't cure."

Brooke was glad that Elena picked that moment to enter
the house with bags of groceries. It kept her and Nic from
plunging back into heated waters. With Elena bustling
around the kitchen they had little need to exchange more
than a few words over a meal of eggs and pastries.

An hour later, they were heading to the windmill. The
paved road that led from the town past Nic's villa gave out
two miles farther. Ahead was the narrow path cluttered
with large rocks and tree roots that led to the three windmills she'd seen on arriving at Ithaca. Nic set a moderate
pace through the irregular terrain, forcing Brooke to focus

on where she stepped, and silence filled the space between them. For once she was grateful for the lack of conversation because she had too many conflicting thoughts circling her mind.

"There are a number of windmills on Ithaca," Nic began as the brush lining the path ahead of them gave way to a flat, rocky expanse. Brooke was glad for her sunglasses as they emerged from the vegetation onto the rocky plateau.

Before them lay the three disused windmills. Twenty feet in diameter, thirty feet tall, their squat, round shapes stood sentinel over all the boats coming and going from the harbor. Their walls once would have been whitewashed, but years of wind and weather had scoured the brick, returning it to shades of gray and tan.

Nic headed toward the structures, his words drifting back to her on the strong breeze. "Corn and wheat would come from all over the islands to be ground here because of the constant winds in this area."

In the lee of the squat towers, Nic gestured to direct her attention through a curved doorway into the windmill's interior. "As you can see, the 1953 earthquake caused the grinding wheel and shaft to break and tumble to the bottom."

"Fascinating." But her attention was only half on the scene before her. A moment earlier she'd stumbled when her toe caught on a half-buried rock and he'd caught her arm to steady her. His hand had not yet fallen away. "Thank you for bringing me here. The view is amazing. I can see why you enjoy coming to the island."

"After this we should take the boat to Vathay and have lunch." He was obviously hoping that by keeping busy they could avoid a repeat of the morning's events.

Brooke wasn't sure she could spend a fun-filled afternoon with him while her heart was in the process of shattering. For the first time since her interest in him had sparked, she was bereft of hope. Even after he'd broken things off a month ago, she hadn't really believed it was over. This morning, she'd finally faced up to reality.

Nic was going to marry someone else and build a life with that person.

"If you don't mind," Brooke said, "I think I'd rather just hang out on the terrace and do a little reading. But you go ahead and do whatever it is you've been doing before I got here."

He frowned, obviously unsure what to make of her abrupt about-face. "If that's what you want to do."

"It is." The words sounded heavy.

"Very well."

For the next fifteen minutes, he inundated her with facts about the area, the aftereffects of the 1953 earthquake and other interesting tidbits about the island. Brooke responded with nods and polite smiles when he paused to see if she was listening. Eventually, he ran out of things to say and they headed back down the path. They had to walk single file until they reached the road. Once they got there they strode side by side without speaking. When Nic's villa was less than a mile away, to Brooke's surprise, it was Nic who broke the silence.

"About this morning."

"Please don't," Brooke murmured, expelling her breath in a weary sigh.

"I was wrong to kiss you," he continued, either not hearing her protest or ignoring it. "I'm sending you mixed messages and that isn't fair."

"It was my fault. I shouldn't have intruded on your sleep and thrown myself at you. Most men would have taken advantage of the situation. You showed great restraint."

"Nevertheless." His frown indicated he wasn't happy she'd taken the blame. "I haven't been fair to you. If I'd told you from the start who I really was, you'd never have developed feelings for me."

Brooke couldn't believe what she was hearing. She'd chased this man for five years, teased him, flattered him, poured her heart out to him and received nothing in return until six months ago when he'd kissed her. *He'd* kissed *her.* She hadn't plunked herself onto his lap and tormented him the way she'd done the day before. In fact, she hadn't even flirted with him that night. He'd been the one to draw her away from Glen's party and kiss her senseless.

"I never meant to hurt you."

"You haven't." She wasn't upset with him. She was disappointed in herself. How could she have been such a fool for so long? "If I hurt right now it's because I didn't listen when you told me over and over that we weren't right for each other. I created my own troubles. Your conscience should be clear."

She walked faster, needing some space from Nic. He matched her stride for stride.

"Is this some sort of ploy—?"

She erupted in exasperation. "Get over yourself already. I'm done." She gestured broadly with her arms as her temper flared. "You've convinced me that it's stupid to keep holding on for something that can never be. So, congratulations, I'm never going to ask you for anything ever again."

Her anger wasn't reasonable, but at that moment it was the only way to cope with her deep sadness. She couldn't cry, not yet, so she took refuge in ferocity. This was a side of her she'd never let Nic see. She always kept things light and fun around him. Even when she showed him her temper, it was followed by a quicksilver smile.

Right now she had no lightness inside her, only shadow.

Nic caught her arm to slow her as she surged forward. "I don't want us to end like this."

She was not going to say nice things so he could ease his

conscience about her. "End like what? Me being upset with you? How do you think I felt a month ago when you told me that sleeping together had been the wrong thing to do?"

"I was wrong not to tell you the truth about what was really going on." The intense light in his eyes seared through her defenses. "I'm sorry."

Unbidden, sympathy rose in her. Brooke cast it aside. She didn't want to accept that he was as much a victim of circumstances as she. With a vigorous shake of her head she pulled free and began walking once again.

"What happened isn't fair to either one of us," he called after her. "Don't you think if I could choose you I would?"

She swung around and walked backward as she spoke. "The trouble is, you didn't choose me. Nothing is really forcing you to go home and make this huge sacrifice for your country. This is your decision. You feel honor bound. It's who you are. It's why I love you. But don't blame circumstances or your family's expectations for the choice you are making."

Leaving him standing in the middle of the road, Brooke ran the rest of the way back to the villa.

<u>Six</u>

Nic lay on his back, forearm thrown over his eyes. Moonlight streamed into his room like a searchlight, but he couldn't be bothered to close the shutters. A soft breeze trailed across his bare chest, teasing him with the memory of Brooke's fingers tantalizing his skin this morning.

The regret he'd been trying unsuccessfully to contain for the past twelve hours pounded him as relentlessly as the Ionian Sea against the cliff below the villa. Any sensible man would have taken Brooke to bed rather than inflict on her a long sightseeing adventure to busted-up windmills. Instead he'd rejected her not once but twice this morning, and then disregarded the pain he'd caused.

She'd eaten lunch by herself on the terrace and barely spoken to him during dinner. When she did speak, her tone had been stiff. He didn't blame her for being upset. Any apology he might make would've been way too little and far too late. But he'd been relieved when she'd escaped as soon as the dishes had been piled in the sink.

He gusted out an impatient breath and sat up. Sleeping without the benefit of too much alcohol had been hard enough before Brooke arrived. Knowing she slept thirty feet away made unconsciousness completely impossible. Hell. It used to be that if he couldn't sleep, he would work. That outlet was lost to him now. Still, he hadn't yet looked at the forty emails restored to his inbox. Maybe a few hours of technical questions would take his mind off his problems.

Padding barefoot downstairs, he stopped short as he neared the bottom, his skin tingling in awareness that he wasn't alone.

Beyond the open French doors, the full moon slanted a stripe of ethereal white across the harbor's smooth surface and reached into the living room to touch the couch. Beside the shaft of moonlight, a dark shadow huddled, an ink spot on the pristine fabric.

Brooke.

His breath lodged in his throat and her name came out of him in a hoarse whisper. His body went into full alert. This was bad. Very bad. A late-night encounter with her was more temptation than he was prepared to handle.

"How come you're not in bed?" he demanded, stepping onto the limestone tile. He took two steps toward the couch, his impulses getting the upper hand. He'd come close enough to smell vanilla and hear her unsteady breathing. He set one hand on his hip and rubbed the back of his neck with the other.

"I couldn't sleep." Her voice emerged from shadow, low and passionless with a slight waver. "I haven't been able to stop thinking about what I said to you earlier. You're doing the right thing where your family and country are concerned."

"This whole thing is my fault. You came a long way

not knowing who I was or what my family has been going through."

If circumstances were different...

But it wasn't fair to patronize her with meaningless platitudes. Circumstances were exactly what they were and he'd made his decision based on what he'd been taught to do.

"Still, I shouldn't have hit you with a guilt trip."

"You didn't." Nic took another two steps and stopped. His breath hissed through clenched teeth. What was he doing? The longing to gather her into his arms and comfort her stunned him with its power. His body ached to feel her soft body melt against him. Madness.

"I just wanted you to choose me for once."

Her words slammed into his gut and rocked him backward. He'd been a first-class bastard where she was concerned. How many times had he rebuffed her when all she wanted was to help him work through a problem? So what if her methods sounded illogical and ineffective? She'd been right the time she'd badgered him into playing miniature golf with her when he was busy trying to solve a difficult technical problem. On the fourth hole the solution had popped into his head with no prompting. Had he bothered to thank her before rushing back to his workroom at the hangar and burying himself in the project once more?

And now, it was too late to make everything up to her.

"You should head back to bed. You have a long flight back to California tomorrow."

Her shadow moved as she shook her head. "I'm not going home tomorrow."

"Where are you going?"

"I don't know yet. I have a few weeks before I have to be back at UC Santa Cruz. I thought maybe I'd head to Rome and meet up with some friends."

"What about your Berkeley interview?"

"It's the day after tomorrow."

"But you said it was in a few weeks."

"It was rescheduled."

"Why didn't you tell me?" Annoyance flared, banishing all thoughts of comforting her.

"I thought if you knew, you'd put me on a plane right away and I wanted these two days with you."

Two days during which they'd argued and he'd done nothing but push her away. Irritation welled.

"But why aren't you going right home for the interview? Teaching at Berkeley is all you've talked about since I've known you."

Her temper sparked in response to his scolding. "Plans change. It's just not the right time for me to take the position."

"Are you giving up something as important as Berkeley because of me?"

"Seems foolish, doesn't it?" she countered without a trace of bitterness.

Nic clenched his fists. She was going to be so much better without him.

And he was going to be so much worse.

"You should take your own advice about going to bed," she told him. "Sounds like your mother planned a grueling week for you. It will be better if you're well rested."

Nic had the distinct impression he'd just been dismissed. His lips twitched. He could always count on Brooke to do the last thing he expected. After her assault on his willpower this morning, he'd been lying awake half expecting her to launch another all-out attack tonight.

From the way he'd been with her this morning, she had to know he was having a harder and harder time resisting her. Resisting what he wanted more than anything. With each beat of his heart, the idea of taking her back upstairs and tumbling her into his bed seemed less like a huge mistake and more like the right thing to do.

Walk away.

"What are you going to do?" he asked, knowing that prolonging this conversation was the height of idiocy. It would only make going back to bed alone that much harder.

"Sit here."

"I won't be able to sleep knowing you're down here in the dark."

A small smile filled her voice as she said, "You've never had trouble putting me out of your mind before."

If she only knew. "You weren't sitting on my couch in your pajamas before."

Her sigh was barely audible over the blood thundering in his ears.

"Good night." Calling himself every sort of fool, he headed back upstairs. Leaving his bedroom door open in a halfhearted invitation, he fell onto the mattress. Hands behind his head, eyes on the ceiling, he strained to hear footfalls on the stairs. The house was completely silent except for the breeze stirring the curtains on either side of his window.

His nerves stretched and twisted, but she didn't appear. He caught himself glancing at the doorway, expecting her silhouette. As the minutes ticked by, Nic forced his eyes shut, but he couldn't quiet his mind and the past two days played through his thoughts with unrelenting starkness.

With a heated curse, he rolled off the bed and stalked downstairs. It didn't surprise him to find her exactly where he'd left her.

"You are the most stubborn woman I've ever known," he complained. "I don't know what the hell you expect from me."

Even his mother had given up trying to keep him in Sherdana when his heart belonged in an airplane hangar in the Mojave Desert. But for years Brooke had relentlessly pushed herself into his life until he couldn't celebrate achievements or face failures without thinking about her.

"My expectations are all in the past," she said, pushing to her feet.

And that's what was eating him alive.

They stared at each other in motionless silence until Brooke heaved a huge sigh. The dramatic rise and fall of her chest snagged Nic's attention. The tank top she wore scooped low in front, offering him the tiniest hint of cleavage. Recalling the way her breasts had tasted this morning, he repressed a groan.

"Brooke."

"Don't." She started past him. Nic caught her wrist. At his touch, she stilled. "I thought I was pretty clear this afternoon when I said that I've given up on you."

"Crystal clear." Nic cupped her face, his fingers sliding into the silky strands of russet near her ear.

"Then what are you doing?"

"Wishing you didn't have to."

He brought his mouth down to hers, catching her lips in a searing kiss that held nothing back. She stiffened, her body bracing to recoil. He couldn't let that happen. Not now. Not when he'd stopped being principled and noble. Not when he wanted her with a hunger that ate at him like acid.

Taking a tighter grip on her wrist, he slowly levered it behind her back, compelling her hips forward until her pelvis brushed against the jut of his erection. The contact made him moan. He deepened the kiss, sweeping his tongue forward to taste her. Her lips parted for him. A soft whimper escaped her throat as she writhed in his grasp, but whether she fought to escape or move closer he couldn't be sure.

"I want you," he murmured, setting his mouth on her throat and sucking gently.

Her body trembled, but her muscles remained tense. Labored, uneven breaths pushed her breasts against his bare chest.

"Damn you, Nic." It was in her voice, in the way she tilted her head to allow him better access to her neck. She was furious and aroused. "It's too late for you to change your mind."

"It's too late when I say it is." He released her wrist and cupped her small, round butt in his palm. The cotton pajama bottoms bunched as he gave a light squeeze.

She gasped, set both hands on his chest and shoved. It was like a kitten batting at a mastiff. "This isn't fair."

"Fair?" He growled the word. "Do you want to talk about fair? You've tormented me for five years. Strutting around the hangar in your barely there denim shorts. Coming to peer over my shoulder and letting your hair tickle my skin. How hard do you think it was for me to keep from pulling you into my lap and putting my hands all over you?"

"You never..." She arched back and stared up into his face. "I had no idea."

"I made sure you didn't. But it wasn't easy." He wrapped his fingers around her red curls and gave a gentle but firm tug. "And it wasn't fun."

Brooke was electrified by Nic's admission; the twinge in her scalp when he pulled her hair merely enhanced her already overstimulated nerves. She welcomed the discomfort. The fleeting pain chased the last vestiges of self-pity from her mind and grounded her in the moment.

Taking her silence and stillness as surrender, Nic bent to kiss her again, but Brooke turned aside at the last minute. Even though this was what she'd wanted when she'd bought her plane ticket, she wasn't the same woman who'd gotten on the plane in San Francisco.

Nic wasn't deterred by her evasion. He kissed his way across her cheek and seized her earlobe between his teeth. Her knees wavered as his unsteady breath filled her ear. Meanwhile, his hands moved over her back, gliding beneath her tank top to find her hot skin and trace each bump of her spine.

"What's wrong?" he murmured as his lips investigated the hollow made by her collarbone.

"You want me to give in." He was doing whatever it took to make her putty in his hand. "Just like you used to want me to leave you alone. It's always about what you want."

She felt as much as heard his sigh. His hands left her body and bracketed his hips. He regarded her solemnly.

"I thought this was what we both wanted."

A breeze puffed in from the terrace, chilling Brooke. Where a second earlier the room had been dark, moonlight now poured over the tiled floor and bathed Nic's splendid torso in a white glow. Her mouth went dry as her gaze traced the rise and fall of his pecs and abs, the perfect ratio of broad shoulders to narrow hips. Although still in shadow, the planes of his face seemed more chiseled, his jaw sharper.

Her pulse began to slam harder, throbbing in her wrist, her throat and between her thighs. She found his eyes in the dimness, fell beneath the hypnotic power of his gaze. A rushing filled her ears, the incessant movement of a stream as it surges past boulders and fallen trees, unstoppable. Once upon a time, she'd been like that, full of purpose and joy. Then she'd let her doubts bottle her up.

Was she really going to stand here being annoyed with him and waste another second of the limited time she had left bemoaning the cards fate had dealt?

She held out her hand to Nic. He linked his fingers with hers and drew her toward the stairs. Without saying a word they entered his bedroom and came together in a slow, effortless dance of hands, lips and tongue. Pajamas landed on the floor and Brooke stretched out on Nic's king-size bed, his strong body pressing her hard into the mattress as they kissed and explored.

Words were lost to Brooke as Nic's fingertips rode her rib cage to the undersides of her breasts. She couldn't remember ever feeling so heavy and so light at the same time. Arching her spine, she pushed her nipples against his palms. Stars burst behind her eyelids as he circled the hard buds, making them ache with pleasure before at long last drawing one, then the other, into his hot mouth.

The sensations snapping along her nerves made Brooke quiver and gasp. She was hungry for Nic to touch her more intimately, but her senses had gone fuzzy, her body languid. His hand rode upward along her inner thigh with torturous precision and she followed its progress with breaths growing ever more faint. By the time his finger dipped into her wet heat, her lungs had forgotten how to function. She lay with her eyes closed, her head spinning as he filled her first with one, then two fingers, stretching her, finding the spot that caused her hips to jerk and the first shuddering moan to escape her throat.

And then he replaced his hand with his mouth and adored her with tongue and teeth. Sliding his hands beneath her butt, he lifted her against the press and retreat of his kiss. She tried to squirm, to escape the tongue that drove her relentlessly toward pleasure so acute it hurt, but Nic dug his fingers into her skin and held her captive. Mewling, Brooke surrendered to the slow, tantalizing rise of ecstasy.

Nic hadn't made love to her like this the first time they were together. Five years of anticipation had made their lovemaking passionate and impatient. Nic had satisfied her three times that night, his large body surging into hers, filling her completely. She'd come with desperate cries, unable to articulate the incandescent heights to which he'd lifted her.

But the rush upward had been followed by only a brief respite to catch her breath and savor the afterglow. Nic had proved insatiable that night and when at last they'd spent the last of their passion, she'd fallen into a deep, dreamless slumber.

This was different. As if recognizing this was their last time together, he made love to her with his eyes first and then his hands. Languid sweeps of his lips across her skin soothed her soul and set her skin aflame. Words of appreciation and praise poured over her while his fingers reverently grazed the lines of her body.

By the time he slipped on a condom and settled between her thighs, Brooke wasn't sure where she ended and he began. He moved slowly into her, easing in just the head of his erection, giving her time she didn't need to adjust to him.

Tipping her hips as he began his second thrust, she ensured that his forward progress didn't end until he was fully seated inside her. He groaned and buried his face in her neck. She dug her fingernails into his back, reveling in the fullness of his possession. For a long moment neither of them moved. Brooke filled her lungs with the spicy tang of his aftershave and the musk of their lovemaking. She closed her eyes to memorize the feel of his powerful body as he began moving.

Measured and deliberate, Nic rocked against her, thrusting in and out while pleasure built. He kissed her hard, his tongue plunging to tangle with hers. Their hips came together with increased urgency. Brooke let her teeth glide along Nic's neck. He bucked hard against her when she nipped at his skin. The thrust rapped her womb where their child grew and sent her spiraling toward climax. She must have clenched around him because suddenly Nic picked up the pace. Together they climbed, hands pleasuring, bodies striving for closeness. Brooke came first, Nic's name on her lips. He drove into her more urgently and reached orgasm moments later.

His strong body shook with the intensity of his release and a hoarse cry spilled out of him. What followed was the deepest, most emotionally charged kiss he'd ever given her. Brooke clung to him while her body pulsed with aftershocks and surrendered to the tempest raging in Nic. If she'd thought their lovemaking had forever branded her as his, the kiss, tender one moment, joyous the next, stole the heart right out of her body.

"Incredible." He buried his face in her neck, his breath heavy and uneven, body limp and powerless.

Brooke wrapped her arms around his shoulders, marveling that this formidable man had been reduced to overcooked noodles in her arms. Grinning, she stroked the bumpy length of his spine and ran her nails through his hair in a soothing caress.

"Am I too heavy?" he murmured, lips moving against her shoulder as he spoke.

"A little, but I don't want you to move just yet." She was afraid any shift would disrupt this moment of perfect harmony.

"Good. I like it just where I am."

They stayed that way for a long time. Legs entwined, his breath soft and steady on her neck, his fingers playing idly in her tangled curls. Brooke couldn't recall if she'd ever enjoyed being so utterly still before. She didn't want to talk or to think. Only to be.

But as with all things, change is inevitable. Nic heaved a mighty sigh and rolled away from her to dispose of the

condom and pull a sheet over their cooling bodies. The
breeze had shifted direction and the air that had seemed
dense and sultry an hour earlier was swept away.

With her head pillowed on his shoulder and Nic's fingers absently gliding across the small of her back, the leth-
argy she'd experienced earlier didn't return.

"I can feel you thinking," Nic said, his eyes closed, a
half smile curving his lips.

"That's illogical."

His chest moved up and down with his sigh. "If I was
in a logical frame of mind, I wouldn't be lying naked with
you in my arms."

"I suppose not."

"What's on your mind?"

Not wanting to share her true thoughts, she said the first
thing that popped into her head. "If you must know I was
thinking about getting a cat when I get home."

"Really?" He sounded genuinely surprised. "I thought
Glen said you guys grew up with dogs."

"We did, but dogs are so needy and some of my days
can go really long with classes and office hours. I think a
cat would be a wiser choice."

"I like cats."

"You do?" She couldn't imagine Nic owning anything
that needed regular feeding or care. "Wouldn't a snake be
a more suitable pet for you?"

"A snake?"

"Sure, something you only had to feed once a week."
She chuckled when he growled at her.

"No snakes." He yawned. "A cat. Definitely."

Brooke could tell by the sleepiness of his voice that
she was losing him. "But a cat is going to jump on your
worktable and knock things off. It's going to wake you in
the middle of the night wanting to be petted and yowling

at you for attention. They ignore you when you give them commands and never come when they're called."

Nic cracked open one eye and smirked at her. "Yeah, a cat. They're definitely my favorite kind of nuisance."

It took Brooke a couple seconds to realize he had connected her behavior to what she'd just said about cats. In retaliation, she poked him hard in the ribs and he located the ticklish spot behind her knees that had her squirming. It didn't take long for their good-natured tussling to spark another round of lovemaking.

Much later, while Nic's breathing deepened into sleep, Brooke lay awake in the predawn stillness and tried to keep her thoughts from rushing into the future. The hours she had with him grew shorter every second. So instead of sleeping, as the sky grew lighter, Brooke lost herself in Nic's snug embrace, savored the way his warmth seeped through her skin and awaited the day.

The nausea that had plagued her the day before began as the sun peeked over the horizon and gilded the window ledge. She breathed through the first wave and sagged with relief when her stomach settled down. Remembering how the previous morning had gone, Brooke knew she had to get back to her room. Nic might not be the most observant of men, but even he'd be hard-pressed not to notice if she was throwing up in his bathroom.

Last night while in the grip of insomnia, she'd decided not to tell him she was pregnant. If he hadn't made love to her with such all-consuming emotion, she might have accepted that they could go back to being friends, affectionate but disconnected by distance and circumstances. But now she realized that they had to make a clean break of it. It would be best for both of them if he didn't know the truth.

Before her stomach began to pitch and roll again, Brooke untangled herself from Nic's embrace and eased from his bed. Her head spun sickeningly as she got to her feet and snatched up her pajamas. Naked, the soft cotton pressed to her mouth, she raced from the room and down the stairs.

If Elena was shocked to see her streak by, Brooke never knew because her focus was fixed on crossing the twenty feet of terrace to the guesthouse and reaching the bathroom in the nick of time. Panting in the aftermath, she splashed cold water on her face and waited to see if the nausea had passed. When it appeared the worst was over, Brooke climbed into the shower.

She was dressed and repacking her suitcase when a soft knock sounded. Heart jumping, she eased the door open, expecting to see Nic standing there, and was surprised to see Elena bearing a tray with a teapot and a plate of bread and assorted preserves.

"Ginger tea is good for nausea," she announced, slipping the tray onto the dresser. "I understand you are leaving for Sherdana today."

"Nic is going. I'm heading for Italy." But her plan to visit friends in Rome had lost its appeal. More than anything she wanted to head home to family and friends and start the process of healing in their comforting embrace.

Elena's eyes narrowed. "You let me know if you need anything before you leave."

Seven

Awaking to an empty bed hadn't been the best start to Nic's day, but he reasoned he might as well get used to disappointment because he wouldn't ever wake to Brooke's smile again. The sun was high by the time Nic finished his shower and headed to the first floor. Elena was dusting the already immaculate furniture. She shot him an intensely unhappy look as he poured himself a cup of coffee and he wondered at her barely veiled hostility.

"Have you seen Brooke this morning?" he asked, carrying his cup to the terrace doorway and peering in the direction of the guesthouse. The trip to Kefalonia's airport would take forty-five minutes by boat and another hour over land. They would need to leave soon.

"She has eaten breakfast and had some last minute packing to do."

"Is Thasos ready with the boat?"

Elena nodded. "She is a nice girl. You shouldn't let her go to Italy by herself."

"She is going to visit friends," he explained to the housekeeper, while guilt nibbled at the edges of his conscience. "She knows her way around. She lived in Rome and Florence for a year."

"You should take her home."

Nic was startled by Elena's remark. He'd been thinking the same thing all morning. Unfortunately that wasn't possible. Reality dictated he should distance himself from Brooke as soon as possible, but the thought of letting her go off by herself disturbed him.

If she didn't get on a plane bound for California, he would spend the next two weeks worrying about her traveling alone in Europe instead of focusing on the issues at home and the necessity of finding a wife. Nor did he have time to escort her to the gate and satisfy himself that she was heading to San Francisco. He was expected back in Sherdana this afternoon.

Nic's chest tightened. He was doing a terrible job of lying to himself. In truth he wasn't ready to say goodbye. It was selfish and stupid.

"I need to make a phone call," Nic told Elena. "Will you let Brooke know we'll be leaving in ten minutes?"

Calling himself every sort of idiot, Nic dialed Gabriel. When he answered, Nic got right to the point. "I'm bringing someone home with me. She's come a long way to see me and I don't feel right leaving her alone in Greece."

"She?" Gabriel echoed, not quite able to keep curiosity out of his voice. "Is this going to cause problems?"

Nic knew exactly what Gabriel meant and decided not to sugarcoat it. "That's not my intention. She's Glen's sister. I think I've mentioned her a few times."

"The one who drives you crazy?" Gabriel sounded intrigued.

"The interfering one who flew here to convince me to come back to the *Griffin* project."

"Just the project?"

"What's that supposed to mean?" Nic didn't intend to be defensive, but with last night's events still reverberating across his emotions, he wasn't in the best shape to fence with a diplomat as savvy as Gabriel. "She's Glen's little sister."

"And you talk about her more than any woman you've ever known."

"I know what you're getting at, but it's not an issue. Things got a little complicated between us recently, but everything is sorted out."

"Complicated how?"

"I didn't tell her who I was until she came here looking for me and that upset her. I shouldn't have left her in the dark. We've been…friends…for a long time."

"Why didn't you tell her?"

Nic rubbed his temples where an ache had begun. "I know this is going to be hard for you to understand but I liked being an ordinary scientist, anonymously doing the work I'm really good at."

"You're right. I don't understand. I grew up knowing I belonged to the country. You never did like being in the spotlight. So you didn't tell her you're a prince. Do you think she would have looked at you differently if she'd known all along?"

"Brooke values a person for how they behave not who they are or what they have."

Gabriel laughed. "She sounds like your sort of girl. I can't wait to meet her."

"Honestly, it's not like that." He didn't want his brother giving the wrong idea to their parents. "She understands my situation."

"She knows that you're coming home to find a bride? And she wants to accompany you, anyway?"

"I haven't spoken with her this morning." Not exactly a

lie. "She doesn't know I'm bringing her with me to Sherdana yet."

"Well, this should make for an interesting family dinner," Gabriel said. "I'll make sure there's a place set at the table for her beside Mother."

And before Nic could protest that arrangement, Gabriel hung up. Nic debated calling him back, but decided it would only exacerbate his brother's suspicions about Brooke. Playing it cool and calm around his family would be the best way to handle any and all speculation.

Grabbing his bag from his bedroom, Nic made his way toward the steps that Brooke had used to access the terrace two days ago. They led down the steep hillside in a zigzag that ended at a private dock. Brooke had already arrived at the boat and was settled onto the seat opposite the pilot's chair. The smile she offered Nic was bright if a little ragged around the edges.

Thasos started the engine as soon as Nic stepped aboard and quickly untied the mooring ropes. Nic settled into the bench seat at the back of the boat and watched Brooke pretend not to be interested in him. He knew the signs. He'd spent years giving her the impression he was oblivious to her presence. Yet how could he be? She lit up every room she entered. Her personality set the very air to buzzing. Sitting still was probably the hardest thing she did. Yet when her brain engaged, she could get lost in a book or her writing for hours.

They'd shared many companionable afternoons while she was working on her second doctorate. Not surprisingly, she enjoyed sitting cross-legged on the couch in his workroom, tapping away at her computer keyboard or with her nose buried in a book. If he managed to accomplish any work on the weekends she visited, it was a miracle. Most of the time, he'd pretended to be productive while he watched her surreptitiously.

Forty-five minutes after leaving Ithaca, the boat maneuvered into an open space at the Fiskardo quay. A car would be waiting to carry them on the thirty-one-kilometer journey to the airport outside Kefalonia's capital, Argostoli. If traffic was good, they would get there in a little less than an hour.

Thasos carried their bags to the waiting car and with a jaunty wave turned back to the boat. As soon as he'd driven out of sight, Nic turned to Brooke.

"I don't feel comfortable heading home to Sherdana and leaving you on your own."

"Good Lord, Nic." She shot him a dry look. "I'm perfectly capable of taking care of myself."

"I agree. It's just that with everything that has happened in the last few days—"

"Stop right there." All trace of amusement vanished from her tone as she interrupted him. "After everything that's happened...? I am not some delicate flower that has been crushed by disappointment."

"Nevertheless. I'm not going to leave you stranded in Greece. You are coming home with me."

After five years of teasing and cajoling, bullying and begging, Brooke thought she had Nic all figured out. He preferred working in solitude, hated drama and rarely veered from a goal once he'd set his mind to something. But this announcement left her floundering. Had she ever really known him at all?

"What do you mean you're taking me home with you?" The notion thrilled and terrified her.

"Exactly what I said." Nic's jaw was set in uncompromising lines. "You will fly with me to Sherdana and from there I will make sure you get a flight back to California."

The knot in Brooke's stomach didn't ease with his clarification. "I assure you I'm perfectly capable of getting a flight home from Greece." With morning sickness plaguing her, she'd given up the idea of a summer holiday in Italy. She wanted to be surrounded by familiar things and her favorite people. Maybe she'd spend a week in LA visiting her parents.

"Don't make this difficult on yourself."

"Isn't that what I should be saying to you?" Seeing he didn't comprehend her meaning, Brooke clarified. "Have you considered what happens when we land? How fast can you get me on a plane to the States? In the meantime are you planning on leaving me waiting at the airport? Putting me up in a hotel? Or perhaps you think I'd be more comfortable at the palace?"

Expecting her sarcasm to be lost on him the way it usually was, Brooke was stunned by his matter-of-fact retort.

"My brother said he'll make sure the staff sets an extra place for you at dinner next to my mother." Lighthearted mischief lit his eyes as her mouth dropped open.

"I can't have dinner with your family." Her throat clenched around a lump of panic.

"Why not?"

"I have nothing to wear."

"You look perfect to me."

With lids half-closed, his gaze roamed over her body, setting off a chain reaction of longing and need. The July morning had gone from warm to hot as the sun had crested the horizon and Brooke had dressed accordingly in a loose-fitting blue-and-white cotton peasant dress with a thigh-baring hem and a plunging neckline. The look was fine for traveling from one Greek Island to another or catching a short flight to Rome, London or anywhere else she could snag a connection home to California. But to go to Sherdana and be introduced to Nic's family?

"Why are you really bringing me along?"

"Because I'm not ready to let you go." As light as a

feather, he slid his forefinger along her jaw. It fell away when it reached her chin. "Not yet."

But let her go he would. Her skin tingled where he'd touched her. Brooke saw the regret in his eyes and her heart jerked. Heat kindled in her midsection as she recalled what had taken place between them the night before, but desire tangled with anxiety and sadness. How was she supposed to just walk away?

She jammed her balled fists behind her to hide their shaking and estimated she had half an hour to talk him out of his madness. "Have you considered how unhappy your parents are going to be if you show up with some strange girl in tow?"

"You're not a strange girl. You're Glen's sister."

"And how are you going to explain what I was doing on the island with you?"

"I've already contacted Gabriel and briefed him."

Briefed him with the truth or a diplomatic runaround? "You don't think anyone is going to be suspicious about the nature of our relationship?

"Why would they be? I've spoken of you often to my family. They know you're Glen's annoying baby sister whom I've known for the last five years."

Seeing his wicked smile, she relaxed a little. "Okay, maybe we can do this. After all, Glen knows us better than anyone and he has no idea anything changed between us." If they could fool Glen, they could keep his family from guessing the true nature of their relationship.

"He knows."

Brooke shook her head. "Impossible." Her mind raced over every conversation she'd had with her brother in the past month. "He hasn't said a word."

"He had plenty to say to me," Nic replied in a tight voice, and Brooke suddenly had no trouble imagining how that conversation had gone.

Glen was the best older brother a girl could have. Born eighteen months before her, he'd never minded when she'd tagged after him and his buddies. The guys had accepted her as one of them and taught her how to surf and water-ski. She'd grown up half tomboy, half girlie-girl. They'd all had a great time until Glen graduated high school two years early and headed off to MIT where he'd met Nic.

"The morning after we were together," Nic continued, "your brother cornered me in the lab and threatened to send me up strapped to the rocket if I hurt you."

"No wonder you got out of town so fast after breaking things off with me." Her words were meant to be funny, but when Nic grimaced, she realized her insensitivity. He'd actually left not long after the rocket blew up. "I'm sorry." She looked down at her hands. "I shouldn't have said that."

Nic set his fingers beneath her chin and adjusted the angle of her head until their eyes met. "I'd like to show you my country."

And then what? She received the royal treatment and another goodbye? Already her heart was behaving rashly. She'd opened herself to heartache when she'd surrendered to one last night in his arms. To linger meant parting from him would be that much harder. Did she have no self-control? No self-respect? Hadn't she already learned several difficult lessons?

The need in his gaze echoed the longing in her heart. "Sure," she murmured, surrendering to what they both wanted. "Why not."

"Then that's settled."

An hour later, Nic led her onto a luxurious private plane and guided her into a comfortable leather seat beside the window. With his warm, solid presence bolstering her confidence, Brooke buckled her seat belt and listened to the jet's engine rev. As the plane began to taxi, her chest compressed. Try as she might, she couldn't shake the notion that she should have refused Nic's invitation and just gone home to California.

The instant he'd set foot on the plane his demeanor had changed. Tension rode his broad shoulders and he seemed more distant than ever, his bearing more formal, his expression set into aloof lines. Before leaving Ithaca he'd donned a pair of light beige dress pants and a pale blue dress shirt that set off his tanned skin. On the seat opposite him, he'd placed a beige blazer that bore a blue pocket square. Brooke stared at the oddity.

Nic in stylish clothes. And a coordinating pocket square.

He'd always been sexy, handsome and confident, but he now wore a mantle of überwealthy, ultrasophistication. Ensconced in the luxurious plane, his big hands linked loosely in his lap, he looked utterly confident, poised and...regal. For the first time she truly accepted that Nic was no longer the rocket scientist she knew. Nor was he the ardent lover of last night. Swallowed by helplessness, Brooke stared straight ahead unsure who he'd become.

Maybe leaving him behind in Sherdana was going to be easier than she realized. This Nic wasn't the man she'd fallen in love with. A shiver raced up her spine as his hand covered hers and squeezed gently. Obviously, her heart had no problem with the changes in Nic's appearance. Her pulse fluttered and skipped along just as foolishly as ever.

"Are you okay?" he asked.

Did she explain how his transformation bothered her? To what end? He could never be hers. He belonged to a nation.

"This is quite a plane." Feeling out of place sitting beside such an aristocratic dreamboat on his multimillion-dollar aircraft, Brooke babbled the first thought that entered her head. "Is it yours?"

"If by 'yours' you are asking if it belongs to Sherdana's royal family, then yes."

"Well, that's pretty convenient for you, I guess." She mustered a wry grin. "I suppose the press knows the plane pretty well and that your arrival won't exactly be a state secret."

"Your point?"

"Aside from the fact that we're trying to maintain a low profile on our whole relationship thing, I'm dressed like someone's poor relation. The press is bound to be curious about me. Please can I stay on the plane after you get off until the coast is clear?"

He looked ready to protest, but shook his head and sighed. "If you wish. I'll arrange for someone to meet you at the hangar. That way there won't be any press asking questions you don't want to answer."

It hit Brooke what some of those questions might be and her brain grew sluggish. She'd spent most of her life with her nose buried in books. Glen was the sibling who relished the spotlight. He didn't freeze up in front of large crowds, but put people at ease with his charismatic charm and dazzled them with his intelligence. Numerous times she'd stood back during press events and marveled at his confidence. Not even the difficult questions fired at him after the rocket blew up had rattled him. He'd demonstrated the perfect blend of sadness and determination.

"As for clothes," Nic continued, "I'm sure either my sister, Ariana, or Olivia, Gabriel's wife, will be able to lend you some things."

Brooke would be borrowing clothes from princesses. This wasn't an ordinary family he was taking her home to meet. His mother was a queen. His father was a king. Nic was a prince. What the hell was she doing? She clutched at the armrests, suddenly unable to breathe.

The whirr and clunk of landing gear being locked into place startled her. They were minutes from landing. Nothing about this trip was working out the way she'd planned.

She'd stepped onto the plane in San Francisco thinking she would fly to Greece, tell him about the baby and bring Nic back with her so they could be one big happy family.

The full impact of her foolishness now hit her like a mace. Even if Nic were madly in love with her, he couldn't offer her anything permanent. In fact, he was so far out of her league that they could be living on separate planets.

"I need to know details about your family so I'm prepared," she blurted out, her stomach flipping as the plane lost altitude.

"Sure. Where would you like to start?"

So many questions whirled in her mind that it took her a moment to prioritize them. "Your parents. How do I address them?"

Eight

Nic emerged from the plane and hesitated before descending the stairs to the tarmac. In a tight knot, thirty feet away, a dozen reporters held up cameras and microphones all focused on him. He approached the assembled crowd—the prodigal son returning to the bosom of his family—and answered several questions before heading toward the black Mercedes that awaited him.

Although he'd known it was the sensible thing to do, separating from Brooke even for a short period of time didn't feel right. It wasn't as if he expected her to run off and hop a plane back to California. Enough security surrounded the royal aircraft hangar that she wouldn't get five feet from the plane before she was stopped and questioned.

No, it was more the sense that by traveling separately to the palace, he was acknowledging that there was something to hide. And yet, wasn't there? During the car ride to the airport when she'd asked him why he wanted her to come home with him, he'd told her the truth. He wasn't ready to let her go. The answer had distressed her.

Last night she'd accused him of always demanding things be his way. Now, once again he was acting selfishly.

Nic passed the crowd of reporters without another glance. A familiar figure stood beside the car's rear door. Stewart Barnes, Gabriel's private secretary, offered a smile and a nod as Nic approached.

"Good afternoon, Your Highness. I hope you had a good flight from Greece." The secretary's keen blue eyes darted toward the plane. "Prince Gabriel mentioned you were bringing someone with you. Did she change her mind?"

"No. She's just a little skittish about public appearances. Could you arrange a car to pick her up at the hangar?"

If Stewart was surprised that Nic was sneaking a girl into the country, his expression didn't show it. "Of course." He bowed and opened the car door.

Because the car windows were tinted, Nic had no idea anyone besides the driver was in the vehicle. Therefore, when he spotted Gabriel sitting in the backseat and grinning at him, Nic was overcome by an unexpected rush of joy.

"Good heavens, what are you doing here?" Nic embraced his brother as Stewart closed the door, encasing the princes in privacy.

"It's been three years since you've come home and you have to ask? I've missed you."

The genuine thrum of affection in Gabriel's voice caught Nic off guard. As tight as the triplets had been as children, once on their divergent paths, circumstances and distance had caused them to drift apart. Nic hadn't realized how much he'd missed his older brother until this moment.

"I've missed you, too." The car began to move as Nic asked after the youngest of the three brothers. "How's Christian?"

"Unpredictable as always. Right now he's in Switzerland talking to a company that might be interested in bringing a nanotechnology manufacturing plant here."

"That's wonderful." Nic couldn't help but wonder at the timing of Christian's absence given the series of events his mother had designed for the purpose of finding brides for her sons. "When is he due back?"

"In time for the wedding or Mother will skin him alive."

"And the rest of the parties and receptions?"

Gabriel laughed. "All eyes will be on you."

Nic marveled at the change in his earnest brother. Although young Gabriel had been as full of curiosity and mischief as Nic and Christian, somewhere around his tenth birthday it had hit him that the leadership of the country would one day be his. Almost overnight, while his inquisitive nature had remained, he'd become overly serious and all too responsible.

"You're different," Nic observed. "I don't remember the last time you were this…"

"Happy?" Gabriel's eyes glinted. "It's called wedded bliss. You should try it."

A woman had done this to Gabriel? "I'm looking forward to meeting your wife."

"And speaking of fair women, what happened to your Brooke?"

"She's not my Brooke." Nic heard gravel in his voice and moderated his tone. "And she's staying in the plane until it's taxied into the hangar."

"Your idea or hers?"

"Hers. She was concerned that she wasn't dressed properly and wanted to maintain a low profile."

Gabriel's eyes widened in feigned shock. "What was she wearing that she was so unpresentable?"

"I don't know. Some sort of cotton dress. She thought she looked like someone's poor relation."

"Did she?"

Nic thought she looked carefree and sexy. "Not at all, but what do I know about women's fashion?"

The two men fell to talking about recent events including the incident where the vengeful aunt of Gabriel's twin daughters had infiltrated the palace intending to stop him from marrying Olivia.

"And you have no idea where she's gone?" Nic quizzed, amazed how much chaos one woman had created.

"Interpol has interviewed her former employer and visited her flat in Milan, but for now she's on the run."

As the car entered the palace grounds, Nic's mind circled back to the woman he'd left at the airport. "Have you told anyone besides Stewart that I brought Brooke with me?"

"Olivia and her secretary, Libby, know. They are prepared to take charge of her as soon as she arrives."

"Thank you." Nic was relieved that Brooke would be taken care of.

"Oh, and Mother is expecting you in the blue drawing room for tea. She has an hour blocked out for you to view the first round of potential wives. Stewart interviewed several secretary candidates for you. Their résumés will be waiting in your room. Look them over and let Stewart know which you'd like to meet."

"A secretary?"

"Now that you're back, we've packed your agenda with meetings and appearances. You'll need someone to keep you on schedule."

Nic's head spun. "Damn," he muttered. "It feels as if I never left."

Gabriel clapped him on the shoulder. "It's good to have you back."

From the backseat of a luxurious Mercedes, Brooke clutched her worn travel bag and watched the town of

Carone slip past. In the many years she'd known Nic, which she'd spent alternately being ignored and rejected, she'd never once been as angry with him as she was at this moment.

What had he been thinking to bring her to Sherdana? She didn't belong here. She didn't fit into his world the way he'd fit into hers. No doctorate degrees could prepare her for the pitfalls of palace life. She'd be dining with his family. What fork did she use? She would stand out as the uncouth American accustomed to eating burgers and fries with her fingers. Brooke frowned as she considered how many of her favorite foods didn't require a knife and fork. Pizza. Tacos. Pulled pork sandwiches.

And what if she couldn't get a flight out in the next day or two? As Nic's guest, would she be expected to attend any of the parties his mother had arranged? Were they the sort of parties where people danced? Nic had already shown her a dance specific to the country. They'd laughed over her inability to master the simplest of steps. She'd never imagined a time when she'd be expected to perform them.

And the biggest worry of all: What if someone discovered she was pregnant? Now that morning sickness was hitting her hard, what excuse could she make to explain away the nausea?

Brooke gawked like any tourist as the car swung through a gate and the palace appeared. Nic had grown up here. The chasm between them widened even further. It was one thing to rationalize that her brother's business partner was in reality the prince of a small European country. It was another to see for herself.

During her year abroad in Italy she'd been fortunate enough to be invited to several palaces. A few of the older volumes of Italian literature she'd used in her doctoral thesis had been housed in private collections and she'd been lucky enough to be allowed the opportunity to study them. But those residences had been far less grand and much smaller than the enormous palace she was heading toward right now.

The car followed a circular driveway around a massive fountain and drew up in front of the palace's wide double doors. Surprise held Brooke in place. Given her stealthy transfer from the royal private plane to this car, she'd half expected to be dropped off at the servants' back entrance.

A man in a dark blue suit stepped forward and opened the car door. Brooke stared at the palace doors, unable to make her legs work. One of the tall doors moved, opening enough to let a slim woman in a burgundy suit slip through. Still unsure of her circumstances, Brooke waited as the woman approached.

"Dr. Davis?" She had a lovely soft voice and a British accent. "I'm Libby Marshall, Princess Olivia's private secretary."

"Nice to meet you." Brooke still hadn't budged from the car. "Nic didn't mention he intended to bring me here when we left his villa this morning so I'm not really sure about all this."

The princess's secretary smiled. "Don't worry, all has been arranged. Princess Olivia is looking forward to meeting you. Armando will take your bag. If you will follow me."

If she hadn't flown hundreds of miles in a private jet, Brooke might have been giddy at the thought that a princess was looking forward to meeting her. Instead, it was just one more in a series of surreal experiences.

Brooke slipped from the car and let herself gawk at the sheer size of the palace. Her escort moved like someone who knew better than to keep people waiting and had disappeared through the tall doors by the time Brooke surrendered her meager possessions to Armando. She trotted to catch up, but slowed as soon as she stepped inside.

The palace was everything she'd expected. Thirty feet before her a black-and-white marble floor ended in a wide staircase covered in royal blue carpet. The stairs were wide enough to let an SUV pass. They were split into two sections. The first flight ascended to a landing that then split into separate stairs that continued their climb to the second floor.

She envisioned dozens of women dressed in ball gowns of every color, gliding down that staircase, hands trailing along the polished banister, all coming to meet Nic as he stood, formally dressed, on the polished marble at the bottom of the stairs awaiting them. His gaze would run along the line of women, his expression stern and unyielding as he searched for his perfect bride.

Brooke saw herself bringing up the rear. She was late and the borrowed dress she wore would be too long. As she descended, her heel would catch on her hem. Two steps from the bottom, she'd trip, but there would be no Nic to catch her. He was surrounded by five women each vying for his attention. Without him to save her, she would make a grab for the banister and miss.

Flashes would explode in her eyes like fireworks as dozens of press cameras captured her ignominy at a hundred frames per second.

"Dr. Davis?" Libby peered at her in concern. "Is something amiss?"

Brooke shook herself out of the horrifying daydream and swallowed the lump that had appeared in her throat. "Call me Brooke. This is—" Her gaze roved around the space as maids bustled past with vases of flowers and two well-dressed gentlemen strode by carrying briefcases and speaking in low tones. "Really big. And very beautiful," she rushed to add.

"Come. Princess Olivia is in her office."

Normally nervous energy would have prompted Brooke to chatter uncontrollably. But as she followed Libby past the stairs and into a corridor, she was too overwhelmed. They walked past half a dozen rooms and took a couple more turns. In seconds, her sense of direction had completely failed her.

"You really know your way around." She'd lost the battle with her nerves. "How long have you worked in the palace?"

"A few months. I arrived with Princess Olivia."

"Be honest. How long did it take until you no longer got lost?"

Libby shot a wry smile over her shoulder. "Three weeks."

"I'm only expecting to be here a couple days. I don't suppose there's a map or something."

"I'm afraid not. And I was under the impression that you'd be with us until after the wedding."

Brooke stumbled as she caught the edge of her sandal on the marble floor. "That's not what Nic and I agreed to." But in fact, she wasn't sure if they'd discussed the length of her stay. It certainly couldn't stretch to include a royal wedding.

"I could be mistaken," Libby told her, turning into an open doorway.

The office into which Brooke stepped was decorated in feminine shades of cream and peach, but the functional layout spoke of productivity. On her entrance, a stunning blonde looked up from her laptop and smiled.

"You must be Dr. Davis," the woman exclaimed, rising to greet her. She held out a manicured hand. "Lovely to meet you. I'm Olivia Alessandro."

"It's nice to meet you, as well." The urge to curtsy overwhelmed Brooke and only the knowledge that she'd fall flat on her face if she tried kept her from acting like an idiot. "Your Highness."

"Oh, please call me Olivia. You're Nic's friend and that makes you like family."

It was impossible not to relax beneath Olivia's warm smile. "Please call me Brooke. I have to tell you that I'm a little overwhelmed to be here. This morning I was on a Greek island with no real destination in mind. And then Nic informs me that he intends to bring me to Sherdana."

"Something tells me he didn't plan much in advance, either." The way Olivia shook her head gave Brooke the impression that the future queen of Sherdana believed strongly in preparation and organization.

"Your secretary mentioned something about me staying until after your wedding," Brooke said, perching on the edge of the cream brocade chair Olivia gestured her into. "But I think it would be better if I caught a flight to California as soon as possible."

"I'm sure that could be arranged, but couldn't you stay for a while and see a little of the country? Gabriel and I have plans to tour some of the vineyards in a couple days and it would be lovely if you and Nic could join us."

"As nice as that sounds…" Brooke trailed off. Never before had she hesitated to speak her mind, but being blunt with Nic's sister-in-law seemed the wrong thing to do. "I'm just worried about overstaying my welcome."

"Nonsense."

Brooke tried again. "I got the impression from Nic that his mother had arranged quite a few events in the next week or so that he's expected to attend. I wouldn't want to distract Nic from what he needs to do."

Olivia looked surprised. "You know why he came home?"

"He needs to get married so there can be…" It suddenly occurred to Brooke that the woman who was supposed to

produce Sherdana's next generation of heirs but couldn't
was seated across from her.

"It's okay." Olivia's smile was a study in tranquillity.
"I've made peace with what happened to me. And I consider myself the luckiest woman alive that Gabriel wanted
to marry me even though I wasn't the best choice for the
country."

"I think you're the perfect princess. Sherdana is damned
lucky to have you." Brooke grimaced at her less than elo-
quent language. "Sorry. I have a tendency to be blunt even
when I'm trying not to."

"Don't be sorry. It was a lovely compliment and I like
your directness. I can't wait for you to meet Ariana. She
has a knack for speaking her mind, as well."

"I saw her artwork at the villa. She's very talented. I'm
looking forward to talking with her about it."

"She's been vacationing with friends in Monaco for a
few days and is expected home late tonight. She's very
excited that you've come to visit. When I spoke with her
earlier today, she told me she'd met your brother when he
and Nic stayed at the villa."

That was something else Glen had neglected to mention. Brooke intended to have a long chat with her brother
when she returned to California.

"And now, I expect you would like to go to your room
and get settled. Dinner will be served at seven. If you need
anything let a maid know and she can get it for you."

Brooke gave a shaky laugh. "Like a whole new wardrobe? I'm afraid I packed to visit a Greek island. Casual
things." She imagined showing up to dinner in her tribal
print maxi and winced. "I really don't have anything I
could wear to dine in a palace."

"Oh." Olivia nodded. "I should have realized that from
the little Gabriel told me. It looks like you and I are the

same size, I'll send some things down for you to choose from."

Unsure whether to be horrified or grateful, Brooke could see protesting was foolish so she thanked Olivia. Then she followed a maid through the palace in a journey from the royal family's private wing to the rooms set aside for guest use. After five minutes of walking Brooke knew she'd never find her way back to Olivia's office and hoped someone would be sent to fetch her for dinner. If her presence in the palace was forgotten and she starved to death, how long would it take before her body was discovered? She lost count how many doors they passed before the maid stopped and gestured for Brooke to enter a room.

"Thank you."

The instant Brooke stepped into the bedroom she'd been given, she fell instantly in love. The wallpaper was a gold-and-white floral design while the curtains and bedding were a pale blue green that made her think of an Ameraucana chicken egg. In addition to a bed and a writing desk, the room held a settee and a small table flanked by chairs against the wall between two enormous windows. The room had enough furniture to comfortably seat the students in her class on Italian Renaissance poetry.

On the bench at the foot of her bed sat her well-worn luggage. To say it looked shabby among the opulent furnishings was an understatement.

"Can I unpack that for you, Dr. Davis?" The maid who'd brought Brooke here had followed her into the room.

"I've been traveling for quite a few days already and most of what's in here is dirty."

Brooke sensed that she would scandalize the maid by inquiring if there was a laundry machine she could use.

"I'll sort through everything and have it back to you by evening."

Brooke dug through the bag and pulled out her toiletries

and the notebook she always kept close by to write down the things that popped into her head. Her mother was fond of saying you never knew when inspiration would strike and some of Brooke's best ideas came when she was in the shower or grabbing a bite to eat.

Once the maid had left, Brooke picked up her cell phone and checked the time in California. At four o'clock in Sherdana it would be 7:00 a.m. in LA. Theresa would be halfway to work. Brooke dialed.

When Theresa answered, Brooke said, "Guess where I am now…"

Nic hadn't been in the palace more than fifteen minutes before his mother's private secretary tracked him down in the billiards room where he and Gabriel were drinking Scotch and catching up. The room had four enormous paintings depicting pivotal scenes in Sherdana's history, including the ratification of the 1749 constitution that was creating such chaos in Nic's personal life.

"Good afternoon, Your Highnesses." A petite woman in her midfifties stood just inside the door with her hands clasped at her waist.

Gwen had come to work for the queen as her personal assistant not long before the three princes had been born and more often than not, regarded the triplets as errant children rather than remarkable men.

"Hello, Gweny."

"None of that."

Nic crossed the room to kiss her cheek. "I missed you."

Her gaze grew even sterner, although a hint of softness developed near the edges of her lips. "You missed tea."

"I needed something a little stronger." Nic held up his mostly empty crystal tumbler.

"The queen expected you to attend her as soon as you arrived in the palace. She's in the rose garden. You'd better go immediately." Gwen's tone was a whip, driving him from the room.

Knowing better than to dawdle, Nic went straight outside and found his mother in her favorite part of the garden. Thanks to the queen's unwavering devotion, the half acre flourished with a mixture of difficult-to-find antique rose varieties as well as some that had been recently engineered to produce an unusual color or enhanced fragrance.

"It's about time you got around to saying hello," the queen declared, peering at him from beneath the wide brim of her sun hat.

"Good afternoon, Mother." Nic kissed the cheek his mother offered him and fell into step beside her. He didn't bother to offer her an explanation of what he'd been doing. She had no tolerance for excuses. "The roses look beautiful."

"I understand you brought a girl home with you. She's the sister of your California friend." She paused only briefly before continuing, obviously not expecting Nic to confirm what she'd said. "What is your relationship to her?"

"We're friends."

"Don't treat me like an idiot. I need to know if she's going to present a problem."

"No." At least not to anyone but him.

"Does she understand that you have come home to find a wife?"

"She does. It's not an issue. She's planning on heading home after the wedding."

"I understand you are taking her along with Gabriel and Olivia on a trip to the vineyards?"

"Gabriel mentioned something about it, but I haven't spoken with Brooke."

"I don't think it's a good idea that you get any more involved with this girl than you already are."

"We're not involved," Nic assured her.

"Is she in love with you?" Nic waited too long to answer and his mother made a disgusted sound. "Do you love her?"

"It doesn't matter how we feel about each other," Nic said, his voice tense and impatient. "I know my duty to Sherdana and nothing will get in the way of that." From his conversation with Gabriel, Nic knew she hadn't gone this hard at Christian. Why was Nic alone feeling the pressure to marry? Christian was just as much a prince of Sherdana. His son could just as easily rule. "I assume you have several matrimonial candidates for me to consider."

"I've sent their dossiers to your room in the visitors' wing. Did Gabriel mention the problem in your suite earlier today? Apparently your bathtub overflowed and flooded the room."

"Gabriel thought it might have been the twins although no one caught them at it."

His mother shook her head. "I don't know why we're paying a nanny if the girl can't keep track of them."

"From what I understand they are a handful."

"There are only two of them. I had three of you to contend with." His mother took Nic's hand in hers and squeezed hard. "It's good to have you home." She blinked rapidly a few times and released her grip on him. "Now, run along and look over the files I sent to your room. I expect you to share your thoughts with me after dinner tonight."

"Of course." He bent and kissed her cheek again. "First I'm off to see Father. I understand he has a ten-minute gap in his schedule shortly before five."

After reconnecting briefly with his father, Nic headed to the room he'd been given until his suite could be dried out. The oddity of the incident left him shaking his head.

How could a pair of two-year-old girls be as much trouble as everyone said?

As his mother had promised, a pile of dossiers had been left on the desk. Shrugging out of his blazer, Nic picked up the stack and counted. There were eight. He had twenty minutes before the tailor arrived to measure him for a whole new wardrobe. The clothes he'd traveled in today had belonged to Christian, as had most of what he'd worn the past ten days. Of the three brothers, Christian spent the most time at the Greek villa.

Nic settled into a chair in front of the unlit fireplace and selected a file at random. The photo clipped to the inside showed a stunning brunette with vivacious blue eyes and full lips. She was the twenty-five-year-old daughter of an Italian count, had gotten her MBA at Harvard and now worked for a global conglomerate headquartered in Paris. She spoke four languages and was admired for being fashionable as well as active on the charity circuit. In short, she was perfect.

He dropped the file onto the floor at his feet and opened the next one. This one was a blonde. Again beautiful. British born. The sister of a viscount. A human rights lawyer.

The next. Brunette. Pretty with big brown eyes and an alluring smile. A local girl. Her family owned the largest winery in Sherdana. She played cello for the Vienna Philharmonic.

Then another blonde. Bewitching green eyes. Daughter of a Danish baron. A model and television personality.

On and on. Each woman strikingly beautiful, accomplished and with a flawless pedigree.

Nic felt like a prize bull.

Replaying the conversation with his mother, he recognized he shouldn't have ignored Brooke's concerns that their relationship would come under scrutiny. He'd deliberately underestimated his mother's perceptiveness. But he didn't regret bringing Brooke to meet his family.

What he wasn't so happy about, however, was how little time they would have together in the days between now and her eventual departure. Being forced by propriety to keep his distance would be much more difficult now that he'd opened the door to what could have been if only he wasn't bound to his country.

At the same moment he threw the last folder onto the floor, a knock sounded on his door. Calling permission to enter, Nic got to his feet and scooped up the dossiers, depositing them back on the desk before turning to face the tailor and his small army of assistants who were to dress Nic.

While the suits he tried on were marked and pinned, Nic fell to thinking about Brooke. He hadn't seen her since leaving the plane and wondered how she'd coped in the hours they'd been apart. Despite the nervousness she'd shown during the flight, he suspected she'd figured out a way to charm everyone she'd encountered. He knew she was supposed to meet with Gabriel's wife right away and wondered how that had gone.

He was eager to meet Olivia. He already knew she was beautiful, intelligent and a strong crusader for children's health and welfare. The citizens loved her and after the drama surrounding her emergency hysterectomy and her subsequent secret elopement with Gabriel so did the media. But Nic was fascinated by how she'd caused such drastic changes in his brother.

The tailor finished his preliminary work and departed. Alone once more, Nic dressed for dinner. Family evenings were for the most part casual and Nic left his room wearing navy slacks and a crisp white shirt he'd purchased at a department store in California. His fashionable younger brother would be appalled that Nic was dressing *off the rack*. Nic was smiling at the thought as he joined Gabriel and his new bride in the family's private drawing room.

"You've made my brother a very happy man," Nic told Olivia, kissing her cheek in greeting. "I haven't seen him smile this much since we were children."

From her location snuggled beneath her husband's possessive arm, the blonde stared up at Gabriel with eyes filled with such love that a knot formed in Nic's gut. At that instant, any lingering resentment he'd felt at the uncomfortable position Gabriel's choice had put him in vanished. His brother deserved to be happy. The responsibility of the country would one day rest on Gabriel's shoulders and being married to the woman he loved would make his burden lighter.

This drew Nic's thoughts back to the dossiers in his room. He was glad there hadn't been a redhead among them. Brooke was a singular marvel in his mind. Marrying a woman with similar hair color was out of the question. He couldn't spend the rest of his life wishing his wife's red hair framed a different face.

Brooke hadn't made an appearance by the time Nic's parents entered the drawing room and he wondered for one brief moment if she'd let her anxiety get the better of her. He was seconds away from sending a maid to check on her when the door opened and Brooke stumbled in, unsteady in heels that appeared too large for her.

She wore a long-sleeved, gold, lace dress that flattered her curves, but conflicted with her usual carefree style. She wasn't wearing her usual long necklace that drew attention to the swell of her breasts, and she'd left her collection of bracelets behind. The look was sophisticated, elegant and formal, except for her hair, which spiraled and bounced around her shoulders like a living thing.

"Dr. Davis, welcome." Gabriel and Olivia had approached her while Nic stood there gaping at her transformation.

"I'm so sorry I'm late," Brooke was saying as he finally approached. "I only meant to close my eyes for fifteen minutes. Then next thing I know it's six-thirty. Thank heavens I showered before I sacked out. Of course this is what happens to my hair when I just let it go. If I'd had a few more minutes, I could have done something to it but I had such a hard time deciding which dress to wear. They were all so beautiful."

"You look lovely." Olivia gave her a warm smile and drew her arm through Brooke's in a show of affection and support. "Why don't I introduce you to Gabriel and Nic's parents."

"You mean the king and queen?" Brooke whispered, her gaze shooting to the couple enjoying a predinner cocktail. They appeared to be ignoring the knot of young people.

"They are eager to meet you," Gabriel said.

Brooke's lips quirked in a wry smile. "That's sweet of you to say." She took a clumsy step and smiled apologetically at Olivia. "I'm usually less awkward than this."

"The shoes are a little large for you," Olivia said, giving the gold laser-cut pumps a critical look. "I didn't realize your feet were so much smaller than mine. Perhaps you have something of your own that would fit better? I could send a maid to fetch something."

"Are you kidding me?" Brooke retorted, her voice feverish as she took her next step with more deliberation and improved grace. "These are *Louboutin glass slippers*. I'm Cinderella."

Gabriel waited a beat before following his wife. He caught Nic's eye and smirked. "I like her."

"So do I," Nic replied, his voice low and subdued.

Not that it should have mattered to Nic, but his brother's words sent gratitude and relief rushing into his chest. It was good to know he had at least two people in the palace, Gabriel and Olivia, who would understand how wretched doing the right thing could feel.

"It's very nice to meet you," Brooke was saying to his parents as Nic and Gabriel caught up to the women. "Thank you for letting me stay at the palace for a few days."

Nic felt the impact of his mother's gaze as he drew up beside Brooke. He set his palm on her back and through her dress felt the tension quivering in her muscles.

"We are happy to have you," Nic's father said, his broad smile genuine.

When it came to matters affecting his country, the king was a mighty warrior defending his realm from all threats social, economic and diplomatic. However, he was a teddy bear when it came to his wife and children. But the queen ruled her family with an iron fist in a velvet glove. All four of her children knew the strength of her will and respected it. In exchange she allowed them the opportunity to figure out their place in the world.

This meant Nic had been allowed to attend university in the United States and stay there living his dream of space travel until Sherdana had needed him to come home. But while he'd appreciated his ten years of freedom from responsibility, it made his return that much harder.

"Very happy," the queen echoed. "I understand, Miss Davis, that you are the sister of the man Nic has been working with for the last five years."

"Yes, my brother is in charge of the *Griffin* project."

"Perhaps you will join me for breakfast tomorrow. I'd like to hear more about the project Nic has been working on with your brother."

"I would be happy to have breakfast with you."

"Wonderful. Is eight o'clock too early for you?"

"Not at all. Unlike Nic, I'm an early riser."

Nic knew she'd meant the jab for him. It was an old joke between them on the mornings when he'd worked late into the night and then crashed on the couch in his workroom. But he could see at once that his mother was wondering how Brooke knew what time Nic got out of bed in the morning.

Even without glancing toward his brother, Gabriel's amusement was apparent. Nic kept his own expression bland as he met his mother's steely gaze.

Olivia saved the moment from further awkwardness. "And after breakfast perhaps you could come to the stables and watch the twins take a riding lesson. They are showing great promise as equestrians. Do you ride, Brooke?"

"I did when I was younger, but school has kept me far too busy in recent years."

"Brooke has two doctorates," Nic interjected smoothly. "She teaches Italian language and literature at the University of California, Santa Cruz."

"You're young to have accomplished that much," Gabriel said.

Brooke nodded. "I graduated high school with two years of college credits and spent the next ten years immersed in academia. After my brother went off to college my parents hosted a girl from Italy. She stayed with us a year and by the time she went home, I was fluent in Italian and learning to read it, as well."

Olivia spoke up. "Have you spent much time in Italy?"

"While I was working on my second doctorate, I spent a year in Florence and Rome. Before that my mother and I would visit for a week or two during the summer depending on her deadlines. She writes for television and has penned a mystery series set in sixteenth-century Venice that does very well." Talking about her mother's accomplishments had relaxed Brooke. Her eyes sparkled with pride.

This relaxed Nic as well, but as the family made their way toward the dining room, the queen pulled him aside.

"Lovely girl, your Miss Davis."

"Actually it's Dr. Davis." Although he had a feeling his mother already knew that and had spoken incorrectly to get a rise out of her son. And since Nic had already denied that he and Brooke were anything but friends, why did his mother put the emphasis on *your*? "I'm glad you like her."

"Did you look at the files I gave you?"

"Yes. Any one of them would be a fine princess." He couldn't bring himself to use the word *wife* yet. "You and your team did a fine job of choosing candidates that lined up with my needs."

"Yes we did. Now, let's see if you can do an equally fine job choosing a wife."

Nine

At her first dinner with Nic's family, Brooke sat beside Nic on the king's left hand and ate little. Part of the reason she'd been late to dinner was another bout of nausea that struck her shortly after she'd risen. So much for morning sickness. Brooke wasn't sure why it was called that when it seemed to strike her at random times throughout the day.

"You're not eating," Nic murmured, the first words he'd spoken directly to her since the meal had begun.

"I'm dining with royalty," she muttered back. "My stomach is in knots."

"They're just people."

"Important people." Wealthy, sophisticated, intelligent people. "Normally I wouldn't get unsettled by this sort of thing, but this is your family and I want them to like me."

"I assure you they do."

"Sure." Brooke resisted the urge to roll her eyes. His mother had been observing her through most of the meal, making each swallow of the delicious salmon more trial than pleasure. Brooke sensed that the queen had a long list of questions she wanted to ask, starting with: When are you going home? Not that Brooke blamed her. Nic's mother had plans for her son. Plans that she must perceive as being threatened by an uncouth redhead who regarded Nic with adoring eyes.

Despite the fact that the meal was a relaxed family affair and not the formal ordeal Brooke had feared, by the time the dessert course concluded, she was more than ready to escape. She was relieved, therefore, when Gabriel and Olivia offered her a quick tour of the public areas of the palace before escorting her back to her room.

Strolling the hall of portraits, Brooke realized the extent of Sherdana's history. Some of the paintings dated back to the late-fifteenth century. Thanks to all those years when she'd accompanied her mother to Italy and helped her research the Italian Renaissance period, Brooke had developed a love of history that partially explained why she'd chosen the same time period for her second doctorate.

"I imagine you have a library with books on Sherdana's history," she said to Gabriel as he and Olivia led the way to the ballroom.

"An extensive one. We'll make that our next stop."

A half an hour later the trio arrived at Brooke's door. She was feeling a touch giddy at the idea that she could return to the library the next day and check out the collection more thoroughly. The vast amount of books contained in the two-story room was an academic's dream come true. She could probably spend an entire year in Sherdana's palace library and never need to leave.

"Thank you for the tour."

"You are very welcome," Olivia said. "If you need anything else tonight, let one of the maids know. There is always someone on call."

Brooke bid the prince and princess good-night and entered her room. As she did, she noticed the store of crackers she'd nibbled on prior to dinner had been replenished. With a grateful sigh, Brooke grabbed a handful and went to the wardrobe. As the maid had promised earlier, her clothes had been laundered and returned. Brooke grinned as she slipped off her borrowed shoes, guessing the staff wasn't accustomed to washing ragged denim shorts and cotton peasant blouses. Regardless, they'd done a marvelous job. Her clothes looked brand-new.

A knock sounded on her door. Brooke's pulse kicked up. Could Nic have come by to wish her good-night? But it wasn't her handsome prince in the hall. Instead, her visitor was a beautiful, tall girl with long chocolate-brown hair and a welcoming smile.

"I'm Ariana." Behind Nic's sister were two maids loaded down with six shoe boxes and four overstuffed garment bags.

"Brooke Davis."

"I know that." Ariana laughed. "Even if the palace wasn't buzzing about the girl Nic brought home, I would have recognized you from the pictures Glen emailed me from time to time. He's very proud of you."

"You and Glen email?" Earlier Brooke had learned that Nic's sister had met Glen in Greece, but an ongoing correspondence was something else entirely. "I thought you'd just met the one time."

"Yeees." She drew the word out. "But it was *quite* a meeting."

Brooke didn't know what to make of the other girl's innuendo and made a note to question Glen about Nic's sister.

"Olivia told me her shoes were too big for you, so I brought you a few pairs of mine," Ariana said, indicating the maids behind her. "They should fit you better—and I included some dresses, as well. That's one of Olivia's, isn't it?"

Brooke couldn't figure out what about the gold lace could possibly have caused Ariana to wrinkle her nose. "Nothing I brought with me is suitable for palace wear. I had no plans to come here with Nic."

For a moment Ariana's eyes narrowed in the same sharp expression of assessment her mother had aimed at Brooke all evening. At last the princess smiled. "Well, I'm glad you did."

"So am I." And for the first time in eight hours, Brooke meant it. "I've really been looking forward to meeting you. I thought your artwork at the villa was amazing."

"Then you'd be the first." With a self-deprecating hair flip, Ariana slipped her arm through Brooke's and drew her into the bedroom.

"What do you mean?" Brooke let herself be led. From the way Nic had talked about his sister and from studying Ariana's art, Brooke felt as if she and the younger woman might be kindred spirits. "Your use of color gave the paintings such energy and depth."

Ariana's eyebrows drew together. "You're serious." She sounded surprised and more than a little hopeful.

"Very." Brooke didn't understand the princess's reaction. "I did my undergrad work in visual and critical studies."

"My family doesn't understand what I paint. They see it all as random splashes of color on canvas."

"I'm sure it's just that they are accustomed to a more traditional style of painting. Have you ever had your work exhibited anywhere?"

"No." A laugh bubbled out of her. "I paint for myself."

"Of course. But if you're ever interested in getting an expert's opinion, I have a friend in San Francisco who runs a gallery. He likes finding new talent. I took some pictures of your work. With your permission I could send him the photos."

"I've never thought…" Ariana shook her head in be-musement. "I guess this is the moment every artist faces at some point. Do I take a chance and risk failing or play it safe and never know if I'm any good."

"Oh, you're good," Brooke assured her. "But art is very subjective and not everyone is going to like what you do."

"I guess I've already faced my worst critics. My family. So why not see what your friend thinks."

"Wonderful, I'll send him the pictures tomorrow morning."

"And in the meantime—" Ariana gestured toward the wardrobe "—show me what you brought from home and let's see if I have anything that will appeal to you."

Brooke suspected the stylish princess wouldn't be at all impressed with the limited contents of her closet, but she knew her fine speech about art being subjective would be hypocritical if she couldn't back it up with action. For what was fashion but wearable art and even though Brooke's wardrobe wasn't suitable for a palace, it worked perfectly in her academic world.

The maids who'd entered behind Ariana deposited their burdens on Brooke's bed. If the princess had brought anything like what she was wearing—a sophisticated but fun plum dress with gold circles embroidered around the neckline and dotted over the skirt—Brooke braced herself to be wowed.

"It feels like every day is Christmas around here," Brooke said as dress after gorgeous dress came free of the garment bags. The variety of colors and styles dazzled Brooke. Of course, with her skin tone, Ariana could wear just about anything.

When the maids finished, Brooke pulled out her own dresses, shorts, skirts and her favorite kimono. Ariana narrowed her eyes in thought and surveyed each item.

"You have a great eye for color and know exactly what suits you."

Coming from the princess, this was a huge compliment. Ariana wasn't at all what Brooke imagined a princess would be like. She was warm and approachable. Not at all stuffy or formal. Brooke warmed to her quickly, feeling as if they had known each other for years instead of minutes.

"In California I blend in dressed like this." Brooke slipped into the tie-dyed kimono. It looked odd over the gold lace dress she'd borrowed from Olivia. "Here I stick out like a sore thumb."

"Hardly a sore thumb, although definitely a standout. No matter how you dress, your unique hair color will keep you from being a wallflower. No wonder my brother finds you irresistible."

Brooke felt Ariana's comment like a blow. "We're just friends," she explained in a rush, but her cheeks heated as the princess arched one slim eyebrow.

"But he talks about you all the time and he brought you to meet us."

"It's not what you're thinking. I went to the island to convince him to return to California. To Glen and the *Griffin* project. And when he was summoned back here sooner than expected, he didn't want to leave me alone in Greece."

"He must be in love with you. He's never brought a woman home before."

Brooke relaxed a little. "That's because the love of his life wouldn't fit inside an airplane." Seeing she had confused Ariana, Brooke explained. "As long as I've known him, Nic has been committed to the rocket he and my brother hope will one day carry people into space. There's been no room for an emotional connection with any woman."

"And yet here you are."

"Until a few days ago I didn't know he was a prince or that he needs to marry a citizen of the country or an aristocrat so his children can rule someday. Obviously I'm neither."

"He wouldn't have kept something like that from you unless he was worried about hurting you."

"That much is true." Here Brooke hesitated, unsure how much to explain. In the end, she decided to trust Ariana. "I've had a crush on him for years. When I showed up on Ithaca, he told me everything. He didn't want me to hope for a future we could never have together."

"Did it work? Did you stop hoping?"

"I'd be crazy if I didn't."

Like her brothers, Ariana had her father's warm brown eyes flecked with gold, but she'd inherited the intensity of her gaze from her mother. "But you two have been intimate."

Hating to lie, Brooke pretended she hadn't heard the soft question. Instead she chose a dress at random and announced, "I love this."

Luckily her selection was a flirty emerald-green dress that she could see herself wearing. Brooke held it against her body. As she looked at her reflection, she noticed the dress had no tags, but Brooke doubted it had ever been worn.

"I'll take your nonanswer as an affirmative." Ariana's musical laughter filled the room. "Try on the dress." While Brooke obeyed her, the princess continued, "I'm sorry if I was blunt and please don't be embarrassed." The gold bracelets on her slender wrists chimed. "My brothers are very hard for the opposite sex to resist. Thank goodness Gabriel and Nic are honorable and not ones to take advantage. Christian is like a child in a toy store wanting everything he sees."

And getting it, too, Brooke guessed. "Please don't tell

anyone about Nic and me. It's over and I wouldn't want to cause any needless problems."

Ariana nodded. "That dress is amazing on you."

The empire bodice cupped her breasts, the fabric ending in a narrow band of a darker green ribbon. From there, the layers of chiffon material flowed over her hips, the hem ending just above her knee. Brooke stared at herself in the mirror as Ariana guided her feet into strappy black sandals.

"It brings out the green in your eyes."

"I feel like a princess." Brooke laughed. "I guess I should because it's a dress fit for a princess. You."

Next, Ariana urged Brooke into a hot-pink sheath with a V-shaped neckline and bands of fabric that crisscrossed diagonally to create an interesting and figure-slimming pattern. It had a sophisticated, elegant vibe that Brooke wasn't sure she could pull off.

"I understand you are having breakfast with my mother tomorrow. This will be perfect, and I think you should pair it with these."

Ariana grabbed a box and pulled out a pair of white suede and black velvet lace ankle boots that were amazing, Brooke waved her hands in protest. "I can't. Those are just too much."

"You must wear them or the outfit will not be complete."

At Ariana's relentless urging, Brooke slipped her feet into the boots and faced the mirror, accepting immediately that she'd lost the battle. "I never imagined I could look like this."

Ariana's eyebrows lifted in surprise. "Why not? You are very beautiful."

"But not refined and effortless like you and Olivia."

With a very unladylike snort, Ariana rolled her eyes. "This is just how I appear here in the palace. When I go to Ithaca, I assure you, I'm so different you'd never recognize me."

"Do you spend a lot of time on the island?"

"Not as much as I'd like. It's an escape. I go to paint. To forget about the responsibilities of being a princess."

"I imagine there's a lot that keeps you busy."

"It's less now that Olivia is here." Ariana selected five more dresses and put them into Olivia's wardrobe with three more pairs of shoes. "That will do for now, but you will need a long dress for a party we must attend the day after tomorrow. It's the prime minister's birthday."

"Are you sure I will be going?"

"Absolutely. The event is always deadly dull and having you along will make the whole thing bearable."

While the maids returned the rest of the dresses to the garment bags, Ariana squeezed Brooke's shoulder. "I am sorry you and Nic cannot see where things might lead between you. I think you would make him very happy."

"Actually, I drive him crazy."

"Good. He has always been too serious. He needs a little crazy in his life." And with that, Ariana said good-night and left Brooke to her thoughts.

The corridors of the visitors' wing were quiet as Nic made his way back to his temporary quarters. The tranquillity would vanish over the next few days as guests began to arrive for the week of festivities leading up to the royal wedding. The conversation he'd had with his parents after dinner had highlighted their expectations for him. The women in the dossiers had been invited to the palace. He was to get to know each of them and make his selection.

As he'd listened to his mother, Nic realized he'd been in America too long. Although he'd grown up in a world where marriages sometimes were arranged, he'd grown accustomed to the notion of dating freely without any expectation that it might end in marriage.

He'd almost reached his suite when the door to the room

beside his opened and two maids emerged carrying garment bags. Their appearance could only mean he had company next door. It hadn't occurred to Nic that Brooke had been placed on this floor, much less in the room beside his, and his suspicion was confirmed when his sister came out of the room a few seconds later.

"Nic!" She raced across the few feet that separated them and threw herself into his arms. "How good that you're home."

She smelled of the light floral perfume he'd sent her the previous Christmas. He'd asked Brooke to help him pick out the perfume because he'd sensed the two women were a lot alike. Seeing his sister's good mood upon leaving Brooke, he knew he'd been right.

"I'm happy to be here."

Ariana pushed back until she could see his expression, and then clicked her tongue. "No you're not. You'd much rather be in California playing with your rocket."

"I'm done with that." The accident and Gabriel's marriage had seen to that.

"It's not like you to give up."

Her remark sent a wave of anger rushing through him. The emotion was so sharp and so immediate that he could do nothing more than stand frozen in astonishment. The loss of *Griffin*. His obligation to give up his dream and come home to marry a woman he didn't love. None of it was of his choosing.

But without this call to duty, would he have stayed in California and started over? The accident had been a disaster and his confidence was in shreds. Was that why he wasn't fighting his fate or figuring out a way around the laws that were in place so he could choose whom he married?

"Nic?"

As quickly as it had risen, his rage subsided. He shook

himself in the numb aftermath. "Sorry. I'm just tired. It's been a long day. And I didn't give up." He gave her nose an affectionate tweak the way he used to when she was an adorable toddler and he an oh-so-knowing big brother of ten. "I was called home to do my duty."

Ariana winced. "You're right. I'm sorry." Her contrite expression vanished with her next breath. "I met Brooke tonight. She's wonderful."

He was starting to wish his siblings would find something about Brooke to criticize. It was going to be hell bidding her goodbye and it would have been easier on him if they behaved as if falling for her was a huge error in his judgment.

"I'm glad you think so."

"If you're going to visit her, you might want to hurry. I think she was getting ready for bed."

For a second Nic wasn't sure if he should take his sister's statement at face value or if she was trying to get a reaction out of him. He decided it was the latter.

"This is my room." He indicated the door to his left. "I didn't know where she was staying in the palace."

"Why are you in the visitors' wing?"

"Something about my room flooding."

She gave him an incredulous look. "Who told you that?"

"Gabriel." Nic was starting to suspect something might be up. "Why?"

"Because I stopped by your suite earlier and it looked fine to me." She smirked. "I think our brother is trying to play matchmaker. You and Brooke all alone in the visitors' wing with no one to know if you snuck into each other's rooms. Very romantic."

"Damn it." Now he had another dilemma facing him. Confront Gabriel and return to his suite in the family wing or pretend he and Ariana never had this conversation and do what his heart wanted but his brain protested against.

"Honestly, stop being so noble." It was as if Ariana had read his mind. "Gabriel followed his heart. I think he wants the same for you."

"And then who will produce the legitimate heirs to ascend the throne?"

His sister shrugged. "There's always Christian. He isn't in love with anyone. Let him be the sacrificial lamb."

Nic hugged his sister and kissed the top of her head. "You are the best sister in the world."

"So are you going to choose Brooke?"

"You know I can't and you know why."

With a huge sigh, Ariana pushed him away. "You are too honorable for your own good."

"I know how this whole thing is making me feel. I can't do that to Christian." He paused and looked down at her. "Or to you."

"Me?"

"Have you considered what would happen if both Christian and I failed to produce a son? The whole burden shifts to your shoulders."

Ariana obviously hadn't considered this. Even though the constitution wouldn't allow her to rule as queen, she was still a direct descendant of the ruling king and that meant her son could one day succeed.

"Okay, I see your point, but I think it's terrible that you and Brooke can't be together."

"So do I."

Nic watched as his sister retreated down the corridor. For several heartbeats he stood with his hand on the doorknob to his room, willing himself to open the door and step inside, while Ariana's words rang in his head. *Brooke was getting ready for bed.* They were isolated in this wing of the palace. He could spend the night with her and sneak out before anyone discovered them. But how many times could he tell himself this was their last time together? Just that morning he'd been on the verge of saying goodbye.

He pushed open the door to his room, but didn't step across the threshold. He'd invited Brooke to Sherdana; it would only be polite to stop by and find out how her day had gone. If he stood in the hall, they could have a quick conversation without fear that either of them would be overcome with passion. That decided, Nic strode over and rapped on Brooke's door. If he'd expected her to answer his summons looking disheveled and adorable in her pajamas, he was doomed to disappointment.

The stylish creature that stood before him was nothing like the Brooke he'd grown accustomed to. Even the dress she'd worn at dinner tonight, as beautiful as she'd looked in it, hadn't stretched his perception of her as much as this strapless pale pink ball gown that turned her into a Disney princess.

Obviously enjoying herself, Brooke twirled twice and then paused for his opinion. "What do you think?"

"That's quite a dress."

She laughed, a bright silvery sound he hadn't heard since before the day he'd put an end to their fledgling romance. His heart lifted at her joy.

"I never imagined dressing like a princess would be so much fun."

His gut clenched at her words. She didn't mean them the way they'd sounded. The last thing she'd ever do was pick on him for rejecting her as unsuitable. Brooke wasn't the sort to play games or come at a problem sideways. It was one of the things he appreciated about her.

But that didn't stop regret from choking him.

"You look incredibly beautiful."

She shot him a flirtatious grin. "Aw, you're just saying that because it's true. Ariana brought the dress. I simply had to try it on since I'll never get the chance to wear it in public."

"Why not?"

"We both know the answer to that."

She drew him into the room and closed the door. Her actions had a dangerous effect on Nic's libido. He really hadn't come to her suite to make love to her, but it wouldn't take more than another one of her delicious smiles for him to snatch her into his arms and carry her to the bed.

"I don't think I follow you," Nic said, crossing his arms over his chest, his gaze tracking her every move as she enjoyed her reflection. He caught himself smiling as she shifted from side to side to make the skirt swish.

"Your mother and I are having breakfast tomorrow. I'm certain she's going to politely but firmly give me the heave-ho."

"She'd never be that rude."

"Of course not. But she can't be happy that her son brought home some inappropriate girl when he's supposed to be focused on selecting a bride."

"You're not inappropriate."

"I am where your future is concerned." Brooke reached for the dress's side zipper and gave Nic a stern look. "Turn around. I need to get out of this dress."

Blood pounded in his ears. "You are aware that I've seen you naked many, many times."

"That was before I was staying beneath your parents' roof. I think it would be rude of us to take advantage of their hospitality by getting swept up in a passionate moment. Don't you?" She set her hands on her hips. "So, turn around."

"My not watching you strip out of your clothes isn't going to prevent us from getting swept up in a passionate moment. I have memorized every inch of your gorgeous body."

"Turn around." Although her color was high, her firm tone deterred further argument.

At last Nic did as she'd asked. For several minutes the only sound in the room was the slide and crinkle of fabric as she undressed and the harsh rasp of his breath. He berated himself for acquiescing. If she was going to return to California in a few days, they were fools not to steal every moment they could to be together.

Bursting with conviction, Nic started to turn back around. "Brooke, we should…" He didn't finish because she gave him a sharp shove toward the door.

"No we shouldn't."

"One kiss." The irony of his demand wasn't lost on Nic. How many times had she teased, tormented and begged for any little bit of attention from him over the years? Time after time he'd refused her. "I missed waking up with you this morning."

"Whose fault was that?"

"Mine." It was all his fault. The five years when they could have been together if he hadn't been so obsessively focused on work. The way he'd hurt her because he'd chosen duty to his country over her. The emotional intimacy he couldn't give her because he was afraid his heart would break if he opened up.

"One kiss." He was pleading now.

"Fine. But you need to be in the hall with your hands behind your back."

A muscle ticked in his cheek. If she wanted to be in control, he would do his best to let that happen. "Agreed," he said and stepped out of her room.

Given the way he'd yielded to her conditions, Nic expected more demands from her.

"Close your eyes. I can't do this with you glaring at me."

In perfect stillness she waited him out. At last Nic let his lashes drift down. Years of working toward a single possibly unattainable goal would have been impossible without a great deal of fortitude, but Nic had recently discovered a shortage of patience where Brooke was concerned.

"Dear Nic." Her fingertips swept into his hair and tugged his head downward until their lips met.

Sweetness.

The tenderness of her kiss sent his heartbeat into overdrive. The desire previously driving through his body eased beneath her gentle touch. For the first time he acknowledged what existed between them wasn't born out of passion alone, but had its origins in something far deeper and lasting. A sigh fluttered in his chest as she lifted her lips from his and grazed them across his cheek.

"Good night, sweet prince."

Before he'd recovered enough to open his eyes, she was gone.

Ten

Thanks to Ariana's help with her wardrobe, Brooke had gone to bed feeling confident about her breakfast meeting with the queen. However, when she woke at dawn plagued by the increasingly familiar nausea, she plodded through her morning routine, burdened by anxiety.

By the time she'd swept her straightened hair into a smooth French roll, Brooke had consumed half a package of crackers in an effort to calm her roiling stomach. It seemed to be working because by the time she finished applying mascara and lipstick, she was feeling like her old self.

A maid appeared promptly at ten minutes to eight and Brooke dredged up her polite interview face as she followed her downstairs and into the garden. The girl pointed to a grassy path that curved past flower beds overflowing with shades of pink and purple. Brooke's destination— a white gazebo overlooking a small pond—appeared to be about fifty feet away. As she neared the structure, she noted that the queen had already arrived and was seated at the table placed in the center of the space. Rose-patterned china and crystal goblets were carefully arranged on a white tablecloth. The whole display reminded Brooke of a storybook tea party.

"Good morning, Your Majesty," Brooke said cheer-fully as she neared.

The queen turned her attention from the electronic tablet in her hand and her keen gaze swept over Brooke, lingering for a long moment on the low boots. Brooke withstood the queen's assessment in silence, wondering if custom required her to curtsy.

"Hello, Dr. Davis. Don't you look lovely. Please sit down."

Noticing the change from last night in the way the queen addressed her, Brooke perched on the edge of a mint-green damask chair and dropped her napkin on her lap. Two maids stood by to wait on them. Brooke accepted a glass of orange juice and a cup of very dark coffee lightened with cream which she sipped until her stomach gurgled quietly. To cover the noise, Brooke began to speak.

"Your garden is beautiful." Ariana had offered Brooke several safe subjects on which to converse. "I understand you have several rare varieties of roses."

"Are you interested in gardening?" the queen asked, offering a polite smile. A diplomat's smile.

Brooke's whole digestive track picked that moment to complain. She pinched her lips tight in response. After a second she took a deep breath. "I love flowers, but I don't have much of a green thumb."

"I suppose you've been busy earning your two doctor-ates. That's quite impressive for someone your age." Most people thought it was impressive, period, but it made sense that the queen of a country would be hard to impress. "And now you teach at a university."

"Italian language and literature."

"Olivia tells me you've traveled around Italy quite a bit."

"As well as France, Austria and Switzerland. I love this part of the world."

"Have you ever wanted to live in Europe?"

At that moment Brooke wished she'd never agreed to come. Nic's mother obviously regarded her as an intruder, or worse, an opportunist. Should she explain that she understood Nic was off-limits? She couldn't imagine that was the sort of polite conversation one made with the elegant queen of Sherdana.

"I love California. I did my undergraduate work in New York City." Brooke knit her fingers together in her lap lest she surrender to the urge to play with her silverware. "I couldn't wait to get back home."

"Home is a wonderful place to be. Are you hungry?" The queen gestured to the maids and one of them lifted the lid off the serving dish. "Crepes are my weakness," the queen said. "There are also omelets made with spinach and mushrooms or the chef would be happy to prepare something else if you'd prefer."

"I don't want to be any trouble." The crepes looked marvelous. Some were filled with strawberries, others with something creamy and covered in apples or...

"Pears roasted in butter and honey over crepes filled with ricotta cheese," the queen said, her eyes softening for the first time in Brooke's company.

If Brooke hadn't been so queasy, she could have easily eaten her way through half a dozen of the thin fluffy pancakes. As it was, she took one of each kind and nibbled at them.

"Olivia tells me you spoke of leaving in the next few days," the queen remarked in her delightfully accented English. "But when I spoke with Nicolas last night, he wishes you to remain through the wedding." She tucked into her breakfast with relish, obviously enjoying herself. "I think my son believes himself in love with you."

Brooke's coffee cup rattled against the saucer as she set it down too abruptly. Her stomach seized and suddenly eating the crepes didn't strike her as the smartest idea. The queen's words repeated themselves several times in Brooke's head. *He believes himself in love with you.* Not *he's in love with you.* Brooke recognized the difference. In high school and college she'd believed herself in love any number of times. Then she'd met Nic and began the discovery of what love truly was.

"I'm sorry, but you're wrong." Brooke put her napkin to her lips as her body flushed hot. It wasn't embarrassment or guilt, but her system reacting to stress and being pregnant. "Nic knows his mind like no man I've ever met. His heart belongs to this country and his family."

The queen sighed. "And you are in love with him."

The edges of Brooke's vision darkened. What was Nic's mother trying to establish? Already Brooke had accepted that she and Nic had no future. She knew he would never give his mother any cause to believe otherwise so she guessed the queen's protective instincts were kicking in. She understood. In a little more than seven months she would have her own child to keep from harm. Heaven help anyone who got in her way.

"He's my brother's best friend..." Brooke said, her voice trailing off. "I've known Nic for years. Did I once want something more? Yes. But that was before I knew who he was and what was expected of him."

"Are you trying to tell me you didn't know he was a prince?"

Brooke held still beneath the queen's penetrating regard. The older woman's face became difficult to stay focused on. Brooke wanted nothing more than to lie down until the spinning stopped.

"I didn't know until a few days ago. He left California without a word after the accident. I tracked him down to Ithaca because he wouldn't return my phone calls or emails. I was worried about how he was coping in the aftermath." She hoped the queen was satisfied with her reason for following Nic to Greece and would refrain from probing further.

The queen nodded. "The rocket ship was very important to him. But it's gone and he needs to put it behind him." Her tone was matter-of-fact as she dismissed her son's driving passion.

"He can't just put it behind him. He feels responsible for the death of one of his fellow scientists." Brooke endured a sharp pinch of sadness that Nic's mother didn't understand this about her son. "Walter hadn't been with the team long, but he worked closely with Nic. I think part of the reason why Nic was so willing to come home and let you marry him off was because he felt as if he'd failed Walter and Glen and even you and the king. I think the reason he worked so hard was to justify being away from Sherdana. He spent every day proving that his work would benefit future generations, driving himself beyond exhaustion in order to contribute something amazing to the world. So that his absence from you had meaning."

Brooke didn't realize she'd gotten to her feet until the gazebo began to sway around her. She clamped a hand over her mouth as the unsettled feeling in her stomach increased. She couldn't throw up. Not now. Not here. Sweat broke out on her body. She was about to ruin Ariana's gorgeous dress in an inglorious way the palace would be talking about for weeks. Brooke blinked and gulped air to regain her equilibrium. But she was too hot. Too dizzy.

"I have to..." *Go.* She didn't belong here. She'd been unbearably rude to Nic's mother, who was the queen of a nation. But she could no longer tell in which direction lay escape.

"Dr. Davis, are you all right?" The queen sounded very far away.

Brooke tried to focus on the queen's voice but she stumbled. Abruptly a wood column was beneath her fingers and she clutched the rough surface like a lifeline as darkness rushed up to claim her.

Nic exploded through the green salon's French doors and raced toward the gazebo as soon as Brooke stood and began to weave like a drunken woman. For the past fifteen minutes he'd been positioned by the windows that overlooked the garden so he could observe the exchange between his mother and Brooke and step in if things appeared as if they were going badly. Like Brooke, he'd expected his mother to diplomatically encourage her to leave as soon as possible and he was worried that Brooke might say something she'd immediately regret. Never could he have predicted that he'd be just in time to catch Brooke's limp body before it hit the gazebo floor.

"What happened?"

For once his mother looked utterly confounded. "She was going on and on about you and the rocket and then she turned bright pink and collapsed."

Nic scooped Brooke into his arms and headed toward the palace. Whereas she'd been flushed a moment earlier, her skin was now deathly pale. He entered the green salon and crossed the room in several ground-eating strides. His heart hammered harder in his chest each time he glanced down at Brooke's unconscious face. What was wrong with her? As far as he recalled she'd been sick a mere handful of times and it had certainly never been this drastic. A cold. Sinus infection. Once a bad case of food poisoning.

He didn't realize his mother had followed him until he

pushed open the door to Brooke's suite and carried her to the bed.

"Is there something wrong with her that caused her to pass out?" the queen demanded, sitting on the bed to feel Brooke's skin. "She's clammy."

"She's perfectly healthy." He pulled out his phone, unsure if this was a true emergency. "She was anxious about coming here, but seemed all right at dinner last night. What did you say to her at breakfast? She seemed agitated before she passed out."

"You were watching us?"

"I was worried about how you two would get along. Seems I was right to be."

"I merely told her that I thought you believed yourself in love with her."

Nic closed his eyes briefly and shook his head. "What would possess you to tell her that?"

"I needed her to understand that what was between you wasn't real."

"How would you know? You barely know her and I haven't been around for ten years so you scarcely know me, either."

His mother looked shocked. "You are my son. I raised you."

With effort, Nic reeled in his temper. "None of this is helping Brooke. She hasn't awakened yet. I think she needs a doctor."

He was texting Gabriel when a single word from his mother stopped him.

"Wait."

"Why?"

She pointed at a package of crackers on the nightstand. "How long has she been eating these?"

"I have no idea." And what did it matter? "Do you think there's something wrong with them?"

"No, but when I was pregnant I used to eat crackers to fight nausea." His mother looked thoughtful. "She barely ate any of her dinner last night and she was picking at breakfast today. Pregnancy could explain her fainting spell."

"Pregnant?" Nic shook his head to clear the sudden rushing in his ears. "Impossible."

"Impossible because you haven't been intimate or because you thought you were being careful."

The blunt question shocked him for a moment before comprehension struck. Of course his mother knew he'd been involved with Brooke. They hadn't kept their relationship secret and no doubt Ariana had mentioned that he was seeing someone in California.

"We've been very careful."

"Then perhaps she has someone else in her life."

Nic glared at his mother. "There's no one else."

The queen pressed her lips together and didn't argue further. "I suggest we wait for her to come around and ask her. If there's something more serious going on, we can call the doctor then." His mother stood and smoothed her skirt. "I'll give you some privacy. Please let me know how she's doing when she wakes."

And with that, the queen left and Nic was alone with Brooke.

Pregnant.

With his child. The thought of it filled him with warmth. But all too quickly questions formed. Had she realized it yet? She wasn't showing and he guessed that she was between five and eight weeks along. Was that too early for her to suspect? Yet she'd obviously been queasy and had to wonder why.

Brooke began to stir and Nic went to sit beside her. She blinked and slowly focused on him.

"What happened?"

"You passed out."

"Damn." She rubbed her eyes. "I yelled at your mother. She must hate me."

"She doesn't." He skimmed his knuckles against her cheek. "What's going on with you? I've never known you to be sick."

She avoided his gaze. "Nothing, I'm just really over-wrought and I think my blood sugar is low because I was too nervous to eat much at dinner."

"Is that why you were eating these?" He picked up the crackers and held them before her.

"Whenever my stomach gets upset, I eat crackers to ab-sorb the acid." Her words made sense, but something about her tone told him she wasn't giving him full disclosure.

"My mother told me she used to eat crackers when she was pregnant," he said. "She claimed it helped with nau-sea."

Brooke's body tensed. "I've heard that before. I think if you keep something bland in your stomach it settles it."

Nic's irritation was growing by the second. Brooke was a terrible liar because she believed in being honest. So much so it had gotten her into trouble a number of times. Her behavior while answering his questions demonstrated that while she hadn't actually said anything false, she was keeping things from him.

"Are you pregnant?"

"We've been careful."

"That didn't answer my question." He leaned down and grabbed her chin, pinning her with his gaze. "Are you pregnant?"

"Yes." Her voice came out small and unsure.

He sat back with a muffled curse. "Why didn't you tell me?"

"That was the plan when I came to Ithaca." She pushed into a sitting position and retreated away from him as far as the headboard would allow. "I couldn't tell you something like that over the phone, but then I showed up and you were so unhappy to see me." She wrapped her arms around herself and stared at her shoes. "And then you announce that you are a prince and you need to get married so your country could have an heir and that your wife needed to be an aristocrat or a citizen of Sherdana."

"So you were planning on leaving without ever telling me?" Outrage gave his voice a sharp edge.

"Don't say it like that. You made a choice to come back here and do the honorable thing. I made a decision that would save you from regret."

"But to never see my child?"

She put her hands over the lower half of her face and closed her eyes. After a long moment she spoke. "Don't you think I considered that? But I knew you would have other children, hopefully lots of them."

Her every word slashed his heart into ribbons. The woman he loved was having his child and he'd been days away from never knowing the truth. "Well, there's no question of you going home now."

"What? You can't make that decision for me. My job, friends and family are in California. That's where I belong. Just like you belong here in Sherdana with your family and your future *wife*."

She was crazy if she thought he was just going to let her vanish out of his life. "You belong with me just like I belong with you and our child."

"Maybe if you were the ordinary scientist I first fell in love with, but you are a prince with responsibilities that are bigger than both of us combined. Do the right thing and let me go. It's the only thing that makes sense."

"I refuse to accept that." Nic got to his feet and stared down at her. Where a moment earlier she'd seemed fragile and lost, her passionate determination to do what she perceived as the honorable thing gave her the look of a Valkyrie. "Get some rest. We will talk at length later."

Nic should have gone straight to his mother to deliver the confirmation of Brooke's condition as he'd promised, but found he needed some privacy to absorb what he'd just learned. He headed to his suite in the royal wing, curious to see if it was in the condition Gabriel had said. But just as Ariana had said, there was no leak.

The rooms that had been his growing up couldn't feel any less familiar than if he'd never seen them before. The past ten years of his life, first living in Boston, then California, felt much more real to him than the first twenty-two being Sherdana's prince. But that had been the case before he'd found out Brooke was pregnant. If he put aside duty and engaged in an honest conversation with himself, he'd accept that he no longer felt connected to his birth country. Yet his failure in the Mojave Desert meant that California was no longer a welcoming destination, either.

Never had he felt so conflicted about his future path. No matter what direction he chose, he was destined to leave disappointment and regret in his wake. Staying in Sherdana and marrying a suitable bride would require him to give up the woman he loved and abandon his child. But if he chose to make a life with Brooke could he convince her that he would never regret turning his back on his country when he knew it would always haunt him? And what would he do in California without the *Griffin* to work on? Teach at a university? He frowned.

When an hour of self-reflection passed without a clear solution presenting itself, Nic left his suite and sought his mother. He found her and his father in the king's private office deep in discussion.

"Well?" the king demanded, his eyes reflecting disappointment. He was seated behind a large mahogany desk that had been a gift from the king of Spain back in the early eighteenth century. "Is Dr. Davis pregnant?"

"Yes." Nic refused to feel like a chastised teenager. "And the child is mine." This last he directed to his mother, who sat on one of the burgundy sofas in the office's sitting area.

She was in the process of pouring a cup of tea and sent a pained look to her husband. "It seems as if none of my grandchildren are going to be legitimate."

"I won't apologize for what happened," he told his parents. "And I won't shirk my responsibility to Brooke."

"What does that mean?" his father said, his deep voice charged with warning.

"I don't have all the details worked out yet."

"You're not planning to marry her."

"It would take both of us to be on board for that to happen and at this point she's determined to return to California alone."

"You must let her," his mother said. "We will make sure she and the child are well taken of, but news of this must not get out. You need to marry and produce children that can one day succeed Gabriel."

The press of duty had never felt more overwhelming. Nic wanted to struggle free of the smothering net of responsibility that his parents cast over him.

"And what about Christian?" Nic asked, his heart burning with bitterness. "Will he not be expected to do the same?"

"Of course." The king nodded. "We are calling on both of you."

And with that, Nic accepted that one decision had been made for him.

Embarrassment and remorse kept Brooke from venturing out of her room the rest of the day. She put her pajamas back on, pulled the curtains closed and huddled in bed. A maid brought her lunch, which she barely touched, and when Ariana poked her head in the room sometime in the late afternoon, Brooke pretended to be sleeping.

She couldn't hide like this forever. For one thing it wasn't her style to avoid problems, and she really wouldn't shake the despair gnawing at her until she apologized to the queen for her outburst.

Around five she roused and phoned Theresa, needing to pour her heart out to someone who was 100 percent on her side. Unfortunately, the call rolled to voice mail and Brooke hung up without leaving a message. This was her problem to solve and the sooner she faced the music, the better.

A maid came by around six and found Brooke dressed in her tribal print maxi dress and sandals. Wearing her own clothes was like wrapping herself in a little piece of home. She didn't fit into Nic's world and trying to appear as if she did had been silly. Better to face the queen's displeasure as her authentic self, a woman who knew her own mind and was determined to do what was best for her and for Nic.

"Princess Olivia sent me to ask if you felt well enough to have dinner with her in half an hour," the maid said.

"Tell her yes."

When Brooke entered Prince Gabriel and Princess Olivia's private suite thirty minutes later, she wasn't surprised to discover Olivia had heard all about the morning's events. Up until now the princess had seemed like an ally, but would that continue? Brooke regarded Olivia warily as the princess indicated a spot on the gold couch. Brooke sat down while Olivia poured a cup of something that smelled like peppermint from a silver tea set.

The princess's kindness brought tears to Brooke's eyes. "How badly have I messed everything up?"

Olivia's eyes grew thoughtful. "Your pregnancy has

created quite a stir as you can imagine, but you shouldn't feel responsible. I doubt either you or Nic planned this."

"I don't mean that. I mean how mad is the queen that I yelled at her?"

"I didn't hear anything about that." Olivia's lips twitched and her eyes glinted with merriment. "What happened?"

"It's a bit of a blur. She said something dismissive about Nic needing to forget about the rocket and I straight up lost it." Brooke cradled the teacup, hoping the warmth would penetrate her icy fingers. "I started ranting about how he worked so hard because he wanted to justify his being away from his country for so long." Brooke shook her head as her heart contracted in shame. "It's none of my business. I shouldn't have said anything."

"You were defending the man you love. I think the queen understands."

"You didn't see her face." Brooke squinted and tried to summon a memory of the queen's reaction, but all she recalled was the garden pitching around her and the descent into darkness. "I was so rude."

"You are being too hard on yourself," Olivia said. "No wonder you and Nic get along so well. You're both such honorable people."

"I don't feel very honorable at the moment. But I'd like to change that. I made arrangements for a flight leaving the day after tomorrow at nine in the morning. I could use some help getting to the airport."

"You can't really mean to leave."

"You can't possibly think it's a good idea for me to stay. The longer I'm here the more likely it will leak that I'm pregnant. Better if I disappear from Sherdana so Nic can move forward with his life."

"What makes you think he's just going to let you go? When faced with the same choice, Gabriel fought for me.

Nic is no less an Alessandro and I don't think he's any less in love."

Olivia's words provoked many questions as Brooke realized that the princess had been confronted by a similar choice of whether to marry her prince when doing so put the future line of Alessandros at risk. But as much as curiosity nipped at her, Brooke feared asking would insult the princess.

"I think Gabriel is more of a romantic than Nic," Brooke said. "Your husband's heart led him to choose you and he will never question whether he made the right decision. Nic approaches matters with logic, listing the pros and cons, assigning values so he can rank what's most important. I think he takes after his mother in that respect."

Olivia's beautiful blue eyes clouded. "You know him well so I will just have to accept that you're right, but I hope for your sake that you're wrong."

Eleven

Both Olivia and Ariana had ganged up on Brooke and convinced her to go to the prime minister's birthday party the next evening. As it was her last night in Sherdana—she was due to fly out the next morning—the princesses were opposed to her spending any more time alone. Their concern was a balm to Brooke's battered spirit and because Ariana had tapped into her contacts in the fashion world and found Brooke the perfect Jean-Louis Scherrer gown to wear, she'd caved with barely a whimper.

Trailing into the party behind the crown prince and princess with Ariana beside her for support, Brooke experienced a sense of wonder that made her glad she'd come. The gown Ariana had found for her had the empire waist Brooke loved and a free flowing skirt. With every stride, the skirt's bright gold lining flashed and showed off the most perfect pair of Manolo Blahnik shoes with tasseled straps. The bodice was crusted with bronze beading that made her think of Moroccan embellishment and the gown's material was a subdued orange, gold and pink paisley pattern that exhibited Brooke's bohemian style.

After meeting the prime minister and wishing him a happy birthday, Brooke relaxed enough to gaze around at the guests. With Ariana at her side, no one seemed overly interested in her. It wasn't that she was ignored. Each person she was introduced to was polite and cordial, but no one seemed overly curious about the stranger from California. Brooke suspected that Ariana's social nature brought all sorts of individuals into her sphere.

Of Nic she saw nothing. The party was crowded with Sherdanian dignitaries and Brooke was determined not to spend the entire evening wondering which of the women Nic might choose to become his wife.

"Do you see what I mean about dull?" Ariana murmured to her an hour into the party. "We've made an appearance. Anytime you're ready to leave, just say the word. A friend of mine owns a club. It's opening night and he'd love to have me show up."

Brooke had been finding the party anything but dull. Unlike Nic, she liked to balance hours of study and research with socializing. People-watching was the best way to get out of her head and the prime minister's party was populated by characters.

"Sure, we can leave, but this isn't as dull as you say."

"I'm sorry, I forget that you are new to all this."

"I suppose you're right. Who is the woman in the black gown and the one over there in blue?" Each of them negotiated the room on the arm of an older gentleman, but Brooke had observed several telling glances passing between them.

"That's Countess Venuto." Ariana indicated the woman wearing blue. "And Renanta Arazzi. Her husband is the minister of trade. The men hate each other."

"Their wives don't share their husbands' antagonism."

"What do you mean?"

"I think they're having an affair." Brooke grinned. "Or they're just about to."

Ariana gasped, obviously shocked. "Tell me how you know."

Brooke spent the next hour explaining her reasoning to Ariana and then commented on several other things she'd picked up, astonishing the princess with her observations and guesses.

"You have an uncanny knack for reading people," Ariana exclaimed. "Gabriel should hire you to sit in on his meetings and advise him on people's motives."

Flattered, Brooke laughed. "I'm trained as an analyst. Whether it's art, literature or people, I guess I just dig until I locate meaning. Just don't ask me about anything having to do with numbers or technology. That's where I fail miserably."

"But that's what makes you and my brother such a perfect pairing. You complement each other."

At the mention of Nic, Brooke's good mood fled. "If only he wasn't a prince and I wasn't an ordinary girl from California." She kept her voice light, but in her chest, her heart thumped dully. "I didn't tell you earlier, but I made arrangements to fly home tomorrow morning."

"You can't leave." Ariana looked distressed. "At least stay through the wedding."

The thought of delaying the inevitable for another week made Brooke shudder. Plus, she hadn't yet been offered the opportunity to apologize to the queen in person and didn't feel right taking advantage of the king and queen's hospitality with that hanging over her. "I can't stay. Coming here in the first place was a mistake."

"But then I'd never have met you and that would have been a tragedy."

Brooke appreciated Ariana's attempt to make her feel

special. "I feel the same way about you. I just wish I'd handled things better." By which she meant the incident with the queen and Nic's discovering that she was pregnant.

She hadn't spoken to him since he'd left her room the day before. She'd dined that night with Olivia and taken both breakfast and lunch in her room. Ariana had joined her for the midday meal, bringing with her the gown Brooke was wearing tonight and reminding her of the promise she'd made to attend the birthday party.

Suddenly the crowd parted and Nic appeared, looking imposing and very princely as he strode through the room. Brooke stared at him in hopeless adoration, still unaccustomed to the effortless aura of power he assumed in his native environment. What was so different about him? He'd always radiated strength and confidence, but he'd been approachable despite his often inherent aloofness. What made him seem so inaccessible now? Was it the arrogant tilt of his head? The way he wore the expensive, custom tuxedo as easily as a T-shirt and jeans? The cool disdain in his burnished gold eyes?

And then he caught sight of her and the possessive glow of his gaze melted the chill from his features. Brooke's heart exploded in her chest and she abandoned Ariana with a quick apology, slipping through the party guests in Nic's direction before she considered what she would say. When she'd drawn to within five feet of him, her path was blocked by a petite brunette in a shimmering black mini.

"Nicolas Alessandro, I heard you returned home." The woman's cultured voice stopped Brooke dead in her tracks.

She turned aside and spotted French doors leading onto a terrace. Moving in that direction with as much haste as she dared, Brooke chastised herself. What had she been thinking? She and Nic couldn't act as friends or even acquaintances at this public event. All eyes were on the returning prince. During her self-imposed incarceration, she'd pored over the local gossip blogs and read several news articles speculating on Nic's abrupt return. The media were having a field day detailing all the women who'd been invited to the royal wedding the following week and speculating on who might be the front-runner to become the next Sherdanian princess.

Not one of the news sources had mentioned a girl from California. For that Brooke was grateful, but if she threw herself at Nic during this party, how long would it be before someone started wondering who she was.

Brooke had about five minutes of solitude on the terrace before she was joined by Olivia.

"Are you all right?" the princess inquired, her concern bringing tears to Brooke's eyes.

"I almost made a huge mistake out there. I saw Nic and raced through the crowd to get to him." Her story came out in uneven bursts as her heart continued to pound erratically. "If someone hadn't beaten me to him, I don't know what I would have done." Brooke braced herself on the metal railing as hysterical laughter bubbled up, making her knees wobble. "I am such an idiot."

"Not at all. You are in love. It makes us behave in strange and mysterious ways."

Brooke loved Olivia's British accent. It made even the most impossible statements sound plausible. Already calm was settling back over her.

"I'm so glad I had the chance to get to know you," Brooke said. "Ariana, too. Nic is lucky to have you."

"He'd be lucky to have you as well if only you wouldn't be so eager to rush off."

"I know you mean well." Brooke shook her head. "But Nic needs me to go."

"What if instead he really needs you to stay? He's been locked in the library since yesterday morning. His mind is a hundred miles away from anyone trying to have a conversation with him. He called Christian and could be heard yelling at him to get home all the way across the palace."

That didn't sound much like the Nic she knew, but then he'd been through a lot in the past month. Was it any surprise that having his entire world turned upside down would cause a crack in his relentless confidence?

"It's my fault," Brooke said, her own confidence returning. "I dropped a huge bomb on him yesterday when I said I was going back to California without consulting him."

"You should speak to him. He wants badly to do right by everyone and it's tearing him apart."

As it had torn Brooke apart, until she'd concluded that Nic would be better off not knowing about her pregnancy. "But I'm leaving in the morning. It will have to be tonight." Brooke considered. "Ariana's friend has a club opening tonight and she wants to go. I'll have her drop me at the palace. If you'll let Nic know, I'll be waiting for him in the library at midnight."

She didn't want him to leave the party early. His mother would expect him to spend the evening getting acquainted with all the available women there. Brooke turned to go, but Olivia stopped her.

"If Nic could marry you, would you accept?"

The princess asked the question with such poignant sincerity that Brooke faced her and answered in kind. "I love him with everything I am. Which is why it's both incredibly simple and impossibly hard to let him go so he can be the prince his family needs him to be."

Olivia wrapped her in a fierce hug and whispered, "If he asks you to stay, please say yes."

Brooke smiled at the beautiful princess without answering and then squared her shoulders and went to find Ariana.

* * *

Trapped in a tedious conversation with one of Christian's former girlfriends, Alexia Le Mans, Nic watched Brooke exit the ballroom for the less populated terrace and was just extricating himself to go after her when Olivia beat him to it. He'd only come to the party tonight in the hopes of seeing Brooke and demanding they have a conversation about the child she carried. He might not be able to marry her, but he'd be damned if the child would disappear out of his life. Nic had seen Gabriel's regret at not knowing his daughters during their first two years and Nic wasn't going to let that happen to him.

Ten minutes after Brooke left the room, she was back, and almost immediately he lost her in the crush. He moved to intercept her, but was stopped three times before he reached where he thought Brooke had been headed.

"Nic."

He turned at Olivia's voice and saw that she and Gabriel were coming up behind him. "I can't talk right now, I'm looking for Brooke."

Olivia exchanged a wordless look with her husband. "Ariana was heading to a club opening and she offered to give Brooke a lift back to the palace. But before she left, she gave me a message for you. She said she'll be waiting to speak to you in the library at midnight."

"Thank you." Nic had no intention of waiting until then to talk with Brooke. "And thank you for all you've done for her."

"No need to thank me," Olivia said, her smile affectionate. "She's lovely and I've enjoyed being her friend."

"Yes," Gabriel added. "Too bad she couldn't become a permanent fixture in the palace. I think she'd make an outstanding princess."

The temptation to say something disrespectful to the future king sizzled in Nic's mind, but he quelled his frustration and thanked Olivia with as much courtesy as he could muster. Bidding them goodbye, Nic headed downstairs to reclaim his car and follow Brooke to the palace.

The drive from the hotel where the prime minister's party had taken place back to the palace only took ten minutes, but Nic discovered Brooke had already disappeared into the visitors' wing by the time he arrived. He'd hoped to catch her before she went upstairs so they could have their conversation someplace that wouldn't invite gossip, but that wasn't going to stop him from tracking her down.

As he knocked on her door, he was a little out of breath from his rush up the stairs to the third floor. Listening to his heart thunder in his chest as he waited for her to answer, he made a note to drink less and exercise more than had been his habit in the past month. But when Brooke answered the door, snatching his breath away as he stared down into her soft gray-green eyes, he knew it wasn't stamina that had his heart and lungs to labor, but excitement at being close to her again.

"Nic? What are you doing here?"

"You wanted to talk." He stepped forward, forcing her to retreat into her room. As soon as he cleared the door, he shut it behind him. His hands made short work of his tie and slipped the first buttons of his shirt free. "Let's talk."

Brooke's body immediately began to thrum with arousal at Nic's apparent intent in entering her room. Her lips couldn't form protests as he removed his tuxedo jacket and unfastened his gold cuff links. Those went into his pocket before he set the jacket on a convenient chair while still advancing on her.

"Didn't Olivia tell you midnight in the library?"

"I considered it a suggested time and place." He pulled his shirt free of his pants and went back to work on the buttons. Each one he freed gave her a more evocative glimpse of the impressive chest beneath. "I prefer this one."

The gold shards in Nic's eyes brightened perceivably when his temper was aroused. Because she enjoyed riling him, Brooke had noticed this phenomenon a lot. She could judge the level of his agitation by the degree of the sparkle. At the moment his gaze was almost too intense to meet.

She thought about Olivia's words and wished he'd ask her to stay in Sherdana. No, she didn't. She ached for him to ask her. But he wouldn't. He shouldn't. From the start he'd been right to keep her at bay.

Nic closed the distance between them and swept her into his arms. As he bent her backward, his lips gliding along her temple, Brooke's senses spun.

"Stay in Sherdana a while longer."

He wasn't asking for forever, but every second with him was precious. "I don't belong here."

"Neither do I," he whispered an instant before his lips met hers.

With a moan, she sank her fingers into his thick black hair and held on as he fed off her mouth. Desire lashed at her, setting her pent-up emotions free. She met him kiss for kiss, claiming him as he sought to brand her with his passion.

Both were breathing unevenly when he lifted his lips from hers and captured her gaze. With her heart thundering in her ears, Brooke barely heard his words.

"You and I belong together."

"In another life. As different people. I'd give up everything to be with you," she murmured, the last of her resistance crumbling as he slid his hands down her back and aligned her curves to his granite muscles. "But not here and now."

"Yes to here and now," he growled. "It's tomorrow and

all the days beyond we can't have. Don't deny either of us this last night of happiness."

Brooke surrendered to the flood of longing and the demanding pressure of his arms banded around her body. Tomorrow would come all too soon. She wanted him for as long as possible.

With her face pressed against his bare chest, her ear tuned to the steady beat of his heart, she said, "I love you."

His arms crushed her, preventing any further words. For a long moment his grip stopped her from breathing, and then his hold gentled.

"You are the only woman I'll ever love."

Brooke lifted up on tiptoe and pushed her lips against his. He immediately opened to her and she matched the fierce hunger of his kiss with a desperation she couldn't hide. He loved her.

Working with deliberation that made her ache, he eased down the zipper of her dress, his lips sending a line of fire along her skin as he went. She'd never felt so adored as he unwrapped her body, treating her as if she was a precious gift. By the time his fingers lifted away the exquisite designer gown, exposing all of her, she was quivering uncontrollably.

Nic stripped away the last of her clothes, pushed her to arm's length and stared. Looking at her excited him and that set her blood on fire. She licked her dry lips and his pupils flared, almost vanquishing his gold irises. Her legs trembled. She couldn't take much more without ending up in a heap at his feet.

Without warning he surged back to life, lifting her into his arms and carrying her to the bed. As she floated down to land on the mattress, Brooke's thighs parted in welcome and Nic quickly stripped off the rest of his clothes and covered her with his body. She expected him to surge inside her, such was the intensity of his erection, but instead, he went back to work on her body with lips and hands, driving her to impossible levels of hunger.

At long last, she'd gone light-years past the point of readiness and gathered handfuls of his hair. "I can't wait any longer to have you inside me."

"Are you asking or commanding?" He sucked hard on her neck and she quaked.

"I'm begging." She reached down and found him. Her firm grip wrenched a satisfying moan from his lips. "Please, Nic."

His hands spanned her hips and in one swift thrust he answered her plea. She flexed her spine and accepted his full length while he devoured her impassioned groan. Before she could grow accustomed to the feel of him filling her, Nic rolled them over until she sat astride his hips.

This new position offered a different set of sensations and freed his hands to cruise across her torso at will. She took charge of their lovemaking and began to move. Whispering words of encouragement, he cupped her breasts, kneading and rolling her hard nipples between his fingers to intensify her pleasure.

When she came, it was hard and fast. If she could have lingered in the moment forever, she would have known perfect happiness, but such profound ecstasy wasn't meant to last. And there was a different sort of joy in the lazy aftermath of being so thoroughly loved. As Nic nuzzled his face in the place where her neck met her shoulder, Brooke savored the synchronized beat of their hearts and knew no matter where her body existed, her soul would stay with Nic where it belonged.

Morning brought rain and the distant rumble of thunder. Nic woke to the soft, fragrant sweetness of Brooke's naked body curved against his and held his breath to keep from disturbing the magic of the moment. Last night had been incredible. And it had been goodbye. He'd tasted it in the desperation of her kisses and felt it in the wildness of his need for her.

"What time is it?" she asked, her voice a contented purr.

"A little before seven."

"Oh." She practically sprang out of bed and began to hunt around for her clothes. "I have to go."

Nic sat up, automatically admiring the fluid movement of her nude form as she dressed. "Where are you going?"

"Home. My flight leaves in two hours."

Shock held him motionless and she'd almost reached the door before he caught up with her. If he hadn't barged into her room and spent the night would he have even known she was gone?

"And if I ask you to stay?" He thought he was ready to set her free, but now that the moment had arrived, he was incapable of saying goodbye.

"Don't you mean command?" Her smile was both wicked and sad.

Despite his solemn mood, Nic's lips twitched. "You aren't Sherdanian. I have no way to make you behave."

"And throwing me in the dungeon would create an international scandal that would upset your mother."

"Is that why you're running away? Because you think either I or my family would be bothered by some adverse publicity?"

Her body stiffened. "I'm not running away. I'm returning to California where I live. Just like you are staying in Sherdana where you belong. Besides, the longer I stay the more I risk becoming fodder for the tabloids and that wouldn't do your marriage hunt any favors."

"No. I suppose it wouldn't. But I still don't want you to go."

"And yet I must."

"You're breaking my heart," he said, carrying her hand to his lips and placing her palm against his bare chest.

"I'm breaking *your* heart?" She tugged her hand from beneath his, but his free arm snaked around her, and pulled her resistant body against him. "Do you have any idea how unfair you're being right now?"

He knew and didn't care. Nic tightened his hold, letting his heat seep into her until there was no more resistance. And then he kissed her, long and slow and deep, while in the back of his mind he acknowledged that this would be their final goodbye. By the time he broke away they were both gasping for breath.

Brooke spoke first. "You were right."

"About?" He nuzzled her cheek, feathering provocative kisses along her skin. His teeth grazed her earlobe, making her shudder.

"Starting something that had no future." Her pain and grief tore at him.

"I didn't want there to be regrets between us."

"I don't regret it."

"But you can't help thinking if we'd never been together that leaving would be easier." His arms tightened. "And you might be right. But for the rest of my life I will cherish every second we've spent together." And now he had to be strong enough to let her go. Only knowing that their child would connect them together forever gave him the courage to set her free. "There's no getting you out of my system," he said. "Or my heart."

"I love you." She kissed him one last time. "Now let me go."

Twelve

"You let her go?" Gabriel Alessandro, crown prince of Sherdana, was furious. "What the hell is the matter with you?"

From her seat behind the ornate writing desk, Olivia watched her husband storm around the living room of their suite, her expression a mask of sadness and resignation.

"Why are you yelling at me?" Nic demanded, pointing at Gabriel's princess. "She's the one who arranged to have a car take her to the airport."

It was shortly before lunch and Brooke's flight had departed Carone International over two hours prior. By now she would be over the Atlantic Ocean on her way to New York's JFK airport and her connecting flight to San Francisco.

"It's not my wife's fault that she was leaving in the first place. You were supposed to stop her before she ever got into the car." Gabriel raked his fingers through his hair in a gesture of acute frustration. "Do you realize what you've done?"

"I did what the country required of me."

Silence greeted his declaration, but Nic refused to feel bad that he'd at long last addressed the elephant in the room. He'd let Brooke get away because Gabriel hadn't acted in the country's best interest when he'd married Olivia.

"For the first time in your life," Gabriel shouted back. "How the hell do you think I felt having to carry the burden of responsibility for both you and Christian all these years? Maybe I would have enjoyed being an irresponsible playboy or playing at an impossible dream like building a rocket ship."

"Playing at—"

"Enough." Olivia's sharp tone sliced through the testosterone thickening the air and silenced both men. "Tossing accusations back and forth is not solving our immediate issue."

Gabriel was the first to back down. He turned to his wife and the love that glowed in his gaze made Nic's heart hurt.

"She's right." Gabriel's attention returned to his brother. "I know you were doing amazing things in California and I wish you were still there doing them. I really don't begrudge you any time you've spent chasing your dream."

Nic was seeing a different side of his brother. Never before had Gabriel spoken so eloquently about what he was feeling. The crown prince could speak passionately about issues relating to the country and he had a fine reputation for diplomacy, but he'd always been a closed book with regard to anything of a personal nature.

"I've lost my nerve." Since Gabriel felt comfortable sharing, Nic decided it was only fair to give a little in return. "Since the accident, I am afraid to even think about what went wrong with *Griffin*. Five years of my life went into designing the fuel delivery system that caused the rocket to blow up. I killed someone. There's no coming back from that for me." Nic's voice was thick with regret as he finished, "It's part of the reason I let Brooke go. Her life is in California and there's no place for me there anymore. I belong here where I can make a difference."

"Oh, Nic." Olivia was at his side, her soft hand gentle on his arm. "I'm sorry you are in so much pain. And what happened to your rocket and that man's death are a horrible tragedy, but you can't let that get in the way of your happiness with Brooke."

Gabriel grabbed his other arm and gave him a shake. "And you really don't belong here."

"Yes, I do. The country needs an heir to the throne." But his protest was cut short as Olivia and Gabriel shared a moment of intense nonverbal communication. "What's going on?"

Olivia shifted her gaze to Nic and offered him a sympathetic head tilt. "We can't get into specifics…"

"About what?" There was obviously an important secret being kept from him and Nic didn't like being left out.

The crown prince's lips quirked in a wry smile. "What if as the future leader of your country I order you to return to California, resume work on your rocket ship and marry the mother of your child?"

Nic spent a long moment grappling with his conscience. He'd come to grips with sacrificing his happiness for the sake of the country and although it had torn him apart to let Brooke go, he'd known it was for the greater good of Sherdana and his family.

Now, however, his brother was offering him a way out. No, Nic amended. Gabriel was directing him to forsake his duty and chase his dreams all the way back to California. The walls he'd erected to garrison his misery began to crumble. He sucked in a ragged breath. Permission to marry Brooke and raise their child with her. The chance to complete his dream of space travel. All on a silver platter compliments of his brother. It was too much.

But as he scrutinized Gabriel's confident posture and observed the secret smile that lit Olivia's eyes, he sensed that whatever was going on, these two were well in control of the country's future.

Nic offered Gabriel a low bow, his throat tight. "Naturally, I'd do whatever my crowned prince commands."

On her way to the Mojave Air and Space Port to visit her brother, Brooke took a familiar detour and drove past the house Nic had rented for the past three years. The place looked as deserted as ever. Nic hadn't spent much time there, sometimes not even sleeping in his own bed for days at a stretch because the couch in his workroom was within arm's reach of his project.

Still, when she could get him to take time off, they'd often had fun barbecuing in the backyard or drinking beer on the front porch while they stared at the stars and Nic opened up about what he and Glen hoped one day to accomplish.

Brooke stomped on the accelerator and her Prius picked up speed. Those days were behind her now that Nic was back in Sherdana, but at least she had the memories.

A ten-minute drive through town brought her to the hangar where Glen and his team were working on the new rocket. Brooke hadn't been here since the day Nic had broken off with her and she was surprised how little work had been done. From what Glen had told her, the inflow of cash hadn't dried up after the first *Griffin* had exploded. In fact, the mishap had alerted several new investors who'd promised funding for the project.

Brooke spent several minutes walking around the platform that held the skeleton of the *Griffin II*, her footsteps echoing around the empty hangar. She wasn't accustomed to this level of inactivity and wondered if she'd misunderstood her brother's text, asking her to meet him at the airfield rather than at his house.

As she made her way to the back of the facility where the workrooms and labs were set up, Brooke detected faint strains of music and figured her brother had gotten caught up in something and lost track of time. Except the music wasn't coming from Glen's office, but from Nic's former workroom.

The wave of sorrow that swarmed over her stopped Brooke in her tracks. Someone had obviously been hired to replace Nic on the team and had been given his office. The shock of it made her dizzy, but she quickly rationalized the unsteadiness away. How could she expect forward progress on the rocket without someone taking on the fuel delivery system Nic had abandoned? With the exception of her brother, no one else on the team could match Nic's brilliance or comprehend the intricacies of his design. Someone new would have to be brought in.

Brooke squared her shoulders and continued down the hallway. She might as well introduce herself to Nic's replacement and start to accept the changes that he'd bring to the team.

"Hi," she called over the music as she first knocked, and then pushed open the unlatched door. "I'm Brooke Davis, Glen's…" Her voice trailed away as the tall man in jeans and a black T-shirt turned to greet her.

"Sister," Nic finished for her. "He told me you might be stopping by today."

Brooke's throat tightened. "What are you doing here?"

"I work here." His smile—at once familiar and utterly different from anything she'd seen before—knocked the breath from her lungs.

"I don't understand." She sagged back against the door frame and drank in Nic's presence. His vibrant, imposing presence made it impossible for her to believe he was a hallucination, but she couldn't let herself trust this amazing turn of fortune until she knew what was going on. "I left you in Sherdana. You were going to get married and make Alessandro heirs."

Nic shook his head. "Turns out I was completely wrong for the job."

"How so?" His wry amusement was beginning to reach through her shock. She was starting to thaw out. The ice water that had filled her veins for the past week heated beneath his sizzling regard. "You're not impotent or something, are you?"

He laughed and reached out to snag her wrist, pulling her away from the wall and up against his hard body. "That was not the problem."

"Then what was?" She wrapped her arms around his neck and arched her back until they were aligned from chest to thigh.

"No one wanted me."

"I can't believe that." And she didn't. Not for a single second.

"It's true. Word got around that a spunky redhead had stolen my heart and left me but a shell of a man."

Brooke purred as he bent his head and nuzzled his lips into her neck. "So you've come here to take it back?"

"No. I've come here to sign it over all legal and such."

Fearing she'd misunderstood what he was saying, Brooke remained silent while her mind worked furiously. He'd left Sherdana and resumed his old position on the team. From the way his lips were exploring her neck, she was pretty sure he intended that their physical relationship would get back on track.

"Brooke?" He cupped her face and stared deep into her eyes. "You're awfully quiet."

"I guess I'm not sure what to say."

"You could start by saying yes."

Relief made her giddy. "You haven't asked me a question."

"You're right." And to her absolute delight, he dropped down on one knee and fished a ring out of his pocket. "Brooke Davis, love of my life and mother of my child, will you marry me?"

She set her hands on her hips and shook her head. "If this is about the baby, I assure you I'm not expecting you—"

"Oh, for heaven sakes," came an explosive shout from the hallway behind them. "Just tell the guy yes."

"Yes," she whispered, leaning down to plant her lips on Nic's.

He wrapped his arms around her and shot to his feet, lifting her into the air and spinning her in circles. She laughed, delirious with joy, and hugged him back. When he let her toes touch the floor once more, Glen was there to pound Nic on the back and offer his congratulations.

Amidst this, Nic slipped an enormous diamond ring onto her left hand. She ogled it while Glen played the brother card and threatened Nic with bodily harm if he didn't take good care of her. Then Glen left her and Nic alone so he could fill her in on what had transpired after she'd left.

"Gabriel almost killed me when he heard that you'd left," Nic explained, sitting on his couch and pulling her onto his lap.

She let her head fall onto his shoulder and savored the contentment that wove through her. "He did?"

"Apparently he decided to play matchmaker and wasn't particularly happy that I failed to do my part."

"Matchmaker?"

"He made sure we were in adjoining rooms in the visitors' wing of the palace and enlisted Olivia and Ariana to convince you not to give up on us."

"They did a pretty good job of that," Brooke agreed, thinking about that last night she'd spent with Nic. "In fact, I almost left without seeing you one final time, but both of them convinced me I owed it to us to say goodbye." But there was something she still didn't understand. "And we did. I left and you didn't stop me. You were determined to do the honorable thing and stay in Sherdana and get married. So what's changed?"

"Two things. First, I thought long and hard about what made me happy. Spending the rest of my life with you and my work. But I couldn't marry you without regretting that I'd decided not to step up when my family needed me and I couldn't see returning to the *Griffin* project when my design had caused a man's death."

"And yet you're here," Brooke pointed out.

"I didn't accept I couldn't live without you until I had to start."

"But what about Sherdana and producing an heir?"

"Gabriel released me from duty. Before I left he explained how it had nearly destroyed him to lose Olivia and he refused to let me go through the same sort of pain."

"But what about an heir for the throne?"

"I guess it's up to Christian."

"And you don't feel bad that he has to carry the full burden of the country's future on his shoulders?" Brooke arched her eyebrow at Nic's poor attempt to conceal a grin.

"If he had to choose between the woman of his dreams and duty to Sherdana, I'd feel horrible." Nic brushed Brooke's hair aside and kissed his way down her neck. "But he's never dated any woman long enough to fall in love and it's time he let someone in."

"Et benedetto il primo dolce affanno ch'i' ebbi ad esser con Amor congiunto."

Nic translated, "And blessed be the first sweet agony I suffered when I found myself bound to Love." He grazed his lips against Brooke's, making her sigh in pleasure. "I only hope the woman who finally breaks through to Christian makes him half as happy as you've made me."

Heart singing, Brooke wrapped her arms around Nic's neck and set her forehead against his. His gaze fastened on hers, letting her glimpse his joy and his need for her. For the first time she truly understood the depth of Nic's love for her. He'd made light of his decision to leave Sherdana, but she suspected even though Gabriel had released him from duty, the king and queen hadn't backed either of their sons' actions.

"I haven't begun to make you happy," she promised, tightening her hold.

"You don't say."

"I do say." And she proceeded to demonstrate how she planned to start.

* * * * *

MILLS & BOON

THE HEART OF ROMANCE

A ROMANCE FOR EVERY KIND OF READER

MODERN

Prepare to be swept off your feet by sophisticated, sexy and seductive heroes, in some of the world's most glamourous and romantic locations, where power and passion collide.
8 stories per month.

HISTORICAL

Escape with historical heroes from time gone by. Whether your passion is for wicked Regency Rakes, muscled Vikings or rugged Highlanders, awaken the romance of the past.
6 stories per month.

MEDICAL

Set your pulse racing with dedicated, delectable doctors in the high-pressure world of medicine, where emotions run high and passion, comfort and love are the best medicine.
6 stories per month.

True Love

Celebrate true love with tender stories of heartfelt romance, from the rush of falling in love to the joy a new baby can bring, and a focus on the emotional heart of a relationship.
8 stories per month.

Desire

Indulge in secrets and scandal, intense drama and plenty of sizzling hot action with powerful and passionate heroes who have it all: wealth, status, good looks…everything but the right woman.
6 stories per month.

HEROES

Experience all the excitement of a gripping thriller, with an intense romance at its heart. Resourceful, true-to-life women and strong, fearless men face danger and desire - a killer combination!
8 stories per month.

DARE

Sensual love stories featuring smart, sassy heroines you'd want as a best friend, and compelling intense heroes who are worthy of them.
4 stories per month.

To see which titles are coming soon, please visit

millsandboon.co.uk/nextmonth

JOIN US ON SOCIAL MEDIA!

Stay up to date with our latest releases, author
news and gossip, special offers and discounts, and
all the behind-the-scenes action
from Mills & Boon...

 millsandboon

 millsandboonuk

 millsandboon

It might just be true love...